THE NEW IBERIA BLUES

Also by James Lee Burke

DAVE ROBICHEAUX NOVELS

Robicheaux
Light of the World
Creole Belle
The Glass Rainbow
Swan Peak
The Tin Roof Blowdown
Pegasus Descending
Crusader's Cross
Last Car to Elysian Fields
Jolie Blon's Bounce
Purple Cane Road
Sunset Limited
Cadillac Jukebox
Burning Angel
Dixie City Jam
In the Electric Mist with Confederate Dead
A Stained White Radiance
A Morning for Flamingos
Black Cherry Blues
Heaven's Prisoners
The Neon Rain

HACKBERRY HOLLAND NOVELS

House of the Rising Sun
Wayfaring Stranger
Feast Day of Fools
Rain Gods
Lay Down My Sword and Shield

BILLY BOB HOLLAND NOVELS

In the Moon of Red Ponies
Bitterroot
Heartwood
Cimarron Rose

OTHER FICTION

The Jealous Kind
Jesus Out to Sea
White Doves at Morning
The Lost Get-Back Boogie
The Convict and Other Stories
Two for Texas
To the Bright and Shining Sun
Half of Paradise

THE NEW IBERIA BLUES

James Lee Burke

ORION

First published in Great Britain in 2019 by Orion Books,
an imprint of The Orion Publishing Group Ltd,
Carmelite House, 50 Victoria Embankment
London EC4Y 0DZ

An Hachette UK company

1 3 5 7 9 10 8 6 4 2

A CIP catalogue record for this book
is available from the British Library.

ISBN (Hardback) 978 1 4091 7649 7
ISBN (Export Trade Paperback) 978 1 4091 7650 3

Printed and bound by CPI Group (UK) Ltd, Croydon, CR0 4YY

www.orionbooks.co.uk

For Julian Higgins, a poet with a movie camera

THE NEW IBERIA BLUES

Chapter One

DESMOND CORMIER'S SUCCESS story was an improbable one, even among the many self-congratulatory rags-to-riches tales we tell ourselves in the ongoing saga of our green republic, one that is forever changing yet forever the same, a saga that also includes the graves of Shiloh and cinders from aboriginal villages. That is not meant to be a cynical statement. Desmond's story was a piece of Americana, assuring us that wealth and a magical kingdom are available to the least of us, provided we do not awaken our own penchant for breaking our heroes on a medieval wheel and revising them later, safely downwind from history.

Desmond was not only born to privation, in the sleeper of a semi in which his mother tied off the umbilical cord and said goodbye forever; he was nurtured by his impoverished grandparents on the Chitimacha Indian Reservation in the back room of a general store that was hardly more than an airless shack. It stood on a dirt road amid treeless farmland where shade and a cold soda pop on the store gallery were considered luxuries, before the casino operators from Jersey arrived and, with the help of the state of Louisiana, convinced large numbers of people that a vice is a virtue.

Like his grandparents, he belonged to that group of mixed-blood Indians unkindly called redbones. His hair was cinnamon-colored, more a characteristic of Cajun women than of men. His skin was as smooth as clay, almost hairless, his eyes a washed-out blue and set too wide, like those of someone with fetal alcohol syndrome. He was self-conscious about his racial background, as most of his people were, and smiled rarely, but when he did, he could light a room. I always had the sense that Desmond was trying to shrink inside his clothes, as though both fear and a great sadness lived inside him. Like Proteus blowing his wreathed horn, Desmond constantly created and re-created himself, perhaps never knowing who he was.

No matter. Even as a little boy, he was not one to accept the world as it was, no more than he would accept the hand he'd been dealt. By the time he was twelve, he seemed destined to remain skinny and frail and a carrier of intestinal worms and head lice. One morning, behind his grandparents' general store, bare-chested under a white sun, his little body running with sweat, he roped a cinder block to each end of a broom handle and lifted. And kept lifting. And squeezing a rubber ball silently on the school bus while the bigger boys laughed at him and often pushed him down on the gravel. By the time he was fourteen, he had the body and the latent animus of a man, and the boys who had bullied him now tried to ingratiate themselves with a weak, self-deprecating smile. He responded with the benign attention of someone watching a stranger blow soap bubbles, until they bowed their heads and went silent, lest they provoke him.

After high school, he waited tables in the French Quarter and became an apprentice to a sidewalk artist in Jackson Square, and discovered that he was better than his teacher. Sometimes I would see him in the early a.m., disheveled, paint on his shirt and in his hair, eating beignets out of a paper bag and drinking café au lait from a Styrofoam cup. On a particularly cold and gray January morning, I saw him hunched on an iron bench inside the fog by St. Louis Cathedral, like an unevolved creature from an earlier time. He was not wearing a coat and his sleeves were rolled high up on his arms, as though in defiance of the weather. He seemed melancholy, his insouciance a pretense for his loneliness, and I sat down beside him without being invited. The air smelled of the river, dead beetles in a storm sewer, the wine and beer cups in the gutters, damp soil and night-blooming flowers and lichen on stone. It was a smell like a Caribbean city rather than America. He told me he was going to Hollywood so he could become a film director.

"Don't you have to study to do that?" I said.

"I already have," he replied.

"Where?"

He pointed a finger to his head. "In here."

I grinned good-naturedly but didn't speak.

"Don't believe me, huh?" he said.

"What do I know?"

"You still go to Mass?" he said.

"Sure."

"That means you believe in the things that are on the other side of the physical world. That's what painting is. That's what making movies is. You enter a magical world others have no knowledge of."

I got up from the bench. I felt old. My war wounds ached. The hardness of the bench was printed on my buttocks. I heard the Angelus ringing in the cathedral's tower, perhaps as a reminder of our mutability and ultimate fate.

"Good luck," I said. "Kick some butt in California."

There was a smear of powdered sugar on his cheek. For just a moment I thought of a pauper child who might have ferreted his way into a bakery. He was smiling when he looked up at me.

"What's the joke?" I asked.

"Anything you get with luck isn't worth owning, Dave. I thought you knew that."

TWENTY-FIVE YEARS LATER, Desmond came home a director, with a Golden Globe Award and an Academy Award nomination. He took up part-time residence in a house on stilts down at Cypremort Point, with oaks and palm trees in the yard and a magnificent view of the bay, where each evening he claimed to see sharks gliding out of the sunset, dipping in the swells, their dorsal fins as etched as broken razor blades. The problem was, nobody else saw them. A long time ago everyone had decided Desmond was not quite of this earth and lived on the edge of a dream from which he derived both his art and his apparent contempt for success and money.

He didn't fit into a categorical shoe box and, consequently, got into trouble with everyone—producers, the politically correct and the non–politically correct, an actor he tossed into a swimming pool, an Arab sheik who kept a dozen automobiles idling twenty-four hours a day in the garage of the Beverly Hills Hotel and to whose cottage Desmond delivered a truckload of goats.

On the burnt-out end of an August afternoon, following a summer of drought and fish kills and dried-out marshland that was turning to ceramic, I drove down to the tip of Cypremort Point with a young uniformed deputy named Sean McClain, who had seven months' experience in law enforcement and still believed in the human race and woke up each day with birdsong in his head. He had been raised in a small town on the Louisiana–Arkansas line and had an accent like someone twanging a bobby pin.

At five a.m. the same day, we had received three 911 calls about a woman screaming from somewhere at the southern end of the Point. One caller said the scream came from a lighted cabin cruiser. The other callers were unsure. The sun was up when the responding deputy arrived. Nobody at the docks or boathouses had heard or seen anything unusual. I could have written the entire incident off, but any time three people report a scream, they're calling not about a sound but about a memory that lives in the collective unconscious, one that goes back to the cave. When we are alarmed to the degree that we have to tell others about it, we're dipping into a primal knowledge about the darker potential of the gene pool. Or at least this has always been my belief.

I pointed out Desmond's house to Sean.

"That's where that famous movie guy lives at?" he said. "That's something else, isn't it?" I'm sure what he said contained a message, but I had no idea what it was.

"Yep, that's where he lives part of the year," I said.

"Is he one of them Hollywood liberals?"

"Ask him. If he's home, I'll introduce you."

"No kidding."

"But let's do some work first."

"You bet," he said. He looked earnestly out the side window at the camps and the palm trees and the oaks hung with Spanish moss. "What are we looking for, anyway?"

"If you see a dead person facedown on the beach, that'll be a clue."

I parked the cruiser on the roadside, and we walked down to the water's edge. The tide was on its way out, the strip of sandy beach slick and rilling with water and tiny crustaceans in the sunrise, the bay glittering like a bronze shield. We walked to the end of the Point, then five hundred yards back north. I saw a tennis shoe floating upside down in the froth. I picked it up and shook out the sand and water. It was lime green, with blue stripes on it, size seven.

"Bag it?" Sean asked. He was slender, over six feet, his shoulders as rectangular as coat-hanger wire inside his shirt, his stomach as flat as a plank. There was an innocence in his face I hoped he would never lose.

"Why not?" I said.

We walked into Desmond's yard and mounted the double flight of wood steps to his front door. I had not seen Desmond in years and wondered if it was wise to invite the past back into my life or into his. I rang the chimes. In retrospect, I wish I had not.

THE HOUSE WAS L-shaped and built of teak and oak, with spacious rooms and sliding glass doors and a widow's peak and a railed deck like the fantail on a ship. The sun was a red ember in the west, the clouds orange and purple, a water spout twisting as brightly as spun glass on the horizon. Desmond shook my hand, his grip relaxed and cool, with no sign of the power it actually contained. "You look good, Dave. I have a roast on the rotisserie. You and your young friend, please join me."

"I'm a big admirer of your films, Mr. Cormier," Sean said.

"Then you came to the right place," Desmond replied.

Sean could not have looked happier. Desmond closed the door behind us. There were potted plants all over the house. The rug was two inches thick, the furniture made from blond driftwood, the chairs and couches fitted with big leather cushions, an onyx-black piano by the sliding glass doors, a Martin guitar and a golden tenor sax propped on stands. But the most striking aspect of the decor were the steel-framed photos extracted from the films of John Ford. They ran the length of the corridor and one wall of the living room.

"We got some 911 calls about a woman screaming early this morning," I said.

"Some kind of domestic trouble?" Desmond said.

"Could be. Maybe the scream came from a cabin cruiser," I said. "Know anybody with a cabin cruiser who likes to knock women around?"

"At Catalina Island I do. Come out on the deck. I want to show you something."

I started to follow him. Sean was staring at a black-and-white still shot from the last scene in *My Darling Clementine*. "That makes me dizzy."

The still shot showed Henry Fonda in the role of Wyatt Earp, speaking to Cathy Downs, who played Clementine Carter, on the side of a dirt trail that led into the wastelands. In the distance was a bare mountain shaped like a monument or perhaps a rotted tooth, its surface eroded with perpendicular crevices. The antediluvian dryness and immensity of the environment were head-reeling.

"The woman is so pretty and sweet-looking," Sean said. "Is he saying goodbye to her?"

"Yes, he is," Desmond answered.

"I don't get it. Why don't he take her with him?"

"No one knows," Desmond said.

"It makes me feel sad," Sean said.

"That's because you're a sensitive man," Desmond said. "Come outside. I have some soft drinks in the cooler. I'd offer you more, but I guess y'all don't drink alcohol on the job."

"That's us," Sean said. "Damn shooting, it is."

Desmond smiled with his eyes and slid open the glass door and stepped out onto the deck, into the wind and the warmth of the evening. A telescope was mounted on the deck rail. But that was not what caught my attention. A barefoot and virtually naked man, his genitals and buttocks roped with a knotted white towel, was performing a slow-motion martial arts exercise, silhouetted against the sunset, his slender physique sunbrowned and shiny with baby oil, his iron-gray hair combed back in a sweaty tangle.

"This is my good friend Antoine Butterworth," Desmond said.

"Ciao," Butterworth said. His eyes lingered on Sean.

"We can't stay," I said to Desmond. "We found a lime-green tennis shoe with blue stripes up the beach. Does that bring anyone to mind?"

"Afraid not," Desmond said.

"Are we looking for a body, something of that sort?" Butterworth asked. The accent was faintly British, smelling of pretense and self-satisfaction.

"We're not sure," I said. "You know a woman who wears green tennis shoes?"

"Can't say as I do."

"Hear a woman scream early this morning?" I said.

"I wasn't here early this morning, so I'm afraid I'm of no help," Butterworth said.

"From the UK, are you?" I said.

"No," he replied cutely, his mouth screwed into a button.

I waited. He didn't continue, as though I had violated his privacy.

"You do mixed martial arts?" Sean asked.

"Oh, I do everything," Butterworth replied.

"You an actor?" Sean said, not catching the coarse overtone.

"Nothing so grand," Butterworth said.

Sean nodded in his innocent way.

I heard Desmond pop two soda cans. "Take a look through my telescope," he said.

I leaned down and gazed through the eyepiece. The magnification was extraordinary. I could see Marsh Island in detail and the opening into Southwest Pass, which fed into the Gulf of Mexico. In the fall of 1942, from almost this same spot, I saw the red glow on the horizon of the oil tankers that had been torpedoed by German submarines. I also saw the bodies of the burned and drowned American seamen who had been dredged up in shrimp nets and dumped on the sand like giant carp.

"The sharks will be coming soon," Desmond said.

"Sure about that?" I said.

"Big fellows. Hammerheads, maybe."

I straightened up from the telescope. "They usually don't come into the bay. It's too shallow, and there's not enough food."

"You're probably right," he said.

That was Desmond, always the gentleman, never one to argue.

I bent down to the eyepiece again. This time I saw a fin slicing through a wave. Then it disappeared. I rose up from the telescope. "I take it back."

"Told you," he said, smiling. "Mind if I look?"

He bent down to the eyepiece, his denim shirt ballooning with wind, his wispy hair blowing. "He's gone now. He'll be back, though. They always come back. Predators, I mean."

"Actually, they're not predators, at least no more than any other form of fish life," I said.

"You could fool me," he said. "Let me fix you and your friend a plate."

I started to refuse.

"I could go for that," Sean said.

Desmond slid the roast off the rotisserie and began slicing it on a platter with a fork and a butcher knife. Butterworth pulled the towel off his loins and began wiping down his skin, indifferent to the sensibilities of others, his face pointed into the breeze, his eyes closed.

I leaned down to the telescope again. The bay and the current through Southwest Pass were glazed with the last rays of the sun. I moved the telescope on the swivel and scanned Weeks Bay. Then I saw an image that seemed hallucinatory, dredged out of the unconscious, a superimposition on the natural world of humanity's penchant for cruelty.

I rubbed the humidity out of my eyes and looked again. The tide had reversed itself and was coming toward the shore. I was sure I saw a huge wooden cross bobbing in the chop. Someone was fastened to it, the arms extended on the horizontal beam, the knees and ankles twisted sideways on the base. The cross lifted on the swell, the headpiece rising clear of a wave. The air went out of my lungs. I saw the person on the cross. She was black and wearing a purple dress. It was wrapped as tightly as wet Kleenex on her body. Her face was wizened, from either the sun or the water or her ordeal. Her head lolled on her shoulder; her hair hung on her cheeks and curled in tendrils around her throat. She seemed to look directly at me.

"What's wrong, Dave?" Desmond said.

"There's a woman out there. On a cross."

"What?" he said.

"You heard me."

He bent to the telescope, then moved it back and forth. "Where?"

"At three o'clock."

"I don't see anything. Wait a minute, I see a shark fin. No, three of them."

I pushed him aside and looked again. A long wave was sliding toward the shore, loaded with sand and organic trash from a storm, its crest breaking, gulls dipping into it.

"You probably saw a reflection and some uprooted trees inside it," Desmond said. "Light and shadow can play tricks on you."

"She was looking right at me," I said. "She had thick black hair. It was curled around her neck."

I felt Antoine Butterworth breathing on me. I turned, trying to hide my revulsion.

"Let me see," he said.

I stepped aside. He bent to the telescope, holding his wadded towel to his genitals. "Looks like she floated away."

I looked once more. The sun was as bright as brass on the water. I could feel Butterworth breathing on me again. "Would you step back, please?" I said.

"Pardon?"

"I'm claustrophobic," I said. "Been that way since I was a child."

"Perfectly understandable," he said. He put on a blue silk robe and tied it with a sash. "Better now?"

"We'll be running along," I said to Desmond. "We'll call the Coast Guard."

Sean looked through the telescope, then stood.

"Let's go, Deputy," I said.

"Hold on," he said. He wiped the eyepiece with a handkerchief and looked again. Then he turned and fixed his eyes on mine.

"What?" I said.

"Son of a bitch is hung on a snag," he said. "Those aren't sharks out there, either. They're dolphins."

I stared at Desmond and Butterworth. Desmond's face blanched. Butterworth was grinning, above the fray, enjoying the moment.

"I've got a boat," Desmond said, collecting himself. "There's really a body there? I didn't see it, Dave."

"My, my, isn't this turning into a lovefest?" Butterworth said.

I punched in Helen Soileau's number on my cell. "Y'all stick around. My boss lady might have a question or two for you."

Chapter Two

We reached the body and the cross with a department rescue boat at 10:34 p.m. In the glare of searchlights, two divers jumped off the bow, freed the cross from a submerged tree, and glided it onto a sandspit, the waves rippling over the dead woman's face. She was tied to the beams with clothesline. Her eyes were open; they were the same pale blue as Desmond's.

Our sheriff was Helen Soileau. She had worked her way up from meter maid to detective grade at NOPD and later became my homicide partner at the New Iberia Police Department. After the city department merged with the parish, she was elected our first female sheriff.

Helen and a paramedic and Sean and I waded through the shallows onto the sand. Helen shone her flashlight on the body. "Jesus."

I'd been wrong in my earlier description. The dead woman was not just fastened to the cross with clothesline. Her ankles were nailed sideways to the wood, which twisted her knees out of alignment with her hips. Helen stooped down and straightened the dead woman's dress and untied her wrists. A paramedic unzipped a body bag. I squatted down beside the cross. "How long do you think she was in the water?"

Helen held her flashlight beam on the dead woman's face. "She wasn't submerged. Hard to say. Maybe eight or nine hours."

"That doesn't compute with the 911 calls about a scream early this morning," I said.

"Maybe this isn't the same woman," Helen said.

"We picked up a tennis shoe from the beach," I said. "A size seven."

"That's about the right size," she said. "No wounds I can see except on the ankles. No ligature marks or bruising on the neck. Who the hell would do this?"

We were both wearing latex gloves. I touched one of the nails that had been driven through the woman's ankles. "Whoever did it knew something about Roman crucifixions. The nails went through the ankles rather than the tops of the feet. The bones in the feet would have torn loose from the nails."

Helen looked down at the body, her face empty. "Poor girl. She can't be more than twenty-five."

I remained on my haunches and took the flashlight from Helen's hand and shone it on the ankle wounds. They were clean, as though they had not bled. There was a cheap metal chain around one ankle. A tiny piece of silver wire barely clung to one of the links.

In South Louisiana, religion is a complex matter. Not all of it originated in Jerusalem or Rome. Some of it has origins in the Caribbean Islands or western Africa. For many poor whites and people of color, the *gris-gris*—bad fortune or an evil spell—can be avoided only by wearing a perforated dime on a string around a person's ankle. I knew a white couple, Cajuns who couldn't read or write, who tied a string around their infant child's throat to prevent the croup from getting into her chest. The child strangled to death in her crib.

"See something?" Helen said.

I stood up, my knees popping. "If she was wearing a charm, it didn't do her much good."

"I don't know about that," Helen said.

A ball of yellow heat lightning rolled through a cluster of storm clouds and disappeared without making a sound. "I didn't catch that."

"There's not a scratch on her," Helen said. "You know what the crabs do to any kind of carcass?"

I looked across the bay at Cypremort Point. All the lights were on in Desmond's house. I wondered if he or his friend was watching us through the telescope. I wondered if I had ever really known Desmond Cormier.

"Let's get out of here," Helen said. "This place gives me the heebie-jeebies."

I WAS THRICE A widower and lived with my adopted daughter, Alafair, in a shotgun house on East Main in New Iberia. When I got back from Weeks Bay, I went straight to bed and didn't tell Alafair where I had been or what I had seen until the next morning. It was raining, and Bayou Teche was over the banks and running through the trees at the foot of our property, and there was sleet inside the rain that struck the tin roof as hard as birdshot. Alafair had spread newspaper on the kitchen floor and brought our warrior cat, Snuggs, and his friend Mon Tee Coon inside and begun feeding them. Her face showed no expression while I told her about the woman on the cross.

"No identification?" she said.

"A tiny chain around the ankle."

"Nothing on the chain?"

"A piece of wire. Maybe a charm had been torn loose."

Her eyes roamed over my face. "What did you leave out of the story?"

"I saw the cross and the woman through Desmond's telescope. So did the deputy. But Desmond and this guy Butterworth said they couldn't see anything."

She put a plate of biscuits and two cups of coffee on the table, then sat down. "Would it make sense for them to lie about what you had already seen?"

"Probably not," I said. "But how smart are liars?"

"The woman had nails through her ankles?"

I nodded.

"But you don't know the cause of death?"

"No. There was no blood in the nail wounds. I hope she was dead when the nails were put in."

"You need to get these images out of your head, Dave."

She had graduated with honors from Reed and at the top of Stanford Law. Before she started writing novels and screenplays, she'd clerked at the Ninth Circuit and been an ADA in Portland, Oregon. But to me she was still the little girl who hoarded her Nancy Drew and Baby Squanto books.

"What's with this guy Butterworth?" I said.

"He started out as an actor and screenwriter, then became a producer. There're some rumors about him, but actually, he has a lot of talent."

"What kind of rumors?"

"Coke and pills, S and M."

I didn't reply.

"He makes pictures that people enjoy," she said. "He casts the biggest stars in the industry."

"I bet he's a regular at his church, too," I said.

"I don't think you got enough sleep."

"I'd better get ready for work."

"It's Saturday," she said.

"Really?"

"I'll get you another cup of coffee," she said.

I put on my hat and went out the back door and walked down the slope and stood under a live oak tree and watched the raindrops dimpling the bayou. I could not get the dead woman's gaze out of my mind, nor the smooth chocolate perfection of her skin—the only visible violations on it, the nail wounds. Helen was right. Marine life is not kind to the dead. But the woman seemed spared. Was it coincidental that dolphins were her escorts?

I have investigated many homicides. It's the eyes that stay with you. And it's not for the reason people think. There is no message in them. Instead, they force you to re-create the terror and despair and pain that marked their last moments on earth. Two kinds of cops eat their gun: the corrupt ones and the ones who let the dead lay claim upon the quick.

LATER THAT AFTERNOON Clete Purcel pulled into my driveway in the restored 1956 Cadillac he had bought the previous week. With its sleek lines and hand-waxed maroon paint job and chrome-spoked whitewall tires and leather interior, it made our contemporary designs look like shoe boxes with wheels. The top was down; two fishing rods were propped on the back seat. He stepped out on the gravel and removed a leaf from the hood and dropped it on the lawn as he might an injured moth. "Want to entertain the fish?"

"I'm meeting with the coroner at Iberia General," I said.

"About that body y'all pulled out of the salt?"

"It's in the paper?"

"Yeah," he replied. He looked down the street at the Shadows—a plantation home built in 1834—his hair freshly barbered, his face pink in the sun's glow through the live oaks. "I need to tell you something."

I knew the pattern. When Clete did something wrong, he headed for my house or office. I was his confessor, his cure-all, his bottle of aspirin and vitamin B, his hit of vodka Collins to sweep the spiders back into their nest. He was wearing pressed gray slacks and a fresh Hawaiian shirt and shined oxblood loafers. He had not come to fish.

"Anything going on?" I asked.

"Ten days ago I put a boat in by the train trestle over the Mermentau. Right at sunset. Nobody around. No wind. The water just right. The goggle-eye were starting to rise in the lily pads. Then I heard the train coming. A freight going about twenty-five miles an hour."

Clete was not given to brevity. "Got it," I said.

"It was a perfect evening, see. It's kind of my private spot. So I was daydreaming and not thinking real sharp."

"What are we talking about, Cletus?"

"I'm talking about the freight. It was wobbling and rattling, and the moon was rising, and about eight or nine cars went by, and then I saw a guy in white pants and a white shirt standing on the spine of an empty boxcar. There was blue trim on his collar and shirt pockets. Then the guy flew off the boxcar into the river. He must have hit in the middle or he would have broken his legs."

"He was wearing a uniform?"

"Yeah." Clete waited.

"What kind?" I said.

"The kind you see in a lot of Texas jails. He popped up from the water and looked right at me. Then he started swimming downstream."

"You had your cell phone?"

"It was in the Caddy," he said. There was a pause. "I wasn't going to call it in, anyway."

"Why not?"

"I wasn't sure about anything. I couldn't think. You know what those for-profit joints are like."

"Let's keep the lines straight, Clete. We can't be sure he escaped from a for-profit jail. Or any kind of jail."

"This is the way I saw it. Why dime a guy you don't know the whole story on? I hate a snitch. I should have been born a criminal."

"That's what I'm saying. So what happened to the guy?"

"He waded through a canebrake and disappeared. So I wrote it off. Live and let live."

"So why are you bothered now?"

"I did some googling and found out a guy who committed two homicides got loose from a joint outside Austin. That was eleven days ago. The guy is supposed to be a religious fanatic. Then there was the story in the *Daily Iberian* today about the woman you pulled out of the drink. There was nothing in the story about the cross. I got that from the reporter. Now I got this guy on my conscience."

"What's the name of the escaped inmate?"

"Hugo Tillinger. He set fire to his house and burned up his wife and ten-year-old daughter because they listened to Black Sabbath."

"Why didn't he get the injection table?"

"He did. He tried to kill himself. He got loose from a prison hospital. What should I do?"

"You saw a guy jump off a freight. You've reported it to me. I'll take it from here. End of story."

"Who's the dead woman?" he asked.

"We have no idea."

"This is eating my lunch, Dave."

What could I say? He was the best cop I ever knew, but he'd ruined his career with dope and booze and Bourbon Street strippers and had hooked up with the Mob for a while and now made a living as a PI who ran down bail skips and looked in people's windows.

"Come inside," I said. "We'll go out for supper."

"You said you were meeting with the coroner."

"I'll talk to him on the phone."

"You don't have to babysit me. I'll see you later."

"Go easy on the hooch," I said.

"Yeah, that's the source of the problem, all right," he replied. "Thanks for the reminder I'm a lush."

CORMAC WATTS WAS our coroner. He had a genteel Virginia accent and wore size-fourteen shoes and seersucker pants high on his hips and long-sleeve dress shirts without a coat, and had a physique like a stick figure and a haircut that resembled an inverted shoe brush.

At Iberia General, in a room without windows, one that was too cold and smelled of chemicals, our Jane Doe lay on a stainless steel table, one with gutters and drains and tubes that could dispose of the fluids released during an autopsy. A sheet was pulled to her chin; her eyes were closed. One hand and part of the forearm were exposed; the fingers were a dark blue at the tips and had started to curl into a claw.

"Beautiful woman," Cormac said.

"You got the cause of death?"

He lifted the sheet off her left foot. "There were three injections between her toes. She was loaded with enough heroin to shut down an elephant."

"No tracks on the arms?"

"None."

"Was there any sexual violation?"

"Not that I could determine."

"Most intravenous users start on the arms," I said. "Those who shoot between the toes usually have a history."

"It gets weirder," he said. He lifted her hand. "Her nails were clipped and scrupulously cleaned. Her hair had been recently shampooed and her skin scrubbed with an astringent cleanser. There were no particles of food in her teeth."

"You can tell all that in a body that was in the water for half a day?" I asked.

"She was floating on top of the cross. The sun did more damage than the water."

"Was she alive when the nails went in?"

"No," he said.

"What do you think we're looking at?" I asked.

"Fetishism. A sacrifice. How should I know?"

I could hear the hum of a refrigeration unit. The light in the room was metallic, sterile, warping on angular and sharp surfaces.

"You'd better get this motherfucker, Dave."

I had never heard Cormac use profanity. "Why?"

"He's going to do it again."

THE IBERIA SHERIFF'S Department was located in city hall, a grand two-story brick building on the bayou, with white pillars and dormers and a reflecting pool and fountain in front. I went into Helen's office early Monday morning.

"I was just about to buzz you," she said. "An elderly black minister in Cade called and said his daughter went missing six days ago. Her name is Lucinda Arceneaux."

"He's just now reporting her missing?"

"He thought she took a flight out of Lafayette to Los Angeles. He just found out she never arrived."

"How old is she?"

"Twenty-six."

"Want me to talk to him?"

"Yeah. What were you going to tell me?"

"About two weeks ago Clete Purcel was fishing on the Mermentau River and saw a guy jump from the top of a boxcar into the water. Clete saw the story in the *Iberian* about our Jane Doe and thought he ought to tell me. The guy was wearing a white uniform with blue trim on it."

"Like a Texas convict?"

"Possibly."

There was a beat. "Clete didn't want to call it in?" she said.

"Ice cream vendors wear white uniforms. So do janitors and cooks. After Clete saw the story in the paper, he found a story on the Internet about a condemned man who escaped from a prison hospital outside Austin. The name is Hugo Tillinger."

Helen got up from her chair and wrote on a notepad that rested on her desk blotter, her jaw flexing. She had a compact and powerful physique and features that were androgynous and hard to read, particularly when she was angry. "What was Tillinger in for?"

"Double homicide. His wife and teenage daughter. He set fire to his house."

"Tell Clete he just went to the top of my shit list."

"He didn't have the information we have, Helen."

"Lucinda Arceneaux's father says she worked for the Innocence Project. They get people off death row."

I let my eyes slip off hers. "What's the father's address?"

"Try the Free Will Baptist Church. Tell Clete I'm not going to put up with his swinging-dick attitude."

"Cut him some slack. He couldn't be sure the guy was an escaped convict. He didn't want to mess up a guy who was already down on his luck."

"Don't say another word."

I CHECKED OUT A cruiser and drove to Cade, a tiny, mostly black settlement on the back road between New Iberia and Lafayette. The church house was a clapboard building with a faux bell tower set back in a grove of pecan trees. A house trailer rested on cinder blocks behind the church. In the side yard stood a bottle tree. During the Great Depression and the war years, many rural people hung blue milk of magnesia bottles on the branches of trees so they tinkled and rang whenever the wind blew. I don't believe there was any reason for the custom other than a desire to bring color and music to the drabness of their lives. Then again, this was Louisiana, a place where the dead are not only with us but perhaps also mischievous spirits you don't want to think about. I knocked on the door of the trailer.

The man who answered looked much older than the father of a twenty-six-year-old. He was bent and thin and walked with a cane, and wore suspenders with trousers that were too large. His cheeks were covered with white whiskers, his eyes the color of almonds, unlike those of our Jane Doe. I opened my badge holder and told him who I was.

"Come in," he said. "You got news about Lucinda?"

"I'm not sure, Reverend," I replied. I stepped inside. "I need more information, then maybe we can make some phone calls."

"I've done that. Didn't help."

I sat down on a cloth-covered stuffed chair. I looked around for photographs on the walls or tables. My eyes had not adjusted to the poor lighting. A fan oscillated on the floor. There was no air-conditioning in the trailer. I hated the possible outcome of the conversation I was about to have.

"Miss Lucinda works for the Innocence Project?" I said.

"She used to. She got a job in California."

"Doing what, sir?"

"What they call organic catering. She always loved cooking and messing with food. She's been working for a caterer about three months."

"How long was she with the Innocence Project?"

"Two years. It was mostly volunteer work. She'd visit men in the penitentiary and interview them and help their lawyers."

"Over in Texas?"

"Yes, suh. Sometimes. Other times in Angola."

"Do you recognize the name Hugo Tillinger?"

"No, suh. Who is he?"

"A man we'd like to find."

He was sitting on a faded couch printed with roses. The coffee table in front of him was stacked with *National Geographic* and *People* and *Sierra* magazines. "I called the airline. They wouldn't give me any information. I called a friend she worked with in Los Angeles. Nobody at her workplace knows where she is."

"Is your wife here, sir?"

"She passed nine years ago. We adopted Lucinda when she was t'ree. She never went off anywhere without telling me. Not once."

"Do you have a photograph?"

He went into a short hallway that led to a bath and a pair of bedrooms, and returned with a framed photo he took from the wall. He put it in my hand and sat down. I glanced at the young woman in the picture. She was standing next to the reverend, a beach and a mountain behind her. She was smiling. A wreath of flowers hung from her neck. I felt the blood in my chest drain into my stomach.

"That was taken in Hawaii two years ago," he said. "We went on a tour with our church." He paused. "You've seen my daughter before, haven't you?"

"Sir, I need you to go with me to Iberia General."

He held his gaze on me, then took a short breath. "That's where Lucinda is?"

"We found a young woman in Weeks Bay."

"Lucinda wouldn't have any reason to be out there."

"Is there someone who should come with us?" I asked.

"It's just me and her here. That's the way it's always been. She was always the sweetest li'l girl on earth."

His eyes would not leave mine. There were moments when I hated not just my job but the human race. I had no adequate words for him.

"You're sure about this?" he asked.

"Let's take care of the identification, sir."

"Help me up, please. My knees aren't much good anymore."

He held on to my arm, weightless as a bird when we walked down the steps to the cruiser. Then he veered away from me as though he could undo our meeting and the message I had brought him. "Who would want to hurt her? She tried to get justice for people nobody cares about. Tell me what they did to her. Tell me right now."

But any comfort I could have offered him would have been based on a lie.

He sat down sideways on the passenger seat of the cruiser, his feet outside, and wept in his hands. I could hear the bottle tree tinkling in the wind, the pecan leaves ruffling. I wanted to be on the other side of the moon.

Chapter Three

CLETE CALLED ME at the department late the same afternoon and asked me to come to his office. It was located on Main Street in a century-old brick building half a block from the Shadows. The receptionist was gone, and the folding metal chairs were empty except for one where a man with long hair as slick and shiny as black plastic was cleaning his nails with a penknife. The floor was littered with cigarette butts and gum wrappers and an apple core and a banana peel. Clete sat behind his desk in the back room, the door ajar. He waved me in. "Close the door," he said.

There were printouts and two folders and a legal pad on his desk. Through the window I could see his spool table and umbrella on the concrete pad behind the building, and the drawbridge at Burke Street and the old convent across the bayou.

"What's up?" I said.

"I made several calls about Hugo Tillinger. It's a complex case. It also stinks."

"I talked with Helen about him, Clete. Let us take it from here."

"Is everything okay? I mean with me not reporting Tillinger right away?"

I avoided his eyes. "Don't worry about it."

"Did you ID the body of the girl on the cross?"

"She's the daughter of a Baptist minister in Cade. Her name is Lucinda Arceneaux. She was a volunteer for the Innocence Project."

He flinched.

"That doesn't mean she knew Hugo Tillinger," I said.

"Stop it."

He got up from his desk and opened the door. "Come in here, Travis."

The man with black hair greased straight back folded his knife and dropped it in his slacks. He had the beginnings of a paunch and cheeks that looked like they had been rubbed with chimney soot. He wore his slacks below the belly button; hair protruded from the top of his belt.

"This is Travis Lebeau," Clete said. "Tell Dave what you know about Hugo Tillinger."

"While he was being held for trial, I'd bring ice to his cell," Travis said.

"Ice?" I said.

"That's what I did in this particular jail. I brought ice from the kitchen and got paid in smokes or whatever."

Three teardrop tats dripped from his left eye. Two blue stars the size of cigar burns were tattooed on the back of his neck.

"Travis was in the AB," Clete said. "Now he's trying to do a few solids to make up for the past."

"I thought the AB was for life," I said.

"They sold me to the niggers. The BGF," he replied. "They claimed I snitched on a guy. I never snitched on anybody in my life."

"Go ahead about Tillinger," Clete said.

"We played checkers on the floor, between the bars," Travis said. "He knew he was gonna get the needle. He said the jury and the judge and cops and his lawyer were working for Satan. I told him they don't need Satan, they're working for themselves, that's bad enough. Can I sit down? I feel like a fireplug that's about to get pissed on."

"Sure," Clete said.

"He went on and on, like all these reborn people, you know, they cain't shut up talking about it," Travis said. "He told me he was a drunk, a rage-a-holic or whatever, then he got saved by the Pentecostals at a tent rival. He was a pain in the ass to listen to."

"You're going a little fast for me, Travis," I said.

"I'm saying Tillinger wasn't a criminal or the kind of guy who burns up his family. He ripped all the posters off his daughter's walls when he was drunk, and yelled and hollered in the yard, but that was it. I believed him. So did the colored girl who showed up."

"Which colored girl?" I asked.

"Her name was Lucinda. She started visiting him right after he got sentenced. She said the people at the Innocence Project were taking his case. She said she knew people in the movie business, maybe some of the people who got Hurricane Carter out of prison. It gave him hope. But I thought he was gonna ride the needle from the jump."

"Why?" I said.

"The governor was running for president. Guys who want to be president don't get elected by being kind to guys charged with murdering their family."

"What was the black woman's last name?" I said.

"He called her Miss Lucinda. That's all."

"A rage-a-holic wouldn't set fire to his house?" I said.

"Maybe a guy like me would. Tillinger didn't belong in the system. Everybody knew it. You know what con-wise is, right?"

I didn't reply.

"I did double nickels back to back. I did them straight up and went out max time. I burnt up my brother-in-law in his car and did a guy inside. In the chow line. For one of these teardrops on my face. I didn't mean to kill my brother-in-law, but that's the way it worked out. I deserved what I got. Tillinger is what we call a virgin. He never got his cherry busted. That means he was never in the life. He belongs in the PTA and shit like that."

"We don't need all that information," I said.

"About the hit in the chow line?" he said. "You don't like that? You think I give a shit if anybody knows?"

I didn't answer.

"Look at me, man," he said. "You got any idea of what those fucking black animals did to me? My best friends sold me for two cartons of smokes. They said, 'Rip his feathers off.' I got to live with what they did every night of my life. Fuck you, asshole."

His eyes were brimming.

AFTER TRAVIS WAS gone, Clete and I walked down the street under the colonnade to Bojangles' and had coffee and a piece of pecan pie in a back corner of the room.

"You believe him?" I said.

"He's on the square most of the time," Clete said. "He doesn't want to lose the few connections he has. He knows the Aryan Brotherhood will probably get him down the road."

"I don't buy Tillinger's innocence."

"Here's what happened," Clete said. "Tillinger's house was a hundred years old and dry as kindling. The flames were in the second story when he came home. The daughter and the mother were upstairs. He claimed he tried to get them out, but the heat was too great. Later, he told the fire inspector some of the wiring in the walls needed replacing, but he didn't have the money for repairs.

"So far, so good. Then the inspector finds signs of an accelerant trailing from the gallery into the hallway, or at least that's what he thought he saw. He said the fire started on the first floor and climbed the walls to the ceiling and up the stairwell. One of the neighbors said Tillinger never tried to go inside the house. Instead, he moved his new Ford F-150 away from the fire.

"On top of it, Tillinger had a fifty-thousand-dollar life insurance policy on both the wife and daughter. He also shot off his mouth in the Walmart and told a group of churchgoers his family had better straighten up or he would burn the house down.

"It looked more and more like arson and homicide. Then an ACLU lawyer showed up and began looking at the evidence. The guy who called himself a fire inspector wasn't certified and had little experience in arson investigation. The accelerant was a can of charcoal lighter that somebody had left next to the portable barbecue pit on the gallery. There was no accelerant trail in the hall. Also, the heat marks on the baseboards were probably caused by an explosion of flame from the stairwell, not from a fire that started on the first floor.

"The defense lawyer was from the ACLU and went over like elephant turds in a punch bowl."

Customers at other tables turned and looked at us.

"What's your opinion?" I said.

"It doesn't matter. I should have called 911 when I saw a guy in jailhouse whites bail off the train."

"We can't be sure the guy was Tillinger. Why would he jump off in the Mermentau River? Why wouldn't he keep going until he was in Florida?"

"I checked that out. There were some gandy dancers working on the track. He could see them from the top of the boxcar. Helen is pretty hot about this, isn't she?"

"You're a good cop, Clete. She knows that."

"I'm not a cop. I blew it."

"Don't say that. Not now. Not ever."

He looked at nothing. The whites of his eyes were shiny and tinged with a pink glaze. He glanced up at the air-conditioning vent. "It's too cold in here. Let's take a walk. I feel like I walked through cobwebs. Sorry about the way Travis talked to you. He was a bar of soap in the shower at Huntsville."

As always, I walked to work the next morning. Desmond Cormier was waiting for me in the shady driveway that led past the city library and the grotto devoted to the mother of Jesus. He was sitting in the passenger seat of a Subaru convertible with California plates driven by Antoine Butterworth.

Desmond got out and shook my hand. His friend winked at me. "I have to talk with you, Dave," Desmond said.

I didn't answer. Butterworth lifted a gold-tipped cigarette from the car's ashtray, took one puff, and flipped it into the flower bed surrounding the grotto.

"I feel so foolish," Desmond said. He was wearing tennis shorts and a yellow T-shirt and a panama straw hat. "About that business with the telescope and the woman on the cross. My right eye is weak and I have a cataract on the left. That's why I didn't see her. I should have explained."

"How about your friend there? He didn't see her, either."

"It's just his way," Desmond said. "He's contrary. He's been in a couple of wars. Somalia and the old Belgian Congo. You'd find him quite a guy if you'd give him a chance. Have lunch with us."

"Another time."

"Dave, you were one of the few I looked up to."

"Few what?"

"The regular ebb and flow."

"There's some pretty good people here, Desmond."

"See you around, I guess."

"You ever hear of a guy named Hugo Tillinger?" I asked.

"No. Who is he?"

"An escaped convict. He knew the dead woman. He may be in the vicinity."

"I wish I could be of help," he said. "This is an awful thing."

"Before you go—that still shot you have on your wall of Henry Fonda standing on the roadside saying goodbye to Clementine?"

"What about it?"

"That scene is about failed love, about the coming of death, isn't it?"

"For me it's about the conflict between light and shadow. Each seeks dominion. Neither is satisfied with its share."

I looked at him. I didn't try to follow his line of thought. "I saw the picture at the Evangeline Theater in 1946. My mother took me."

He nodded.

"I think a scene like that could almost take a guy over the edge," I said.

"I never heard it put that way."

"It's strange what happens when a guy gets too deep into his own mind," I said.

"Maybe you think too much," he said.

"Probably." I reached down and picked up the burning cigarette Butterworth had thrown in the flower bed. I mashed it out on the horn button of the Subaru and stuck it in Butterworth's shirt pocket. "We're heck on littering."

Butterworth grinned. "In Louisiana?"

The pair of them drove away, the sunlight spangling on the windshield.

I couldn't get the still shot of Wyatt Earp and Clementine out of my mind. I could almost hear the music from the film blowing in the trees.

I HAD ANOTHER SURPRISE waiting for me at the rear entrance to city hall. Travis Lebeau was slouched against the brick wall, in the shade, picking his nails. "Hey."

"What's the haps?" I said.

"Need to bend your ear."

"Come upstairs."

"How about down by the water? I'm not big on visiting cop houses."

I looked at my watch. When it comes to encouraging confidential informants, there is no greater inducement than a show of indifference. "I'm under the gun."

"I've got a bull's-eye on my back," he replied.

I walked down the bayou's edge and let him follow. "Say it."

"There's a couple of AB guys who know where I am. Give me five hundred. I'll give you Tillinger."

"The same guy you stood up for?"

"I'm in a spot," he said, his eyes leaving mine. "He liked to drop names."

"People Lucinda Arceneaux knew?"

He looked sideways and blew out a breath. "Yeah, people she knew."

"Which people?"

"How about the money?"

"You haven't given me anything, Travis."

He scratched his forearms with both hands, like a man with hives. "I got to score, straighten out the kinks," he said. "I'll make good on my word."

"You're an addict?"

"No, I'm Dorothy on the Yellow Brick Road."

"Can't help you, partner."

I turned to go.

"Maybe I exaggerated a little," he said.

"About what?"

"Tillinger. He creeped me out."

"In what way?"

"The way sex between men bothered him. He had a crazy look in his eyes when he'd hear a couple of guys getting it on. You ever know a guy like that who probably wasn't queer himself? Sometimes he'd burn himself with matches. He talked about casting out our demons and raising the dead."

"Would he hurt Lucinda Arceneaux?"

He shook his head slowly, as though he couldn't make a decision. "I don't know, man. I can't go in somebody's head."

"In reality, you don't have anything to sell, do you."

He didn't know what to say. I started up the slope.

"Two hunnerd," he said at my back.

I kept walking. He caught up with me and pulled on my shirt. "You don't understand. They'll use a blowtorch. I saw them do it in a riot."

"Sorry."

"Maybe the chocolate drop led him on. Maybe Tillinger lost it. Come on, man, I got to get out of town."

"You need to take your hand off my arm."

"Come on, man. I'm hurting."

"Life's a bitch."

His face made me think of a piece of blank paper crumpling on hot coals. Cruelty comes in all forms. It's least attractive when you discover it in yourself.

I WALKED HOME FOR lunch. A cherry-red Lamborghini was parked in the driveway. Alafair was eating at the kitchen table with a middle-aged man I had never seen. A plate of deviled eggs and two avocado-and-shrimp sandwiches wrapped in waxed paper and a glass of iced tea with mint leaves in it had obviously been set for me. But she had not waited upon my arrival before she and her friend started eating.

"Hello," I said.

"Hey, Dave," she said. "This is Lou Wexler. He has to get to the airport, so we started without you."

Wexler was a tall, thick-bodied man with a tan that went to the bone and blond hair sun-bleached on the tips. He was ruggedly handsome, with intelligent eyes and large hands and the kind of confidence that sometimes signals aggression. He wiped his fingers with a napkin before rising and shaking hands. "It's an honor."

"How do you do, sir?" I said, sitting down, glancing out the window at the bayou. My manner was not gracious. But no father, no matter how charitable, trusts another man with his daughter upon first introduction. If he tells you he does, he is either lying or a worthless parent.

"Lou is a screenwriter and producer," Alafair said. "He works with Desmond."

"Actually, I don't work with Desmond," he said. "I help produce his films. Nobody 'works' with Desmond. He's his own man. In the best way, of course."

"How about this fellow Butterworth?" I said.

"You've met Antoine, have you?"

"Twice."

Wexler's eyes were sparkling. "And?"

"An unusual fellow," I said.

"Don't take him seriously," Wexler said. "Nobody does. He's a bean counter posing as an artist."

"I heard he was in a couple of wars," I said.

"He was best at scaring the natives in the bush, rattling around in a Land Rover, and showing up for photo ops. South Africa was full of them."

"That's your home?" I asked.

"For a while. I was born in New Orleans. I live in Los Angeles now."

If he'd grown up in New Orleans, he had acid-rinsed the city from his speech.

"We pulled a body out of the salt just south of Desmond Cormier's house," I said. "The body was tied to a cross. I spotted the cross through a telescope. Our man Butterworth took a peep but couldn't see a thing. Neither could Desmond, although this morning he told me he had bad eyesight. Butterworth didn't seem bothered one way or another."

The room was silent. Alafair stared at me.

"Can you run that by me again?" Wexler said.

I repeated my statement.

"Well, that's something, isn't it?" Wexler said. "Sorry, I haven't been watching the time. I have to get a new gym bag. Then I need to pick up some fellows in Lafayette. We're searching out a couple of locations. Perhaps you can help us."

His level of self-involvement was hard to take.

"I probably wouldn't know what you're looking for," I said.

He touched at his mouth with his napkin and set it aside. "It's been grand meeting you, Mr. Robicheaux."

"Likewise."

"Don't get up."

I didn't intend to. Alafair walked him to the door. Then she came back into the kitchen, her jaw clenched. "Why do you have to be so irritable?"

"You're a success on your own. You don't need these phony bastards."

"You stigmatize an entire group because of this Butterworth character?"

"They're nihilists."

"Desmond's not. He's a great director. You know why? Because he paid his goddamn dues."

"How about it on the language, Alf?"

"Sometimes you really disappoint me," she said.

I felt my face shrink. I took my plate outside and finished eating at the picnic table with Snuggs and Mon Tee Coon. Then I went back inside. Alafair was brushing her hair in front of the mirror in the bedroom. She was five-ten and dark-skinned, with beautiful hair that fell to her shoulders. She had a black belt in karate and ran five miles every morning. Sometimes I couldn't believe she was the same little El Salvadoran girl I'd pulled from a submerged airplane near Southwest Pass.

"What was that guy doing here, anyway?" I said.

"Inviting me out. For supper. This evening," she said. "Thanks for asking."

Chapter Four

DURING THE NEXT three days I talked with Lucinda Arceneaux's employer and fellow employees at the catering service in Los Angeles, and her former roommate, and a boy in Westwood who used to go to the public library with her. They all spoke of her good character and gentle disposition. None had an explanation for her disappearance.

The Texas Department of Criminal Justice referred me to three correctional officers who had known Hugo Tillinger. Two had no opinion of him; the third, an old-time gunbull, said, "Tillinger? Yeah, I knew that lying son of a bitch. Turn your back on him and he'd gut you from your belly button to your chin. Anything else you want to know?"

On Friday I went into Helen's office and told her what I had.

"What are your feelings about Tillinger?" she said.

"I don't see him as a viable suspect in the murder of Lucinda Arceneaux. An escaped convict in a prison uniform would have more on his mind than committing a ritualistic homicide with a cross and a hypodermic needle."

Helen looked at a legal pad on her desk. "There were break-ins at three fish camps not far from Cypremort Point. A white shirt with blue tabs on it was found half buried by a boathouse. He's here. The question is why."

"He jumped on the first freight he could find going out of Texas."

"What if he had a partner?" she said.

"We're looking at the wrong guy, Helen."

"He burned his wife and daughter to death. Don't tell me he's the wrong guy."

"I want to talk to Desmond Cormier and Antoine Butterworth again."

"You've got a bias, Streak. You don't like Hollywood people."

"That isn't true. I don't like anyone who thinks he's entitled."

She twiddled her ballpoint on her desk blotter. "Okay. By the way, you have a new partner."

"Pardon?"

"Her name is Bailey Ribbons."

"Who is Bailey Ribbons?"

"I hired her two days ago. She's twenty-eight years old. She was a middle school teacher in New Orleans and has a graduate degree in psychology. She was a dispatcher with NOPD for eighteen months."

"That's her entire experience?"

"What she doesn't know, you'll teach her."

"Is this an affirmative-action situation?" I said.

"I hired her because of her intelligence. I'm going to get a lot of criticism for that. I don't need it from you. Stay here."

She left the office and returned three minutes later with a woman who seemed to have walked out of a motion picture that had little connection to the present. She had dark brown hair and clear skin and eyes like light trapped in sherry, and she wore black shoes and a white blouse with a frilly collar buttoned at the throat and a skirt that hung well below the knees. What struck me most were her warm smile and her erect posture. I felt strange, even awkward and boyish, when I took her hand.

"It's a pleasure to meet you, Detective Robicheaux," she said.

"You, too, Miss Bailey," I said. "Call me Dave."

"Hi, Dave."

I started to speak but couldn't remember what I'd wanted to say.

"Bring Bailey up to date on the Arceneaux investigation," Helen said.

"Sure," I said. "Helen?"

"What?"

Again my head went blank. Bailey Ribbons was too young, too inexperienced, too likely to be resented by older members of the department.

"I'll check out a cruiser," I said. "If Bailey is free, we can head down to Cypremort Point."

"She's free," Helen said. "Bye, Dave."

I walked downstairs and out the door with Bailey Ribbons. She smelled like flowers. I felt my palms tingling and a fish bone in my throat.

"Did I say something inappropriate?" she asked.

"No, ma'am, it's a pleasure to have you aboard."

"I appreciate your courtesy. I realize some might think I don't have the qualifications for the job, but I'll give it my best."

I looked at her profile, the radiance in her face, and felt my heart beating.

God, don't let me be an old fool, I prayed.

WE DROVE DOWN to the southern tip of Cypremort Point and walked along the bib of sand and salt grass and concrete blocks where I had found the tennis shoe. The wind was hot and scudding brown waves up on the sand.

"We had three 911 calls about a woman screaming," I said. "One caller thought the scream came from a lighted cabin cruiser. The cabin cruisers that are docked here were all accounted for."

Bailey looked across the long expanse of the water, the humps of greenery and sandspits that resembled swampland rather than a saltwater bay. "This is all disappearing, isn't it?"

"About sixteen square miles of it a year," I replied.

"Why are you bothered by the movie director and his friend?"

"It's the friend, Butterworth, who bothers me more. I think he's a deviant and a closet sadist."

"Those aren't terms you hear a lot anymore," she said.

"He's the real deal."

"Introduce me."

Her hair was feathering on her cheek. My protective feelings toward her were the same as those I had for my daughter, I told myself. It was only natural for an older man to feel protective of a younger woman. There was nothing wrong with it. Absolutely. Only a closet Jansenist would see design in an inclination that's inherent in the species.

What a lie.

I HAD CALLED DESMOND and made an appointment. But that was not all I had done by way of preparation regarding Antoine Butterworth. I had talked with a friend who was captain of the West Hollywood Station of the Los Angeles Sheriff's Department. Butterworth was almost mythic among the film industry's subculture. He hired prostitutes he made degrade each other with sexual devices; he also hung them on hooks and beat them with his fists. He returned to Los Angeles from New Orleans in a rage and berated everyone in his office because he had to sleep with an ugly prostitute. He and a co-producer put LSD in the lunch of the co-producer's Hispanic maid and videotaped her while she stumbled bewildered and frightened around the house; later, they showed the tape at their office. Butterworth lived in the Palisades in a $7 million white stucco home overlooking the ocean; he'd moved a junkie physician into the pool house so he could have a supply of clean dope. The physician had been found floating facedown among the hyacinths, dead from an overdose. Prior to his situation with Butterworth, the physician had been in a twelve-step program.

If Butterworth had a bottom, no one knew what it was.

Desmond opened the door. He took one look at Bailey Ribbons, and the breath left his chest. "Who are you?"

She blushed. "Detective Ribbons."

"I can't believe this," he said.

"I hope we haven't upset you," she said.

"No, my heavens, come in," he replied. He looked over his shoulder at the deck. "Can you give me a second?"

"Is there a problem?" I said.

"We were playing a couple of songs," he said. "Antoine isn't quite dressed. I got my times mixed up."

He went into the bedroom and got a robe and took it out on the deck. Through the glass doors I saw him and Butterworth arguing. Butterworth was wearing a yellow bikini, his tanned body glistening with oil; he put on the robe and cinched it tightly into his hips, then picked up a roach clip from an ashtray and took a hit and ate the roach.

Desmond came back into the living room. "Do you know who you look like?" he asked Bailey.

"My parents, I suspect," she replied.

"Cathy Downs. The actress who co-starred with Henry Fonda in *My Darling Clementine.*"

"I'm not familiar with that film," she said.

"We'll have a showing here. Whenever you like," he said.

"Need to talk to your man out there, Desmond," I said.

He scratched at his eyebrow. "That stuff again?"

"I don't know what you mean by 'that stuff,' " I said. "This is a homicide investigation."

"Antoine had some addictions in the past. You should be able to understand that."

"I just watched him eat a roach."

"He has a prescription for medical marijuana. I won't let him smoke it here again. You have my word."

"Do you play all those instruments?" Bailey asked.

"The saxophone is Antoine's," Desmond replied.

"What songs were you playing?" she asked.

"Some of the Flip Phillips arrangements. You know who Flip Phillips was?"

"No, I'm sorry," she said.

"This isn't a social call," I said.

"Okay," he said to me. "What a hothead you are, Dave. No, I take that back. You're a Puritan at heart. You need buckle shoes and one of those tall hats."

I slid back the glass door and waited for Bailey. "Coming?"

"Yes," she said, smiling.

Desmond's eyes never left the back of her head.

Butterworth was lying on a recliner under a beach umbrella inset in a glass table. "Oh me, oh my, what do we have here?" he said.

His robe had fallen open. The outline of his phallus was stenciled as tautly as a banana against his bikini. He blew me a kiss.

DESMOND WAS RIGHT. My feelings about Butterworth were not objective. An open cooler humped with crushed ice and imported bottles of beer rested on a redwood table. I pulled a bottle of Tuborg from the ice. "Catch."

Butterworth blinked but caught it with his left hand as deftly as a frog tonguing an insect out of the air. "Flinging things around, are we?"

"Your eyesight seems pretty good," I said. "Too bad it seems to fail you when you look through a telescope."

"Aren't we the clever one."

"I recommend you not speak to me in the first-person plural again," I said.

"Bad boy. That excites me," he said.

"I don't think you get it, Mr. Butterworth," I said. "Louisiana is America's answer to Guatemala. Our legal system is a joke. Our legislature is a mental asylum. How'd you like to spend a few days in our parish prison?"

"Some big black husky fellows will be visiting me after lights-out?"

As with all megalomaniacs, he had no handles. He was the type of man the Spanish call *sin dios, sin verguenza,* without God or shame.

"Would you stand up a minute?" I said.

"Are we going to get rough now?" he said.

"No, your robe is open and I don't like looking at you," I said. "I also don't like your general disrespect."

He flipped his robe over his nether regions but didn't move from the recliner. "I told Desmond we made a mistake coming here."

"What are you talking about?" I said.

"We're shooting a film in Arizona, Texas, and Louisiana. I told him we'd have trouble here."

"You're filming in Louisiana because the state will subsidize up to twenty-five percent of your costs," I said. I removed an envelope from my pocket and handed it to him. "Take a look at this."

Butterworth slipped a photo out of the envelope and studied it. His eyebrows were beaded with sweat. "This was taken in a morgue?"

"That's right."

"This is the woman who was on the cross?"

The photo showed the body of Lucinda Arceneaux on the autopsy tray, a sheet pulled to her chin. Butterworth replaced the photo in the envelope and returned it to me, his face solemn.

"Look again," I said. "She worked for a catering service that supplies film companies on the set."

"I don't need to. I've never seen this person."

"Look again, Mr. Butterworth."

"I told you the truth. I think you gave me that envelope to get my fingerprints on it."

I could smell the sweat and grease and weed on his skin. "You like to beat up hookers?"

"That's a lie."

"An administrator at the Los Angeles Sheriff's Department told me you make them strap on dildos and degrade each other, and then you hang them up on hooks or straps and beat the hell out of them."

"I'm done with this," he said.

"Yeah, how about it, Dave?" Desmond said behind me.

"It takes a special kind of guy to use up the life of an innocent young woman in order to re-create the Crucifixion," I said. "We never had anything like this around here. At least not till you brought Mr. Butterworth to town."

"In Rwanda I saw bodies stacked as high as this house and set on fire," Butterworth said. "Some of them were still alive. If you weren't a police officer, I'd break your fucking jaw."

"Why is it I believe nothing you say?" I asked.

"Because you're an incompetent idiot with a crime on your hands that you don't have the training or experience to deal with," he replied. "Please excuse my candor, but I'm bloody tired of your arrogance and insults."

The umbrella was flapping, the air bright with humidity, the deck blistering hot. He was either the best actor I had ever seen or a man who had a cache of dignity that I wouldn't have thought him capable of.

"I'd like you to look at the body," I said.

"You're unrelenting, aren't you," he said.

"That's fair to say."

"Then get a warrant," he said.

He stood up from the recliner. Our faces were six inches apart, a feral light in his eyes. I felt my right hand tighten and close and open again. My mouth was dry, a sound like wind blowing inside my head. I knew the signs all too well. It was the precursor that had come to me many times when I'd superimposed the face of a man named Mack on the faces of Asian men who had done me no harm. Bailey and Desmond were staring at us like witnesses to a car wreck in the making.

"Miss Bailey, please take a look at the photos of Henry Fonda and Cathy Downs," Desmond said, pulling back the sliding door that opened onto the living room. "You, too, Dave. I do want y'all to see the film. It would mean a great deal to me."

Bailey looked truly out of her element. My cell phone throbbed in my pocket. I looked at the caller's number. It was Helen Soileau. "Dave here."

"Are you at Cypremort Point?" she asked.

"Yes."

"You get anywhere?"

"Negative," I said.

"Wind it up," she said. "We've got another one."

Chapter Five

THE DUCK CAMP was an old one, a desiccated shack abandoned in a swampy area southwest of Avery Island, the gum and cypress and persimmon trees strung with dead vines. We parked the cruiser and waded through a bog that was iridescent with oil and gasoline. The paramedics, three uniformed deputies, and Helen and Cormac Watts were already there. Helen and Cormac were wearing rubber boots and latex gloves. A swamp maple that was dying of saline intrusion, its limbs scaled with lichen, stood on the far side of the shack, a huge teardrop-shaped object suspended from one of the thickest limbs. The droning sound in the air was as loud as a beehive.

The 911 had been called in by a fisherman who had run out of gas and pulled up onto the hummock, dumbfounded and sickened by what he saw.

The wind changed, and a smell like a bucket full of dead rats washed over us. I heard Bailey gag. I cleared my throat and spat and handed her a clean handkerchief. "Put it over your nose."

"I'm all right," she said.

"That's a smell no one gets used to. Just do it, Miss Bailey."

"Don't call me 'miss' anymore, Dave."

"You got it."

A deputy was stringing crime-scene tape through the trees. Helen was standing on a high place by the front of the shack. The shack had no door and no glass in the windows. The floor was caked with dirt and the shells of dead beetles. Helen was breathing through her mouth, her chest rising and falling slowly.

"Before we get to that mess in the tree, I want you to see this," she said. "It may be the only forensics we take out of here."

Heavy boot prints led into the shack and out through a hole broken in the boards on the far side, still jagged and unweathered, as though recently splintered. There were drag marks across the floor and stains that red ants were feeding on.

The stench was overwhelming now. I tried to envision the man who wore the boots. They were probably steel-toed, the strings laced through brass eyelets, the leather stiff, even gnarled, from wear in a swamp or on the floor of an offshore drilling rig. Or maybe they were the boots of a man with dark jowls and swirls of body hair who deliberately did not wash or shave and wore his odor like a weapon. I could almost hear his feet on the floor as he dragged his victim outside, the stride measured, his hand hooked in the victim's shirt, his weight coming down with a sound like a wooden clock striking the hour.

Our departmental photographer was clicking away, a scarf wrapped across the bottom half of his face. Then he vomited inside the scarf.

We walked on dry ground to the other side of the shack. The body of a slight man dressed in khaki work clothes hung upside down inside a fish net. His arms were bound behind him. One ankle was roped to his wrists so the calf was pulled tight against the inside of the knee. His facial features were in an advanced state of decomposition and had the squinted look of a newly born infant. Flies crawled over almost every inch of his skin. A knotted walking stick with a sharpened tip had been shoved through the chest and out the back.

"You ever see him before?" Helen said.

"It's hard to say," I replied.

"Why is his leg tied like that?" she said.

The image was familiar, but I couldn't remember where I had seen it. I shook my head.

"It's from the tarot," Bailey said.

"The fortune-telling deck?" Helen said.

"It's a compilation of medieval and Egyptian iconography," Bailey said. "The gypsies carried it through the ancient world into modern times."

"So?" Helen said.

"The victim is positioned to look like the Hanged Man," Bailey said.

"What's the Hanged Man?" Helen said.

"Some say Judas, others say Peter," Bailey said. "Others say Sebastian, the Roman soldier martyred for his faith. In death he makes the sign of the cross. In the deck he's generally associated with self-sacrifice."

Helen stepped away from the tree and stared at the ground, her hands on her hips. "What's your opinion, Dave?" she asked. "You still don't think Hugo Tillinger is our guy?"

"Maybe Tillinger killed his family or maybe he didn't," I said. "But I doubt he's a student of Western symbolism."

"Who the hell is?" Helen said. "I don't think this is about tarot cards. I think this is about a guy who likes to kill people and wants to scare the shit out of the entire community."

I looked at Bailey. She was obviously struggling to hide her discomfort about the odor of the victim; also, I suspected she was wondering if her education and knowledge were about to make her a lonely and isolated member of our department.

"Nobody saw anything except the fisherman who found the body?" I said to Helen.

"No," she said. "This place will be washed away in another year or so. Cormac says the body has probably been here a week."

We went back to the other side of the shack. The sun was shining through the trees, the leaves moving in the wind. I could hear a buoy clanging on the bay.

"Maybe the way the leg is tied is coincidence," I said. "But the walking stick through the chest doubles the coincidence."

"I don't understand," Helen said.

"Our own deck of playing cards comes from the tarot," I said. "The suit of clubs come from the Suit of Wands. The Suit of Wands upside down is associated with failure and dependency."

"I don't want to hear this," Helen said.

"Then I don't know what to tell you," I said.

"Both of you are sure about this?" she said.

"As sure as you can get when you put yourself inside the mind of a lunatic," I replied.

One deputy lifted another deputy so he could cut the rope that bound the net to the tree limb. Neither of them could avoid touching the body nor escape its full odor. The body thudded on the ground in a rush of flies, the jaw springing open, a carrion beetle popping from the mouth.

BY MONDAY THE victim had been identified through his prints as Joe Molinari, born on the margins of American society at Charity Hospital in Lafayette, the kind of innocent and faceless man who travels almost invisibly from birth to the grave with no paper trail except a few W-2 tax forms and an arrest for a thirty-dollar bad check. Let me take that one step further. Joe Molinari's role in life had been being used by others, as consumer and laborer and voter and minion, which, in the economics of the world I grew up in, was considered normal by both the liege lord in the manor and the serf in the field.

He'd lived in New Iberia all his life, smoked four packs of cigarettes a day, and worked for a company that did asbestos teardowns and other jobs people do for minimum wage while they pretend they're not destroying their organs. He'd had no immediate family, played dominoes in a game parlor by the bayou, and, to the best of anyone's knowledge, never traveled farther than three parishes from his birthplace. He had gone missing seven days ago. Cormac Watts concluded Molinari had died from either blunt trauma or a load of opioids or both. The decomposition was too advanced to say.

The only asterisk to Molinari's name was that he had been a janitor at the Iberia Parish courthouse for two years in the 1990s. Otherwise, he could have lived and died without anyone's noticing.

Walking home after work, I saw Alafair and the screenwriter-producer Lou Wexler backing out of my driveway in his Lamborghini, the top down. Wexler braked and raised one hand high in the air. "Join us, sir."

"For what?" I said.

"Dinner at the Yellow Bowl in Jeanerette," he said.

"I left you a note," Alafair said.

"Another time," I said. "I may have to go back to the office tonight."

"Roger that," he said. He gave me a thumbs-up and drove away, his exhaust pipes throbbing on the asphalt. I saw Alafair try to turn around, her hair blowing. I didn't have to go back to the office, and I felt guilty for having lied. I felt even worse for trying to make Alafair feel guilty.

I ate a cold supper on the back steps and watched the gloaming of the day, angry at myself for my inability to accept the times and the fact that Alafair had her own life to live and at some point I would have to let go of her and turn her over to the care of a man whom I might not like. Snuggs and Mon Tee Coon were sitting on our spool table, flipping their tails, checking out the breeze. The air was dense with the smell of the bayou, the way it smells after a heavy rain, and the light had become an inverted golden bowl in the sky, the cicadas droning in the trees. I heard someone walking through the leaves by the porte cochere.

"How's it hanging, big mon?" Clete said.

There was no more welcome person in my life than Clete Purcel. He was the only violent, addicted, totally irresponsible human being I ever knew who carried his own brand of sunshine. "How you doin', Cletus?"

"Is Alafair around?"

"She's with some character named Lou Wexler."

"I get the sense you don't approve."

"I don't have a vote. What's up?"

"I was researching these Hollywood guys. I don't want to believe Tillinger is behind these killings."

"These killings have nothing to do with you. Now give it a rest."

"I should have called 911 when he bailed off that freight."

"Enough."

"All right," he said. He sat down beside me and folded his hands. He looked at Snuggs and Mon Tee Coon. "Something on your mind?"

"On my mind?"

"Yeah, something I can help with."

How do you respond to a statement like that? "I spent the last two days talking to people who knew Joe Molinari."

"The guy in the tree?"

"He probably weighed a hundred and twenty pounds and never hurt a soul in his life. Somebody drove a sharpened walking cane through his heart."

"You're getting the blue meanies."

That was a term from the old days when Clete and I walked a beat on Canal and in the French Quarter, and later, when we were partners in Homicide. "Blue meanies" was our term for depression, or living daily with human behavior at its worst. The blue meanies not only ate your lunch, they chewed you up and spat you out and ground you into the sidewalk.

"How do you read this stuff?" I said.

Clete thought for a moment. "The guy is posing his victims. He might be a photographer. He knows a lot about history and religion and symbolism. He's full of rage, but he lets it out only in controlled situations. He's the kind of white-collar schnook who lives alone and works eight to five in an office, then goes home and plays with a power saw in a basement that has blacked-out windows."

Clete's description made me shudder, not because of his detail but because he was seldom wrong when it came to a homicide investigation.

"That's why Tillinger bothers me," he said. "I found out he was in a drama club in high school. He was also an amateur photographer and dug David Koresh."

"The cultist at Waco?" I said.

"Yeah. There's one other factor. He messed around with acid in high school. In other words, he was into the same heavy-metal bands his daughter was. Later on he sees her as him, and burns down his house with her in it, and the mother for good measure."

"You're thinking too much," I said.

"Travis Lebeau was in my office this afternoon. He says he saw Tillinger in Walmart."

"Stop letting this guy jerk you around. And stop building a case against yourself."

Clete rested his arm across my shoulders. It felt like a pressurized fire hose. "I worry about you. Guys like me can live alone. Guys like you shouldn't. One day Alafair is going to leave for California or New York and not come back."

"Say anything more and I'm going to hit you."

"You got another problem," he said. "You take the weight for others and won't admit it. Just like me."

"I mean it, Clete. Knock it off."

"How's your new partner working out?"

"Fine."

"I saw her in front of city hall today," he said.

I waited.

"She's not your ordinary female plainclothes," he said.

"And?"

"Nothing. I was just wondering how she's working out."

He made a study of Snuggs and Mon Tee Coon, his loafers tapping up and down on the step.

AT 3:17 P.M. on Tuesday, Bailey Ribbons tapped lightly on my office door. She and Helen had spent most of the day at a seminar with an FBI agent in Lafayette.

"Good afternoon," I said.

"I hope I'm not disturbing you," she said.

"Not at all."

I got up and closed the door behind her.

"Desmond Cormier has called me twice," she said. "The first time to invite me to dinner. The second time to apologize for the first time. There's a message on my machine I haven't listened to."

She was standing less than two feet from me, her face lifted to mine, her hands on her purse.

"I'll talk with him," I said.

"He didn't say anything rude."

"He knows he's compromising your situation."

"You won't be too hard on him, will you?"

"No, ma'am."

"You think his friend Butterworth is mixed up with Lucinda Arceneaux's death?"

"There's no evidence of that, except he denied seeing her body through the telescope. But he's one of those guys."

"Which guys?"

"There's a malevolent joy in their eyes. They feed off Kryptonite. They love evil for its own sake."

"That's pretty strong."

"If you underestimate a guy like that, you usually pay the price for the rest of your life."

"Why would Desmond Cormier associate with him?"

"The same reason everyone else does. Money."

She looked at her watch. "I've taken too much of your time."

"I was going over to Victor's for coffee and a piece of pie," I said. "Doing anything right now?"

"I'd love that," she said.

Three uniformed deputies passed us as we walked down the hallway to the stairs. I heard one of them say something under his breath to the others. One of the words began with the letter C.

"Wait for a minute," I said to Bailey.

I caught up with the three deputies. One of them was short and muscular and had a face that reminded me of a hard-boiled egg with a smile painted on it. His name was Axel Devereaux. He had been charged with abuse of prisoners during the previous administration but had been found not guilty.

"You didn't make a reference to my partner, did you, Axel?" I said.

"Not me," he replied. The other deputies looked away.

"So who were you talking about?" I asked.

"Search me. My memory is awful."

"Let's don't have this conversation again, okay?"

His teeth were the size of Chiclets when he grinned. "You're full of shit, Robicheaux."

"Probably," I said. "Want to talk later? After hours?"

"Fuck off," he said.

I rejoined Bailey at the top of the stairs, and the two of us walked down to the first floor and out the door into the sunshine. The wind was blowing in the live oaks by the grotto, the bamboo swaying, the air sprinkled with the smell of rain. We went to Victor's and had coffee and pie. I believed people were staring at us. Under the circumstances and at my age, that's a strange and degrading feeling.

"Are you uncomfortable about something, Dave?" she asked.

"No," I said. "Let's take a ride."

"Where?"

"I know where our Hollywood friends are shooting today."

"Is that a good idea?"

"The movie people are involved in Lucinda Arceneaux's death. I can't prove it, but I know it."

"How?"

"Evil has an odor. It's a presence that consumes its host. We deny it because we don't have an acceptable explanation for it. It smells like decay inside living tissue."

She held her eyes on mine, her mouth parting silently. I wanted to take out my vocal cords.

Chapter Six

THE HELICOPTER, A vintage Huey that had no external armament—what we called a "slick" in Vietnam—came in low over the water, yawing, smoke twisting from the airframe, the Plexiglas pocked from automatic-weapons fire, a bloody bandage taped over one eye of the kid on the joystick.

An actor dressed like a third-world peasant clung to one of the skids. The helicopter roared over our heads, flattening the sawgrass around the levee where we stood. The moment sent me back to the sights and sounds and collective madness of an Eden-like Asian country gone wrong, a place I had consigned to my dreams and hoped I'd never see again.

In the dreams I heard the metallic *klatch* on the night trail but not the explosion. Instead I was painted with light, my body auraed with cascading leaves and air vines and dirt that had a fecund odor, like that of a freshly dug grave. I watched my steel pot roll silently down the trail. To no avail, I opened and closed my mouth to force the deafness out of my ears. Inside the great green darkness of the trail, I could see the silhouettes of my patrol against the muzzle flashes of their weapons and also the weapons of the tiny men in pajamas who lived on one rice ball a day and wore sandals made from rubber tires and drank mosquito-infested water hand-cupped from a stream. The flashes resembled electricity leaping inside a cloud of dust and smoke that blotted out the stars.

A black medic from Jersey City, whom we called Spaceman because he was the bravest kid in the unit and also a Section Eight in the making, was suddenly sitting on top of me, pasting a cellophane cigarette wrapper over the hole in my chest, thumping my chest with his fist. There was a rush of air into my lungs, and my hearing came back, and I heard him say, "Breathe, Loot. Chuck got to breathe. One, two. One, two. My main man goin' back alive in '65. Motherfucker got it made."

My patrol rigged a stretcher with web gear and carried me all night while shells from an offshore battery arced overhead and exploded with a *whump* in the jungle. At first light we could see the LZ in the distance, flames climbing inside the elephant grass on the hillside, men in black picking over the dead. I heard someone say "We're fucked."

Then the slick came out of a molten sun, already loaded with wounded grunts, a Vietnamese civilian dangling from one of the skids. He let go and fell sixty feet into the jungle, grinding his legs like a man on a bicycle. The pilot was a nineteen-year-old warrant officer from Galveston. A compress was tied on one side of his face, his cheek streaked with blood. When he landed, I saw a decal of a death's head on his helmet. Under the image were the words "I am the giver of death."

I became one of many on the floor of the slick. The others had an M for morphine painted on their foreheads. I never had a chance to thank the pilot. I heard later that he did not survive the war.

I was not fond of talking about the war or even remembering it. And grand as the intention might be, I hated ceremonies that took me back to it. I had laid down my sword and shield a long time ago, down by the riverside, and did not want to pick them up again.

"You okay?" I heard Bailey say.

"Sure," I said.

We had just arrived and hadn't spoken to anyone on the set. The helicopter landed on the levee, descending slowly enough to let the stuntman drop safely to the ground. He limped away, holding his back.

"Good job, but we got to shoot it again," Desmond said. "A cloud went across the sun. We need the silhouette of the impaled man against a red sun."

"I'm done, Des," the stuntman said. "I think I tore my sciatica."

"Give me your clothes."

"Here?"

"Where else?" Desmond said.

The stuntman went behind the helicopter to undress. Desmond wasn't so shy. He worked off his golf shirt, stuffed it into a pants pocket, and stripped down to his jockstrap, balancing on one foot.

"You want a codpiece, Des?" someone called out.

"I left it in your mother's bedroom," he replied.

He dressed in the clothes of the peasant and turned around. He had not seen us arrive. His face was bright red, and not from sunburn. "Don't tell me you just watched this."

I shrugged. Bailey's gaze wandered over the set. Desmond closed and opened his eyes like a man who had stepped into an elevator shaft. "I've got to reshoot this scene, then I'm at your disposal."

"Go right ahead," Bailey said. "That's okay, isn't it, Dave?"

"Sure," I said. "I should have called."

Desmond pulled on a pair of leather gloves and stood under the helicopter blades as they began rotating. When the helicopter lifted, he sat on a skid as casually as someone taking a funicular ride. A safety belt was attached to one of the stanchions, but he didn't use it. The helicopter rose higher, then tilted away over the water while Desmond sat with one hand on the skid and the other on the stanchion. After the pilot made his turn and headed back in, Desmond swung under the skid. His body looked twisted and tortured, his legs silhouetted against the sun, kicking as though somehow Desmond had stolen from my dreams and re-created the desperate man I had seen fall into the jungle decades ago.

The helicopter descended far enough for him to drop to the ground. He stooped under the blades and walked toward us smiling while everyone on the set applauded.

"We have champagne and soft drinks and cold cuts and potato salad over on the table," he said. "Let's put something in the tank, shall we?"

"Maybe we should talk business first," Bailey said.

"Whatever I can do to help," he said.

"It's about Lucinda Arceneaux," she said.

The light went out of his face.

"We're pretty sure she knew people among your group," I said. That was a lie, but that's the way it works. You stretch the spider web across the doorway and hope the right person will walk through it.

"Like who in our group?" he said, looking around.

"She was young, idealistic, and naive," I said. "A country girl full of dreams about Hollywood. Think any of these guys would latch on to a girl like that?"

"You're tarring everybody with the same brush, Dave," he said. "You put me in mind of those guys back in the fifties. Joe McCarthy and Nixon and the like."

"Nothing so grandiose," I said. "There's a Texas convict on the ground here. His name is Tillinger. He's a convicted killer. He believed Lucinda Arceneaux knew movie people who could help him get off death row. He headed here, to the place where she lived and where you're making a film."

"This is over my head," Desmond said.

In the background I saw Antoine Butterworth and Lou Wexler arguing. Wexler was wearing white slacks. He had flattened his hands and stuck both of them into his back pockets, like a baseball manager giving it to an umpire. He stepped away from Butterworth and came toward us, flicking his fingers as though looking for a towel. "You've got to get that bloody sod off my back before I shove his head in one of these crawfish holes," he said to Desmond.

"No more of this, Lou," Desmond said.

"Very sorry to bring a problem to you," Wexler said. "I thought you were the director."

"What's the issue?" Desmond said.

"I told him you wanted to pick it up at oh-six-hundred tomorrow," Wexler said. "The weather forecast is perfect. We'll have clouds across a pink sky, the shadows on the salt grass. The tide will be out, the sand slick, and driftwood sticking up like bones. The bastard doesn't get it. He says the union will complain."

"I'll talk to him. We shoot at oh-six," Desmond said. "No more spit fights."

"I knew him in Africa, Des," Wexler said. "He was afraid of the wogs and afraid of his own shadow. You ever meet a coward who wasn't a backstabbing shit?"

"We don't have that language on the set," Desmond said.

Wexler looked at Bailey and me as though seeing us for the first time. "Sorry, all."

"Forget it," Desmond said. He put his arms over both Bailey's shoulders and mine. "Let's have something to eat."

"We'll pass on the food," I said. "What's that stuff about the wogs?"

"Lou likes to throw around mercenary references," Desmond said. "Actually, he and Antoine made their money in video games."

"What kind of video games?" I said.

"Urban guerrilla themes. Blowing things apart. A bit like *Grand Theft Auto,*" he replied.

"Themes?" I said.

"Come on, Dave," he said. "Be a sport and enjoy life. Have some fun on the set. It's like Burt Reynolds once told me: 'Why grow up when you can make movies?' "

"Is that why you make them?" I said.

The sun was like a giant ruby nestled in a clump of purple clouds on the tip of the wetlands. He looked at me, his eyes full of thoughts I couldn't read. "No, that's not why I make them. Not at all."

"So tell us why," Bailey said.

"They allow you to place your hand inside eternity. It's the one experience we share with the Creator. That's what making films is about."

I was sure at that moment that Desmond Cormier lived in a place few of us would have the courage—or perhaps the temerity—to enter.

AFTER WORK THE next day, Sean McClain pulled his pickup into my driveway, a pirogue in the bed. Two cane poles were propped on the tailgate. He didn't get out. "Take a ride with me to Fausse Point."

He had never asked me to go fishing before. "Anything going on?" I asked.

"Thought we'd entertain the bream. Last time out, I hooked myself in the neck with a Mepps spinner. Thought I'd keep it simpler, cane pole–style."

I had no idea what was on his mind, but I knew it wasn't fish. "Why not?" I said.

We drove up the Loreauville Road through fields of green cane channeled with wind, the sky marbled with purple and scarlet rain clouds. We put the pirogue in at Lake Fausse Point. I sat in the bow and he sat in the stern, and we paddled along the edge of dead tupelos that resonated like conga drums when you knocked on them. I unhooked the line at the base of my cane pole and threaded a worm on the hook, and swung the line and bobber and small lead weight next to the lily pads. The wind had dropped, and the water was as flat and still as a painting.

"There's something maybe I should tell you," Sean said.

"I thought you might."

"You did?"

"You shot one of your colleagues?" I said.

"Maybe I was working up to it."

I turned around and looked at him. "I was kidding."

"No, I ain't shot nobody," he said. "Although maybe I was thinking about it. There's some what needs it."

"Can you please tell me what we're talking about?"

"I was having coffee at the doughnut place, and some guys was shooting off their mouths about Miss Bailey. One guy in particular. He said she got her job on her back."

"Which guy?"

"The one who got off on that charge at the parish prison."

"Axel Devereaux?" I said.

"I told him a couple of things maybe I shouldn't have."

"Like what?"

"That he put me in mind of a shit-hog ear-deep in a slop bucket. That he'd better shut his face before I went upside his head."

"Devereaux isn't a man to provoke," I said.

"I done it."

"You did what?"

"Went upside his head with the paper-napkin dispenser. It knocked him out of the chair."

"You hit Axel Devereaux with a napkin dispenser?"

"I also stepped on his face and told him he'd better stay where he was at before I mashed his ear into a grape."

"You're not putting me on?"

"No, sir. He wet his pants. Literally." He glanced at the water by the lily pads. "There's something on your line."

The bobber traveled across the surface in a straight line, without sinking, making a V, then sank out of sight. I lifted the pole and pulled a sunfish out of the water and swung it flopping into the boat. I wet my hand and unhooked the fish and lowered it below the surface and watched it disappear into the murk like a gold and red bubble. I turned around on the seat and looked at Sean. He was too good a kid to get mixed up with men who never should have been given a gun or a badge.

"Talk to Helen," I said.

"I ain't a snitch."

"You don't want a guy like Devereaux as an enemy."

"Him and his friends will let me go through a door and get shot, won't they?"

"That's the way his kind work."

"If you was in the cafeteria, what would you have done?"

"Probably the same thing."

"Somehow that don't make me feel any better."

"You're stand-up, Sean. Nobody can take that from you. Secretly, Devereaux fears you."

"You should have been a preacher."

"If you have any more trouble with these guys, let me know."

"Nope."

"Nope, what?"

"My old man always said you got to carry your own canteen. I only told you because I thought you had a right to know what Devereaux and them others is up to."

He lifted his line and dropped it in a different spot, his forehead pink with sunburn.

TWO DAYS PASSED with no progress in the bizarre murders of Lucinda Arceneaux and Joe Molinari. In fact, there was no evidence to link the two. Arceneaux's death obviously had been committed by someone driven by ritualistic obsession, but the upside-down positioning of Molinari's body in the fish net and the configuration of his legs could have been coincidental and not necessarily related to the tarot. Maybe the victim simply owed somebody money or slept with another man's wife or ran into someone loaded on hallucinogens.

On Friday night Clete Purcel was knocking back shots with a beer chaser in a ramshackle black dump that offered blues from the Spheres and barbecue chicken that could break your heart, when a white man he didn't want to see again came through the door and tried to pick up a black woman at the end of the bar. The man was unshaved and drunk, his face greasy with booze and presumption and a level of lust he didn't try to disguise.

The bartender leaned in to Clete. "You know that guy down there?"

"Yeah."

"Do him a favor."

"He's on his own," Clete said.

"On his own is gonna get him facedown on a cooling board." The bartender tipped a bottle of Jack into Clete's glass. "On the house."

Clete folded a five-spot and tucked it between the bartender's fingers. "Maybe I'll get time off from purgatory."

He walked to the end of the plank bar and rested his hand on the drunk man's shoulder. There were two blue stars tattooed on the back of his neck and a line of green tears dripping from one eye.

"Time to get some fresh air, Travis," Clete said.

Travis's bottom lip hung from his teeth; he resembled a fish with its mouth open. "You look like Clete Purcel."

"I don't believe this," Clete said.

Two white men came through the front door and sat in the corner. Clete recognized one, a deputy sheriff out of uniform. What was the name? Axel Dickwad or something? Both were looking in Clete's direction.

"That's heat over there," Clete said to Travis. "They jamming you?"

"Don't know what you're talking about," Travis said. "Just bought a new car. Wanted to take this lady for a ride."

"A ride, all right," said the woman sitting next to him. Even though it was summer, she wore a short navy blue coat with big brass buttons, maybe because of the air-conditioning blowing on her neck. "This boy in the AB but that don't mean he don't like blackberries and cream."

The two men in the corner had not ordered. The shorter one lit a cigarette, the flame flaring on his features. His nostrils were thick with hair.

"I think they're dogging you, Travis," Clete said.

"Only guy dogging me is you."

"Glad you said that." Clete slapped him hard on the back. A whoosh of BO welled out of his shirt. "Keep fighting the good fight."

Clete went back to his shot glass of Jack and half glass of flat beer. Up on a stage a female guitarist in a purple dress sprinkled with sequins was seated on a high stool, a solitary spotlight trained on her hands and electric guitar. Her hair was jet-black, her lips covered with gloss, her nails arterial red. A scar as thick as a night crawler circumscribed half of her neck. She went into a song Clete had never heard a woman sing: *I have a hard time missing you, baby, when my gun is in yo' mouth.*

Clete poured his shot glass into his beer and drank it to the bottom. He felt the hit spread through his stomach and loins and chest like an old friend putting a log on the fire. Two or three more, and his liver would go operatic. He looked at the singer's mouth, the shine on her breasts, the way her nails seemed to click up and down on the frets. Rain was hitting on a window in back. He could almost smell an odor that was like the smell of a field mortuary in a tropical country, but he didn't know why. *You're zoned, that's all,* he told himself. *Slow it down.*

He went into the restroom and unzipped and propped himself on one arm above the urinal and let go. Someone came through the door and let it slam on the spring. A shadow joined his on the wall.

"Mr. White Trash is in trouble."

He turned around and looked into the face of the black woman Travis had tried to pick up. He zipped up and washed his hands in the sink.

"You deaf?" she said.

"If you haven't noticed, this is the men's room."

"They about to take him off somewhere. When they get finished wit' him, he won't know his name."

Clete dried his hands. "What's it to you?"

"Axel Devereaux stuffed a dirty sock in my brother's mout' at the jail and almost choked him to deat'."

Clete wadded up the paper towel and arced it at the trash can. It bounced onto the rim and fell on the floor. "You shouldn't be in here."

He went back to the bar and ordered a double shot and a longneck, ice-cold and ready to go down as hard as brass. The singer was smoking a cigarette on the stool, blowing the smoke in an upward stream. Her eyes seemed to fasten on his. He saw her lips move, as though she were whispering. He looked around the room. The wood trim was painted red. The lights above the back counter were red, too, although he had never noticed before. He wiped at his mouth, momentarily unsure where he was.

"Can you turn the air conditioner down?" he asked the bartender. "I think I'm getting a chill."

The bartender's head resembled a brown bowling ball that was too small for his shoulders. He dried a glass, not looking up.

"Do I need to use sign language?" Clete said.

"There's bars down the bayou," the bartender said.

"I asked you a question. The place is an icebox. Or maybe my malaria is kicking in."

"Life's a skull-fuck, then you die."

"You learn that in a Buddhist monastery?"

The bartender didn't answer. Clete tipped the shot glass to his lips, then did it a second time and drained it, chasing it with half the longneck. He took out his wallet. The bills in it seemed to go in and out of focus. His stomach was roiling. He knew the signs. Somewhere down in the basement, the cannon on the Zippo track had fired to life, arcing a flame into a straw hooch, the slick hovering overhead, people from the ville splashing into a rice paddy.

"We're square," the bartender said.

"You poisoned my drink?"

"We're kind to people with pickled brains."

Clete picked up his porkpie hat from the bar and put it on. "Don't let me in here again."

He went outside into a misting rain and the smell of the bayou. In the distance he could see lights burning in the sugarcane refinery and smoke rising from the stacks, electricity leaping through the thunderheads. A gas-guzzler was idling in the parking lot, the driver's door open, the ignition wires hanging under the dashboard. Travis Lebeau had assumed the position, both hands on the hood, his legs spread.

Don't do this, said a voice inside Clete's head.

"Why y'all bracing this poor bastard?" Clete said.

"We know you?" Axel said.

"Clete Purcel. I got a PI office on Main Street."

"So you know what 'on the job' means. In your case, it also means get lost."

"This guy's my confidential informant. That makes my lawyer his counsel. That means right of presence extends to me."

Axel laughed. "Where'd you get that?"

"The guy's trying to go straight," Clete said. "Give him a break."

"He stole this car," Axel said. "Check the ignition."

"I got the pink slip," Travis said over his shoulder. "I lost the key."

"I'll take him home," Clete said.

"You're interfering with an officer in the performance of his duty," Axel said.

"You were the guard who stuck a sock down an inmate's throat?"

"No, this is what I did," Axel said. "Because he doesn't know when to leave the wrong broad alone." He inserted a short wood club between Travis's legs and wedged it into his colon. Travis clenched his buttocks, the blood draining from his face. "Got the message?" Axel said.

"Yeah!" Travis said, his knees shaking.

Axel pulled the club loose. "That's better. We're getting there."

"You're on a pad for a pimp?" Clete said to Axel.

"We're telling you this guy is driving drunk and probably driving a stolen car," the other man said. His hair was scalped on the sides. There was a circle of whiskers around his mouth. "We'll put him on a D-ring and have his car towed, then buy you a drink. How about it?"

"Who's the pimp y'all in with?" Clete said.

Axel turned around and rested the point of his club on Clete's sternum. "You're way over the line, lard-ass." He moved the club up Clete's chest to his throat and chin. "You copy?"

Clete's right hand opened and closed in the darkness. He gazed at the rain rings on the bayou, the wobbling reflection of a house trailer on its surface. The wind changed, and he smelled an odor like mushrooms on a grave, like a disturbed bog deep in a swamp, the water swelling over his shoes and ankles. Someone pushed open the front door of the nightclub. Clete heard the woman on the stage singing a tale about the House of the Rising Sun.

"Take the baton out of my face, please," he said.

"No problem," Axel said. "We cool?"

"No."

"You're Robicheaux's cornhole buddy, aren't you."

"We both worked homicide at NOPD. Before that we walked a beat on Canal and in the Quarter."

"He's muffing his new partner?"

"Didn't quite hear that," Clete said.

"Tell him not to let his mustache get in the way. Or maybe he wants to smell it all day."

Clete stepped backward, blood thudding in his wrists. He gazed at the bayou; wind wrinkled the surface. "I'm going to walk back inside."

"I say something wrong?" Axel said. "We're all ears."

"I'll follow y'all to the booking room," Clete said. "My friend Travis better not have any alterations on him."

"I heard you took juice when you worked vice," Axel said. "You also chugged pud for the Mob in Vegas."

"You probably heard right," Clete said.

"You're the great Clete Purcel, huh?" Axel said. "I'd better watch out for you."

He and his partner cuffed Travis and put him into an unmarked car, hitting his head as they pushed him in the back seat. The rain was falling harder now, ticking on Clete's porkpie hat. He thought he heard an electrical short buzzing inside his head. He watched the three men drive away, his viscera turning to water.

He went back inside and sat at the bar. He blotted the rain off his face with his sleeve. "Give the singer whatever she's having. Same with the lady down the bar."

"What happened out there?" the bartender said.

"Nothing. Who's running the action?"

"What action?"

Clete nodded toward the end of the bar.

"Ain't nobody running it. It runs itself. Don't get your necktie in it, man. You'll have your face in the garbage grinder."

Chapter Seven

CLETE DIDN'T TELL me about it until Monday, in my office.

"Did Travis file charges?" I said.

"For what?" he said.

"Axel Devereaux putting a baton up his colon."

"A guy with a sheet like his thinks he's going to get justice?" he said.

"I need to tell Helen about this."

"I just saw Axel Devereaux outside. He looked right through me."

"Get away from these guys, Clete."

"It wasn't me who started it."

He had a point. Cops like Devereaux were part of the system. We created and nurtured and protected them, always to our detriment and never learning from the experience. "Where's Travis?"

"I went his bail."

"So you think we've got a deputy who's a part-time pimp?"

"Who knows? We got black kids selling dope in front of their houses at three-thirty in the afternoon."

"What's the name of the hooker?"

"I never asked. I bought her a few drinks."

He was wearing a loose suit and a crisp sport shirt without a tie. His eyes were smoky green, impossible to read, his face free of alcohol.

"I know what you're thinking," I said. "Clean those thoughts out of your head."

"Which thoughts?"

"Squaring things with Devereaux on your own."

"I shouldn't have told you what Devereaux said about Bailey Ribbons," he said.

"I'll take care of that through the proper procedure."

"Proper procedure? Lovely. Do you know what my greatest fear is?"

"No clue," I said.

"That one day you'll find out who you really are and shoot yourself."

AFTER WORK I drove in my pickup to the blues club on the bayou. The sun was low and red in the west; dust drifted from the cane fields. I went inside and opened my badge holder on the bartender.

"I know who you are," he said.

"Clete Purcel was in here Friday night," I said. "There was a black woman sitting at the end of the bar. She had on a navy blue coat with big brass buttons. She followed him into the restroom."

The bartender popped a counter rag idly in the air, looking down the bar at an empty stool. "Yeah, I remember. What about her?"

"What's her name?"

"Hilary Bienville. She drinks in here. But that's all she does."

"How many nights a week does she come in?"

"Four or five."

"Who does she come in with?"

"I didn't notice."

"Who does she leave with?"

"Same answer."

"Where does she live?"

"Don't know exactly."

"You know who Axel Devereaux is?"

"No, suh."

The bartender began rinsing out a washrag in the sink, his eyes lidded. A black woman with a slim figure in a tight black skirt and a green cowboy shirt with pearl snap buttons and glass Mardi Gras beads in her hair was tuning her guitar on the stage. Her hair hung in her face, but I had the feeling her gaze was on me rather than the tuning pegs.

"Axel Devereaux is a dirty cop," I said to the bartender. "Why carry his weight?"

"Way it is, suh."

"Lose the Stepin Fetchit routine."

He leaned toward me, his head round and slick and small for his big shoulders. "I ain't got to take this."

"You're right." I placed my business card in front of him. "I'll tell Devereaux you're a stand-up guy. I see you've got a mop and pail back there. That might make a great coat of arms."

I went outside and got into my truck. But I didn't leave. The light began to go out of the sky, and birds were gathering inside the oaks along the bayou, the tree frogs singing. Fifteen minutes passed. Then the front door opened and the woman in the cowboy shirt and Mardi Gras beads came out and popped a paper match and lit a cigarette in a holder and flipped the match away. She came to my window, smoke sliding from her lips. "What's goin' on, darlin'?"

"No haps."

"Girl you looking for gonna need some he'p. You'll find her in the trailer court by the drawbridge in Jeanerette, right acrost from the big plantation house."

"Is she in danger?"

"She dimed Axel Devereaux wit' your PI friend."

"Where'd you get the scar on your neck?"

"I'm a Mississippi nigger. I got all kinds of stories."

"You're from New Orleans," I said. "Don't put yourself down, beautiful."

"How you know I'm from New Orleans?"

"You've got an accent like an angel."

She slipped her fingernails into my hair. "Come see me sometime when you ain't working. I can burn away your blues."

"I'm too green to burn," I said.

She smiled, her gold-rimmed teeth glinting. "You got a *gris-gris* on you, baby. Let Mama know when you need some he'p."

She picked my hand up off the steering and tenderly bit my finger.

I WOKE HARD AND throbbing in the morning, filled with all the desire and longing that old men never lose, no matter how dignified they may behave. The manifestation of that desire takes many forms, none of them predictable and none of them good.

At 8:16 a.m., I followed Axel Devereaux into the department men's room. He wet his comb at the sink. I stood behind him but didn't speak. He tapped the water off his comb and put it into his shirt pocket, watching me in the mirror.

"You look a little out of joint. Somebody cross her legs on your nose?" he said.

"I don't like to talk to a reflection."

He turned slowly, his eyes meeting mine. His forearms were thick and solid, wrapped with monkey hair. "Purcel been talking to you?"

I slapped him across the face. His skin was as coarse as emery paper. He stared at me unblinking, his face stark, as if someone had flashed a strobe on it in a dark room. I've known evil men, but I had never seen any man's eyes look the way his did. There was a dirtiness in them that had no bottom.

"Speak disrespectfully about my partner again and I'll hang you by your toes and cut your tongue out," I said. "That's not a metaphor."

His gaze slipped off mine and focused on empty space.

"Did you hear me?" I said.

He walked past me and out the door, causing two deputies to step aside, water dripping from his hair onto his shirt.

I stood in the middle of the room, trembling with anger, my ears ringing. I washed my hands, trying to scrub the feel of his whiskers off my skin.

• • •

AT FIVE P.M., I drove down Bayou Teche to Jeanerette, past Alice Plantation, built in 1803, with its palm trees and elevated wide gallery and twin chimneys, and past another plantation home surrounded by live oaks that were two centuries old. I crossed a drawbridge and turned in to a trailer park that looked transported from Bangladesh.

The manager of the park pointed to the trailer rented by Hilary Bienville. It was set on cinder blocks, the seams orange with rust, the floor sagging. I tapped on the door.

A young black woman answered, hooking the screen door as soon as she saw my badge holder. "What you want?"

"I'm Dave Robicheaux, a friend of Clete Purcel. I'd like to talk with you."

"I'm fixing to eat."

"You tried to help out a worthless man named Travis Lebeau. Not everybody would do that, Miss Hilary."

"Who tole you where I live?"

"A lady who sings the blues."

"Somebody is after me?"

"You know Axel Devereaux?"

"I ain't said nothing about Mr. Axel."

"But you know him?"

"Everybody knows Axel Devereaux."

"I work homicide and felony assault, not vice," I said. I took a photo out of my wallet. It showed Clete and me together at Gulfstream Park in Hallandale, Florida. "Give me five minutes."

She looked at my truck and studied my face, then stared at the other trailers and the clothes flapping on wash lines. She unhooked the screen. "I got to get my dinner out of the micro."

I stepped inside. The walls were covered with pages cut from movie magazines. Most of the actors in the photos were black. A large green bottle of bulk wine stood on her kitchen table. She removed the frozen dinner from the microwave and set it on a place mat.

"I got a baby to feed before my gran'mama come over," she said. "Make it fast, okay?"

"How many nights do you work?"

"Six. Don't work Sundays. Sunday ain't never good in my bidness."

"You're a better person than you think," I said.

"Try to pay your bills with that."

"If you're lucky, the pimp who owns you takes only thirty-five percent. He pieces off another twenty percent to Axel. Once in a while your pimp runs a Murphy scam on a guy and you make a little more. Does that sound like a reasonable way to make a living?"

"It's better than scrubbing a flo' for a white man that spits on it." She peeled the plastic off her dinner, indifferent to the heat, her eyes starting to film.

"The nuns at Southern Mutual Help can get you a new start," I said.

She didn't reply. She bowed her head and began taking small bites. She wiped her nose with her wrist.

I got a roll of paper towels off the drainboard and set it beside her. "It sounds like your baby is up."

She set down her fork. "She needs changing."

"I'll do it."

I went into a tiny side room where a baby of about nine or ten months lay on her side in a crib. I removed the dirty diaper and wiped her down and replaced it with a clean one. She looked curiously into my face and smiled when I rattled a toy and put it in her hand. A piece of red twine with an eight-point cross on it, stamped from brass, was knotted around her ankle.

I went back into the kitchen and sat down at the table without being asked. "That's a sweet baby."

"T'ank you."

"Where'd you get that charm on her ankle?"

"Mine to know."

"Don't put it on the child's neck."

"I ain't gonna do somet'ing like that."

"You believe in the *gris-gris*?" I asked.

"I seen dead people. They got hungry eyes. It's 'cause they cain't eat or drink till they get inside someone and do it t'rew them."

"You see these dead people at night?" I said.

"In the daylight. Standing right next to me in the grocery store. A lot of people ain't what they look like. There's a second person inside them."

She did not speak like an ignorant person or even one who was superstitious. And for that reason she really bothered me. She looked through the window. "There's my gran'mama."

"The charm is called the Maltese cross. You won't tell me where you got it?"

"A bubblegum machine," she said.

"Who's your pimp, Miss Hilary?"

"Like I'm gonna tell *you*?"

"Here's my business card. If you want to get out of the life, call me. Don't let Axel push you around. He's a bully and a coward."

"So how come he's a deputy sheriff?"

HELEN CALLED ME into her office the next afternoon. "Somebody poisoned Sean McClain's pets."

"When?" I said.

"He fed them last night. This morning they were dead. Whoever did it wanted to get both the cat and the dog. There was butcher paper with ground meat in the kennel, and a sardine can on the grass."

"Did Sean have trouble with his neighbors?"

"Sean doesn't have trouble with anyone. Except for a couple of wiseasses in the department."

"Axel Devereaux is one of those wiseasses?"

"Devereaux knows you're protective of Sean."

"It goes deeper than that," I said. "Sean slammed Devereaux in the head with a napkin dispenser at Victor's."

"I didn't know that."

"It doesn't matter. Devereaux shouldn't be a member of the department."

"When I fire him arbitrarily, you can handle the lawsuit," she said.

"I think he may be working with a pimp."

"Which pimp?"

"I don't know," I said. "I talked to a black prostitute in Jeanerette. She wouldn't give him up. Do we have anything more on the escaped convict from Texas?"

"No, why?"

"The prostitute is named Hilary Bienville. Her baby had a Maltese cross tied on her ankle. It was an icon worn by Crusader knights."

"What's the connection?"

"Lucinda Arceneaux had a chain on one ankle. The medal on it had been pulled off."

"I got that. What's the connection with Hugo Tillinger?"

"I don't know, Helen. I'm lost. From everything we hear, Tillinger's head is full of superstition and general craziness."

"Do you know how many people in southern Louisiana wear a charm or religious medal on their body, including you?"

We had reached a point where we were taking out our anger on each other, which, in a police investigation, almost always signals a dead end in the making.

"I'll talk to Sean," I said.

"Here's the rest of it. When Devereaux passed him in the corridor this morning, he went 'Bow-wow' and 'Meow-meow.' "

THAT NIGHT THE weather was hot and dry, the end of summer floating like ash on the wind. The sky flickered with heat lightning, like flashes of artillery that began on the horizon and spread silently through the clouds. A drunk plowed into a power pole and knocked out the electricity on East Main, and the three air-conditioning units in my house made a groaning sound and died like sick animals. I took a jar of lemonade from the icebox and rolled it on my face, then sat in my chair on the bayou and drank the lemonade and watched the stars fall out of the sky.

The phone was ringing and the message light blinking when I came back inside. It was 2:13 a.m.

"Where've you been?" Helen said.

"Outside."

"Need you on Old Jeanerette Road," Helen said. "Between Alice Plantation and the drawbridge. Hang on. I've got to get a news photographer out of here."

The location made my stomach flip-flop. It was a short distance from the trailer of Hilary Bienville.

Helen came back on the line. "We've got a body. Or what's left of it. Haul ass, will you?"

"Man or woman?"

"Good question," she replied.

Chapter Eight

THE MOST SURREAL aspect of the scene was the juxtaposition of the antebellum plantation homes on the road, the carriage lamps glowing like candles on a wedding cake, and the drag on the asphalt. It began by the LSU experimental farm and continued in a wet serpentine line almost to the drawbridge, a journey of about half a mile. That was where the vehicle stopped and someone cut the rope that had been cinched around the victim's neck.

He lay in the weeds on his side, his eyes open, clotted with blood. Most of his face and hair had been sanded off. His teeth and shoes were gone, his jaw broken. His legs looked like bloody sticks clothed in rags.

Emergency vehicles, their flashers rippling, lined the road. "There's no ID on him," Helen said.

"His name is Travis Lebeau," I said.

"Clete's snitch?"

"Just a bumbling, hapless guy."

She shined her light on a green teardrop that still remained on the skin. "He was in the AB?"

"Until they sold him to the Black Guerilla Family."

"I can't believe we've got these guys here," she said. "Wasn't it the AB that dragged a black man in Texas about twenty years back?"

"They had white-supremacist tats. Maybe they were AB, maybe not. This isn't racial."

"Yeah, but it's them."

I walked with a flashlight down the trail of blood and skin. The moon had come from behind the clouds and lit the bayou and the cattails and canebrakes in the shallows. There was blood at the base of two oak trees that grew by the road. I hoped Lebeau had been knocked unconscious when he struck them. I clicked off my flashlight and walked back to where Helen was standing.

"You don't look good," she said.

"Not enough sleep."

"Right."

"Lebeau tried to sell me information so he could score or get out of town," I said. "I blew him off."

"You didn't trust his information?"

"No."

"So what were you supposed to do? Give him the money anyway? Put the cork in it, Pops."

I clicked on my light again and shone it in Lebeau's mouth. "I don't think his teeth were broken on the road."

She stared at me.

"The roots are gone," I said. "I think his teeth were pulled before he was dragged."

I ached for a drink. I think Helen did, too. Wonder why cops bring the job home or to a bar? It's no mystery.

WE HAD NO leads. Travis Lebeau had been staying at a men's shelter in Lafayette. No one there remembered seeing him the day of his death. He was a loner, had no family or friends, and took little interest in the other men at the shelter. We put his mug shots in local newspapers and on television and asked anyone with information about him to call the department.

On Friday I got a call from a bartender in North Lafayette named Skip Dubisson. At one time he had been a pitcher in the St. Louis Cardinals farm system, but he'd lost an arm in Iraq and now worked at a low-bottom bar in Lafayette's old unofficial red-light district north of Four Corners. "I'm pretty sure your guy was in here, Dave. The one whose picture you put on TV."

"Travis Lebeau?" I said.

"He didn't give his name. But yeah, same guy, a week ago. He wanted to set up a tab. I think he wanted to get laid, too."

"Did he come in with anyone? Make any friends, female or otherwise?"

"I didn't pay that much attention," he said. "My regulars keep me busy, know what I mean?"

"You've had some bad dudes in?" I asked.

"Are you kidding?"

"The Aryan Brotherhood?"

"Who knows? Everybody's got sleeves these days, all blue, wrist to the pits, lots of swastikas. Race-baiting is back in style."

"This isn't about race."

"In this place everything is about race," he said.

I drove to Lafayette in my pickup rather than a cruiser and parked in front of the club. It was a wretched place on a backstreet, the parking lot full of flattened beer cans, the trash barrels overflowing and crawling with flies. I went inside and stood at the bar. Skip saw me from the far end and poured a Dr Pepper in a glass packed with ice and dropped two cherries and an orange slice into it and set the glass on a napkin in front of me. His upper left arm was fitted with a prosthesis. The IED that took his arm had also disfigured the side of his face, puckering the tissue like a heat burn on a lamp shade. But he was still a handsome man, as though defined by an internal radiance rather than his wounds. I'd never once heard him complain or even make mention of his war experience. "How's business in New Iberia?" he asked.

"Just the usual effluent. Want to check out some of our clientele?"

My iPhone was loaded with mug shots of outlaw bikers and members of the Klan, Christian Identity, Aryan Nations, the American Nazi Party, and the AB. I watched as Skip scanned through them.

"Is it coincidence that all these guys look stupid?" he said.

"That's a pre-prerequisite."

He shook his head. "No, I've never seen any of them."

"You said Lebeau wanted to get laid."

"He was definitely the guy hanging on to a couple of soiled doves."

"Can I talk to them?"

He scratched his face with his prosthetic hand. "I don't remember which ones he talked to, Dave. He was drunk and didn't have any money. I felt sorry for him."

"He didn't have trouble with anyone?"

"No. What was he inside for?"

"Manslaughter knocked down from first-degree homicide."

"He was actually dragged behind a car?"

"Somebody pulled his teeth first."

"Jesus, I thought Iraq was bad. Sorry I couldn't be more help. You want another Dr Pepper?"

"There're two more photos I'd like you to look at." I clicked on the unshaved front-view and side-view mug shots of a man in prison whites that I had gotten from the Texas Department of Criminal Justice.

"Yeah, he was in here," Skip said. "A nice-looking guy. A little edgy. He wasn't shopping for the trade. I wondered what he was doing here. He drank soda pop."

"That's Hugo Tillinger. He's an escapee from the Texas penal system. You're sure he was here?"

"Yeah, last week."

"Was he with Travis Lebeau?"

Skip looked into space, then back at me. Someone was tapping on the bar for another drink. Skip served him and came back. "I remember him because he sat alone at the end of the bar and ordered a soft drink. When a working girl came on to him, he was polite but not interested. In a dump like this, it's trick, trade, or travel. It puts me in a bad spot sometimes. I mean, telling people to beat it."

"You told Tillinger to leave?"

"I let him slide. He seemed like a nice guy. That attitude gets me in trouble with the boss."

"Think hard. Did you see him talking to Lebeau?"

"Yeah, maybe. I can't be sure." He closed and opened his eyes. "It seemed like they knew each other."

"Did Tillinger leave with anyone?"

"I don't know."

I was about to give up.

"But he said something weird."

"Like what?"

" 'You ought to be in the movies.' I said, 'You wising off?' He said I had him wrong, that he had some movie connections with people who got Hurricane Carter out of jail. He said I was photogenic. I told him to get his eyes examined."

"That's Tillinger. That's our guy."

"What was he in for?"

"Burning his wife and daughter to death."

Skip blew out his breath. He poured the remainder of the Dr Pepper can into my glass. "You know what's the most depressing aspect of my job?"

"No."

"Cleaning the bathroom at two a.m. and thinking about the people who were in there," he said. "Ever have that feeling?"

Every day, I thought. But I didn't say it.

I WENT BACK TO the department. On the way to my office, I passed Axel Devereaux in the corridor. He looked through me. When a guy like Devereaux looks through you, you'd better watch your ass.

"Axel?"

He turned around.

"Want to meet somewhere and talk this out?" I said.

"Talk it out? I feel like ripping your face off."

"Because I hit you?"

"No, because you're a goddamn liar."

"I lied about what?"

"Me killing Sean McClain's pets. You spread it around."

"You mocked him," I said. "You imitated the sounds of his cat and dog."

"Whoever told you that is a liar. Just like you."

"At my age, I don't have a lot to lose, Axel. Know what I mean?"

"You'll see me coming, asshole. I ain't a sneak that goes around bad-mouthing people."

Unless you are familiar with the nature of Southern white trash, you will not understand the following: They are a genetically produced breed whose commonality is a state of mind and not related to the social class to which they belong. Economics has nothing to do with their origins or their behavior. You cannot change them. They glory in violence and cruelty and brag on their ignorance, and would have no problem manning the ovens at Auschwitz. That's not hyperbole. When I looked into Axel's eyes, I knew my slap across his face had been a slap across his soul and that one day I would pay for it.

"You dealt the play when you disrespected my partner," I said. "But I shouldn't have struck you. For that I apologize. That also means I'm done."

He put a toothpick in his mouth, then removed and stared at it, a glint in his eye. "So you got no problem."

I walked away, then glanced back at him before entering my office. He was still standing in the corridor, by himself, silhouetted against a window like a black cutout without features or humanity.

I HAD THREE OPEN homicide files on my desk: Lucinda Arceneaux floated out to sea on a cross; Joe Molinari hanged in a shrimp net from a tree; and Travis Lebeau tortured and dragged to death. In terms of forensic evidence, we had nothing that would necessarily connect one case to the other. But the histrionic nature of each homicide couldn't be denied. There were also threads that seemed to overlap. The man Lucinda Arceneaux tried to get off death row had broken out of a prison hospital and come here rather than a large urban area where he could hide more conveniently. He'd also gone out of his way to tell a bartender he knew people connected to the film industry. The man who had befriended him, Travis Lebeau, had ended up dead. But where did Joe Molinari fit in? His life had been lived almost invisibly. Had he been selected randomly by a lunatic and posed to represent the Hanged Man in the tarot, or had Bailey Ribbons and I let our imaginations go unchecked?

Normally, the motivation in any premeditated homicide involves sex or money or power or any combination of the three. The similarity in the Arceneaux and Molinari homicides was the lack of motivation and the possibility of religious fanaticism bordering on madness. The horrible death of Travis Lebeau may have been simply a revenge killing by the AB. But the fact remained that his friend was the escaped convict Hugo Tillinger, and Tillinger was a friend of Lucinda Arceneaux's. Tillinger had known both people, and now both were dead.

Tillinger was the only lead we had. Skip, my bartender friend, had said Tillinger was a nice guy. A jury in Texas had thought otherwise. But what did we actually know about him?

He may or may not have killed his family. He was argumentative and had inflexible moral attitudes. He had probably broken into three fishing camps but had taken little of value and seemed to have no record of dishonesty. Skip had said he didn't belong in a bar that was one cut above a hot-pillow joint. A Texas gunbull had called him a lying son of a bitch you shouldn't turn your back on.

All of which added up to take your choice.

THAT EVENING I went home late and stood at the back of my property and threw moldy pecans into the current and watched them sink out of sight. Snuggs sat by my foot, sniffing the breeze, his tail draped over my loafer. I heard Alafair walk up behind me. "What's goin' on, big guy?"

"Eighty-six the big-guy stuff, please."

"I signed on with Desmond's group," she said. "I might be going out to Arizona."

"Sorry—what?"

"I'm going to do the rewrite on the script. I'm also going to have a small acting role."

"That's good," I said.

"I'll be flying out to the location with Lou next week."

"Lou Wexler?"

"Yeah," she said. "What about it?"

"He's old."

"He's older than I am. That doesn't mean he's old."

"It's your life, Alf."

"Why do you have to say that, Dave?"

"I don't trust these guys. When they get what they want, they're gone. Every time, without exception."

"So I should stay away from the movie business? How about publishing? Should I stay away from publishing houses?"

I arced a pecan into the middle of the bayou. "I'm at a dead end on three homicides. One thing I'm sure of, however: Antoine Butterworth is mixed up in them."

"I think you're wrong," she said. "Besides, Lou hates his guts."

"Why do you call this guy by his first name?"

"It's what people do when they know each other. I don't mean in the biblical sense, either. You think Desmond is corrupt?"

"No," I said.

"Then maybe you won't mind that he wants to cast Bailey Ribbons."

"That's her business." I threw a pecan into the bayou.

"You have feelings for her?"

"Cut it out, Alafair. When are you leaving?"

"Tuesday. Lou has a private plane."

"Have a good trip."

I picked up Snuggs and put him on my shoulder and walked back to the house and opened a can of cat food for him and fed him on the step. Mon Tee Coon was nowhere in sight. Then I washed my hands in the sink and went out the front door without saying goodbye or telling Alafair where I was going. I walked down East Main in the twilight, under the canopy of live oaks, past the city library, counting cadence in my head, and went inside the Little River Inn and sat at a table at the back of the dining room, my mind filled with thoughts and desires that boded well for no one.

Chapter Nine

"YOU EATING TONIGHT, Dave?" the waiter asked.

"What do you have that's cold?" I said.

"Iced tea?"

"What else have you got?"

"Whatever you want," he replied.

"You have French vanilla ice cream?"

"Sure. Want anything on it?"

I gazed out the window, a fleeting tic in my eye. "What do you have?"

"Crème de menthe, brandy and chocolate, plain chocolate, butterscotch."

There was an oak tree wrapped with tiny white lights in the backyard. The sky was purple, a sliver of moon hanging by the evening star.

"I don't want anything," I said. "Maybe I'll just sit here a minute."

"You got it, Dave," he said. "Let me know if you need anything."

After the waiter was gone, I went to the restroom, then out the door. I kept walking through town, past the Shadows and across the drawbridge at Burke Street, and on up Loreauville Road to an Acadian-style cottage that sat on a one-acre green lot on the bayou. All the lights were on. I twisted the bell.

"Why, Dave. Come in," Bailey said when she answered. She was dressed in sandals and stonewashed jeans and a shirt printed with faded flowers.

I stepped inside.

"Where's your truck?" she said.

"I was out for a walk."

"On Loreauville Road?"

The living room was immaculate. I could smell food on a stove. "I'm sorry if I caught you at supper."

"No, join me."

"I've already eaten. I'll take just a few minutes."

"Come in the kitchen. Is something wrong?"

"I was talking with my daughter this evening."

She pointed at a chair by the table. The kitchen was bright and clean, every surface wiped down. Through the window I could see the long green sweep on the yard and the shadows of the trees on the grass and the reflection of lights on the bayou. My body felt strange, my skin dead, my ears humming. I did not know why I was there. My legs were turning to rubber. I sat down.

"Yes?" she said.

"Desmond Cormier wants to cast you in his film, even though he knows you're investigating a homicide that might involve people he works with."

"He hasn't said anything to me about it."

"I'm sorry for breaking in on you like this."

She put a sandwich and two scoops of potato salad on her plate, then set a pitcher of iced tea and two glasses on the table. "Will you please tell me what's bothering you?"

"There are two or three bad guys in the department," I replied. "One of them is Axel Devereaux."

"What about him?"

"He's a misogynist."

"You think I care about a man like that?"

"He may have poisoned Sean McClain's animals."

"Ugh," she said. "Is somebody going to do something about that?"

"There's no proof."

"Every thought in that man's brain is on his face. What's he doing in the department, anyway?"

"From what I gather, you grew up in a traditional neighborhood in New Orleans, Bailey," I said.

"I'm not making the connection."

"In Vietnam we used to say 'It's Nam.' Same thing here. This is Louisiana. That means we're everybody's punch. Wars of enormous consequence are fought in places nobody cares about."

"You don't have to protect me, Dave. Or patronize me."

"I believe you. I'd better be going."

She looked at her food. She hadn't touched it. "How long has your wife been gone?"

"Three years."

"A car accident?"

"I'd call it a homicide. Why do you ask?"

"My husband died when he was only twenty-five," she said. "He was in Iraq, but he had to come home to get killed. I know what it's like to lose someone and be alone."

"I'm not alone."

"Don't pretend," she said.

"Desmond is right. You look like the actress who played Clementine in the Henry Fonda movie."

"I guess I'll have to see it sometime."

"Stay away from those guys, Bailey. They're sons of bitches."

"I'll try to watch out for myself."

I didn't know if she was being ironic or trying to be polite. I half-filled my glass with tea and drank it down. "I'll see you Monday morning."

"Come by anytime. Can I drive you home?"

"No."

I didn't want to leave. I wanted to be decades younger. I wanted to be everything except what I was. Unfortunately, at a certain age, wanting something you can't be or wanting what you can't have can become a way of life.

WHEN I GOT home, Alafair and Lou Wexler were sitting in rocking chairs on the gallery.

"Where have you been?" Alafair said.

"I took a walk."

"How about telling me next time?" she said.

"How do you do, Mr. Robicheaux?" Wexler said.

"I'm solid. How about you?"

"It's a lovely night," he said.

"Y'all are going to Arizona on Tuesday?" I said.

"Yes, sir," he replied, rocking back and forth.

"In your private plane?"

"Actually, I rent it," he said. "I get a corporate break."

"Is that how it works?" I said. "I think I'll incorporate my pickup truck."

"Come in and let's have some pecan pie, Dave," Alafair said.

"I have to make a call on a bartender I insulted."

"You did what?" she said.

"A black guy who bartends at that blues joint on the bayou," I said. "I told him he should adopt a mop and pail as his coat of arms."

"You didn't," Alafair said.

"I was in a bad mood."

"Don't go there," she said.

"I won't be long."

She got up from the chair. It rocked weightlessly behind her. "Please."

"You worry too much," I said.

"Can we go along?" Wexler said.

"No need. They cater to a rough trade," I said. "You know how Louisiana is."

"Try a couple of ports in West Africa," he said.

"That's right, you and Butterworth were mercenaries," I said.

"I was a security contractor. Butterworth was a degenerate fop."

"You like war, Mr. Wexler?"

"No, I hate it. I also bloody well hate those who profit from it."

"Security contractors don't?" I said.

"With respect, sir, we saved the lives of thousands who would have been massacred in their villages."

"That's a noble endeavor," I said. "Top of the evening to you."

I got into my truck and fired up the engine. Alafair walked to my window. The belt on the fan was squealing, the gearshift knob throbbing in my palm. Wexler remained on the gallery. "You either end this attitude or I won't be back," she said to me.

"Security contractor, my ass," I said.

"I mean it, Dave."

My heart was a lump of ice.

I DROVE TO THE blues bar on the bayou. The night was sliding into the hours when the psychological metabolism in certain people shifts into reverse and the worst in them comes out and they feed fires that warp and reconfigure who they are. The sky was black, the air dry and full of dust, the parking lot lined with gas-guzzlers. A man and woman were arguing by the entrance. The woman hit him and stormed away. He grinned at her, grabbed his package, and said, "Bite."

I went inside and sat in the shadows at the end of the bar. The singer who called herself a Mississippi nigger was playing an instrumental with two Creole men who wore porkpie hats and firehouse suspenders and puff-sleeved pink dress shirts that looked as fresh as roses. My bartender friend with the waxed mahogany knob for a head drummed his fingers in front of me. "What'll it be, chief?"

"I look like I have feathers in my hair?" I said.

"Same question. You want some ribs? You want a beer? What d'you want?"

"I made a crack about a mop and pail and Stepin Fetchit."

"I was all busted up about that."

"I apologize."

"I ain't got all night."

"Give me a diet Dr Pepper."

"This ain't a soda fountain."

"Give me a Dr Pepper and give the lady on the bandstand whatever she's having."

"She drinks double Scotches and milk."

"Then give her that. One other thing?"

"*What?*"

"Has Hilary Bienville been in?"

"The working girl? I hear she not taking any friction, get my meaning?"

"What's your name?"

"Lloyd."

"You're a charmer, Lloyd."

"You need to see a psychiatrist, man."

"You're probably right. Give me a plate of ribs and dirty rice," I said, pushing a twenty at him.

Ten minutes later, the singer with the scar like a snake wrapped around her neck sat down next to me, the double Scotch in one hand, a glass of milk in the other. She wore a black skirt and a cowboy vest and a brocaded maroon shirt and enough jewelry to rattle. She sipped from the Scotch, her eyes fixed on me. "Thanks, baby. Where you been?"

"Hanging around."

She touched my can of Dr Pepper. "You drink that?"

"That's what I'm drinking tonight."

"You go to meetings?"

"For quite a while. I'm not a good example, though."

"Church and all that jazz?"

"I figure it beats blowing my brains out."

"What are you doin' in here, baby?"

"I need to know who Hilary Bienville's manager is."

"Ax her."

"She doesn't want acid in her face?"

"Don't be shopping around for information ain't nobody gonna give you," she said.

"You never told me your name."

"Bella."

"Bella what?"

"Delahoussaye."

"That's a pretty name."

She rattled her jewelry. "Know what that sound is?"

I shook my head.

"Same sound you make when you walk," she said. "You dragging a chain, honey-bunny, just like me."

"You read minds?"

"I can read yours."

"I owe a debt to some people who have no voice," I said. "That's because they're in the cemetery. Or buried in a body bag in a rain forest on the other side of the world."

"You won't do them no good by joining them."

I pushed my plate toward her. "Want some ribs?"

"You think you're too old?"

"Old for what?"

"Me."

"My wife was killed in a car wreck three years ago. I spend most of my time alone."

She looked into space. "The dead don't care. The world is for the living. You got to take your shot."

"That's one way of looking at it," I said.

She poured her Scotch into her milk; it swirled like caramel against the glass. She drank the glass empty, her eyes closed, the lids covered with blue eye shadow. She got up from the bar stool. "I get off at two. Hang around."

"You don't know me. I could be a dangerous man."

"But you ain't."

As I went out the door, I heard her singing a song written by Big Mama Thornton and made famous by Janis Joplin. It was one of despair and loss and unrelieved misery, one that maybe only a black woman of Thornton's era could adequately understand. The song was "Ball and Chain."

At two a.m. I pulled up to the side door of the club.

BELLA DELAHOUSSAYE STARED at me in the headlights, then got in and closed the door without speaking.

"Where's your guitar?" I asked.

"Locked up. What's that you got?"

"A bouquet and a box of chocolates."

"Everything is closed."

"Not Walmart." I started the engine. "Where do you live?"

"In St. Martinville."

"First I want to take you somewhere else," I said.

"I ain't choicey. Except about my men." She touched my thigh.

I drove to a cemetery in St. Martin Parish, not far from a large lake and a wetlands area that bled into the Atchafalaya Swamp. The moon was down, the sky black and swirling with dust from the fields. Oddly, the lake glowed with a luminosity that seemed to radiate from beneath the water. When I was a child, we believed the loup-garou lived under the lake and was responsible for the disappearance of both animals and people.

I cut the engine and took a second bouquet from behind the seat and walked to the passenger side of the truck and opened Bella's door.

"What are we doing?" she said.

"Need to show you something."

She stepped onto the ground, a little off balance. I fitted my hand around her upper arm. I could feel the muscle twitch, see a glint of fear in the corner of her eye. She pulled away from me. I took a penlight from my pocket and clicked it on. "That yonder is my wife's crypt."

"Why you showing it to me?"

"Her name was Molly. She was a Maryknoll nun in El Salvador and Guatemala. Friends of hers were murdered there. Our government abandoned them, even covered up for their killers."

"Why you telling me this?"

"I want you to understand what I mean when I say I owe the dead a debt. My wife spent her life helping others. A bad man T-boned her with his truck at high speed. There were no witnesses. The bad man put the blame on her and got away with it. He's dead now. I didn't kill him, but I wanted to."

Bella pushed her hair into a curl behind her neck. Her eyes were elongated, more like an Asian's than a black woman's; they seemed to take on a wet sheen, like the darkness in the lake. "I don't want to be disrespectful, hon, but I ain't up for this kind of gig."

I walked to the crypt and squatted and placed the flowers in a vase by the name plate. I stood up, my back creaking. "I lost another wife to men who killed her rather than me. Her name was Annie. For the rest of my life, I have to find justice for Molly and Annie. I've killed several men as a result. I'm glad I did, and I think the world is a better place for it. In the nocturnal hours, I sometimes want to kill more men. That's how I feel tonight. But in the morning I won't feel that way."

"Ain't you figured it out yet? I'm in the life. I'm the kind of people you hate."

"No, you're not. You're an artist."

"You learn the blues at the crossroads, darlin'. There ain't no going back once you been there."

"Don't let anyone sell you that crap, Bella. Who's Hilary Bienville's pimp?"

"The pimp is a middleman. Hilary don't have no middleman, just a piece of trash wit' a badge looking out for her."

"Axel Devereaux?"

"Wasn't me said it," she replied. "Take me home, please. I don't sing the blues, I live them. Ain't shooting you a line, darlin'."

We arrived at her small house in St. Martinville just as a thundershower blew through town and clattered like hail on my truck. I put a raincoat over our heads and ran with her to the door, then said good night and drove back to New Iberia.

Chapter Ten

I slept late on Saturday morning and woke to birdsong and sunshine in the trees. Alafair was gone and had not left a note. Snuggs was sitting on the back steps, his white coat smudged with mud, a cut like a three-inch piece of red string threaded through his fur. I wiped him off with paper towels and dressed his wound and took him inside and fed him on the floor. The cut was jagged, as if he'd hooked himself going over a chain-link fence.

"You okay, old fella?" I said, stroking his head.

I went outside and looked for Mon Tee Coon. There was no sign of him. I called Clete and told him of my conversation with Bella Delahoussaye the previous night and my worries about my animals.

"Axel Devereaux is shaking down local hookers?" he said.

"On one level or another. Maybe they're just hauling his ashes."

"You think he hurt your coon?"

"He probably killed Sean McClain's pets."

"Everyone thinks that?"

"That's right."

"And he'd do the same to yours when he'd be the first guy people would suspect?"

"He's a sociopath and a sadist," I said. "He can't change what he is. If he's not cruel to an animal, he'll be cruel to a person."

"How about if I break his wheels?"

"That's out."

"You called *me,* Dave."

"Sorry I did."

"What the hell is the matter with you?" he said.

"I'm like you. I want to do it the old-time way. But we can't."

"Speak for yourself," he said. He hung up.

I called him back. "I apologize."

"Quit tormenting yourself, big mon. We handle the action. They deal the play, we scramble their eggs."

Wish it worked that way, I thought. But I didn't try to argue.

ON MONDAY MY office phone rang at 8:06 a.m.

"Detective Robicheaux speaking," I said.

"I tried to get you all weekend," a man's voice said. "Nobody would give me your number."

"That's because it's unlisted," I said. "Who is this?"

"Never mind who I am. You're the guy working the Travis Lebeau homicide, right?"

"I'm one of them."

"You figure the AB did it?"

"You need to tell me who you are, partner."

"No, you need to listen. Maybe the AB caught up to Travis, maybe not. Or maybe some of your own people did it."

I punched in Helen's number on my cell phone and placed the phone on my desk so she could overhear my conversation with the man as soon as she picked up. "Am I talking to Mr. Tillinger?" I asked.

"Call me Hugo. You know my history, right? The fire, the trial, me busting out of that hospital?"

"Yes, sir."

"I didn't kill either my daughter or my wife. I wouldn't harm a woman or a child under any circumstance."

"Why'd you come here?"

"To find Miss Lucinda. To ask her for money so I didn't have to steal it, then get as much gone from here as I can."

"Who killed her?"

"That's why I called. I aim to get those who done it."

"We don't have any leads," I said. "Maybe I can establish a back channel with you."

"Yeah, in a heartbeat. Who do you think you're talking to?"

"A guy who's con-wise, a fellow who perhaps went down on a bad beef."

There was a brief silence. "Did Miss Lucinda suffer?"

"She wasn't tortured or violated, if that's what you mean."

"But she suffered?"

"She was injected with heroin. Maybe she just went to sleep."

"But she suffered just the same, didn't she?"

"You know the answer to that," I said.

"Who's the last person she saw?"

"We ask the questions," I said.

"It's done a lot of good, hasn't it."

"She was supposed to get on a flight from Lafayette to Los Angeles. She never boarded the plane." Again the line went silent. "Did she talk to you about movie people?" I asked.

"She just said they'd he'p me."

"Which people in particular?"

"She didn't say. There was one local name she gave me, though. A bad cop. He runs whores and such."

"What does the dirty cop have to do with getting you off death row?"

"Nothing. Miss Lucinda said she wanted to put him out of business because he preyed on black women. You recording this?"

"What do you think?" I asked.

"I think y'all cain't find your asses with both hands."

"It's been good talking to you."

"I'm fixing to make a statement, the kind a guy will remember, get my drift?"

"No, I don't. I think talking to you is a waste of time."

I hung up and waited. Five minutes later, he called back. "She left the airport with somebody she knew and trusted, somebody who was more important to her than the catering people or the boyfriend waiting to pick up her in Hollywood," he said. "I'm right, aren't I?"

"You're an intelligent man."

"I'm a dead man walking, and we both know it," he said. "You know what the upside of that is?"

"You've got nothing to lose."

"See? You're a smart son of a buck yourself."

An escapee from death row who didn't use coarse language? This case was getting muddier by the day.

AT DAYBREAK ON Tuesday, Lou Wexler arrived in his Lamborghini to take Alafair to the private jet that would deliver them to Monument Valley, Arizona, in time for a late lunch. She gave me a card with the name and number and email address of the hotel where she would be staying. I asked her to step aside for a moment.

"What is it?" she said.

"I have to ask you something of a personal nature. I don't want to offend you."

She searched my face. "Don't say it, Dave."

"I have to."

"Please don't do this."

"Do you have a single room?"

"You have no right to ask me that."

"I don't care. I'm your father. I don't trust any of these guys."

"That's obvious. Goodbye. I'll call you when we get there. Dave, you really know how to do it."

As they backed out in the street, Wexler lifted his hat in a salute. I squinted one eye and cocked my thumb and aimed my index finger at him.

AXEL DEVEREAUX DIDN'T show up for the 0800 roll call. Instead, he called Helen from his home. She walked down to my office and opened the door without knocking. "Get Bailey and go over to Devereaux's place. Somebody creeped his house."

"You want us to investigate a B and E?"

"It sounds like it's more than a B and E," she said. "Maybe justice is finally catching up with this asshole."

Bailey checked out a cruiser, and the two of us rode up the bayou to the drawbridge south of Loreauville where Axel lived by himself in a smudged stucco house with Styrofoam litter and car parts and two boats and stacks of crab traps in the yard. He met us at the door in a rage.

"Calm down," I said.

"Look at my place. He did it in my sleep," he said.

"Who did?" I said, stepping inside.

"The exterminator," he said.

"Which exterminator?" I asked.

"A freelancer," Axel said. "He was going from door to door yesterday."

"You don't use a regular service?" Bailey said.

So far he had not acknowledged her presence. "I take care of the termites myself. The guy gave me a deal."

"How do you know the exterminator is the vandal?" she said.

"I keep a spare set of keys on the dresser," Axel said. "I didn't notice they were missing until this morning. Nobody else has been in here except me."

The living room was a masterpiece of destruction, one that had obviously been accomplished with silent perfection. The couch and chairs had been sliced, perhaps with an X-Acto knife or a barber's razor, the stuffing pulled out, the cheap decorative prints on the walls and the photos on the mantel slashed and pulled from the frames, the carpets and wood floor layered with paint. In the kitchen and bathroom, the intruder or intruders had poured concrete mix down the drains and oil sludge and glue in the appliances. A deer rifle and a shotgun and a German Luger had been taken from a closet, five hundred dollars from a desk drawer, a gold watch and a derringer from a jewelry box.

Bailey peered out the window at the backyard. A new electric-blue Ford pickup was parked by a tin boat shed. She went out the screen door.

"Where's she going?" Axel said.

"Obviously to look around. You want us here or not?"

"What's with you, Robicheaux? I never had a beef with you."

"You've got a beef with the world, Axel. What was the exterminator's name?"

"I didn't get it. He's an exterminator."

"You didn't look at his license or proof of insurance?"

"Crawling under the house and spraying poison on Formosan termites doesn't take a college degree."

"You didn't hear anything during the night? While he was demolishing your house?"

"I had a couple of drinks. Somebody left a bottle of Dewar's on the gallery."

"That didn't seem odd to you?" I asked.

"People leave me gifts."

"For doing what?"

"For helping them," he replied. "For doing my job."

"What did the exterminator look like?"

"White, medium height, stocky, black curly hair, unshaved."

"From around here?"

"Texas or Mississippi."

"What kind of vehicle did he drive?"

"An SUV, lot of mud on it, Louisiana tag."

"Remember the number?"

"I didn't pay it any mind. I didn't have any reason to."

"Quit dancing around the problem, Axel. You hired an illegal sprayer."

"Oh, I'll live in remorse over that." He bent down to see under the window shade. "What's that bitch doing?"

"You call her that again and I'll take your head off."

"Try it. Either here or anywhere else." He pointed at his cheek. "I haven't forgotten what you did in the restroom. That one isn't going away."

I closed my notebook and clicked on a photo in my iPhone. "You recognize this guy?"

"That's him, the exterminator."

"That's Hugo Tillinger."

"The escapee? Why's he after me?"

"Did you know Lucinda Arceneaux?"

"I saw her around, maybe. She was a do-gooder or something."

"Yeah, or something. Why would Tillinger come after you, Axel?"

"Why does somebody get hit by lightning?"

Bailey came back through the door. "You didn't check your truck?"

"I looked out the window. It was all right. It's all right, isn't it?"

"Sorry I have to tell you this," she said. "You have four slashed tires. Your seats and headliner and door panels are slashed. There's an empty sugar sack by your gas cap. The ignition was on, but the engine had died. The hood is still warm. The engine must have run quite a while."

"The fuck?" Axel said.

She dropped the keys in his palm, releasing them high enough so her hand didn't touch his. She gazed at him silently, in a benign way, as if staring at a stranger in a casket.

"What's going on?" he said. "Why is this happening? Why am I getting treated like I'm the stink on shit?"

"Tillinger had a reason for doing this," I said. "You know what it is. Want to tell us?"

"Get out of here," he said.

"Gladly," I said.

"What are *you* looking at?" he said to Bailey.

"A sad man," she said. "Get some help."

ALAFAIR CALLED ME from Arizona late that afternoon. "You should see it here," she said.

"Beautiful, huh?" I replied, a strange longing in my heart at the sound of my daughter's voice.

"I didn't mean to be hard on you this morning."

"Don't worry about it," I said. "I have a way of saying all the wrong things at the wrong time."

"I have a single room. Lou is just a friend."

"You don't have to explain."

"Yes, I do. You want to protect me. But I'm fine. Give me some credit."

"Is Desmond out there?"

"Yes. Why do you ask?"

"He's decent to women."

"But the people he works with are not?"

"I don't trust Butterworth, that's for sure."

"He's still at Cypremort Point."

"When will you be back?"

"In a few days, probably. Dave, are you sure about Desmond?"

"How do you mean?"

"Sometimes he goes inside himself and doesn't come back for a while."

"He's probably a depressive. Most artists are."

"I asked him about it," she said. "Know what he said? 'Dead poets are always speaking to us. You better listen to them. If you don't, they get mad.' "

I felt like someone had poured ice water on my back.

"Are you there?" she said.

"The last person who said something like that to me was a prostitute who lives in that trailer slum by the Jeanerette drawbridge."

"That's not unusual in Acadiana."

"Her baby had a charm tied on her ankle. It was a Maltese cross. The mother wouldn't tell me where she got it. There was a tiny ankle chain on Lucinda Arceneaux's body, with a piece of silver wire attached."

"You're scaring me, Dave."

"Come on back home."

"I can't do that. I made a commitment. Why don't you come out? You'd love it here. It's like stepping into eternity."

"You were born to be a writer, Alfenheimer."

I was on my cell phone in the backyard. I saw a gator slip under the hyacinths, its serrated tail slicing through the flowers and tendrils.

"I love you, Dave."

"You, too, kid," I replied.

"I have to go now. I'll call in the morning."

I said goodbye and closed my cell. I heard a sound in the oak limbs above me and felt a shower of leaves come down on my head, and I thought perhaps Mon Tee Coon had returned. A hoot owl with an injured wing was caught in the branches. I got a ladder from my toolshed and climbed into the tree and brought him down and placed him in a cardboard box and called a friend in Loreauville who ran an animal sanctuary and would pick up the bird. Then I drove to the University of Louisiana in Lafayette, from which I had graduated in 1960 with a teacher's certificate and a degree in English.

Chapter Eleven

I PARKED MY PICKUP under the oaks by Burke-Hawthorne Hall and walked to the library. The advantage of having a little knowledge about the classical world is that few other people do. The second advantage is your awareness that every problem facing us today has already occurred many times previously, and the behavior of the players is always predictable and the consequences are always the same. It's a bit like going to the track with the names of the winners and losers in your pocket.

Every literary plot is either in the Bible, Greek mythology, or Elizabethan theater. Hemingway said it was all right for an author to steal as long as he improved the material. I felt the same way about a homicide investigation. The externals were cosmetic. The motivations were not a mystery. Avarice, fear, sexual passion, revenge, a desire for power, rage that produced a chemical assault on the brain, this was the detritus floating in the gene pool. Read Charles Dickens's journalistic account of a public execution in London. It will make you want to flee humanity.

I put my notebook and a yellow legal pad on a big table in the archive reading room and tried to give a degree of coherence to the events that had occurred since I first saw the body of Lucinda Arceneaux bobbing in Weeks Bay. The apparent ritualistic hanging of Joe Molinari's fly-infested corpse in a shrimp net, a walking cane plunged through his chest, made no sense unless you linked his death to Arceneaux's. In the meantime, Hugo Tillinger had become a serious presence in our midst. He now had weapons and money courtesy of Axel Devereaux, and a cause to go with them, one involving prostitution.

Hilary Bienville had tied a Maltese cross on her daughter's ankle with a piece of red twine, then claimed—facetiously, I'm sure—that she had gotten it from a bubblegum machine. When I'd pressed her about it, she had said, "Mine to know," in a prideful fashion. In the library I found seven books that dealt specifically with Crusader knights. The Maltese cross was supposedly the sign of a late-sixteenth-century group, although it may have had earlier origins. No matter. It symbolized the ethos of the knight errant who, with body armor and chainmail and spiked mace and broadsword, managed to synthesize the noblest aspects of Christianity with bloodlust.

I stayed in the library until closing time, my eyes burning. At a certain time in your life, you accept the fact that lunacy comes in many forms. Is there a more disturbing sound than hobnailed boots striking a cobblestoned street in unison? Or our penchant for using ritual and procedure to give plausibility to the unthinkable? Baptized Christians ran the ovens in the camps. If we get scared enough we can convince ourselves that snake and nape are selective, and that a scarlet cross painted on a shield can make acceptable the beheadings of Saracens on a scaffold in Jerusalem.

I thanked the reference librarian for her help and walked back to my pickup. The campus was dark, the sky sprinkled with stars. When I reached my truck, I saw that a sheet of spiral notebook paper had been placed under my windshield wiper. The message was printed in ballpoint, each letter a composite of slashes:

Dear Detective Roboshow,

Enjoyed talking to you on the phone. Hope you read the Bible. The following from Psalms is one of my favorite quotes. "Arise, O Jehovah; Save me, O my God: For thou hast smitten all mine enemies upon the cheek bone; Thou hast broken the teeth of the wicked."

Your friend?

H.T.

I folded the note and placed it in my shirt pocket. I had a feeling Tillinger was watching me, but I gave him no indication. The moon was up, the shadows of flooded trees moving on the water of Cypress Lake by the old student center. I slipped my snub-nose .38 special from my snap-on belt holster and held it behind my hip. I walked down to the edge of the water. "You out there, Hugo?"

There was no response.

"You shouldn't be bird-dogging me, partner," I said.

I heard a splash. It could have been either a frog or someone throwing a dirt clod into the lake.

"Maybe we've got the same goal," I said. "Nobody is worried about you creeping Axel Devereaux's house. The firearms are another matter. Maybe you'll beat death row in Texas. Don't blow it by getting into an assault beef in Louisiana."

I thought I saw a silhouette merge with the corner of the student center, but I couldn't be sure. No sound came from the lakeside or the walkways. I got into my truck and started the engine. Then the words from the Book of Psalms came back to me, and I squeezed my eyes shut at their implication.

I WENT INTO HELEN'S office early the next morning.

"The note is from Hugo Tillinger?" she said.

"Who else?"

"Look, I'm not exactly a biblical scholar. Run that quotation by me again."

"It refers to Jehovah breaking the teeth of the wicked."

Her eyes were fastened on mine. "Travis Lebeau," she said. "His teeth were pulled out."

"Yep."

"Lebeau was Tillinger's friend."

"Maybe the quotation is coincidence. Or maybe Tillinger is a real nightmare."

"I hope he's our guy," she said. "I'd like to put all this craziness on one guy and shut him down."

"Except it's a whole lot more complicated, isn't it?"

"To say the least," she replied. "Just before you came in, I got a call from Desmond Cormier. He said he wants to cast Bailey Ribbons in his movie, but he doesn't want to cause her conflict."

"Then why does he create conflict?"

"I said something similar. How's Bailey working out?"

"Good. The best," I said.

"Really?"

"Is that supposed to have a second meaning?" I said.

"Nope. Just asking." She leaned back in her swivel chair, her eyes unfocused, her face wan. "Some fun, huh, bwana?"

WHILE IN NEW IBERIA, Clete Purcel lived on East Main at the Teche Motel, a 1940s motor court with cottages on either side of a narrow strip of tree-shaded asphalt that dead-ended in an oak grove on the bayou. Two or three evenings a week he cooked a pork roast or a chicken on a grill under the oaks, and shared it with anyone who wanted to sit down with him. Late Wednesday afternoon a smoking gas-guzzler gnarled with dents made its way down to the last cottage on the asphalt. Hilary Bienville got out and knocked on the cottage door.

"I'm over here," Clete said.

She twitched at the sound of his voice. "Can I talk wit' you?"

"Yeah. Who told you where I live?"

She walked toward him. She wore jeans and sandals and a man's khaki shirt tied at the waist. "The bartender at the club."

"What happened to your face?"

"Tripped on the stairs."

"You live in a trailer."

"Tripped somewhere else."

"Who did that to you?" he said.

"Ain't important."

"You went to the hospital?"

"I don't mess with them emergency room people."

"Axel Devereaux beat you up?"

"I'm scared, Mr. Clete."

"I'm not a 'mister.' Answer me."

"I don't care about Axel. I'm here about somebody else. What he's doing to me." She pointed at her head. "Inside here."

Clete opened the top on his grill and let a cloud of white smoke rise into the trees. He pulled a longneck from a tub full of half-melted ice and twisted the cap off and set it on the picnic table. "Sit down. I'm going to fix you a sandwich. Dave Robicheaux told me he went to see you. Why don't you talk to him?"

"He's a policeman."

"Axel Devereaux beat you up?"

"You ain't hearing me." She sat at the table and put her hands over her face. "Don't nobody hear me. Don't nobody know what it's like when you're on your own against the world."

Clete picked up the longneck and touched her arm with it. "Drink it."

Her hand was shaking when she lifted the bottle; the beer spilled out of her mouth. He handed her a paper towel. "Who's this guy getting in your head?"

She wiped her chin. "I only went to the ninth grade."

"So?"

"I know what I'm t'inking is the troot, except I cain't find the right words for it. When I'm wit' him, I got no power. I get weak all over. The way he touches me and talks in my ear and looks in my eyes like no man done before. It's like he's putting pictures in my head that ain't supposed to be there, and it makes me scared. I cain't sleep, no."

"Is this a white or a black man?"

"A black man might hit you, but he don't mess up your head."

"He's not a pimp?"

"No, he ain't nothing like that."

Clete sliced the roast and layered two pieces of French bread on a paper plate with meat and sauce and tomatoes and lettuce and onions and set it in front of her.

"I ain't hungry," she said.

"Eat it anyway."

"You ain't gonna he'p, are you."

"Tell me the guy's name, and we might get somewhere."

"He tole me I ain't supposed to do that. He held my chin wit' his fingers and looked into my eyes when he said it."

"This guy sounds like a real piece of shit. Tell me who he is and I'll dial him up."

"He said I'm a chalice. I got to be pure 'cause I'm chosen. Chosen for what?"

"Did you ask him that?"

"I was afraid."

"Listen to me, Miss Hilary. You're giving me half the story and not trusting me with the other half."

He waited for her to speak. She took a small bite from her sandwich and chewed as though it were cardboard. Then she took the food out of her mouth and put it on the plate. "I'm gonna be sick."

"Is he a client?"

"Not in a reg'lar way."

"You don't get it on with him?"

"He gives me money and t'ings. Once he axed me to rub his back."

"Where did you meet this guy?"

"At the Winn-Dixie. His basket crashed into mine. He said, 'Sorry, pretty lady.' "

Clete closed the top of the grill and sat down across from her. "Did you know Lucinda Arceneaux?"

"I don't know nobody named Lucinda."

"Her body was found floating on a wood cross in Weeks Bay."

"I don't know nothing about that."

"You don't read the newspaper or watch the news?"

"It don't have nothing to do wit' me."

Clete shut and opened his eyes. "Describe the pictures that the man without a name puts in your head."

"Horses galloping, people burning up in their shacks, children screaming. If I don't do what he say, t'ings like that are gonna be my fault. He says we're all part of a big plan."

"Are we talking about a guy named Hugo Tillinger?"

"No."

"This guy is not only a bad guy, he's a fake. The only power he has is the power you give him."

She stared at Clete as though he were an apparition and the man who had poisoned her mind were real. Her skin was like dark chocolate, pitted in one cheek, a scar like a piece of white string at the corner of one eye. There was a smear of lipstick on her teeth. Clete wondered whom she had been with before she had come to his cottage. He wondered how many times she had been used as a child and sworn to secrecy by her molester.

"What was Nine/eleven, Hilary?"

"What was *what*?"

"Nine/eleven."

"You mean the convenience store?"

He wrote his cell number on the back of his business card and gave it to her. "When you're ready to give up your guy, let me know."

"I remember what he said now. I'm the Queen of Cups. What's that?"

"Some kind of bullshit he uses to scare people," Clete said. He pulled another longneck from the cooler and screwed off the cap and drank from the bottle. "Is your baby okay?"

"Yes, suh."

"You need any money?"

"What you t'ink?"

He removed two twenties from his wallet and put them in her hand. "Stay out of bars and away from the wrong people for a few days. Call me if Axel Devereaux comes around."

She looked at the money. "You don't want me to do nothing for you?"

"One look at me in the nude and women run for the convent."

He thought she might smile, but she didn't. She walked away without saying thanks or goodbye. He watched her get into her car and drive off, the muffler clanking. He hit the speed dial on his cell phone and got into his Caddy, talking on the phone, then drove down East Main to my house.

WE SAT ON the front steps while he told me everything Hilary Bienville had said. The sun was almost down, and through the trees I could see clouds that were crimson and yellow and half filled with rain in the afterglow.

"You have any idea who this guy could be?" he said.

"The same one who gave her the Maltese cross she tied on her daughter's ankle."

"Yeah, but who's the guy?"

"Anybody can buy tarot cards in the Quarter or on the Internet."

Clete kept fiddling with his hands, running his fingers over his knuckles. They were the size of quarters. "What's he after? It's not sex."

"Maybe she'll get hurt again and tell us."

"So just leave her alone?"

"It's her choice," I said.

"What about this guy Butterworth? Your cop friend in West Hollywood says he's a bucket of vomit."

"He's hard to read. He spends a lot of time hanging out his signs."

Clete stood up. "I got to go."

"Where?" I asked.

"Not sure. Did Mon Tee Coon come back?"

"No."

"I'm going to have a chat with Axel Devereaux."

"Bad idea."

"The guy beats up on women. He's about to stop. Same with hurting people's pets."

I was sitting in his shadow now, the tree limbs above us clicking with hail, the last of the sunset shrinking inside clouds that were dark and swollen with rain and quivering with thunder. "What I say won't make any difference, will it."

"You can't always wait out the batter, Dave. Sometimes you have to take it to him. Devereaux is overdue." Clete's porkpie hat slanted on his forehead, and an unlit cigarette hung from his mouth.

"The key is the tarot," I said. "Devereaux is an asshole and a distraction."

"Not if you're a woman and he's pounding your face into marmalade."

After Clete backed into the street and drove away, the hail stopped and the rain began, big drops flattening on the heat trapped in the sidewalk and the street, filling the air with a sweetness like the summers of our youth. I got up and went inside and turned off the air-conditioning units and opened the windows, letting the house swell with wind. Then a strange sensation overtook me, in the same fashion it had on the evening I'd walked without purpose to the home of Bailey Ribbons and could give no explanation for my behavior other than the fact that I seemed to have stepped into a vacuum in which the only sounds I heard were inside my head.

The rain fell like drops of lead on the tin roof and the bayou. From the hall closet, I removed an old sweat-stained Stetson that had belonged to my father. I put it on and walked down to the bayou, the brim wilting with rain.

I told myself I didn't know why I was standing on the bank of a tidal stream in rain that was coming down harder by the second. That wasn't true. For me, the rain has always been the conduit between the visible and the unseen worlds. Years ago my murdered wife, Annie, spoke to me in the rain, and dead members of my platoon called me on the phone during electrical storms, their voices hardly audible in the static, and my father who died in an offshore blowout appeared in the surf during a squall, still wearing his hard hat and strap overalls and steel-toed boots, giving me a thumbs-up while the waves slid across his knees, the oil rig that killed him stenciled against the sky.

The rain was about death. It defined it. It was an old friend, and I welcomed its presence. I knew its smell when I walked past a storm drain in cold weather, or sat down to rest in an Oregon rain forest filled with lichen-covered boulders that never saw sunlight, or saw a spectral figure on the St. Charles streetcar, his head hooded, his face like gray rubber, his lips curled whimsically in a lopsided figure eight, as though he were saying *Whenever you're ready, sport.*

I heard leaves thrashing and looked upward into the live oak. Mon Tee Coon had just slipped on a branch and crashed on top of the limb below. Looking down at him was a smaller raccoon, her tail hanging off the branch.

"*Comment la vie?*" I said. "*Bienvenu, mon raton laveur et votre tee amis, aussi.*"

Both of them stared down at me, their coats slick with rain.

"How about a celebratory can of sardines?" I said.

They looked at each other, then at me.

"*C'est ce que je pensais,*" I said. "*Allons-allez.*"

I walked back to the house, opened the can over the sink, and emptied it on the steps. Mon Tee Coon and his lady came running.

I thought about calling Clete and telling him that Mon Tee Coon had come home. But I didn't. Clete was Clete, and no power on earth would ever change his mind about anything. I was also tired of trying to protect people like Axel Devereaux. Or maybe I was just tired of everything. Acceptance of death, or at least its presence, is that way sometimes and not the canker on the soul it's made out to be.

I had never worn my father's battered Stetson, and it felt strange. The rain had turned to mist and was blowing through the screens. For some reason, in my mind's eye, I saw a mesa that resembled a tombstone, one that had been placed in the foreground of a wasteland that seemed to dip into infinity.

The phone rang on the kitchen counter. I looked at the caller ID and picked up. "What's goin' on, Baby Squanto?"

"Don't call me those stupid names," Alafair said. "Is everything all right there?"

"Of course."

"It's raining here. It never rains so hard this time of year. I'm looking out at the desert and thinking of you. I don't know why."

"I'm fine."

"Are you sure? I have this terrible feeling."

"You shouldn't. Mon Tee Coon just came home."

"That's wonderful. But don't come here."

"I wasn't planning to."

"Through my window, I can see a huge mesa in the rain. For some reason I felt you were coming here. Maybe because you worry about me."

"Wrong."

"I have to go. Flowerpots and earthen jars are breaking on the patio."

"I'll talk with you later, kid."

"Dave, I have an awful feeling. It's about death. I don't know why I feel this way."

"It'll pass."

"What will?"

"Fear of death."

"My thoughts are about you. Not me."

"I understand. But your worries are misplaced. Hello?"

The line had gone dead.

I sat down and stared through the window at the rain. A bolt of lightning split the gray sky and trembled on the iron flagpole in City Park, like an aberration in the elements that refused to die.

Chapter Twelve

ON SUNDAY, ALAFAIR called me from the airport in Dallas. She had taken a commercial flight and was on her way back home.

"You quit?" I said.

"No, Desmond and Lou had to take care of some union trouble in Los Angeles and New Orleans. I wasn't getting anything done, so I decided to work from home."

"Was that all right with them?"

"I don't know. I didn't ask."

I picked her up in Lafayette. We had slipped into Indian summer without being aware of it. The sky was as hard and blue as porcelain, the oak leaves red and gold and clicking like crickets when they rolled across the lawn in the wind. I knew somehow that better days lay ahead.

I fixed dinner for us when we got home, and later, we fed Snuggs on the kitchen floor and Mon Tee Coon and his girlfriend on top of Tripod's hutch. That night we slept with the windows open, and I could smell the camellias and the dense lemony fragrance of our late-blooming magnolia in the side yard. As I drifted off to sleep, I resolved to capture and protect each spoonful of sunshine allotted me for the rest of my life, and not go with the season or lend myself to doomed causes.

I woke at six-fifteen to the sounds of rain and the phone ringing. I picked up the phone and went into the kitchen so as not to awake Alafair. It was Sean McClain. "I'm in front of Axel Devereaux's place by the drawbridge on Loreauville Road. I need a witness here."

"What for?"

"There's something wrong in that house. People know I don't get along with Devereaux or his buddies. I don't want to be busting in on my own."

"What happened?"

"I was passing his house a half hour ago. All the lights were on and the shades down. A black SUV was in the yard. I saw a woman come running out the back door and thought I heard glass breaking."

"Go on."

"I slowed down but didn't stop."

"Why not?"

"I didn't want to mix in his personal business."

He had already made two mistakes: He had ignored a battery situation in progress, and he hadn't called it in. I didn't want to think about what was coming next.

"What made you change your mind?" I said.

"I go off at oh-seven-hundred. I thought I'd make one more pass. The SUV was bagging down the road. I didn't get a tag. The lights were off in the house, and a front window was broken and the shade and screen hanging outside. Devereaux's truck was in the shed. This time I knocked on the door. No answer."

"Where are you now?"

"In the front yard."

"Try again."

"I pert' near shook it off the blocks already."

"You tried the back?"

"Yes, sir. I hit on the bedroom wall."

"Give me a few minutes."

I brushed my teeth and washed my face and took a small bottle of orange juice and a cinnamon roll out of the icebox and headed up Loreauville Road. The rain had quit and the sky was an ink wash, as though the sun had refused to rise. A blanket of white fog was rolling off the bayou when I turned onto Axel Devereaux's property. Sean was waiting on the gallery. An empty whiskey bottle wet with dew glittered in the yard. I walked up the steps.

"You know Axel's a juicer, don't you?" I said.

"If that's the problem, he must have tied on a whammeroo."

I pounded with the flat of my fist on the door. "It's Dave Robicheaux and Sean McClain! Open up, Devereaux!"

I took out a handkerchief and twisted the knob. It was locked tight. I stepped back and balanced myself with the screen and kicked the wood door with the bottom of my shoe. The second time it splintered off the jamb. Axel seemed to have cleaned up the damage done to his living room by Hugo Tillinger. Through the hallway I could barely make out a figure sitting motionlessly at the breakfast table, his back to us. Then I realized he was wearing a peaked hat, dripping with bells like ornaments on a small Christmas tree.

I walked through the hallway with Sean behind me. He looked over my shoulder. "Oh, man."

"Don't touch anything," I said. "Get Bailey and Helen on the horn. Don't let a photographer get near this."

"They say they got a right."

"Devereaux wasn't worth the spit on the sidewalk. But we don't punish the family."

I BELIEVED A FIGHT or an attempt to flee the house had begun in the living room and ended in the kitchen. Dishes and glassware were broken. Cutlery from a wooden knife block was splayed on the floor. The icebox door was open, a carton of milk on its side, leaking into the vegetable tray. The air-conditioning units were turned on full blast, the back door key-locked, the key gone.

Even in death, Axel's face resembled a boiled egg, the eyes open wide, disbelieving. His wrists were fastened behind the chair with plastic ligatures. A short baton had been shoved down the throat and into the chest, prizing up the chin. But I doubted that was the cause of his death. A leather loop, one with three knots tied in it, had been flipped over his neck. The burns went a quarter inch into the tissue. A Lincoln-green felt cap hung with tiny chrome bells had been snugged on his head.

The medics and the ambulance were the first to arrive, then Helen and Bailey and Cormac Watts. Through the front window I saw a television truck and the automobile of a *Daily Iberian* reporter coming up the road. Sean was in the backyard. He was wearing latex gloves. He bent over and picked up a key and used it to open the back door. "Why would the killer want to lock up a corpse?"

"To give himself as much time as possible to get out of town."

"You suspect he cranked up the air conditioners?"

"That's the way I'd read it."

"Damn, I wish I'd pulled in when I saw that woman run out the back door."

"Axel dealt the hand a long time ago, Sean. He was a cruel, evil man, and he died the death of one."

"Ain't nobody deserves going out like this," he said. "Look at the butt end of the baton."

"What about it?"

Sean nudged a claw hammer on the linoleum with the tip of his shoe. "Whoever done it went at it like he was driving a tent peg."

Helen and Bailey came through the hallway. Both of them stared silently at Devereaux's profile. Neither showed any expression.

"The back door was locked from the outside," I said. "Sean found the key in the backyard."

"You saw somebody leave in a black SUV?" Helen said to Sean.

"Yes, ma'am," he replied. "Hauling ass."

"You didn't get a number?"

"No, ma'am, the headlights was off."

"You didn't go after it or call it in?" she said.

"I didn't have no reason to at that point." He lowered his head, his cheeks coloring.

"What'd you think the hat is about?" Helen said.

"He's the Fool in the tarot," Bailey said.

"The tarot again?" Helen said.

"Bailey is right," I said.

"I didn't say she wasn't," Helen replied. "But what the hell does Devereaux have to do with fortune-telling cards?"

"The Fool represents pride, arrogance, and presumption," I said. "He's portrayed whistling as he's about to step off a cliff. He has a staff over his shoulder. Joe Molinari had a walking cane plunged through his chest."

"I have a hard time buying in to this symbolism crap, Dave," she said.

"Know a better explanation?" I said.

She stared at nothing. "Do the knots mean anything?"

"Our killer probably had commando training of some kind," I said. "The knots are to break the larynx and silence the victim."

"Or maybe he's just a sadist," Bailey said. "The Internet is full of information that Jack the Ripper couldn't have thought up."

Cormac Watts had been standing in the background. "Can I have a look?" he asked.

"Sorry," I said, and stepped aside.

He leaned down and studied Axel's face and the garrote and the baton. He straightened his back and looked at us.

"What is it?" I said.

"The garrote is cosmetic," he said. "It's there to mislead us."

"I'm not following you," I said.

"Look at the discharge on the shank of the baton," he said. "Devereaux was alive when it went down his throat. He looked straight into the eyes of the guy who did this to him. There's a tear sealed in one eye. The killer isn't just a ritualist. He enjoyed this one."

A fly was buzzing on the ceiling. Helen turned to Sean. "You saw a woman run outside?"

"Yes, ma'am," he said.

"White or black, fat or thin, what?" she said.

"I couldn't make her out, Miss Helen."

"That's great," she said.

"Pardon?" he said.

"We look like the dumbest fucks on the planet," she said. "We can't even protect our own."

Sean's face seemed to shrink and the blood to go out of his cheeks.

"Devereaux wasn't one of our own," I said.

I felt her eyes on the side of my face. I walked out to the front yard. The medics were wheeling in the gurney, a body bag folded on top. Helen followed me. "Don't ever correct me in front of others again, Pops."

"You were too hard on Sean," I said.

Her head seemed to wobble like a balloon on a string, her eyes blazing. "He blew it. He has to man up and take his medicine."

"You're putting this in his jacket?"

"He should have called it in. We could have had this lunatic in custody."

"We should have flushed Devereaux from the department years ago. The onus is on us."

"I can't help what happened 'years ago.' The guy who killed Devereaux is going to kill again, and we could have had him, but now we have nothing. Excuse me if I'm not as charitable as you. You not only piss me off, Dave, you disappoint me."

"Sean went back after he passed the house," I said. "Had he gone in earlier, thinking Devereaux was involved in a domestic argument, he'd probably be dead, too."

Her face was pinched, her fists balled on her hips. "All right."

"All right, what?" I said.

"I'll talk with Sean. No paperwork."

The forensic team was dusting the house, the medics bagging up Devereaux, the fog breaking up on the bayou. It was a new day for everyone except Devereaux. I almost felt sorry for him. But I suspected his own victims were many and that most of them would never tell others of the degradation he had put them through. *Anyway, have a good trip to the other side,* I thought, and walked to my truck.

"Where you going?" Helen said.

"To work," I replied.

I WASN'T SURPRISED BY Hugo Tillinger's phone call to my office later that day. There is a subculture in this country that seems to have no antecedent—a conflation of reality television, *National Enquirer* journalism, fundamentalist religion, militarism, and professional football. At the center is an adoration of celebrity, no matter how it is acquired or in what form it comes. Women line up to marry Richard Ramirez and the Menendez brothers; the Jerry Springer clientele will degrade themselves and their families and destroy any modicum of dignity in their lives for ten minutes in front of the camera. Tillinger had probably stumbled into his role as the innocent man on death row, then decided after a few headlines that a frolic in the limelight might be worth the grief. Check out the story of Caryl Chessman.

"What do you want this time?" I asked him.

"Y'all gonna try to put the Devereaux job on me?"

"You'd be a logical candidate."

"On what grounds?"

"You already burglarized his house?"

"I did that for Miss Lucinda."

"Maybe you shoved a baton down his throat for the same reason."

"That's how he went out?"

"Don't worry about it," I said. "Did you mutilate Travis Lebeau before he was dragged?"

"Where in the hell did you get that?"

"You used a quote from the book of Psalms about Jehovah breaking the teeth of His enemies."

"That doesn't mean I go around mutilating people."

"You're a nuisance, Mr. Tillinger. I wish you would go away."

"The AB probably killed Travis. But I think the order came from Devereaux."

"Devereaux was hooked up with the AB?"

"They kept his whores in line. How come you don't know this?"

"I'm not that smart," I said. I looked at the second hand on my watch. Eight seconds passed before he spoke again.

"I don't want to go back to Texas, Mr. Robicheaux."

"That's not an unreasonable attitude."

"Every night I dream about being injected."

"I don't have the power to influence your situation, sir."

"You could get me to the right people. Actors, celebrities, hereabouts. People are making films all over the state these days."

"A bartender in Lafayette told me you already knew those kinds of people."

"Miss Lucinda knew them," he said.

My attention was starting to fade.

"She was working on her genealogy," he said. "She was an orphan. Her foster daddy is a preacher."

"So?"

"She thought maybe she was related to a famous guy in Hollywood. She didn't say who."

"When you find out, tell me, will you?" I said. "I'm done here."

"You're a hard-nosed bastard."

"Just self-destructive. You stole firearms out of Devereaux's house. What do you plan to do with them?"

"Cancel the ticket of anyone who tries to take me back to Texas."

Spoken like a real idiot, I thought. "Don't call here again unless you have some useful information."

I hung up. This time he didn't call back. Helen opened my door. "The prints from the Devereaux crime scene are no help. The door key was clean. The killer was probably wearing gloves when he went inside. Anything on your end?"

"Tillinger called. He was on a cell phone. He's not our guy."

"How can you be sure?"

"He's a five-star peckerwood. What you see is what you get."

"You don't believe he burned his family to death?"

"If I'd been on the jury, I'd have reasonable doubt."

"So we've got nothing."

"There's Antoine Butterworth," I said.

"Why Butterworth?"

"His soul probably resembles the La Brea Tar Pits."

"What are you going to bring him in on?"

"He's a long way from his usual resources," I replied. "Let's see how he likes being one of the little people."

Chapter Thirteen

I CALLED MY FRIEND the captain of the West Hollywood Station of the Los Angeles Sheriff's Department and asked more specifically about Butterworth's record. Butterworth's reputation for deviancy was ubiquitous. But legend and legal reality don't always coincide. Prostitutes told outrageous stories about him. One claimed he hung her from a hook and beat her bloody, but she had been in Camarillo twice and hadn't filed charges. As gross as his behavior was, most of it seemed thespian, more adolescent and obscene than criminal.

"He's never had to register as a sex offender?" I asked.

"Twelve years ago he got nailed on a statutory," my friend said. "She was sixteen, although she looked twenty-five. The DA was going to put him away, but the girl got a big role in a South American film and left town."

"Butterworth got her the role?"

"That's how it usually works."

"What's the status on the charge now?"

"It doesn't have one. The case died in the file drawer."

"That's all I need," I said. "Thanks for the help."

"I don't see how I helped."

"This is Louisiana, Cap. The language in our sex offender registry laws would give you an aneurism."

By noon the next day I had a warrant for Butterworth's arrest and a warrant to search Desmond's house. I dialed Desmond's unlisted number, hoping he would be there. Unfortunately, Butterworth answered.

"Is Desmond there?" I said. "This is Dave Robicheaux."

"Oh, my favorite detective," he replied.

"I need to speak to him, please."

"He's taking a break today and sailing. The light is all wrong for the scene we're shooting, anyway. Could I be of assistance?"

"I have to take some photos from your deck. I'm putting together a report on the discovery of the Arceneaux body."

"This isn't about the telescope again, is it?"

"No, it has to do with tidal drift. Will you be there for the next hour?"

"I'll make a point of it," he said. "Ta-ta, cute boy."

Bailey and I checked out a cruiser and headed for Cypremort Point, with me driving and Sean McClain following in a second vehicle. There was a heavy chop on the bay, the moss straightening in the trees and boats rocking in their slips like beer cans in a wave.

"I'm not sure what we're doing, Dave," Bailey said.

"We're on shaky ground, but Butterworth doesn't know it."

She looked straight ahead, thoughtful. "I'm not sure I'm comfortable with this."

"You ever hear of a rich man going to the chair or gas chamber or the injection room?" I said.

"I guess that doesn't happen often."

"It doesn't happen at all."

I waited for her to say something, but she didn't. "We cut the bad guys off at the knees, Bailey."

"What we do is punish the people who are available," she said.

I looked at her profile. She was one of those people whose composure and self-assurance gave no hint of arrogance or elitism. But I couldn't forget that Ambrose Bierce, a war veteran, once defined a pacifist as a dead Quaker, and that Bailey was young for the job and I was old for it, and old for her, and on top of it I wondered if she didn't belong in the public defender's office.

"You're a good fellow, Dave."

"Why do you say that?"

"I'm a good judge of people."

All my thought processes went down the drain.

As we neared the tip of the peninsula, I saw a solitary figure on the deck of Desmond's house, the wind flattening his slacks and Hawaiian shirt against his body. He was playing his saxophone, obviously indifferent to the sounds of the surf and the wind and seagulls, the gold bell of the sax as bright as a heliograph in the sunlight.

"Why does that guy remind me of an upended lizard?" I said.

"Because he looks like one," she replied.

I RANG THE CHIMES. When Butterworth answered, I stepped inside without being asked and held up both warrants. Bailey and Sean followed me. "You're under arrest for failing to register as a sex offender, Mr. Butterworth," I said. "Please turn around and place your hands behind you."

Without pause I cuffed him and began reading him his rights.

"I'm not a sex offender," he said. "Where do you come off with that?"

"I'm going to walk you to the couch and sit you down," I said. "Which bedroom is yours?"

"At the end of the hall. Why are you interested in my bedroom?"

"Our search warrant is limited to part of the house," I said.

"Did you hear what I said? I'm not a sex offender. I have never been charged with a sexual offense."

I eased him down on the leather couch. He was barefoot. The tops of his feet were laced with green veins.

"Under Louisiana law, a sex offender in another state has to register here as soon as he takes up residence, even though the charge in the other state has fallen into limbo," I said. "The statutory beef you skated on in California would be considered a 'deferred' charge in Louisiana. Deferred offenders have to register. You pissed on your shoes, Mr. Butterworth."

"I want to call my attorney," he said.

"You can call from lockup," I said.

"Mr. Butterworth?" Bailey said.

He looked up. His forehead and pate were tan and greasy, the pupils of his eyes like black marbles.

"Are you high?" she said.

"Me?" he replied. "Who cares? I have prescriptions for mood modifiers."

"You're an intelligent man," she said. "You know we're not here about that statutory business of twelve years ago."

"Then why say you are?" he asked.

"Our problem is the young woman on the cross, and an indigent man hanged like a piece of rotted meat in a shrimp net, and a deputy sheriff who had his esophagus and larynx and lungs slowly punctured and ripped apart with a baton," she said. "Your history indicates that you have sadistic inclinations. If you were in our position, whom would you be talking to now?"

"Nice try, love," he said.

"Don't speak to me in that fashion," she said. "Where were you in the early a.m. on Monday?"

"Asleep. In my bedroom. Desmond will confirm that. Was that when the deputy consummated his appointment in Samarra?"

"Stay with him," I said to Bailey.

I stepped out on the deck and called Desmond's cell phone. The wind was hot and full of spray and the smell of salt and seaweed. Desmond picked up on the first ring.

"This is Dave," I said. "We're serving two warrants at your house. One on Butterworth's living area and one on Butterworth."

"You're kidding," Desmond said.

"He says he was asleep in his bedroom in the early morning yesterday. Is he lying?" There was no answer. I put the phone to my other ear. "Did you hear me?"

"He went to bed early Sunday night. His door was closed when I got up in the morning."

"Did you see him?"

"I had to meet some guys with the rain tower in Lafayette. I left at about six-thirty."

"So you don't know if he was in the bedroom or not?"

"Not for certain."

But there was something he was not telling me.

"Where was his Subaru when you left?"

"I didn't see it. That doesn't mean anything, though."

"Does he drive a black SUV sometimes?"

"He has access to them. We rent a number of them. Look, maybe he was out. He's got a girlfriend or two. Locals. Sometimes they drop him off and he lets them tool around in his convertible. He lives a bachelor's life."

"He's hunting on the game farm?" I said.

"No. This is harassment, Dave. You've got the wrong guy. You may not like to hear this, but Antoine is not the evil bastard he pretends he is."

"He fooled me."

"He majored in sackcloth and ashes."

"Sell it to someone else, Des."

"This is why I don't live here anymore. You taint every beautiful thing in your lives and put it on outsiders. Y'all would strip-mine Eden if the price was right."

"Then why make your films here?" I said, my heart thudding.

"Louisiana is anybody's blow job," he replied. "You can buy it for chump change."

I closed the phone and looked across Weeks Bay to where I had first seen the body of Lucinda Arceneaux floating with her arms spread on the cross, her hair undulating like serpents around her throat. Then I went back inside, the wind whistling in my ears.

"You're out of luck, partner," I said to Butterworth. "Desmond doesn't back you up. Your bedroom door was closed when he left yesterday morning, but your car was gone."

"Because I gave it to a lady friend to use," he said.

"Des mentioned that as a possibility," I said. "Who is she?"

"A lady who works in a blues joint."

"A singer?" I said.

"Yes."

"What's her name?"

"Bella Delahoussaye."

I kept my face empty.

"You got it on with her?" Bailey asked him.

"What is this?" he said.

"You know how it is out here in the provinces," I said. "Family values, total abstinence, prayer meetings, Friday-night lights and such. We try to set the bar."

"I realized that the first time I went to a cockfight in Breaux Bridge," he said.

"Is there anything in your room you want to tell us about before we find it?" I said. "Hallucinogens, uppers, China white?"

He twisted his neck, his skin pulling tight on his face like a turtle's. "You're behind the times. What was the name of the deputy who was killed?"

"Axel Devereaux," I said.

Butterworth nodded. "He was mixed up with the Aryan Brotherhood."

"How do you know that?" Bailey said.

"Some of them tried to get jobs as extras with us," he replied. "Devereaux sent them. He had prostitutes working for him. Five hundred dollars a night. He thought he was going to be a friend to the stars."

"What was your connection to Devereaux?" I asked.

"I didn't have one," he replied. "I wouldn't let him on the set. Desmond banned him, and Lou Wexler walked him to his car. We had to do your job."

"Get started," I said to Sean.

I put my hand under Butterworth's arm and walked him into the bedroom. I pulled up a chair for him to sit in while Sean began opening drawers and placing the contents on the bed.

"You have a phone number for Bella Delahoussaye?" I asked.

"You don't?" he said.

"Say again?"

"Cut the charade, Detective," he said. "You took her home."

Bailey looked at me.

"That's right, I did," I said.

"I suspect she was giving you a guitar lesson," he said.

"Y'all had better take a look at this," Sean said.

I didn't know whether Sean had deliberately interrupted Butterworth. Butterworth had gotten the knife in. My face was burning, my wrists throbbing. I saw the shine of disappointment in Bailey's eyes.

"What do you have?" she asked Sean.

He dumped a hatbox onto the bedspread. A pair of sheep-lined leather wrist cuffs fell out, along with a purple hood, a flagellum strung with felt thongs, a black leather vest, and women's undergarments. A hypodermic kit and several bags of dried plants or herbs followed.

"These are yours?" I said to Butterworth.

"I've used a couple of items in intimate situations. Actually, they're stage props." He studied a spot six inches in front of his eyes.

"How about the spike?" I said.

"My medicines are homeopathic in nature. There's nothing unlawful in that box."

"I think your sense of reality is from the other side of Mars," I said.

"You wear your hypocrisy nicely," he said.

"Let me clear up something for you," I said. "I took Miss Bella home in an electric storm. I took her to her front door, and then I drove to my house. I have the feeling she told you that, but you used the information to embarrass me and to cast doubt on the integrity of this investigation."

"I couldn't care less about your peccadilloes," he said. "The issue is otherwise. You're trying to degrade me while pretending you're not."

"Did you put LSD in the food of a housemaid so you could film and ridicule her?"

Then he surprised me. "Yes, it was unconscionable. I've done many things I regret." His gaze fixed on me, then he looked away, detached, as though he had gone somewhere else.

Sean removed stacks of books from a shelf and placed them on the bed, then began searching the closet. The books included titles by Lee Child, Frederick Forsyth, Somerset Maugham, Joseph Conrad, Graham Greene, and a history of the Crusades. But the one that caught my eye was an ostrich-skin-bound scrapbook stuffed with photographs and postcards and handwritten and typed letters, yellowed with age and pasted to the pages.

"I would prefer that you not look at that," Butterworth said. "Nothing in it is related to your investigation."

I began turning the pages. Each was as stiff as cardboard. The backdrop was obviously Africa: wild animals grazing on grasslands backdropped by mountains capped with snow, army six-bys loaded with black soldiers carrying AK-47s and Herstal assault rifles, arid villages where every child had the same bloated stomach and hollow eyes and skeletal face. I could almost hear the buzzing of the flies.

"Which countries were these taken in?" I asked.

"Many of these places don't even have names," he replied.

"The guys in those trucks look like friends of Gaddafi and Castro," I said.

"They're friends of whoever pays them," he said.

The next page I turned was pasted over with an eight-by-ten color photograph that slipped in and out of focus, as though the eye wanted to reject it. The huts on either side of a dirt road were burning. A column of troops was walking into a red sun, some of the men looking at bodies strewn along the roadside. A withered and toothless old man wearing only short pants and sandals was sitting with one leg bent under him, his arms outstretched, begging for mercy. The bodies of a woman and a child lay like broken dolls next to him. A soldier stood behind him, a machete hanging from a thong on his wrist.

I held the page open in front of Butterworth. "You had a hand in this?"

"Did I participate in it? No. Was I there? I took the photograph."

"Did you try to stop it?"

"My head would have been used for a soccer ball."

"Who was the commanding officer?"

"An African thug who was a friend of Idi Amin."

"What was your role?"

"Adviser."

I closed the book and dropped it on the bed. "Get up."

"What for?"

"You need to be in a different place."

I walked him through the living room and out on the deck, my fingers biting into his arm. I unlocked his cuffs and hooked him around the rail, the sun beating down on his face, his eyes still dilated and now watering. He was clearly trying not to blink. "Why are you doing this?"

"I don't like you. How often do you shoot up?"

"Sorry, I won't discuss my private life with you."

"Did you shoot up Lucinda Arceneaux?"

"Alafair told me your friend Purcel fought on the side of the leftists in El Salvador."

"What about it?"

"He never told you what went on down there? The atrocities committed by the cretins your government trained at the School of the Americas?"

"I'm going to leave you out here for a few minutes, and then we'll be taking you to the jail. In the meantime I think it would be to your advantage if you shut your mouth."

"You don't know why you hate and fear me, do you?" he asked.

"What?"

"I symbolize the ruinous consequence of America's decision to abandon the republic that the entire world admired and loved. You see me and realize how much you have lost."

I wanted to believe he was mad, a sybaritic, narcotic-fueled cynic determined to transfer his pathogens to the rest of us. With his hands cuffed to the deck rail, the wind flattening his clothes against his body, he looked like the twisted figure in the famous painting by Edvard Munch.

"Tell me I'm mistaken," he said.

I went back into the bedroom.

"What was that about?" Bailey said.

"Nothing," I said. "Did you find anything else?"

She shook her head.

"Bag up the scrapbook and the stuff in the hatbox," I said to Sean. "I'll put Butterworth in the cruiser."

"This bust bothers me," Bailey said. "We might have some legal problems. Like a liability suit."

"Not if Lucinda Arceneaux's DNA is on that needle," I said.

"But you know it's not, don't you?" she said. "Why do you have it in for this guy?"

I didn't answer. I collected Butterworth from the deck and hooked him to a D-ring in the back of the cruiser. Bailey and I got in the front and drove up the long narrow two-lane toward New Iberia, the palm fronds on the roadside rattling dryly in the wind, the waves chopping against the boats in their slips. She glanced sideways at me.

"What?" I said.

"Nothing," she said, and winked. "I think you're a nice guy. That's all."

That was when I knew that the folly of age is a contagion that spares no man, not unless he is fortunate enough to die young.

Chapter Fourteen

WE BOOKED BUTTERWORTH and transferred him to the parish prison. That evening Desmond turned in to my driveway in a new Cherokee. He seemed to wear his contradictions as you would a suit of clothes. I had a bell, but he tapped lightly on the door. I had a sidewalk, but he walked on the lawn, even though it was damp from the sprinkler. The lightness of his touch on the door was not in sync with the intensity in his face and the corded veins in his forearms.

I looked at him through the screen. "If this is about Butterworth, I'll talk to you at the department during office hours."

"Antoine is my friend," he said. "So are you. I'd like to speak with you in that spirit."

I stepped out on the gallery. The light had pooled high in the sky, like an inverted golden bowl; the oaks in the yard were deep in shadow, the trunks surrounded by red and yellow four-o'clocks that bloomed only in the shade.

Desmond's wide-set pale blue eyes were unblinking and yet simultaneously veiled; they had the vacuity you see in the eyes of sociopaths.

"Let Butterworth take his own fall," I said.

"He hasn't done anything."

"Have you seen the photos in his scrapbook?"

"Maybe he does a different kind of penance than the rest of us. Hollywood is a place of second chances. More important, it's a place where there are no victims. Everyone there knows the rules and the odds. Why beat up on Antoine?"

"On the phone you said we'd strip-mine the Garden of Eden if the price was right. You grew up in Eden?"

"What are you saying, Dave?"

"You lived on a piece of reservation hardpan that was given to the Indians only because the whites didn't want it."

"Better put, they wouldn't spit on it," he said. "What's your point?"

"The casino made life a little better for some of your people. You think that was a bad idea? Why don't you cut the rest of us some slack? Most of us do the best we can."

"I thought I could reason with you," he said. "That was a mistake. I'd better go before I say something I'll regret."

"Say it anyway."

"I see the way you look at Bailey Ribbons. I don't blame you. For me, she's Clementine Carter. She takes us into the past, into our first love, into America before the railroad guys and the industrialists got their hands on it. When you're with her, every day is spring, and death holds no dominion in your life."

How do you get mad at a man who speaks in Petrarchan sonnets? "I talked with Bella Delahoussaye this afternoon."

"Who?"

"She's Butterworth's alibi. He told the truth about lending her his Subaru. There's a problem, though."

"What?"

"She said he also drives a dark-colored SUV. An SUV fled the Devereaux murder scene."

"I already explained that," Desmond said. "We have several in the car pool. For God's sake, get away from this obsession with Hollywood. You're all alike. You can't stand success. You can't stand art or reason or anything that isn't like your putrid way of life. All of you are searching for a house with no mirrors."

"Good try," I said.

He looked at the sweep of leaves on the street, the electric lamps burning inside the oak boughs, the dreamlike shade that was stealing across the lawns of homes that Jefferson Davis's widow once visited. "I apologize. This is my birthplace, too. You have more claim on it, though. I've done wrong by all of you. I wish I could change that. But I probably never will."

There was nothing grandiose or thespian or saccharine in his voice or expression. He walked to his car, his physicality barely restrained by his thin slacks and wash-faded shirt.

I was convinced that, like Helen Soileau, many people lived inside Desmond's skin, male and female, child and adult. He had never married, nor was he ever long in the company of one woman. For certain he was an egalitarian, an aesthete, an actor, and a painter. He had the flame of a mad artist, the voice of a singer, and the indifference to criticism that all great artists possess without being aware of it. I said earlier that he could light a room with his smile. It had been a long time since I had seen him do that. Were Clementine Carter and Bailey Ribbons his keys to resurrection, the rolling away of a rock that blocked out the sun and stole the air from his lungs?

The next morning Antoine Butterworth bailed out of jail. There was no DNA of any kind on the hypodermic needle. His lawyer had our trumped-up charges dropped.

SIX WEEKS PASSED without significant incident, and we found ourselves in the softly murmuring heart of Indian summer and the drowsy days and cool nights that grant us a stay against winter and the failing of the light. I began to think that our investigation into the bizarre homicides of Lucinda Arceneaux and Joe Molinari and Travis Lebeau and Axel Devereaux was overwrought and heavily influenced by speculation. I also wondered if Bailey and I had unknowingly superimposed symbols on each case in order to link them together. It happens. The best example is the murder of President Kennedy and the conspiratorial theories that are still with us. As the mind wearies, the temptation is to simplify and move on. The collective consciousness does not like detail and complexity. Besides, isn't it better to let evil die inside its own flame?

I wanted to slip away with the season and the smell of burning leaves and the vestiges of an innocent youth. In a moment of reverie, I would recall a college dance at Southwestern Louisiana Institute, the music provided by Jimmy Dorsey and his orchestra, a fall crawfish boil under the oaks in the park next to the campus, the thrill of the kickoff at an LSU–Ole Miss football game, where every coed wore a corsage and ached to be kissed.

I was not simply tired of the world's iniquity. I was tired of greed in particular and the ostentatious display of wealth that characterizes our times, and the justifications for despoiling the earth and injuring our fellow man. The great gift of age is the realization that each morning is a blessing, as votive in nature as a communion wafer raised to the sky. I made a habit of letting the world go on a daily basis, but unfortunately, it didn't want to let go of me. The engines of commerce and acquisition operate seven days a week, around the clock, granting no mercy and allowing no tender moment for those who grind away their lives in sweaty service to them.

I'm talking about the avarice at the heart of most human suffering. Yes, revenge is a player, and so are all the sexual manifestations that warp our vision, but none holds a candle to cupidity and the defenses we manufacture to protect it.

Clete would not have used the same words, although he knew them and their meaning. But his thoughts were the same when he decided to drop by the blues club on the bayou and eat barbecued chicken and dirty rice and drink a frozen mug of beer like he had in his youth at Tracey's Bar on Third and Magazine in the Irish Channel.

Because it was Friday night, the bar and tables and the small dance floor were bursting at the gunwales. Bella Delahoussaye was singing "Got My Mojo Working" while a black man backed her up with a harmonica that moaned and whined like a train inside a church house. A bald man on the stool next to Clete leaned in to his face, yelling to be heard. His lips were sprinkled with spittle, his tie pulled loose, his stomach hanging out of his suit coat. Clete wiped his own cheek with a paper napkin and tried to lean in the opposite direction.

"Did you hear me?" the man shouted. "What do you think about the monuments thing?"

"What monuments?"

"They're taking down the Confederate monuments in New Orleans. They just took down Robert E. Lee's statue. What's your opinion?"

A piece of spittle hit Clete on the chin. "I think they're idiots. They want to turn New Orleans into Omaha. They're doing the same thing that the Taliban and ISIS do."

"Yes, but don't you think it's time to—"

"Quit yelling in my face."

"You don't have to get in a huff," the man said, and swung his paunch off the stool.

Clete tried to get back to his food but looked at it and thought about what had probably just happened to it and pushed it away and reordered.

"It's on the house, man," the bartender said.

"Thanks," Clete said. He put a ten on the bar. "Give the fat guy whatever he's having. Just don't tell him where it's from. Keep the change."

Bella went into "The House of the Rising Sun," the song Eric Burdon and the Animals had turned into arguably the most haunting blues depiction of bordello life and spiritual despair ever sung. Though its message of utter hopelessness was like a dull nail driven into Clete's heart, he had never known why. Sometimes he ascribed the feeling to the drowning of the city during Katrina, or the crack cocaine that had turned the city into the murder capital of America, or the T-shirt shops and the affectation of debauchery that impersonated the city's earlier tradition of eccentricity and bohemian culture and Dixieland blowdowns.

The song's influence on him had nothing to do with any of these things, or even with New Orleans. The song was about exploitation and the anonymous fate that seemed the destiny of all those who are used for the convenience of others. The song had no author. The person narrating the tale could have been male or female but had no name. The rising sun did not dispel the night, serving only to illuminate the harshness of the morning, the broken glass in the gutters, a passed-out drunk in an alley.

Clete looked up and down the bar and at the tables and at the dancers on the floor and wondered how many of them would leave the earth as ciphers, would even have a marker on a grave ten years after they were gone. His first night back in New Orleans from Vietnam, he got loaded in the Quarter and met a famous Beat writer who was feeding the pigeons on a bench in Jackson Square. The writer challenged him to name five slaves from the tens of millions who had lived and died in bondage.

Clete got as far as Spartacus and Frederick Douglass.

"What's that say?" the writer asked.

"I don't know much about history?" Clete said.

"No man, it means there's no history. Just humps in the ground wanting somebody to tell their story. Think I'm blowing gas?"

Bella finished her song and walked down the length of the bar. She drew a fingernail along the back of Clete's neck. "Where's your friend?"

"Dave?" he said.

"Who else? I ain't seen him around. Tell him he hurt my feelings."

"He's been busy with a few things. People getting killed, stuff like that."

"Don't mean he cain't drop by." She winked. "Tell him he got the moves and I got the groove."

"Show some respect for yourself," Clete said.

"Talk like I want, baby."

Clete looked down the bar. "There's somebody sitting down there who shouldn't be in here."

Bella lifted her chin and gazed at a black woman ten stools down. The black woman was wearing a white dress and a necklace with red stones that hung between her breasts. "Hilary Bienville? I ain't my sister's keeper."

"She might listen to you," he said.

"That girl is looking for a box. She gonna find it, too."

"She's still messing around with some white guy?"

"She been on her knees since she was a li'l girl. You cain't fix them kind. Messed-up girl becomes a messed-up woman."

"Who's the guy?"

"I ain't axed. I get off at two. Give me a ride? I could sure use one."

She walked away from Clete, looking back over her shoulder. He ordered a shot of Jack and dropped it into his beer, jigger and all. He drank the mug to the bottom, the jigger clinking against the glass. He looked down the bar and saw a sight that made him squint and rub his eyes and look again.

The man's hair was steel-gray, cut tight, top combed straight back with gel, as though he wanted to look younger. He had grown a full beard and lost weight, but the profile was the same Clete had seen in the mug shots he had gotten off the Internet. The man was talking to Hilary Bienville and wore navy blue trousers and the kind of plain short-sleeve khaki shirt that a filling station mechanic might wear.

It can't be him, Clete thought. *Not a guy who escaped death row and should be looking for a cave in Afghanistan.*

Clete got off the stool just as the front door opened and two carloads of revelers poured in. By the time Clete had worked his way through them, the man was gone.

Hilary stared blankly at Clete. She had a Collins glass in her hand. Her eyes were out of focus. "What you want?"

"Was that Hugo Tillinger?" he asked.

"I don't know no Hugo Tillinger."

"What are you doing in here?"

"I come in to see my friends. What it look like?"

"The last time I saw you, you were in meltdown. Where's your baby?"

"Ain't nothing wrong wit' me being here. My baby doing fine."

"Where is she?"

"At Iberia General. She got the croup."

"Go home, Hilary. Don't do this to yourself."

"It's my life. It ain't yours. I got the *gris-gris*. I'm hell-bound. Ain't nothing can he'p me."

"Where'd the guy go?"

"I don't know. You look like a cop. I t'ink he saw you."

"He knows who I am?"

"I don't know about none of this."

"You wait here."

"You like all the rest. 'Shut your mout'.' 'Cook my food.' 'Suck my dick.' Where you going?"

Clete looked in the men's room. A man at the urinal grinned at him. Clete went out the back door just as an SUV motored slowly out of the parking lot, the headlights on, the driver silhouetted behind the wheel. The driver turned onto the asphalt. Clete couldn't see the tag.

He got into his Caddy and followed. The SUV stopped at the four corners and crossed the drawbridge and headed for the four-lane, never exceeding the speed limit. The windows were down. The radio was playing. Clete thought he recognized "Rock of Ages."

HE FOLLOWED THE SUV in and out of traffic all the way to Lafayette. Twice he got close enough to confirm that the driver was the same man he'd seen talking to Hilary Bienville. The driver gave no indication that he knew he was being followed. Just outside Lafayette, the man pulled into a truck stop and got out of his vehicle and began to gas up. Clete parked behind the building with a view of the fuel island and cut the engine. He took his binoculars from the glove box and adjusted the focus on the driver's face. He had no doubt he was looking at Hugo Tillinger.

He put his sap and cuffs in his coat pocket and pulled the .25 semi-auto from the Velcro holster strapped on his ankle.

Sorry, Mac, he thought, getting out of the Caddy. *If you got to ride the needle, it's your misfortune and none of my own.*

A lopsided gas-guzzler oozing oil smoke pulled up to the pumps. The driver was a tiny gray-haired black woman who wore a colorless shift and men's tennis shoes. A girl of eight or nine years was in the back seat. A Mississippi tag hung from the bumper by a single screw. The woman got out and stuck a credit card in the pump and struggled to pull the hose from the hook. Suddenly, the child burst from the back door and ran for the restrooms, just as a pickup truck swerved off the highway and headed for a parking slot in front of the casino.

Clete felt the wind go out of his chest. The scene freeze-framed in his head like a movie projector locking down. Within two or three seconds the girl would be impaled on the truck's grille. The truck driver's face was turned toward a woman in the passenger seat. The elderly black woman had dropped the hose on the concrete, spewing gasoline across her shoes. The little girl was skipping, one knee cocked, one barely touching the concrete, her mouth open, as though she were painted on air. Clete couldn't bear to look.

Tillinger bolted from behind his vehicle and grabbed the girl under both arms and held her to his chest and leaped forward like a quarterback crashing over the line. He twisted his body so he landed on his side, taking the full hit on the concrete, never letting go of the girl.

He got to his feet and picked up the girl and handed her to the elderly woman. He smiled, brushing off her attempts to thank him, and headed for the driver of the truck. The driver turned off his lights, floored his vehicle, and roared into the darkness.

Tillinger went inside the convenience store and bought a package of Fritos and a quart of chocolate milk and ate and drank them at a small table. This was the guy Clete was going to send to the injection table?

Clete followed him to a motel rimmed with pink and green neon tubing north of Four Corners and watched him park in front of the last room in the row. Tillinger went inside and clicked on a lamp. Clete pulled his Caddy under a tree and waited five minutes. Then he got out with his .25 semi-auto and tapped lightly on the door.

"Who is it?" Tillinger said.

"Security. Someone may have tried to open your vehicle."

Tillinger unhooked the chain and opened the door. He was barefoot and wearing boxer shorts and a clean white T-shirt. "I saw you in the club. What are you doing at my motel?"

Clete stepped inside and stiff-armed Tillinger in the chest, knocking him backward over a chair. He kicked the door shut behind him. "Don't get up."

"What the hell! Who are you?"

"A guy you caused a lot of grief."

"Grief? I got no idea who you are."

Clete picked up a pillow. "Look at the gun I'm holding. It's a throw-down. No serial numbers, no history. Don't fuck with me. I'll pop you and in one minute be down the road and gone, and the cleaning lady will smell a strange odor in the morning and you'll be bagged and tagged and in a meat locker. *Diggez-vous,* noble mon?"

"Noble what?"

"You got loose from death row in Texas. I thought you had some smarts."

"Tell me who are you, and maybe something you say will make sense."

"I'm a guy who already cut you slack you didn't deserve. I was fishing by the trestle over the Mermentau River when you bailed off the freight car. I should have dimed you, but I didn't, and I've been paying for it ever since."

"You got the wrong room."

Clete stuck the .25 semi-auto in the back of his belt and grabbed Tillinger by the T-shirt and swung him into the wall so hard the room shook. Tillinger fell to the floor. His expression looked like someone had crashed two cymbals on his ears.

"Next stop is the toilet bowl," Clete said.

Tillinger pushed himself up on his arms. "Do your worst. Then put yourself on a diet. You got a serious weight as well as a thinking problem."

"Why were you hitting on Hilary Bienville?"

"You a cop?"

"I used to be," Clete said. "You been putting shit in Hilary's head? It takes a special kind of white man to do that to a woman of color."

"I was a friend of Lucinda Arceneaux. Lucinda told me how some colored women were being used by some bad cops. You know who Travis Lebeau was, right?"

"He was in the Aryan Brotherhood," Clete said. "He got dragged to death."

"I've been trying to find out who killed Lucinda. It's got something to do with prostitution."

"Who shoved the baton down the throat of Axel Devereaux?"

"I don't know. I don't care. Can I get up?"

"An SUV like yours was seen hauling freight down the road right after Devereaux shuffled off."

"I was there. But he was already dead. You got a beef because I messed up your fishing?"

"Where'd you get the wheels?"

"Boosted them."

"Why'd you go to Devereaux's house? You already creeped it once."

"I was going to beat it out of him."

"Beat what out of him?"

"The name of a movie guy Devereaux was scared of. That's what a couple of stagehands said. Devereaux even got slapped around by this guy. The guy threw him off the set."

"Because Devereaux was pimping?"

"I don't know. That's what I was going to find out. Miss Lucinda was tight with all those people. You ever see *The Thin Blue Line*? It saved an innocent man's life. That could be my story."

"I'm going to give you five minutes to get dressed and get out of here," Clete said. "Then your ass is grass."

Tillinger got to his feet cautiously, wobbling, pressing one hand against the wall. "You know what I was down for?"

"Killing your family."

"That doesn't bother you?"

"No."

"Why not?"

"My guess is you're innocent. But you're still an asshole," Clete said. "You've used up one minute."

Chapter Fifteen

CLETE WAS AT my back screen early on Saturday, freshly showered, his hair wet-combed, his clothes pressed. But his ebullience and his attempt to blend with the coolness of the morning and the dew-drenched fragrance of the flower beds were a poor disguise for the guilt he always wore like a child would, at least when he thought he had wronged me, which he had never intentionally done.

Alafair was still asleep. I fixed biscuits and coffee and waited for Clete to get to whatever was bothering him. It took a while. Clete had a way of talking about every subject in the world until he casually mentioned a minor incident such as smashing an earth grader through the home of a mafioso on Lake Pontchartrain, blowing a greaseball with a fire hose into a urinal at the casino, or pouring sand into the fuel tank of a plane loaded with more greaseballs, all of whom ended up petroglyphs on a mountainside in western Montana.

"You let Hugo Tillinger slide because he saved the little girl?" I said.

"He's not a killer."

We were seated at the breakfast table. The window was open, the wind sweet through the screen, Snuggs and Mon Tee Coon sitting on Tripod's hutch.

"You're not going to say anything?" he asked.

"This conversation didn't happen. We bury it right here. Got it?"

"You're not upset?"

"I probably would have done the same thing. The guy got a bad deal in Texas."

"You don't think he could have done the baton job on Devereaux?"

"These murders are about money, Clete."

"You lost me, big mon."

"The tarot and the floating cross have private meaning to the killer, but the motivation is much larger. It's not sex, it's not power or control. That leaves money."

"I think you're taking too much for granted," Clete said.

"The killer injected Arceneaux with a fatal dose of heroin. The others went out hard. Why would he make distinctions in the way he killed his victims? It's because he's created a grand scheme. Think about it. A serial killer wants to paint the walls and enjoy every minute of it. He's driven by compulsion. Unless his motivation is misogynistic, his targets are random. Our guy has a plan. Tillinger is a simpleton who wants to be a celebrity. He's not our guy."

Clete had a biscuit in his jaw. He looked at me for a long moment, then drank from his cup, his eyes not leaving mine. "Why only in our area?"

"That's the big one," I said. "He's sending us a message."

"Lucky us," Clete said.

MY SPECULATIONS PROBABLY seemed grandiose. In reality, I wasn't talking about our local homicides. I believed then, and I believe now, that our poor suffering state is part of a historical ebb tide that few recognize as such. Southern Louisiana, as late as the Great Depression, retained many of the characteristics of the antediluvian world, untouched by the Industrial Age. Our coast was defined by its pristine wetlands. They were emerald green and dotted with hummocks and flooded tupelo gums and cypress trees and serpentine rivers and bayous that turned yellow after the spring rains and lakes that were both clear and black because of the fine silt at the bottom, all of it blanketed with snowy egrets and blue herons and seagulls and brown pelicans.

We had little money but didn't think of ourselves as poor. Our vision, if I can call it that, was not materialistic. If we had a concept about ourselves, it was egalitarian, although we would not have known what that word meant. We spoke French entirely. There was a bond between Cajuns and people of color. Cajuns didn't travel, because they believed they lived in the best place on earth. But somehow the worst in us, or outside of us, asserted itself and prevailed and replaced everything that was good in our lives. We traded away our language, our customs, our stands of cypress, our sugarcane acreage, our identity, and our pride. Outsiders ridiculed us and thought us stupid; teachers forbade our children to speak French on the school grounds. Our barrier islands were dredged to extinction. Our coastline was cut with eight thousand miles of industrial channels, destroying the root systems of the sawgrass and the swamps. The bottom of the state continues to wash away in the flume of the Mississippi at a rate of sixteen square miles a year.

Much of this we did to ourselves in the same way that a drunk like me will destroy a gift, one that is irreplaceable and extended by a divine hand. Our roadsides are littered with trash, our rain ditches layered with it, our waterways dumping grounds for automobile tires and couches and building material. While we trivialize the implications of our drive-through daiquiri windows and the seediness of our politicians and recite our self-congratulatory mantra, *laissez les bons temps rouler,* the southern rim of the state hovers on the edge of oblivion, a diminishing, heartbreaking strip of green lace that eventually will be available only in photographs.

That afternoon Alafair asked if Clete and I wanted to take a trip to northern Arizona. Clete said he'd pass. I said, "Why not?"

I TOOK FOUR DAYS' vacation time and flew with her and Lou Wexler and Desmond Cormier in a Learjet to a tourist town on the edge of Monument Valley. Wexler slept, and Desmond was on his laptop most of the time, and Alafair and I played Monopoly. On several occasions, even when she was little, she and I had spent time in Hollywood with movie people we had met in Louisiana. We were always treated graciously, and I relearned an old lesson about judging. People in Hollywood are often egocentric, but nonetheless they dream and many of them are wedded to a perception of the world that they never share with others lest they be thought odd or eccentric or dishonest. Perhaps there's a bit of the secular mystic in them. Not unlike Desmond's.

I didn't know how to read Lou Wexler. Certainly he was a fine-looking man, with his bronze skin and rugged profile and sun-bleached hair and wide shoulders that tapered to a twenty-eight-inch waist. Immediately upon arrival at our faux-Navajo hotel, he put on swim trunks and walked on his hands to the tip of the diving board, then did a somersault into the water. Although I suspected he was close to forty, there was hardly a blemish on his skin except for a ragged white scar where his kidney would have been. When others ordered drinks before supper on the terrace, he went behind the bar and fixed his own power shake and drank it foaming from the stainless steel container. I suspected he would be a formidable man in a confrontation, the kind of fellow who had fire in his belly.

He sat next to me at the table. People I didn't know joined us. Several had obviously gotten an early start. North of us lay the vastness of the desert, the sky a seamless blue in the fading light, the sandstone buttes rising like castles from the mountain floor. Wexler glanced at my iced tea. "Looks like we're two of a kind."

"In what way?" I replied.

"Abstinence," he said. "I can't say it's a virtue with me, though."

"How's that?"

"I never saw the attraction. More liability than asset. My father was on the grog all his life and asked for a bottle of porter on his deathbed."

I didn't reply.

"You're a quiet one, sir," he said.

Like most recovering drunks, I didn't like to talk about alcohol or alcoholism with what we call earth people or flatlanders. "Call me Dave, please. What kind of movie are y'all making? How do you tie Arizona to Louisiana?"

"It's an epic film about three generations in a legendary family," he said. "Southerners who migrated to the frontier, then ruined the frontier the way they ruined everything else they got their hands on."

"I take it you're not a fan of manifest destiny."

He loaded a taco chip with guacamole and put it into his mouth and studied Desmond at the end of the table, talking to two beautiful women. A silver bowl filled with water and floating tropical flowers was in front of Wexler. The crumbs from his taco chip fell into it.

"This film means a lot to Desmond," he said. "In fact, it's an obsession. He has seventy-five million dollars of other people's money and thirty million of his own riding on it."

"Who put up the seventy-five?" I asked.

"We used to soak the Japs until they figured out they were still paying for Pearl Harbor. The Arabs are a good source if you don't think too hard about what they do in Saudi jails or to women who get out of line."

"You didn't answer the question," I said.

"That's because I don't intend to." He laughed.

"I saw your scar. You picked it up in Africa?"

"A fellow hooked me with a machete. I thought it was time to find a better line of work. So now I do this stuff. Desmond is a good one to work for. No nonsense. If you're wired, you're fired."

"Why does he tolerate Antoine Butterworth?"

"He thinks Antoine's an artist rather than a sadistic degenerate with his head up a woman's dress."

I looked around to see if anyone had heard him. If they had, they showed no sign. Wexler turned his face to a puff of cool air from the desert floor. "Tomorrow we're shooting a remarkable scene. Probably few will take much heed of it, but if it works, it will be an extraordinary moment, the kind that brought to a close *My Darling Clementine*. It comes from the final scene of the novel that's at the core of the script."

It had been a while since I had read the book or books from which the film was adapted, so I had a hard time tracking his line of thought.

"Don't pay attention to me, Mr. Robicheaux—I mean Dave," he said. "I'm not a bad screenwriter, but I'm best at adapting the work of others. And like most producers, I'm great at calling up the caterer and taking wealthy bozos to lunch."

He looked at the final rays of sun streaking across the desert floor, the pools of shadow at the base of the buttes, the dust rising like strings of smoke from the crests into the light. "It's like staring into infinity, isn't it? Desmond believes death lies on the other side of the horizon, where the earth drops off and the sky begins. I think he's wrong. It's not death that's waiting out there. Not at all."

The people who had gotten an early start were getting louder, their laughter cacophonous and disjointed. The evening air was suddenly cooler, the sandstone formations more lavender than red, more like tombstones than castles.

"If it's not death, what is it?" I asked.

"Something unknowable." His eyes were hollow, sightless, even though he was staring straight at me. "We drown in it. This is the omphalos, the center of it all. You were there, sir. You know what I'm talking about."

"I was where?"

"You bloody well know what I mean. Where you see the realities and never tell anyone."

I wondered if I was talking to a madman. Or someone who had been in the Garden. Or someone who shot up with hallucinogens.

"Sorry. After seven in the evening I develop logorrhea," he said.

"You're fine. I need to take a walk."

"What about dinner?"

"I'll be back in a few minutes. I have sciatica trouble sometimes."

"I'll come along," he said.

"Sure," I said.

"I see you walk with a purpose," he said. "I can always tell a military man. You ever count cadence? It puts your blood to pumping, by God. Orwell said it. Maybe there's something beautiful about war after all."

Wrong, I thought. But why argue with those who are proud of their membership in the Herd?

AT FIVE-THIRTY A.M., I went down to breakfast inside the hotel restaurant and thought I was seeing an apparition at a table by a big glass window that gave onto the desert. Clete was wearing his powder blue sport coat and gray slacks and shined oxblood loafers, his porkpie hat crown-down on the tablecloth. He was surrounded by a stack of pancakes inserted with sausage patties, scrambled eggs, hash browns, a bowl of milk gravy, toast, coffee, a pitcher of cream, and a glass of tomato juice with an orange slice notched on the rim.

"What are you doing here?" I said.

"Thought I'd get out of town in case Helen wanted to chat about Hugo Tillinger. Maybe I'll hike in the hills. Lose a few pounds."

I sat down. "Are you up to something?"

"No, you got my word."

"I know you, Clete."

"Bailey Ribbons is on her way. I heard Helen is beaucoup pissed."

"Bailey is coming here?"

"Cormier is casting her. I didn't know how you'd feel about that."

"She can do whatever she wants. Stop trying to micromanage my life."

"Want some pancakes?"

I WENT TO ALAFAIR'S room. She was just coming out the door. I told her what Clete had just told me.

"Clete is here?" she said.

"Helen isn't in the best of moods."

"And Bailey Ribbons is joining the cast?" Alafair said.

I didn't reply. I didn't want to say it again.

"She's hanging it up with the department?" Alafair said.

"I don't know. I don't care, either."

She pulled me inside the room and closed the door. "How do you want me to say it? You lost two of your wives to violence and one to lupus. You'll never get over your loss. But you won't cure the problem with Bailey."

"We have four unsolved homicides on our desks," I said. "That's not an abstraction or part of a soap opera. I need her. I mean at the job."

"The homicides are not the issue, so stop fooling yourself and stop acting like a twit."

"Give it a rest, Alafair."

Her face was pinched, her hands knotting. "Okay, I'm sorry. I get mad at Bailey."

"Why?"

"She went to the head of the line. She's attractive and intelligent and has charm and an innocent way that makes men want to protect her. Helen Soileau earned her job. Bailey didn't. Now she hangs you out to dry and leaves you at war with yourself."

"I'll survive," I replied, and tried to smile.

"Pardon me while I go to the bathroom and throw up," she said.

I went to the window and looked at the miles and miles of mountain desert to the north, pink and majestic and desolate in the sunrise. It was a perfect work of art, outside of time and the rules of probability and governance of the seasons, as if it had been scooped out of the clay by the hand of God and left to dry as the seas receded and the dinosaurs and pterodactyls came to frolic on damp earth that, one hundred million years later, became stone. As I stared at the swirls of color in the hardpan, the sage clinging for life in the dry riverbeds, and the solemnity of the buttes, massive and yet miniaturized by the endless undulation of the mountain floor, I felt the pull of eternity inside my breast.

I heard Alafair return from the bathroom and felt her standing behind me. "What are you thinking about?" she said.

"Nothing. I bet Desmond casts Bailey as the IWW woman in the book. The one who was at the Ludlow Massacre." Alafair was looking at me with an expression between pity and anger.

"Can I visit the set?" I asked.

"Of course."

"I'd like to wish her luck."

"Better give your well wishes to Desmond. I think he might lose his shirt."

"I thought he had the Midas touch."

"He mortgaged his home and vineyard in Napa Valley. He reminds me of Captain Ahab taking on the white whale. He's always talking about 'the light.' He says it's a Plotinian emanation of the unseen world."

My attention began to wander. "Clete's probably still in the dining room. Let's join him."

"I have to confess something," she said. "I think the killings in New Iberia are connected to us."

"Who's 'us'?" I asked.

"Hollywood. The evil we can't seem to get out of our lives. The legacy of slavery. Whatever."

"Quit beating up on yourself. We pulled the apple from the tree a long time ago, Alf."

"Yeah, that bad girl Eve. Save it, Dave."

Chapter Sixteen

ON PRIVATE LAND just inside the Utah border, Desmond had constructed an environment meant to replicate nineteenth-century Indian territory and a stretch of the Cimarron River just north of the Texas Panhandle. He had diverted a stream and brought in water tanks and lined a gulley with vinyl and layered it with gravel, then placed a solitary horseman five hundred yards from the improvised riverbank.

Wexler was standing next to me. "This scene is going to cost the boys in Jersey over fifty grand. I hope they enjoy it."

"Pardon?" I said.

"It's the last scene in the picture, although we're only a third into the story. The guy who wrote the book says it's the best scene he ever wrote, and the last line in the scene is the best line he ever wrote. I bet our Jersey friends would love that."

"Who are your Jersey friends?"

"Not the Four Seasons," he answered.

The rider was a tall and lanky boy who looked no older than fifteen. His horse was a chestnut, sixteen hands, with a blond tail and mane. Desmond was talking to the camera personnel; then he flapped a yellow flag above his head. Through a pair of binoculars, I saw the boy lean forward and pour it on, bent low over the withers, his legs straight out, whipping the horse with the reins, his hat flying on a cord. The sun was low and red in the sky, the boy riding straight out of it like a blackened cipher escaping a molten planet. Two leather mail pouches were strung from his back, arrows embedded in them up to the shaft.

"The scene is about the Pony Express?" I said.

"On one level," Wexler said. "But actually, it's about the search for the Grail."

I looked at him.

"Don't worry if you're confused," he said. "Probably no one else will get it, either. Particularly that lovely bunch of gangsters on the Jersey Shore."

"It's an allegory?"

"Nothing is an allegory for Desmond. He hears the horns blowing along the road to Roncesvalles. Worse than I."

The rider went hell for breakfast across the stream, the horse laboring, its neck dark with sweat, water splashing and gravel clacking.

"Cut!" Desmond said. "Wonderful! Absolutely wonderful!"

After the boy dismounted, Desmond hugged him in a full-body press. I felt embarrassed for the boy. "Where'd you learn to ride?" Desmond said.

"Here'bouts," the boy said, his face visibly burning.

"Well, you're awfully fine," Des said. "Get yourself a cold drink. I want to talk with you later. With your parents. You're going somewhere, kid."

That was Desmond's great gift. He made people feel good about themselves, and he didn't do it out of pride or compulsion or weakness or defensiveness or a desire to feel powerful and in control of others. He used his own success to validate what was best in the people around him. But there is a caveat implied in the last statement. The people who surrounded him were not simply employees, they were acolytes, and I suspected Bailey was about to become one of them. For that reason alone, I felt a growing resentment, one that was petty and demeaning.

"What'd you think, Dave?" Desmond said.

"That young fellow is impressive," I replied.

"Come on, you're a smart man. What do you think of us, tattered bunch that we are, talking trash about Crusader knights and trying to sell it to an audience that wants a fucking video game?"

"What do I know?"

Bailey Ribbons was standing thirty feet away, dressed like a fashionable pioneer woman. I had not spoken to her yet.

"What do you think of that scene, Bailey?" Wexler asked.

"I think it's all grand," she said. She walked toward us. Her hem went to the tops of her feet. Her frilly white blouse was buttoned at the throat, her hair piled on her head. "Aren't you going to say hello, Dave?"

"You have to forgive me. I was hesitant to speak on the set."

"You're surprised to see me here?" she asked.

"If I'd known you were coming, I wouldn't have asked Helen for some vacation days. She's shorthanded now."

"It wasn't my intention to inconvenience anyone," she said.

I looked at my watch. "I'd better get back to the hotel. I have to make some calls."

"Will you have lunch with us?" she said.

"Let me see what Clete is doing."

"Clete Purcel is here?" she said.

"He gets around," I said.

"Well, I'm happy he was able to come out," she said.

I didn't know what else to say. I felt disappointed in Bailey and in myself. "Thanks for having me here, Des. I'll see you later."

I walked away, feeling foolish and inadequate, as though I were starting to lose part of myself.

"Don't you want a lift?" Wexler said.

I had forgotten I'd ridden to the set with him and Alafair. "I'll hitch a ride," I said.

Three miles down the road, a man driving a chicken truck with glassless windows picked me up, and we drove across the state line into Arizona and a dust storm that turned the sun to grit.

AT THE HOTEL I called Helen and apologized for leaving her shorthanded.

"Forget it," she said. "I'm going to have a talk with Bailey when she gets back."

"Why'd you let her come out here?"

"I figured what's the harm? What are the things you regret most in your life, bwana?"

"Constantly taking my own inventory."

"You know what I'm talking about. We regret the things we didn't do, not the things we did. All the romances we didn't have, the music we didn't dance to, the children we didn't parent. So I let her have her fling with Lotusland. Then I got mad at myself about it. By the way, I got a phone call from a federal agent regarding Hugo Tillinger."

Of all the subjects she could bring up, Tillinger was the one I least wanted to hear about.

"This agent grew up with him," she said. "He believes Tillinger may have killed a biker in the Aryan Brotherhood about ten years ago. The biker raped and broke the neck of an old woman in Corsicana. She belonged to the same church Tillinger did. Somebody tore the biker apart with a mattock."

I felt my stomach constrict. "What's the evidence?"

"None. The crime remains unsolved. Some fellow church members asked Tillinger about it. His answer was 'I, the Lord, love justice.' It's from Isaiah."

My head was coming off my shoulders.

"Are you there?" she asked.

"Yes."

"What's wrong?"

"I'll let Clete tell you."

This time she went silent. Then she said, "Dave, did Clete see Tillinger again?"

"He saw him save a little girl's life at a filling station in Lafayette. Clete followed him to a motel north of Four Corners but cut him loose."

"Son of a bitch," she said. "How long have you known this?"

"A couple of days."

"Why didn't you report it?"

"I thought no good would come out of it."

"No, you thought you'd write your own rules. You put your friendship with Clete ahead of the job. I'm pulling your ticket, Pops. I'm not going to take this shit."

"I'm on the desk?"

"You're on leave without pay. I'm referring this to Internal Affairs."

"What about Clete?"

"He'd better get his fat ass back to New Orleans and stay there for a long time."

"I made a mistake. So did Clete. We didn't know about the biker murder."

"You made your bed," she said. "Dave, you use a nail gun on the people who love you most. You don't know how much you hurt me."

AT MIDDAY, ALAFAIR was still at the set. I ate lunch by myself and then lay down in my room and fell asleep. An hour later, I woke from a disturbing dream about a mountainous desert that was not a testimony to the curative beauty of the natural world but instead a crumbling artifice inhabited only by the wind. I sat on the side of the bed, gripping my knees, my head filled with a warm fuzziness that felt like the beginning of malarial delusions, a condition I've dealt with since childhood.

Perhaps I fell asleep again. I can't remember. Then I went downstairs and sat for a long time by the entrance to the lounge and took a table in the dining room by the big window that gave onto the swimming pool and a vista like the long trail disappearing into the buttes in the final scene of *My Darling Clementine*. The waitress asked if I would like anything from the bar.

"A glass of iced tea," I said.

She was pretty and young and had thick soft brown hair and an innocent pixie face. "Sure thing."

She walked away, yawning slightly, looking through the window at the swimmers in the pool. I wondered if she dreamed about being among them. Many of them were celebrities, or the children or the lovers of celebrities, and those who were not celebrities were obviously well-to-do and carefree and, like the celebrities, enjoying the coolness and turquoise brilliance of the water and the heat of the sun on their bodies, as though all of it had been invented for them, as though the wind-carved shapes to the north had no connection to their lives.

The waitress put the tea and a coaster by my hand. "Are you with the film crew?"

"Afraid not. I'm just a tourist," I said.

"Must be nice, huh?"

"What must be nice?"

"To live like that. To make movies and not have to worry about anything."

"Could be," I said.

"Let me know if you want anything."

I watched her walk away and tried not to look below the level of her waist, then put the charge on my room and left a five-dollar bill under my glass, even though that was more than my personal budget allowed. I used the stairs rather than the elevator to reach my floor and spent the rest of the afternoon in my room. A faucet was ticking in the bathroom as loudly as a mechanical clock, with the same sense of urgency and waste. I tried to tighten the faucet but to no avail. I lay down and put a pillow over my head, the afternoon sun as red as fire behind my eyelids.

ALAFAIR WAS LATE getting back from the set. I had dinner with Clete in a Mexican restaurant and told him about my phone call to Helen and the information I had given her about Clete's decision to let Hugo Tillinger go. I also told him about the penalty she had imposed on me, as well as her feelings about Clete's cutting Tillinger slack a second time.

"A fed says he tore up somebody in the AB with a mattock?" Clete said.

"Which means maybe he put the baton down Axel Devereaux's throat."

"Why didn't the fed do something about it?" Clete said. "Why's he dropping this on us?"

"Nobody is dropping anything on us. You made a choice, and so did I. It was the wrong choice."

"Dave, I don't have the legal power to arrest anyone. I can take skips into custody because they're considered property, but that's it. Helen is wrong on this."

"No, she isn't."

"I'm sorry you got your ticket pulled, big mon."

"Like you say, we're getting too old for this crap."

"Come in with me. We'll put the Bobbsey Twins from Homicide back in business."

"I'll think about it."

"No, you won't. You'll sit around and suffer," he said.

"Lay off it, Cletus. I don't feel too well right now."

"You really believe Tillinger would take out a guy with a mattock?" he asked.

"I think Tillinger and a few like him could found a new religion that would make radical Islam look like the teachings of Saint Francis."

THE TAILINGS OF the monsoon season moved across the sun that evening, darkening and wetting the land and lighting the sky with electricity that quivered and disappeared between the buttes and the clouds. It was Desmond Cormier's birthday. The party began on the terrace, under canopies hung with Japanese lanterns. As the storm dissipated, the celebrants moved down the slope into a picnic area that had a wood dance floor and kiva fireplaces. A band featuring conga drums and horns and a marimba and oversize mariachi guitars played inside a gazebo. Desmond was soused to the eyes and dancing by himself with a bottle of champagne, dressed in tight cutoffs and a T-shirt scissored across the midriff, the smooth firmness of his physique and his wide-set washed-out eyes and his tombstone teeth and the bulge in his shorts and the solipsistic glaze on his face a study in sensuality.

Clete and Alafair and I sat at a table by one of the clay fireplaces and rolled lettuce and tomato and shredded cheese and strips of steak inside tortillas and watched Desmond dance. The flames from the gas lamps painted his body with bands of yellow and orange like the reflections of an ancient fire on a cave wall. A tall, very thin woman with jet-black hair and milk-white skin and a dress slit to the top of the thigh tried to dance with him, her eyes fastened on his. But if she desired to make use of the moment and become a soul mate with Des, she had underestimated the challenge. He scooped her up, one arm under her rump, and waltzed in a circle, holding up the magnum bottle with his other hand, while everyone applauded and the thin woman tried to hide her surprise and embarrassment.

I felt a shadow fall across the side of my face. I turned and looked up at Antoine Butterworth.

"Good evening, all," he said.

"Hello, Antoine," Alafair said. She looked worriedly at me and then at Clete. "I thought you were holding down things in New Iberia."

"I had enough of the mosquitoes and humidity for a while," he said.

Alafair looked at me again, then back at Butterworth. "Would you like to join us?"

"I didn't mean to crash in on you," he said.

"Sit down," I said to him.

"Change of attitude?" he said. "Saw a revelation in the sky, that kind of thing?"

"I'm suspended from the department," I said. "You're safe."

He pulled up a chair and fingered his chin. The skin on his face and his shaved head looked as tight as latex on a mannequin. "Could I ask why?"

"The sheriff likes to flush out the place on occasion," I said. "Kind of like a reverse affirmative-action program."

"Nothing to do with us, the California infidels?" he said.

"No, it has everything to do with me," Clete said. "I cut slack to an escaped convict. Dave didn't report me, so he took my weight. Know who Hugo Tillinger is?"

"Saw his picture in the paper. Man who burned up his wife and daughter," Butterworth said. "Charming fellow, I'm sure. You say you turned him loose?"

"That's the kind of thing I do," Clete said. He was on his fourth Heineken. "I screw up things. You ever do that? Screw up things?"

"We all have our special talents," Butterworth said.

"See, what bugs me is Tillinger was buds with a former Aryan Brotherhood member named Travis Lebeau, a guy who got chain-dragged on Old Jeanerette Road," Clete said. "See, the AB might have been mixed up with a bad sheriff's deputy who was pimping off some local working girls that maybe some Hollywood guys would dig as a change of pace. Know what I'm saying?"

"That's enough, Clete," Alafair said.

"It's okay, isn't it, fellow?" Clete said to Butterworth. "You guys float in and take a dip in the local pond, then head back to Malibu. Splish-splash."

"Cool your jets, Clete," I said.

"My bad," he said, still talking to Butterworth. "That's an expression you guys started. Samuel Jackson says it in a film, then all the locals are saying it. You guys have a big influence on Hicksville, did you know that?"

"Let's go, Alf," I said, getting up.

"Don't bother," Butterworth said. "I'll be running along. Oh, look. Des seems to have found another dancing partner. My, my, and yum, yum."

Desmond and Bailey Ribbons were waltzing in a wide circle. All the other dancers had left the floor, maybe realizing, as I did, that Des and Bailey had become Henry Fonda and Cathy Downs waltzing in the exaggerated fashion of frontier people in *My Darling Clementine*. In fact, the band had gone into the song; I didn't know if they had been told to do so. I felt as though I had stepped into the film, but not in a good way. I should have been witnessing a tribute to a seminal moment in the history of film and the American West, but instead, Desmond's drunkenness, the inscrutability of his eyes, the rawness of his half-clothed body, were all like a violation of a sacred space, one that had been hollowed out of a vast burial ground.

Alafair pulled on my arm. "Come on, Dave. Finish your supper."

"Sure," I said. "I'm just a little off my feed today."

But the moment wasn't over. Bailey and Desmond sat down with their friends, and someone fired up a fatty and passed it. When it was Bailey's turn, she leaned forward and took a toke, then passed it on, laughing as she exhaled. I dropped my napkin on the table and went to my room.

Fifteen minutes later, Bailey was at my door.

"What's the haps?" I said.

"I was going to talk with you, but you stormed off," she replied.

"Long day. I'm on the bench."

"May I come in, or should I just stand here in the hall?"

I stepped aside and let her in. I could smell her perfume as she passed me. I closed the door.

"What do you mean, 'on the bench'?"

"Helen has me on suspension without pay."

"For *what*?"

"Dereliction of duty, I suspect. I held back information to keep Clete Purcel out of trouble."

"Why are you angry with me?"

"Who said I was?"

"You're filling the room with it right now."

"You were smoking weed."

"Clete Purcel doesn't?"

"He's not a cop. If you show contempt for your shield, why should anyone else respect it?"

Her face was tight, her eyes burning with anger, the rim of her nostrils white. "I didn't know I could give you such discomfort."

"It's not about me. You took an oath. We set the standard or we don't. If we don't, dirty cops like Axel Devereaux do."

"I won't be an embarrassment to you again."

"Are you going to throw in with these guys?" I said.

"Throw in with them? I'm going to have a small part in the film: a union woman who was at the Ludlow Massacre. Why are you talking to me like this?"

I thought more of you. "I read the book. It's not a small part. You become the lifelong companion of a Texas Ranger who put John Wesley Hardin in jail."

"Don't look at me like that," she said.

"Like what?"

"Like you're ashamed of me."

I went to the window and opened the curtains and gazed at the buttes in the distance. The heat lightning had died, and the heavens were bursting with stars. I was sure the trail that Henry Fonda had followed into the buttes was still there, stretching over the edge of the earth, teasing us into tomorrow and the chance to build the life we should have had. I felt the room tilt under my feet. When I turned around, Bailey Ribbons was gone.

Chapter Seventeen

I FLEW HOME IN the morning on a commercial flight, although I could sorely afford the cost. The next day I called Helen and the head of Internal Affairs and left messages saying I was at their disposal. Then I sat in the silence of the kitchen and stared at the leaves dropping from the oaks in the backyard. It felt strange to be home alone in the middle of the workday, separated from my profession and all the symbols of my identity: my badge, the cruiser that was always available for me, the deference and respect that came from years of earning the trust of others. I looked at myself in the mirror and wondered whom I was about to become.

That afternoon I walked downtown and across the drawbridge and into the park and sat by myself at a picnic table next to the softball diamond. The park was empty, the grass blown with tiny pieces of leaves chopped up by the mower, a plastic tarp stretched across the swimming pool. At dusk I walked back home and passed people on the bridge whom I did not know and who did not respond to my greeting. Clete would not return from Arizona until the next day, and Alafair was staying on with Desmond until the weekend. I fed Snuggs and Mon Tee Coon, then showered and shaved and dressed in a pair of pressed slacks and a Hawaiian shirt I let hang over my belt. Rain was falling out of the sky, which seemed turned upside down, like a barrel of dark water with stars inside it. I put on a rain hat and drove to the club on the bayou where the blues weren't just music but a way of life.

• • •

BELLA DELAHOUSSAYE WAS singing a song by a Lafayette musician named Lazy Lester. Inside the din, the only line I could make out was *Don't ever write your name on the jailhouse wall.* I sat at the end of the bar in the shadows and ordered a chicken barbecue sandwich and a 7Up with a lime slice. Ten minutes later, a heavyset man spun the stool next to me as though announcing his presence, then sat on it, a cloud of nicotine and dried sweat whooshing out of his clothes. "I think they fucked you, Robicheaux."

His head had the dimensions of a football, swollen in the center and tapered at the top and the chin. His small mouth was circled with salt-and-pepper whiskers he clipped daily. When he spoke, his mouth looked both bovine and feral. His name was Frenchie Lautrec. He ordered a shot and a water back. Before joining the department, he was a brig chaser in the Crotch and a bondsman. He was also a longtime friend of Axel Devereaux.

"Did you hear what I said?" he asked.

"Yeah," I said. "So who fucked me?"

"The Queen Bitch, Helen Soileau. Who else?"

"Don't talk about her like that."

"No problem. I still think she stuck it to you. What are you drinking?"

My glass was half empty. "Nothing."

"You staying off the hooch?"

"What are you after, Frenchie?"

"I hear IA has got you by the short hairs. You been over the line too many times. I heard the prick running your case say it."

"Who's the prick running my case?"

"I'm trying to cut you a break, Robicheaux. You need some help, maybe a job, a little income, I'm here. That's what old school is about. We take care of each other."

"I'll get by."

"I admire that. But if you need a gig, let me know."

"Doing what?"

"Greasing the wheels."

"What kind of wheels?"

"This is the Cajun Riviera, right? Use your imagination."

"Maybe I'll get back to you."

"That's the spirit." He hit me on the back and got up from the stool. "If you want a little action, it's on the house. Know what I'm saying?"

I watched him walk away, his shoulders humped, his hands knotting and unknotting. I finished my sandwich and ordered another 7Up. After her set, Bella Delahoussaye sat down next to me. "That guy who was here, you hang around wit' him?" she said.

"I worked with him."

Her gaze went away from me, then came back. "What do you mean, you *did*?"

"I'm suspended without pay. That means canned."

"What for?"

"Screwing up," I said. "You want a drink?"

"You shouldn't be here, baby."

"How am I going to listen to you sing?"

"You know what I mean. You ain't supposed to be around the wrong kind of liquids."

"What do you know about Frenchie Lautrec?"

She twisted a strand of hair around her finger. She touched the scar that circumscribed half her neck and looked down the row of faces at the bar. "Walls got ears."

"What time you get off?" I said.

"Like you don't know. I ain't giving you an excuse to sit at a bar. Go home. Don't get yourself in no trouble."

I smiled at her. She squeezed my thigh and went back on the stage. She hung her guitar on her neck and gazed into the shadows. "Mean and lean, down and dirty, y'all. I'm talking about the blues."

I KNOCKED ON HER door in St. Martinville at ten the next morning. She opened the door, a bandana on her head. "My favorite boogie-woogie man from *la Louisiane*."

"Thought I'd take you to breakfast," I said.

She looked out at the street. "Ain't nobody followed you?"

"Why would anybody follow me?"

She pulled me inside and closed the door. "Frenchie Lautrec and Axel Devereaux was running the working girls. Now Devereaux is dead, and Frenchie got it all."

"Prostitution?"

"Boy, you right on it."

"It can't be that big."

"They got girls get five hundred a night, some up to a thousand. Most of the johns are in New Orleans and Baton Rouge. Frenchie's got a plane."

Her living room was tiny, the doorways hung with beads, an ancient Victrola against a wall, the couch and stuffed chairs maroon and purple and tasseled, incense burning in a cup on the coffee table. Bella wore sandals and jeans and an oversize Ragin' Cajuns T-shirt and a gold chain around one ankle, a charm balanced on the top of her foot. I could smell ham and eggs cooking in the kitchen.

"Sit down. I got something to ax you," she said.

"Sure."

"I got a son in Angola. He's just a li'l-bitty boy. One of the wolves put him on the stroll."

"What's he down for?"

"Murder. During a robbery, him and another guy. The other guy pulled the trigger, but it didn't matter. I went to see Harold two days ago. He cain't hardly walk. That what the wolves are doing to him. They don't use no grease, nothing."

"I can make a call."

She nodded and put a Kleenex to her nose as though she had a cold. She went into the kitchen. I followed her and sat at a table by the window.

"I got enough for two here," she said.

There was a live oak in the backyard, a broken swing hanging from a limb, an alleyway strewn with trash and spiked with banana plants. "I already ate," I said.

"I thought you wanted to go to breakfast."

"Not really."

"You just wanted to pump me about Frenchie Lautrec."

"No. You're nice to talk to."

There was a beat. She worked the spatula in the frying pan, her back to me. "How long your wife been dead?"

"Three years."

"Ain't been nobody else?"

"No."

She put a piece of browned toast and a cup of coffee in front of me. She filled her own plate and sat down across from me. "I got to say this: I was raised up to believe a redbird don't sit on a blackbird's nest."

"That's what white people taught your ancestors, then forgot their own admonition. I saw the chain on your ankle. What kind of charm is that?"

"A cross."

"Where'd you get it?"

"From Hilary Bienville."

"Where'd she get it?"

"Don't know, didn't ax. No matter what you say, you ain't here about me, are you?"

"I like you and admire you, Miss Bella. Believe what you want."

She got up and raked her food into a trash can, then washed the plate in the sink and set it in a drying rack. She leaned on the counter, her face covered with shadow. I stood up and spread my hand on her back. I could feel her breath rising and falling, her heat through the T-shirt, her blood humming.

"Are you all right?" I said.

"No, I ain't ever gonna be all right. They gonna kill him in there. That li'l boy that never had no daddy and no real mama." She turned around and took my hand and placed it on the scar on her neck. It felt as firm and thick as a night crawler. "A policeman in New Orleans done that. A black one. I was seventeen. I killed him. I done it with a razor blade. Ain't nobody ever knowed about it."

"Why are you telling me?"

"'Cause I ain't never tole nobody. 'Cause my li'l boy is paying for my sin, if it was a sin. I didn't think it was one at the time."

"You're not a sinful person."

She stepped close to me, then buried her face in my shirt and put her arms around me and pressed herself against me. "Hold me."

I laid my arms lightly across her back, my inner self rising, an empty space in my thoughts, her fingers digging into my skin.

"Hold me," she repeated. "Hold me, please. Oh, Lordy, what am I gonna do about my li'l boy?"

When I left, I thought I saw a white man in the alley with a camera. His back was turned. He disappeared behind a clump of banana plants. I walked to the alley, but he was gone.

ON FRIDAY, THE following day, Helen Soileau called me at home. "You're on social media," she said.

"I'm not up on that stuff," I replied. "What are we talking about?"

"You're with a black woman. I can't tell if you're getting it on or not. Thought you ought to know."

"So now I know. Seen any good movies lately?"

"You're not bothered?"

"No."

"Who's the woman?"

"Ask people in Internal Affairs," I said.

"This isn't about me, Pops."

"Don't call me Pops anymore."

"You and Clete put me in a corner. Quit blaming me because you fucked up."

"I don't blame you. What you don't understand is I didn't have an alternative. Clete cut Hugo Tillinger loose because to do otherwise would have sent Tillinger to the injection table. If I reported Clete, he could be charged with aiding and abetting. If I had it to do over again, I'd make the same choice. That means I'll take my own fall. That means you don't have to say anything."

"I think you're enjoying this."

"I'm tired of other people's bullshit."

"Who do you think took the pictures?"

"A friend of Axel Devereaux."

"Like who?"

"Maybe it was Madman Muntz."

"Who's Madman Muntz?"

"Google the name next time you're playing around on the Internet."

I eased the receiver into the phone cradle. She didn't call back. I waited until after supper, then put a throw-down in the pocket of my khakis and rolled my cut-down twelve-gauge Remington pump in a raincoat and placed it on the floor of my truck. I drove to the little settlement of Cade, where Lucinda Arceneaux had grown up as the daughter of a Free Will Baptist preacher who probably never could have guessed his daughter would die upon the symbol of his religion.

I PASSED A TRAILER and a small church with a faux bell tower in a pecan orchard. On a dirt road, behind the remnants of a motel called the Truman, built for colored in the 1940s, was the neat brick house of Frenchie Lautrec, flat-topped and as squat and ugly as a machine-gun bunker. Maybe it was coincidence that Frenchie lived close to the father of Lucinda Arceneaux, a woman who tried to get the innocent off death row. I had no doubt, however, that Frenchie had posted photos of me and Bella Delahoussaye on the Internet and that his agenda was straight out of the pit.

I parked under the pecan trees and watched the sun descend like an orange globe in the dust; a shadow seemed to crawl across the land. Then I saw the electric lights glowing inside Frenchie's house. As far as I knew, he was a single man who lived with various women at various times. Most of them were drunks or addicts or battered wives or women he busted for soliciting. They didn't hang around long, nor did they tell others what he did to them.

I got out of my truck with the shotgun wrapped in the raincoat, and walked across a coulee on a wood bridge and up the steps of his gallery. I could hear a television in the front room. I banged on the door with the flat of my left fist, the cut-down still in the raincoat hanging from my right hand.

Frenchie opened the door. He was barefoot and wore a faded long-sleeve flannel shirt; his shoulders were knobbed with muscle, his chest flat like a boxer's, the veins in his forearms as thick as soda straws. He was smiling. "Just at the right time. I was fixing to call up some pussy. You game?" He pushed the screen wide.

I stepped inside. "Thanks."

I shook the raincoat from the cut-down and slammed the stock across his mouth. I heard his teeth clack against the wood. He crashed against the wall, his lips gushing blood. When he tried to get up, I brought the butt down on his forehead and split the skin at the hairline. He rolled into a ball, his forearms clamped around his ears. I tossed the cut-down on the couch and peeled one arm from his head and mashed his head under my foot.

The inside of his house looked like a collection of synthetic junk someone had bought at the dollar store. There was even a plastic birdcage with a cloth canary in it.

"Who else is in the house?" I said. "If you lie, I'm going to crack your skull."

"Ain't nobody here."

"Where's the camera?"

"I don't have one."

I lifted him to his feet and shoved him across the coffee table, breaking it in half.

"Eat shit," he said.

I lifted him again and threw him through a bedroom door. There was a desk against one wall with a computer and a camera on top. I picked up the camera. "Is this the one you used?"

"*Fuck* you."

"I want to explain something to you. I couldn't care less if you put photos of me on the Internet. But you did it to an innocent woman and made her an object of scandal and ridicule."

"I'm getting up now," he said, one hand raised in front of him.

"I cock-blocked you. You'll have to find a new knothole. I win, you lose. Now get out of here."

"Better stay where you are, Frenchie."

"My dick in your ear."

I felt my old enemy kick into gear, not unlike a half-formed simian creature breaking the chains from its body. The transformation always began with a sound like a Popsicle stick snapping inside my head; then the world disappeared inside a wave of color that resembled the different shades of a fire raging in a forest. I was now in a place bereft of mercy and charity, drunk on my own adrenaline, the power in my arms and fists of a kind that, in certain people, age does not diminish.

When I finished hitting him and throwing him against the wall, I dropped his camera on the floor and smashed it into junk. Then I picked up a handful of parts and pushed them into his mouth and stepped on them.

He began crawling away from me on his hands and knees. Both my hands were bleeding. The wallpaper was splattered with blood.

"Get up!" I said.

He didn't answer. I thought I heard him weeping. Then I realized he was probably choking to death. I dragged him into the bathroom and hung him over the rim of the bathtub and hit him between the shoulder blades. I could hear the pieces of the camera tinkling in the bottom of the tub. I wet a towel and wiped his face and eased him down on the floor, his back against the wall. His whiskers were bright red, his shirt plastered with blood against his chest.

I squatted down in front of him. "You want an ambulance?"

He shook his head.

"If I was you, I'd call for one," I said.

"They're gonna clean your clock."

"Who's 'they'?"

"People wit' big money. More than you can dream about. Axel was gonna tap into it."

"Axel Devereaux was into something besides pimping?"

"Something to do with Arabs and uranium," he said. He spat a piece of metal off his tongue.

"This is southern Louisiana. We don't have Arabs or sand dunes or centrifuges."

"I told you what I know. Axel thought he was gonna be in the movies. He got to eat his baton instead. Maybe they'll do that for you."

"The movie people are going to hurt me?"

"Maybe it's those guys out of Jersey. The ones backing the casinos. Guys who knew Nicky Scarfo. You think the Indians run their show? The wiseguys wouldn't wipe their ass on them."

"The foster father of Lucinda Arceneaux lives a few hundred yards from here. Did you know her?"

"Saw her around. She thought her shit didn't stink."

I got to my feet. My knees were weak, my eyes stinging with sweat.

"Tell me something," he said.

"What?"

"Did you get into her bread?"

"Whose bread?"

"Bella Delahoussaye's. She fucked my brains out. You ought to give it a try, if you haven't already." He was grinning. Two of his teeth were broken off. He spat a clot of blood onto the floor and laughed to himself.

"I've got to give it to you," I said.

"For what?" he replied.

"I never met a worse cop. You give shit a bad name."

I filled a water glass that was on the wash basin and placed it in his hand. I stared at him a long time, until he had to look away.

"*What?*" he said.

"I killed Asian men I had nothing against," I said. "Speak disrespectfully of Miss Bella again, and what happened here tonight will be just a tune-up."

I took the glass from his hand and threw the water in his face.

Chapter Eighteen

CLETE AND ALAFAIR were both back from Arizona, but I told neither of them about my troubles with Frenchie Lautrec. Clete came to my house Monday night. "I saw Bella Delahoussaye at the Winn-Dixie. She said this creep Lautrec smeared you with some photographs on the Internet. The message was supposed to be racial."

"That sounds right," I replied.

"What happened?"

"I dropped by his house."

"And did what?"

"Maybe he swallowed some camera parts. A couple of teeth, too."

"He didn't dime you?"

"I heard he took sick leave. He's a dirty cop. He can't afford to dime anybody."

"He photographed you getting it on with Bella?"

"Her son was being gang-raped at Angola. I tried to comfort her."

"Horizontally?" he said.

We were in the kitchen. It was dark outside. I could see the stars above the park; the trees resembled black cutouts. "Why is your elevator always stuck in the basement, Clete?"

"Answer the question. Are you getting it on?"

"No. Lautrec wanted to do some payback for Axel Devereaux. Or maybe he wanted to get me fired so I'd hook up with him."

"Pimping?"

"Who knows? Get this. He says Devereaux knew something about Arab money and uranium. He learned about it through the movie people."

"This is from outer space, Dave."

"That's what I told him. He said the Jersey guys might be mixed up in it. Nicky Scarfo's crowd."

"Little Nicky is dead," Clete said.

"I know. So forget it."

It was quiet in the room. I could hear the tree frogs down on the bayou.

"You kicked Lautrec's ass pretty bad?" Clete said.

"You could say that."

"But it wasn't about the pictures on the Internet, was it?" he said.

"Nope."

"Bailey Ribbons let you down?"

"I had higher expectations of her."

"Cut her some slack, for Christ's sake. How about the women I've dated? I'm lucky I haven't woken up with my throat slit." He waited for me to reply. "Come in, Earth."

"She was smoking dope. With sycophants and frauds."

"That's not the equivalent of original sin," he said.

"What say we talk about something else?"

"Helen's not going to drop the IA referral?"

"I didn't ask."

"You're planning to square all this on your own?"

"It had crossed my mind."

"Can I have one of your diet Docs?"

"Help yourself."

He went to the icebox and popped a can of Dr Pepper. "Mind if I tag along, do oversight, make sure things stay under control?"

"I wouldn't have it any other way, Cletus."

THERE ARE LESSONS you learn in the military or jail or any other institutional situation where survival is dependent on your ability to think more clearly than your enemies or the people around you. Here are a few admonitions from the bottom of the food chain. They can be interpreted literally or metaphorically, depending on the situation.

1) Don't silhouette on a hill.
2) Get rid of your jewelry, particularly civilian junk. Ostentation can put you in a box.
3) Don't make enemies with anyone in records.
4) Don't threaten anyone who knows your location when you don't know his.
5) Never piss off the people who prepare or serve your food.
6) Be aware that clerks and secretaries run the world and own rubber stamps that can turn your life into a broken pay toilet.
7) Never sass a hack or drill sergeant or any dull-witted white Southerner who has authority over others.
8) Grin and walk through the cannon smoke. It drives the bad guys up the wall.
9) Get the right people on your side. Who would you rather have covering your back in a back-alley brawl, an academic liberal or a hobnailed redneck?
10) Never buy into the acronym FEAR (fuck everything and run). Swallow your blood and don't let others know you're hurt. If that doesn't work, spit it in their faces.
11) Even in the most desperate of situations, stay away from the Herd. Situating yourself between loud oinking sounds and the trough is a surefire way to get trampled to death.
12) Burn this list before anyone catches you with it.

In my vanity, I wanted to think of myself as a vigilante or, even worse, a knight errant. But I was flailing at the dark. Men like Lautrec and Devereaux were surrogates. The person who'd murdered Lucinda Arceneaux and mounted her on a cross and floated her out to sea was either a master manipulator or someone with motivations that were armor-plated in the unconscious. My badge was in limbo. I had no legal power. How could I proceed in a case that had become a room without doors?

On Tuesday morning, I was sitting on my back steps with Mon Tee Coon and Snuggs, throwing pecans into a hat, when I heard someone walk through the porte cochere and come around the side of the house. Mon Tee Coon scampered up an oak tree. Bailey Ribbons walked across the grass, her small black shoes crunching on the patina of red and orange and yellow leaves I had not raked up. "Good morning," she said.

I stood up. "How you doin', Bailey?"

"May I sit down?" She was wearing a dark skirt and a lavender blouse and a gold chain with small heart charms on it.

"Let me get you a chair. The steps are dirty."

"That's all right," she said, sitting down on the steps. She looked up at the oak in front of us. "Did I scare off your coon?"

"He doesn't know you yet."

"I feel very bad, Dave. I got the stars in my eyes out there in Arizona. I was acting like an idiot. It's an honor to be your partner."

"I wouldn't get carried away with that," I said.

"Look at me."

"What is it?"

"I don't want to seem forward."

"About what?" I said.

She picked up my hand in hers. "I don't want to sit by and watch while you hurt your career. You're doing things that make no sense, and I think they have something to do with me."

"I'm an expert at messing up things on my own."

She squeezed my hand, hard. "You listen to me. I've worked with cops who should be in cages. We can't afford to lose people like you."

"Who's 'we'?"

She released my hand. "The human race. That's what it's about. The good guys against the bad guys. I said that to Desmond. That's what the last scene in *My Darling Clementine* is about. Wyatt Earp has a higher destiny."

"That scene is about death," I said.

She stood up and swiped off her rump. I stood up also. She looked up in my face. "Can I say something?"

"Go ahead."

"I don't care about convention."

I looked away from her, then back at her face. My mouth was dry. I couldn't read her expression. I cleared my throat but didn't speak.

"I don't measure people by their age," she said. "I think those things are stupid. Am I getting through here?"

"Yes, ma'am, you are," I said. I picked up my hat and dumped the pecans on the ground, put my hat on my head, then removed it. "Bailey Ribbons. Did I ever tell you I love that name?"

"I think that is one of the nicest things anyone has ever said to me," she replied.

I heard Mon Tee Coon springing from limb to limb overhead. I wanted to believe the natural world had given me an exemption that people my age do not earn and are seldom granted.

I HAD LUNCH WITH Clete at Victor's and told him of Bailey's visit. His eyes roamed around the room as though the earth were shifting. "Are you thinking what I think you're thinking?"

"I'm just quoting what Bailey said."

"There are two types of broads who get involved with old guys: gold diggers and basket cases who don't mind sleeping with mummies or guys in adult diapers."

People at the next table turned and stared.

"Will you lower your voice?" I said.

"When you stop lying to yourself," he said.

"She was trying to be kind."

"What, you're a charity case?"

I didn't try to argue. My behavior and thinking were foolish, and I knew it.

"We're simpatico?" he said. "All thoughts about boom-boom with the wrong woman out of your head?"

The people at the next table moved.

"Yes," I said.

"Good. I don't know what you'd do if I weren't around." He

rubbed his eyes, his face tired. "Know what the real problem is? You hear the clock ticking. You want to go out like a Roman candle instead of dripping into a can."

I had just started on my dessert. I put my spoon down.

"You mentioned Little Nicky Scarfo," he said. "There's a guy I want to talk to on that subject."

"Which guy?"

"Remember Cato Carmouche?"

"The midget who got fired out of a circus cannon into a steel pole?"

"Eat up and let's boogie," he said.

ACADIANA, LIKE NEW ORLEANS, is filled with eccentrics, primarily because it has never been fully assimilated into the United States. It's a fine place to be an artist, a writer, an iconoclast, a bohemian, or a drunk. Some Cajuns are virtually unintelligible to outsiders, yet nurse their accent and inverted sentence structure and forget the outside world. If you wish, anonymity is only a boat ride away. The Atchafalaya Basin is the largest wetland and swamp in the United States. With the purchase of a houseboat, you can live in places that have no name because they didn't exist yesterday and can be gone tomorrow.

Modernity has always been our undoing. Our ancestors were farmers and fisher people expelled from Canada by the British in 1755. Unlettered and pacifist in nature and unable to understand the clash of empires, the Acadians wandered for years before they found a home on Bayou Teche. Maybe for that reason, we have a greater tolerance for others who are different or who have been collectively rejected. The disposition and mind-set of Acadiana is little different from those of San Francisco. Maybe that's why Cato Carmouche lived on a houseboat on the bayou south of Jeanerette, in violation of any number of state and parish regulations.

Most Cajuns don't like to travel. Many will admit they have never been out of the state. Not Cato. He hooked up with a circus and became a human cannonball, until the night the cannon was slanted too high and Cato was sent flying over the net into the audience.

When he came out of a six-week coma, he discovered that his brain had taken on a facility with numbers no one could explain. He could process percentages and numerical probabilities as fast as a computer. One week after he was released from the hospital, he flew to Atlantic City. Then to Reno and Vegas and Puerto Rico. Cato found paradise in the glitter and cheapness and garish mix of fountains splashing with colored lights and the air-conditioned stink of cigarette smoke. The dice jumping across the felt, the coins rattling in the slots, the snap of a card on the blackjack table, the women whose breasts bulged from their evening gowns, the smell of fine liquor, the ball bouncing inside the roulette wheel—where had these gifts been all his life? At four-feet-one, with a scar like a lightning bolt on his shaved head, he stood or sat at the gaming tables and let the blessings of a meretricious deity shower down on him.

For the first six months on the circuit, he kept his wins low. Then he got greedy at Harrah's and went into the Griffin Book. Not to be undone, Cato hired on with the casinos and sat with the brass and monitored the eye in the sky and identified the grifters and card counters who thought they knew every hustle in the game. By anyone's standards, Cato became well-to-do and could have lived anywhere. Instead he came back to Southwest Louisiana and lived by himself on a houseboat painted with the green and purple colors of Mardi Gras and bedecked with glass beads that tinkled in the breeze.

"How's it hanging, Cato?" Clete said as we walked across the reinforced plank onto the houseboat.

"It's hanging very nicely, t'anks," Cato said. "How about yours?"

Cato always had a scrubbed look, and took meticulous care with his clothes and hair, the part as exact as a ruler, each oiled strand a gleaming piece of wire. His voice sounded like it came out of a tin box with gears and springs inside. His eyes were tiny lumps of coal. For some reason he reminded me of Desmond Cormier, as though they shared a similar loneliness, the kind that is usually the fate of the artistically talented.

"What can I do for youse gentlemen?"

" 'Youse'?" Clete said.

"I spent a lot of time in Jersey."

"We know your history with the casino industry, Mr. Cato," I said. "We're wondering about the funding for a motion picture group."

"Go ahead and ax me your questions," he said. "And you don't got to call me mister, either."

His houseboat was moored in the shade of an oak. A cheap rod and reel was propped against the deck rail, the bobber and line floating in an *S* next to the lily pads in the shallows.

"We hear Desmond Cormier is being financed by the gaming industry," I said.

"Gaming it is not. Getting soaked it is," Cato said.

"You got some information for us, sir?" I said.

"Jersey money is Jersey money. The tracks are full of it. Some of it is hot, some not. The track and the casino are the washeterias. I got to check my line. Then I got to shower and change. A lady friend is picking me up, if you know what I mean, no crudeness intended here."

Clete looked at me, clearly trying not to laugh.

"Did you know a woman named Lucinda Arceneaux?" I asked.

"The name is not familiar." Cato pulled his bobber and small lead weight and baited hook from the water and swung them to a different spot.

"She was murdered, Mr. Cato."

"I call other people mister, but I don't ax the same of them. Know why that is?"

"Afraid not," I said.

"Because people who need titles need somebody else to tell them they're worth something. No judgment intended."

"You hear anything about Arab investments around here?" I said.

"I have to confess I haven't seen no A-rabs of recent. You're talking about people who ride camels?"

"That doesn't really answer the question," I said.

He looked at his watch. It was gold, the size of a half dollar, inlaid with jewels. "Can I get you gentlemen coffee or a drink before my lady friend comes? It's fixing to rain. That means the goggle-eye perch gonna be biting soon."

"Thanks for your time, Cato," I said.

"Yes, suh. It was very nice of youse to come by."

I walked back on the plank with Clete, then paused under the tree. "Wait here a minute, will you?"

"Whatever he knows, he's keeping it to himself. Let it go," Clete said.

"Be right back."

I crossed back onto the houseboat. Cato was sitting in a folding canvas chair. The sky had darkened, and I could hear thunder in the distance and feel the barometer dropping and smell the fish bunching up under the lily pads. A big gar rolled as smoothly as a serpent by a flooded canebrake.

"I need to share something with you," I said. "Up the bayou, under a big oak like that one on the shore, I caught my first fish when I was seven years old."

I paused. Cato gazed at the lightning striking silently in a sky that was like purple velvet. The air was damp and sweet and heavy with the smell of sugarcane and the bayou at high tide.

"This is a special place," I said. "Guys like us remember the way it used to be. But a lot of bad guys got their hands on us, Cato."

"I know what you mean, suh."

"Why'd you come back to South Louisiana?"

"I ain't lost nothing in them other places."

"Desmond is tight with the casino guys?"

"They go back. Desmond grew up on the Chitimacha Reservation."

"Is somebody making a big move?"

"It's about money from overseas. Laundering, that kind of t'ing. Politicians are mixed up in it. It's stuff I don't want to know about."

"Who are the players?"

He looked up at me. "You better not have no truck with them, Mr. Robicheaux."

"Call me Dave. Why should I not have any truck with them?"

"I'm talking about hundreds of millions of dol'ars. You know what people will do for that kind of money? Not just here, anywhere. Them A-rabs didn't invent greed and the mean t'ings people can do."

He reeled in his line, his gaze fixed on the sky, and refused to speak again, even to say goodbye.

I'VE ALWAYS BELIEVED the dead roam the earth for many years after we try to weigh them down with stones. I also believe they outnumber us. For that reason I've never quarreled with the notion that they enter and try to shape our lives in order to redeem their own. So I was not surprised by the vision I had when I looked out my bedroom at three a.m. the day after my visit with Cato Carmouche.

The clouds of fog on the bayou were as white as cotton, bumping along the ground between the trees, a tug working its way toward the drawbridge, running lights on, glistening with mist. The figure was no more than five-four; he looked made of sourdough. The roundness of his face and limbs and stomach and soft buttocks seemed sketched by an artist. His mouth was a slice of watermelon, his hair as wispy as corn silk.

I wanted to believe I was watching an apparition, a wandering soul trying to unshackle the fetters of the grave and reclaim the coolness and oxygenated vibrancy of the air that the quick take for granted. I knew better, though. I had seen the figure before. I put my hand under my mattress and retrieved the army-issue 1911-model .45 automatic I had bought for twenty-five dollars in Saigon's Bring Cash Alley. I slipped on my khakis and loafers and went through the kitchen into the mudroom. The sky was clear above the fog bank, the tops of the trees lit by the moon. I stepped into the yard. The figure moved behind an oak that was three feet across.

"Is that you, Smiley?" I asked.

There was no reply.

"You gave me quite a start," I said. "I hope one of us is dreaming."

The wind gusted through the trees, giving second life to the raindrops on the leaves, filling the air with the tannic smell of autumn and gas and nightshade in a forest that seldom saw sunlight.

"I hope you're not mad at me," I said. "It was never personal."

"Please don't come any nearer to me, Mr. Robicheaux," the figure said. His voice had a lisp, a discomfiting wet one, like that of an oversize child nursing.

"I know it's you, partner," I said. "Tell me what you're doing here. It'll make us both feel better."

"You made me do things I didn't want to," he said.

"You killed a female detective. A good woman who didn't deserve to die."

"That is not true. People were shooting at me. I did not ever aim in the woman's direction. Do not make up stories."

"She died just the same. Do you want me to call you Chester or Smiley?"

"My friends call me Smiley. But if you're not my friend, call me something else."

"You need to leave the area," I said. "Then all this will be just a dream."

"I'll leave when my work is done."

"What is your work?"

"You don't know?"

"You get even for people who can't defend themselves," I said. "That's a noble mission, Smiley. But you need to move on. Maybe back to Florida. Work on your tan."

"Are you making fun of me?"

"I know better."

I was sweating inside my clothes. Smiley's real name was Chester Wimple. He had no category. Not even a partial one. In a harsh light his body seemed to take on the translucence and flaccidity of a jellyfish. He sounded like Elmer Fudd and ate Ding Dongs for breakfast and Eskimo Pies and Buster Bars around the clock. He had done hits with an ice pick on a New York subway and in the box seats of a racetrack and at a chamber of commerce meeting in New Jersey. He had never spent one day in jail.

I heard his feet move in the leaves. I held up my weapon so it silhouetted in the moonlight. I released the magazine and stuck it into my pocket, then ejected the chambered round, letting it fall on the grass. "I'm no threat to you, Smiley. I'm suspended from the sheriff's department. I'm going to walk toward you now. Is that okay?"

The wind died. The leaves on the trees were as still as stamped metal. I walked toward the place where Smiley had been standing; the fog enveloped the lower half of my body. I saw a pirogue glide away from the bank, a solitary man seated and stroking evenly in the stern. He waved goodbye without turning around, as though he knew I would follow him to the water's edge but offer no more protest about his presence in Acadiana.

I could hear myself breathing in the dark.

Chapter Nineteen

THE SUN CAME up like thunder, a yellowish bloodred in the smoke of a runaway stubble fire. I did not tell Alafair or Clete about my encounter with Smiley, in part because they would think me unhinged. Also I did not trust my own perceptions. For good or bad, my preoccupation with death and the past had defined much of my life, and a long time ago I had made my separate peace with the world and abandoned any claim on reason or normalcy or the golden mean. Waylon Jennings said it many years ago: *I've always been crazy but it's kept me from going insane.*

I did make a call to a former CIA agent I knew from the program. His name was Walter Scanlon. For forty years he pickled his brain and liver with a fifth of vodka every night while he moved like a threadworm through the underside of the New American Empire. Now he chain-smoked and attended the "Work the Steps or Die, Motherfucker" meeting in New Orleans, sitting silently in the back with a face that looked as old as papyrus and eyes that were the color of raw oysters. Few had any idea of the deeds stored in the basement of his soul.

"Yeah, Chester Wimple," he said. "He goes by Smiley or something."

"Was he ever one of yours?" I asked.

"We didn't use guys like that."

"But you've run across him? You know about him?"

"We thought he took out one of our informants in Mexico City. A child molester. No big loss. You didn't talk to the FBI?"

"They don't know much more than we do."

"Let me ring a couple of people."

He called back that evening. "When's the last time you had contact with this guy?" he said.

"I thought I might have seen him earlier today."

"Better visit your optometrist. Chester Wimple was blown all over a café with a fifty-cal in Venezuela eight months ago."

"Must be a mistake."

"The guys I got this from use DNA."

"I appreciate your time," I said, my mouth dry. "How you doing with the program?"

"I haven't slept since the fall of Saigon," he replied. "Thanks for bringing it up."

AT SEVEN-THIRTY THE next morning Helen Soileau was at my door.

"What's the haps?" I said through the screen.

"Need to get you on the clock," she said. "I killed the IA beef. How about it, Pops?"

I pushed the screen open. "Come in." I let her walk ahead of me into the kitchen. I took the Silex carafe and two cups off the counter and sat down at the breakfast table. "Why the change of heart?"

"I was wrong," she replied.

"I held back information I should have reported."

"And done Texas's dirty work for them. I probably wouldn't have dimed Tillinger either." She took my badge out of her coat pocket and set it on the table. It was gold and inset with blue letters.

"Something hit the fan?" I said.

"I need every swinging dick on the line."

"You know how to say it, Helen."

"In or out?"

I palmed my badge but didn't put it into my pocket. "I had a visitor in the early a.m. yesterday. Chester Wimple, alias Smiley."

"He was just passing through on his way to killing someone?"

"He was standing under the trees in the backyard. He left in a pirogue."

"I don't want to listen to this," she said.

"It gets worse. I called a friend who was CIA for forty years. He says Smiley was shredded into dog food by a fifty-caliber eight months ago."

"I don't know which story is worse, yours or your friend's."

"Take it any way you want. I told Smiley he was unwelcome. I unloaded my weapon in front of him. I watched him paddle his pirogue down to the drawbridge. The CIA isn't made up of stupid people."

I saw the heat go out of her face.

"Okay," she said.

"Okay, what?"

"Maybe it explains something."

"Explains what?"

"We've got another homicide."

"Who is it?"

"You and Clete did what you could. There are people you can't help, Dave."

"Cut the doodah, Helen. Who are we talking about?"

She tapped the table with her knuckles and lifted her gaze to mine. Her eyes were damp. "Fuck me."

HELEN'S HARD-CORE PERSONA was often cosmetic and disguised the humanity that defined her. That said, the scene inside Hilary Bienville's trailer was the kind no cop wants to see. It was the kind that forces you to re-create the suffering and fear of the victim; it also installs itself in your memory and becomes the catalyst for your first hit of Jack that night and the images you'll drag like a chain the rest of your days.

Hilary had been savagely beaten, her blood slung all over the walls and furniture. The blows were of such force that her face was hardly recognizable, and I don't mean in terms of personal identification. Her skull and facial construction no longer looked human. I went back outside. Bailey Ribbons was knocking on doors. Sean McClain had been the first at the scene. He was staring at the drawbridge and the immaculate white antebellum home couched among the live oaks on the far side of the bayou. His mouth was small and gray, his skin pale. There was blood on his trousers and the rims of his shoes. He saw me look at it.

"It looked like somebody kicked over a bucket of paint," he said. "I found her baby and took it to the grandmother's."

"You got the 911?" I said.

"The neighbor said he heard somebody busting up the trailer about five a.m. He thought it was a john. The baby kept crying, so he called it in at six-fifteen."

"He didn't see a vehicle leave?"

"He says he heard one but didn't see it."

"You believe him?"

"Probably not."

"Let's have a talk with him."

The 911 caller wore flip-flops and shapeless pants and a strap undershirt with holes in it. His jowls were spiked with whiskers, his race undeterminable, his eyes pools of suspicion. "I done tole you already. I didn't see nothing and I don't know nothing. She was always having johns in her place. I don't get mixed up in dat."

"You weren't curious enough to glance out the window?"

"For what? You t'ink I don't know what kind of dump this is?"

Hard argument to contest.

Sean and I went back inside Hilary Bienville's trailer. Two plainclothes detectives from Jeanerette were there. The forensic team was already at work. Bailey followed us inside. The broken glass and kitchenware, the splintered furniture, and the dents in the walls were the marks of a killer whose rage was so great it was always on the edge of bursting through his skin; he was the kind of man who had a jitter in his eyes. The paramedics were waiting for Helen to tell them to remove the remains. I looked down at what used to be Hilary Bienville's face. Her killer had stuck a sequined star on her forehead, like you'd mount atop a Christmas tree.

"The Suit of Pentacles," Bailey said.

"What was that?" Helen said.

"It's our guy," Bailey said. "Pentacles, or diamonds, represents prosperity and personal esteem. Or making things grow or increase in value."

"A hooker making things grow in value?" Helen said. She looked at me for reinforcement. I shook my head neutrally.

"Our guy is enraged because she didn't meet the standard," Bailey said. "At least that's my guess."

It was hot and quiet in the trailer, as though we were all caught inside a photograph none of us wanted to be in. In moments like these, you know Treblinka and Nanking and Hiroshima are not abstractions.

"How about it, Sheriff?" one of the paramedics said.

"Take her out," Helen said.

I went back outside. Most of the children who lived in the trailer park had left on the school bus. No adults came out of their trailers. A few looked through the windows. Cormac Watts, the coroner, was standing by his car, his foot on the bumper. He watched me walk toward him, his face empty.

"Glad to see you back," he said.

"This is going to be a funny question."

"You want to know if she was unconscious when the perpetrator tore her up?" he said.

I waited.

"Massive internal bleeding," he said. "I think he probably stomped and kicked her after she went down."

"How do you figure this guy?"

"I can't."

"We've got another player involved," I said. "I think you should know."

"Who?"

"Smiley. I saw him. I talked with him."

His eyes hazed over. "I'll have something on your desk by tonight. Have a good one, Dave."

He got into his car and drove away.

• • •

SMILEY HAD BEEN raised in an orphanage in Mexico City. By all accounts, including his, he had been severely abused, both in the orphanage and on the streets of the city, where he was passed from hand to hand in alleys that specialized in child prostitution. Probably in his late teens, he found his way to southern Florida and discovered that he possessed an enormous talent—namely, an ability to float like a piece of ectoplasm among the criminal culture and be disregarded or dismissed up to the moment someone got it in the ear with a .22 auto or an ice pick in the brain.

His activities seemed to be a labor of love. His hits were contracted and paid for at drop boxes, his weapons provided by UPS. He bought children ice cream wherever he went, and on one occasion he hijacked a truckload of it and passed it out to black children in a park down by Bayou Lafourche while a bound and gagged man he planned to dispose of later struggled impotently inside the refrigerator.

He also tried to kill a local politician whose antecedents were Huey Long and George Wallace. Secretly, I always thought Smiley had his moments.

But Smiley was also responsible for the death of a female detective who paid her dues in Afghanistan. For a short time she was the lover of Clete Purcel. I really didn't want to tell him about Smiley's visit. Nor did I wish to contemplate the results if Clete got his hands on him. But at five that afternoon I drove to Clete's motor court on East Main. He was sitting in a deck chair down by the bayou, a quart of stoppered beer in a bucket by his side. He was reading a novel by Michael Connelly.

"How you doing, Cletus?" I said.

He looked at me over his reading glasses. "Whenever I hear that tone of voice, I know I'd rather be somewhere else."

"I'm back on the job. I also had a visit from Smiley."

"Tell me you've been drinking."

"He's back and ready to rock."

"Why is he back?"

"He says he wants to be our friend."

Clete stood up slowly and set his book on the chair. He removed his glasses and put them away. The warmth of the sunlight on the side of his face contradicted the coldness in his eyes. He stared at the cattails bending in the breeze, the surface of the bayou wrinkling like old skin. "Where do you think I might find him?"

"No idea."

He put a cigarette into his mouth but didn't light it. The worst part of my visit had not begun. Obviously, he had been out of town during the day or he had not listened to the news or seen a local newspaper.

"Hilary Bienville is dead, Clete."

He turned around and removed the cigarette from his mouth. "Say again?"

"Early this morning. She was beaten to death in her trailer. Her killer pressed a Christmas-tree star on her forehead."

His face seemed poached, the color fading, his teeth showing behind his lips. His eyes were green marbles. "Same guy who did Lucinda Arceneaux?"

"That's what it looks like."

"What about her kid?"

"The kid is all right. Sean McClain took her to the grandmother's place."

"Witnesses?"

"None we could find."

"How bad was it?"

"As bad as it gets."

He folded his deck chair and picked up his book and cradled his ice bucket with one arm. "I want to see the crime scene."

"You know the rules."

"Forget I asked," he said. "I'll handle it by myself."

WHEN WE ARRIVED at the trailer park, the sun was low on the horizon, orange and dust-veiled. There were no children at play. I took down the crime scene tape on the small gallery and opened the door to Hilary Bienville's trailer with a key Helen had given me. Clete and

I stepped inside, both of us with latex on. Clete shone his flashlight on the broken glass, the smears and splatter on the walls, the broken table and chairs. "Who was the responder?"

"Sean McClain."

"Wasn't he the responder on the Devereaux homicide?"

"More or less."

"No tie there?"

"No."

"The door was key-locked?" he asked.

"Right."

"So it wasn't a barroom john? It was somebody she trusted?"

"That'd be my guess."

"The baby must have been crying when he left, but he locked up the place anyway?"

"What are you thinking?" I said.

"The guy didn't want Hilary found right away, but he didn't care if the baby sweltered to death or choked on her vomit."

"The guy who killed Hilary doesn't care about anything or anyone," I said.

Clete clicked off his flashlight. "I've seen enough."

"What do you make of it?"

"He had some kind of working relationship with her. But something set him off. She was in pajamas?"

"Yes."

"Maybe he wanted to get it on and she told him to fuck off. Violence like this is almost always sexual. There was no sign of rape or biting or any of that crap?"

"Not according to the coroner."

Clete stared at the sun and the Greek revival home in the trees across the bayou. "Why does this place make me think of a killing ground on the Cambodian border?"

"Because this was a slave cemetery," I said. "They're under your feet."

"Christ," he said, his face twitching.

• • •

LATER THAT EVENING I sat down in the living room with Alafair. The windows were open, the streetlights on. I could see leaves smoldering like red coals in a rain gutter, and smell impending rain and the heavy odor of the bayou. I did not want to think any more about Hilary Bienville or the evil that humans do. I once had a friend who worked with the criminally insane in Norwalk, California. He was a Quaker and a humanist and seemed to be unscathed by his experience with patients who had committed crimes that were unthinkable. I asked him what his secret was.

"I conceded," he answered.

"Conceded what?" I said.

"There are people who are at peace with malevolence. It's in their eyes. It keeps them warm. That's the way they come out of the womb."

There was a reading lamp above Alafair's head. She kept looking at me in a peculiar way. "Are you all right?"

"I'm a little tired. I brought a dessert home."

I went into the kitchen and cut a wet slice of chocolate cake for each of us, then put them on plates and brought them back into the living room. She had been on location in Morgan City all day and had not heard about Hilary Bienville. So I told her, then I told her about Smiley. The room was quiet.

"You don't believe me about Smiley?" I said.

"I'm not sure, you see things other people don't. You haven't said anything about the Bienville crime scene."

"It's better not to talk about it."

"Who's doing this, Dave?"

"I have no idea. There's no single thread that runs through all the cases. We don't know if we're dealing with one killer or more than one."

But her mind seemed somewhere else. "There's something wrong with Desmond."

"Like what?"

"Today somebody said something about the Lucinda Arceneaux

homicide, like working the floating cross with the body on it into the movie. Desmond snapped the guy's head off."

"Maybe he was just out of sorts," I said.

"There's something else bothering me. Des got wet today and was changing his socks. There's a Maltese cross tattooed on his ankle. Didn't you say Bienville tied a charm shaped like a Maltese cross on her daughter's ankle?"

"I did."

"Just coincidence?" she said.

"That's a word liars use often," I said.

Chapter Twenty

EARLY THE NEXT morning I drove to the location outside Morgan City that Desmond had turned into a replica of an early 1950s prison farm. Mounted gunbulls in gray uniforms and shades, their skin as dark as saddle leather, were silhouetted against the sunrise atop the levee, while down below, men in prison stripes and straw hats that had been painted red were pulling stumps with mules and chains.

Part of the set included a two-story barracks with barred windows, constructed in the distance, and two upended cast-iron sweatboxes set in concrete. Alafair had left the house before I had and was sitting behind a camera with a clipboard on her knee. Desmond had interrupted a scene and was telling an actor to start over again. The actor was young and handsome and did not look like a convict who would have been on the Red Hat gang at Angola Farm many decades ago.

"You're putting me to sleep, Zeb," Desmond said. "This is a hara-kiri moment. When you get in the hack's face, you know you're headed for the sweatbox. We're talking about hundred-and-thirty-degree heat, a shit bucket between your ankles, a hole the diameter of a cigar to breathe through, your butt and knees frying against hot metal. But you hate the captain so much you'll accept all that pain in order to keep your self-respect. So far you're not showing either me or the audience the brave man you're supposed to be."

"I'll try to do better," the actor said.

" 'Try' is the wrong word," Des said, his pale blue eyes widening.

"Yes, sir," the actor said.

Desmond stepped behind the camera. "Start," he said.

The captain sat astride a horse that must have been seventeen hands. He wore a long-sleeve crimson shirt and a Stetson and shades. Unlike the other personnel, he was not armed. A quirt was stuck in his boot. Farther down the levee, three women were picking buttercups and placing them in a straw basket. The captain's shadow fell across the young actor named Zeb.

"Was you eyeballing them ladies?" the captain asked.

"No, sir," Zeb said.

"I think you was. One of them is the warden's wife, son."

"I ain't eyeballed no free people, boss," Zeb said.

"Calling me a liar?"

Zeb shook his head.

"I didn't hear you," the captain said.

"No, sir, I ain't said that."

"Captain LeBlanc says you was talking during bell count."

"Wasn't me, Cap."

"You've seen me make a Christian out of a nigger. I can do it to you, too."

"Wasn't eyeballing. Wasn't talking at morning count. Wasn't doing nothing but my fucking time, boss man."

"Cut," Desmond said.

Zeb waited expectantly.

"I could get more vitality out of an electrified corpse," Desmond said. He walked to the captain's horse. "Give me your quirt."

The actor playing the captain slipped the quirt from his boot and handed it to Desmond. The handle was knurled; a leather tassel hung from the tip. Desmond stuck the quirt in Zeb's hand. "Hit me."

"Pardon?" Zeb replied, half smiling.

"Hit me! In the face! Hard!"

"I cain't do that."

Desmond clenched Zeb's fingers into the handle of the quirt. "You think this is funny?"

"No, sir."

Desmond released Zeb's hand and popped him in the face. "Now hit me with the quirt."

"No."

Desmond popped him again. The crew and the other actors stared at the ground. "Either hit me or say your lines like you're supposed to," he said. "You've got booze on your breath, Zeb. Don't show up wired again."

There were tears in the actor's eyes. Alafair laid her clipboard on her chair and walked past me, away from the set.

They recommenced the scene. It was powerful and real and visceral and painful to watch. Zeb virtually spat in the captain's face, then the other gunbulls beat him senseless and carried him on his knees to the sweatbox and flung him inside and slammed the iron door as though they had just hung a hog in a smokehouse.

Desmond yelled, "Cut," and everyone applauded. My stomach felt sick. I walked up behind Des and tapped him on the shoulder. He was grinning when he turned around.

"I need to talk to you," I said.

"I'm a little busy right now," he replied.

"Yeah, I saw you in action."

"You think I'm too rough?"

"That was chickenshit."

"I don't see Zeb complaining."

I looked away, as you do when you can't hide your disgust for someone's behavior. "I'd appreciate your walking over here with me."

"Whatever makes you happy," he said.

We went into the shade of a tarp stretched on four poles. The canvas was popping in the wind, the fall weather both cool and warm at the same time. The cast and crew were drinking coffee and eating beignets at the commissary window.

"We've got another homicide on our hands," I said.

"I heard."

"Her name was Hilary Bienville. She hung out in the same blues joint Butterworth does."

"So talk to him."

"Waste of time. He's a pathological liar and a wiseass on top. I understand you have a Maltese cross on your ankle."

"Would you like to see it?"

"I wondered if you were in the Knights Templar. Or the Nazi Party."

"Maybe I rode with a biker group."

"The Hells Angels?"

"I said maybe. Get off my back, Dave."

"You're lying, Des."

"I don't let people talk to me like that."

"How about the way you just talked to that kid?"

"Titty babies don't make it in the movie industry."

"And bullies thrive?"

"Fuck you, Dave."

"Next time you say that to me, I'll knock your teeth down your throat."

I walked to my truck. I saw Alafair watching me by the commissary trailer. She mouthed the Clete Purcel mantra *Take names and stomp ass, big mon.*

LATE SATURDAY NIGHT Smiley turned his rental car in to a lonely motel on a two-lane asphalt road that dead-ended in a bog far south of Lake Charles. The moon was up, the Gulf the color of pewter, the waves sliding through sand dunes and salt grass and a shrimp dock that had been wrecked by Hurricane Rita. The motel sign was off, the office dark; a panel truck was parked midway down the line of rooms. Smiley cut his headlights and engine and got out of his car with a black physician's bag and stepped up on the concrete walkway, his skin marbled with the orange and yellow neon that circumscribed the motel. The window and the red metal door of his target were pasted with insects. He slipped a screwdriver into the doorjamb and wedged the lock loose, then eased back the door and stepped inside.

A compact unshaved man was sleeping on his side in his underclothes on top of the covers, snoring spasmodically. Smiley removed a hypodermic needle from his bag and inserted it into the man's carotid and pushed down the plunger. The sleeping man made one startled gasp, his eyes springing open, then he dropped into a well.

Twenty minutes later, the man awoke and discovered the ligatures binding him leg and arm to the bedframe. A Brillo pad had been stuffed into his mouth, which was sealed with pipe tape. When he tried to talk, his face looked like a grape about to burst. Smiley sat in a chair by the bed, eating ice cream from the carton he had taken from the icebox. A container of Liquid-Plumr sat on the nightstand.

"My friends call me Smiley," he said. "You're Hugo Tillinger, and you have been very bad. I do not like people who do what you have done. Can I use your bathroom. Blink your eyes for 'yes.' "

Tillinger stared at him like a statue. Smiley dropped his ice cream carton into the wastebasket and went to the bathroom to relieve himself and flushed the toilet and washed his hands and pulled on latex gloves, then returned to the bedside and gazed down at Tillinger. "This might hurt a little." He peeled the tape loose from Tillinger's face and lifted the steel wool from his mouth. "That wasn't so bad, was it? Comfy now?"

Tillinger twisted his head and spat soap and pieces of steel wool on the sheets. "What are you doing in my room?"

"You killed your family."

"I did not."

"Lying will not help you."

"How'd you know I was here?"

"You called an uncle in Denver. Somebody was listening. You should have run far away and not made that call. Why do you remain in this area?"

"Because I wanted to find a black woman who tried to help me. But somebody killed her. You're a hit man?"

"No. You'd better not call me that, either."

"Then what are you?"

"I get rid of people who hurt children or who hurt me. You burned up your family. I saw pictures of their bodies."

"You some kind of ghoul?"

Smiley removed a funnel from his black bag and unscrewed the cap on the Liquid-Plumr. Tillinger pulled against the ligatures, his brow oily with sweat. "I don't know who you are or why you're after me, but I didn't kill my family," Tillinger said. "No matter what happens here, you get that straight, you little shit."

"You're making me mad."

"See what happens if I catch up with you later, gerbil boy," Tillinger said.

Smiley stuffed the Brillo pad back into Tillinger's mouth and stretched a strip of tape across his cheeks, letting the roll dangle on the pillow. He took a ballpoint from his shirt pocket and clenched it like a dagger. He stared down into Tillinger's face. In his mind's eye, he saw a female caretaker in a Mexico City orphanage strike him full across the face. He disconnected from the image in his head and went to the window and looked outside. The Gulf was black and roiling and strung with foam and moonlight. The waves on the jetty made a sound like someone shuffling a deck of cards. He felt tired, his sense of mission gone, his arms as flaccid and useless as rolls of dough. The release he sought in his work was becoming more and more elusive. Why couldn't he be free?

He walked back to the bed and ripped the tape loose from Tillinger's mouth. "Call me names again and you'll wish you were dead. You're a cruel man. I want to do horrible things to you."

"It was an electrical short," Tillinger said. "I tried to save them. You seem like you got a brain. Why do you think you turned out the way you did?"

"I don't know what you mean."

"I was on death row with guys like you. They all got a bad story. Here's the funny part. Their stories are true. That's how they ended up freaks like you. It's not y'all's fault."

"You need a lesson." Smiley removed an electric drill from his bag and hunted for the wall socket. He could hear Tillinger fighting against the ligatures. He inserted the plug into the wall and squeezed the trigger on the drill. It whined and vibrated in his palm. "Open wide."

"Don't," Tillinger said.

"You killed the deputy sheriff, didn't you?"

"No."

"The colored lady on the cross?"

"Anybody who says that is a damn liar."

"Let me put this closer to your eye. Don't blink. Would you say that again? Want to call me a gerbil now? You want me to start on your eyes or your eardrums or your nose? Tell me what you want. What's that sound I hear? Are you going wee-wee in your pants?"

Tillinger's eyes were bulging, his face quivering. "Kiss my ass."

Smiley grinned. "Bad boy. I just want a tiny nick. So I won't feel guilty about not doing my job." He touched the drill tip to Tillinger's earlobe. "There. A little red flower on the pillowcase to remember me by."

Tillinger's lungs seemed to collapse. Smiley clicked off the drill and pulled the plug from the wall, then wrapped the cord around it and placed it and the Liquid Plumr in his bag. He took a switchblade from his tennis shorts and pushed the release button on the blade.

"What are you doing?" Tillinger said.

Smiley sliced one of the ligatures in half. He stepped back from the bed and folded the blade into the case, all the while gazing at Tillinger.

"I don't get it," Tillinger said.

"Did you ever make your daughter cut a switch?"

"What's that mean?"

"Make her participate in her own punishment. Make her hate herself."

"The man who does that isn't a father."

"I need to talk to the people I work for. They will be angry with me when they hear what I have to say."

"What people? Angry about what?"

"You get to live. That's because somebody has lied about you. Don't be here in the morning."

"You're talking about wiseguys in New Jersey or Florida washing money, something like that?"

"They're from everywhere. Maybe I'll see you again. You could be my friend. Most of my friends are colored people."

"Why colored?"

"They accept you for what you are. They're hated and made fun of, just like I am."

Smiley opened the door and filled his lungs with the salt in the wind. He gazed back into the room. His expression was vacuous, his eyes lit with a blue glow, as though the moon were shining through a hole in the back of his head. "You're my friend now. Don't betray me. Nobody had better ever betray me."

He pulled the door shut behind him and walked away, a mindless smile on his lips.

IF YOU'RE A real drunkard, you don't need alcohol to mess up your life. A real drunkard knows his saloon is available inside his head twenty-four hours a day, and he can light up his viscera and give free rein to the gargoyles in the basement and access the whole drunkard's menu—alcoholic psychosis, unprotected sex, messing with guns and knives and dangerous people, all of it as fast as you can snap the cap on a bottle of brew. Or let me use another metaphor. You simply turn yourself into a human pinball, bouncing pell-mell off the flippers and crashing into the bumpers while electrified thunder roars and bells jingle and jangle and all the colors of the rainbow flash in celebration of your self-destruction.

Sunday afternoon Bailey Ribbons invited me to her house for a barbecue. I shined my loafers and put on a pair of gray slacks and a long-sleeve dress shirt and a tie and drove to her house in my truck. A pink balloon was tied with a ribbon to the mailbox by the road. The shale driveway leading to her cottage was an immaculate white against the freshly clipped deep green St. Augustine grass. Through the oak trees I could see the bayou glinting in the sunlight, the smoke from a barbecue pit rising into a hard blue sky that you could scratch a match on.

I thought others had been invited, but the only vehicle on the property was her compact, parked in the porte cochere. I twisted the bell. She answered the door almost immediately. She was wearing huaraches and khakis that accentuated her long legs and a purple blouse and an apron and light lip gloss. "You didn't need to dress up," she said.

"I thought it was a formal lawn party," I said, stepping inside.

"Nothing so grand," she said, closing the door behind me. "I thought we'd just hang out. I bowed out of my situation with Desmond."

"You're not going to do the film?"

"It was a bad idea. It seems like an intriguing world, but it's not. It's just like ours, except worse."

"I wouldn't give up on it. It's quite an opportunity."

"No, there's something kinky about that whole bunch. Come in the kitchen and help me make the salad. I have two chickens on the grill and some lemonade and soft drinks on ice."

She walked ahead of me into the kitchen. Her hair was thick and brown and clean, and tiny strands hung like particles of light on her cheeks. I had a hard time separating her from Clementine Carter standing on a desert road that dipped into eternity.

She turned and smiled but didn't speak. Her eyes were mysterious and had a radiance that seemed to have no source.

"Do you know you have a habit of staring?" she said.

"I think you were born for the screen," I said.

"Not me."

"You don't have to work with Desmond. Louisiana is full of movie people. The state subsidizes movies up to twenty-five percent."

"Let's slice some apples."

I rolled my sleeves and went to work next to her. I could not help glancing at her profile. There was not a line on her face or throat. I know this may seem foolish to some, but I could not associate the image of her toking on a joint with the woman standing beside me. In fact, I hated the thought.

"I know what you're thinking about," she said. "I'm sorry for taking the hit off that joint. My feelings are the same as yours. Fashionable vice is usually the mark of a self-important dilettante. Besides, I'm a cop."

"It's not the end of the world," I said.

She put her knife down and looked through the window at the smoke from the barbecue pit breaking apart in the wind. A cottontail rabbit was couched among the camellia bushes, brown and fat, ears folded back, eyes bright. "Want to go outside?" she said.

"This is fine," I replied.

She dried her hands on a dish towel and hung it over the handle on the oven. "I was married when I was sixteen. My husband was killed one year later in a stock car race. Entertaining people who carry Styrofoam spit cups."

"I'm sorry."

"I know about the loss of your wives," she said. "I don't know how you lived through all that."

I didn't answer. She stood in the silence until my eyes found hers. "I don't care about age differences," she said.

"The woman pays the price, Bailey. Men skate. The scarlet letter didn't die out with the Puritans."

She looked up into my face. She touched my cheek. "You won't give in, will you?" she said.

"Give in to what?"

"Principle, vanity, whatever you call it. You and your friend Clete pretend to be rebels, but you're traditionalists. You know what a traditionalist is, don't you? Someone who lets dead people control his life."

She turned on the cold water in the sink and put her hands and wrists under the faucet, her back rigid. I rested my hand on her shoulder. She turned off the water and looked at me. I thought I heard a sound like train-crossing bells clanging in my head.

I placed my arms lightly around her back and spread my fingers between her shoulder blades and touched her hair with my cheek. I was afraid to pull her against me. "I love your name."

"That's all you can say?" she asked.

How could one not? I thought. But I couldn't say the words.

I went out the door and down the steps to the shale drive. She walked out on the gallery and lifted one hand by way of saying goodbye. There was a hurt in her face that made me want to paint my brains on a ceiling.

I WENT UP LOREAUVILLE Road, my windows down, the rain ditches and cane fields and horse farms and nineteenth-century shotgun houses flying by me, and a vision in my mind I could barely resist. I saw a cool dark saloon with a long foot-railed bar and wood-bladed fans hanging from a stamped-tin ceiling, and domino and bourree tables, maybe a blackboard chalked with racing results, pool balls clattering on green felt, football betting cards scattered on the floor. I saw myself sitting in the shadows, starting the afternoon with a double shot of Jack poured on shaved ice with a sprig of mint, an ice-caked mug of draft or a sweating bottle of Bud for a chaser. I even saw the aftermath, the awakening at dawn to a bloodred sun and a flaming thirst and the first drink of the day, vodka and Collins mix and cherries and orange slices and half-melted ice sliding down the pipe with a beneficence I can only compare to a hit of morphine in a battalion aide station after you've been blown to shit.

There were any number of places in Iberia or St. Martin parish where I could get loaded with people who knew I shouldn't be there but were wise enough to know that no power on earth can keep a drunk from drinking once he decides to take the asp in hand and twine it around his arm.

The bar I found was not like the one I just described. It was a lounge in St. Martinville, one as dark as black satin whose refrigerated air was as cold and unforgiving as a tomb's. I sat at one end of a horseshoe bar and drank a Barq's Red Creme Soda in a mug and tried to finish a ham sandwich that had too much mustard on it. I had never seen the bartender before. I spat a bite of sandwich into a paper napkin and put it on my plate.

"I got some chicken gumbo in the kitchen," the bartender said.

"I'm halfway to the cemetery as it is," I replied.

"It is what it is, Mac," he said.

"I'd appreciate it if you'd call me Dave. I really don't like the name Mac. What's that stink? You always leave the men's room door open?"

He walked away, knowing a losing situation when he saw one. I looked down a hallway and out the back window and saw the sky darkening and a streetlight come on and then the rain beginning to fall, followed by hail that bounced on the asphalt in a white mist. I called the bartender back. "Give me four fingers of Jack in a mug, straight up, no ice. A Budweiser back, with a raw egg in a glass."

"I think you're in the wrong bar."

I opened my badge. "Will this earn me the stool I'm sitting on?"

"We don't serve eggs."

"So forget the egg."

"It's your funeral."

I watched him fill two double-shot glasses to the brim and snap the cap off a Budweiser. He set the shots and the longneck and a beer glass in front of me. My head was thundering. I squeezed my temples. The outside world seemed drained of color, a palm tree whipping across the street, the hail bouncing and rolling like mothballs.

"I asked for the Jack in a mug."

"Are you going to be a problem?" the bartender said.

"Not me. You know what the Evangeline Oak is about?"

"No clue. I'm from Big D. That's in Texas, in case you haven't checked recently."

"This is where the Acadians came by boat over two hundred years ago," I said. "Evangeline lost her lover on the trip from Nova Scotia. She went insane and waited by that tree every afternoon the rest of her life."

"You finished with your sandwich?" he said.

"Yeah. Why don't you wrap it up and take it home for your dog?"

"Anything else?"

"For real, you never heard of Evangeline?"

He leaned close enough for me to feel his breath on my face. "Badge or no badge, we don't take shit in here."

I got off the stool and took my wallet from my back pocket. "What's your name?"

"Harvey."

I put twenty dollars on top of my half-eaten sandwich. "Tell you what, Harvey, give my drinks to the guy at the end of the bar. If there's any change, it's yours." I winked at him.

He looked over his shoulder. "There's no one at the end of the bar, asshole."

I stared into the gloom. A faux-1950s Wurlitzer against the far wall glowed on the empty stools. "So you and your dog drink up for me," I said. "If that's not cool, maybe you and I can stroll outside and have a chat."

"You'd better get out of here, fuckball."

I felt as though something had pulled loose inside my head. In AA we call it a dry drunk. The room was tilting. I wanted to break Harvey up, stomp his face and break his teeth and leave him in a ball on the floor. I wanted to fill my hand with the heavy coldness and lethality of my 1911-model .45 auto. I walked unsteadily out of the lounge and kept going bareheaded in the rain to the town square and the great spreading live oak on Bayou Teche, where some claimed to have seen Evangeline waiting for her lover. The bayou was at high tide, the tops of the elephant ears floating like a green carpet at the edge of the banks. Above my head, the enormous sheltering limbs of the oak, scaled with lichen as coarse as a dragon's hide, seemed to reach into the clouds and the stars and rain like a conduit into both the past and endless black space.

It was under this tree, at age nineteen, that I first kissed Bootsie Mouton. Later that same evening, in a rain just like this one, we lost our virginity on top of an inflated rubber cushion in a boathouse on the bayou while hailstones clattered on the roof. After the murder of my wife, Annie, Bootsie and I married, but I lost her to lupus. Then Molly's life was taken by a benighted, ignorant man who rounded a curve on squealing tires with the joy of a Visigoth smashing works of art in a cathedral.

I watched the bayou rise and the ducks huddling in the cattails and the steam rising off the graves in the cemetery between the great oak and a church built in 1836. But the past is the past, and you don't get it back. Unfortunately, I've never learned that lesson. Maybe no one does. Or maybe you have to murder your heart in order to extract yourself from your own memories. If that's the case, I've never had the courage.

I knew where I was going. Even before I went to the lounge, I knew. Maybe it was wrong and I'll be judged for it. But the world I came from is dead and the land I've loved all my life is strewn with litter and our water is polluted and our principles are for sale. At least these are the things I told myself as I walked through the rain to Bella Delahoussaye's house.

It took her a long time to answer the door. She was wearing hoop earrings, and her hair was tied on top of her head. "You look like you went down with the ship."

"The ship wouldn't have me."

She studied my face. "I ain't no Polk Salad Annie, baby."

"I believe you."

"Ain't got nothing to offer you but the blues."

"That would be more than enough," I said.

She hooked her finger into my shirt and raised her face to mine, her lips parting.

Chapter Twenty-One

I WOKE ON THE couch at four in the morning. The rain was sluicing off the roof. Bella's acoustic guitar was propped facedown on a stuffed chair. Her bedroom door was open. She was sleeping on her side, the covers half on the floor.

I had dried my clothes in front of a fan and put them back on. I barely remembered coming to her house and believed for a moment that I was losing my mind. I had heard about dry blackouts but had never experienced one. I closed her door and went into the kitchen and started a pot of coffee. Through the window I could see the first glimmer of light in the east, water pooling in the alley, raindrops sliding off a banana frond that was bumping against the glass.

"You ain't leaving wit'out saying goodbye, are you?" she said.

I turned around. She was wearing a bathrobe. A thick strand of her hair hung across the scar on her throat. The Maltese cross given to her by Hilary Bienville was tied around her neck. Her lipstick was purple, the features of her face like carved ebony.

"Sorry for barging in on your life, Bella."

"Nobody barges in on my life. They get invited."

"You're the best."

"You wouldn't let me do nothing for you. You hurt me a little bit."

"It's not because of you. I'm bad news."

She stepped closer and fitted her hand around the back of my neck, sinking her nails into my hairline. She kissed me on the mouth, pushing her tongue inside. Then she stared into my eyes. "They gonna kill you, baby."

"No, they're not."

"You don't get it. It's what you're looking for."

"That's not true."

"You won't blow out your own wick because you're a churchgoing man. You think Mr. Death don't know what you're doing?"

I stepped back from her, hitting the stove.

"Stay wit' me," she said.

"I have to work."

"We're alike. You know the world ain't real. You know what most people believe ain't real."

"I think you're right."

She kneaded my throat with her thumbs, pressing on my windpipe, her eyes searching inside my head. "You don't need to come back. You don't need to feel guilty, neither."

"Don't say that. I mean about not coming back."

"Take care of yourself. You're stacking time on the hard road. You just ain't heard that ball and chain clanking."

I WENT OUT THE door and walked to my truck. The hood was open, my battery gone.

The streets and the town square were almost empty, the gutters running. A cherry-red convertible, the top up, pulled alongside me. The driver rolled down his window. "Engine trouble?"

It was Lou Wexler. His thick body, his craggy good looks and tangle of sun-bleached hair, his physicality, if you will, seemed too large for the car he drove. He reminded me of other mercenaries I had known. At heart they were secular Calvinists and believed their fellow man was born in a degraded state; consequently, they oversaw atrocities with equanimity and substituted pragmatism for compassion and slept the sleep of the dead.

I don't know why I had all these thoughts about Lou Wexler. I was unshaved, unshowered, my body clammy, my self-respect tattered. There's nothing like having a scapegoat show up when you need him.

"Somebody helped himself to my battery," I said. "I didn't know you lived in St. Martinville."

"I rented a place just up the bayou. I'll treat you to breakfast and we'll get a Triple A fellow out here."

"I'm not a member, but I'll take a ride back to New Iberia."

"Hop in," he said.

I got into the passenger seat. The rain had quit, and the leather felt warm and snug and comfortable. I looked back at the Evangeline Oak and the small church and the cemetery next to it and the bayou running smooth and high and yellowish brown in the gloom, and for some reason I felt a large piece of my life slipping away from me, this time forever.

As we drove toward the black district, I saw Bella in her yard, still in her bathrobe, waving my wallet at us.

"Pull over, will you?" I said. "This will take just a minute."

"Got a car behind me," Wexler said. "I'd better pull into the drive."

I looked behind us. The car behind us was halfway down the street. We bounced into Bella's driveway. I looked hard at Wexler's profile. He showed no reaction. I rolled down my window. Bella leaned down and handed me my wallet. "You dropped this on the floor."

"Thank you," I said. "This is Lou Wexler, Bella. He's a movie producer."

"Can I have a role?" she asked.

"Anytime," he said.

She laughed and went back inside. Wexler backed into the street and drove through the black district to the state road that led to New Iberia. He looked straight ahead. He turned on the radio and turned it off.

"Bella is a friend of mine," I said.

"She's a musician?"

"How'd you know?"

"Antoine Butterworth is always talking about blues musicians. I think he mentioned her name. She's attractive."

"She is."

"I keep it simple and take care of my side of the street, Mr. Robicheaux. Where would you like to eat?"

"What do you mean, you take care of your side of the street?"

"I have no quarrel with the world and the way it operates."

"That still begs the question, partner."

His teeth were white, maybe capped. "Not for me. One thing intrigues me, though: the Maltese cross on her neck. You don't see many of those around here."

"Desmond has one tattooed on his ankle," I said.

"He made a documentary on some bikers. Desmond doesn't know the first thing about the subculture."

"I think he can handle his own."

"Des likes to be a man of the people. I could take him to places that would make him puke his guts. I suspect you could, too."

"Not me," I said.

"You didn't get a whiff of the tiger cages or Charlie when he soiled himself after someone hooked him up to a telephone crank?"

"I never saw anything like that."

"Lucky man."

The ride was becoming an expensive one. I wondered how committed Alafair was in her relationship with Wexler. The images I had in my mind were the kind no father likes to look at.

"Hope I didn't say anything offensive," he said.

"Not a bit."

We entered the tunnel of oak trees that led into the north end of New Iberia, and passed a home that had been built by a man of color who owned slaves and operated a brick factory prior to emancipation. The wood was desiccated, eaten from within by Formosa termites, painted over, the building stained an ugly off-white by dust clouds and smoke from stubble fires. To change the subject, I mentioned the origins of the house to Wexler.

"That's nothing," he replied. "You should have seen what the wogs could do with a burning tire. They're at their worst when they turn on their own kind."

I had him drop me off at a filling station on the edge of town, and I called Alafair for a ride home.

AT FOUR-THIRTY P.M. the same day, Helen called Bailey and me into her office. She was walking up and down in front of the window, her hands on her hips, her face conflicted. A yellow legal pad scrawled with blue ink lay on her blotter. "The sheriff of Cameron Parish called. Early this morning a couple of guys driving an expensive car with a Florida tag went into a motel room and fired two rounds through a shower curtain. The water was running, but the motel guest must have gone out the window. The shooter probably used a silencer. The sheriff thought it looked like a professional hit, so he dusted the sill and sent the latents to AFIS. Guess whose name popped up."

"Tillinger?" I said.

"It gets better. Somebody in another room saw a weird-looking guy leave Tillinger's room several hours earlier."

"Weird-looking in what way?" Bailey asked.

Helen read from her legal pad: " 'A guy who looks like he was squeezed out of a toothpaste tube.' "

"Smiley?" I said.

"I don't get the guys with the Florida tag," Helen said. "Why would Smiley be with Tillinger? Why do the Florida guys want to pop Tillinger?"

"I think it has something to do with money laundering," I said.

"But what the hell does Tillinger have to do with it?" Helen said.

"Maybe he's a thorn in their side," I said. "He's got an obsession with Lucinda Arceneaux's death. He also wants to have a documentary made about his life."

Helen looked at Bailey. "What do you think?"

"None of this explains the tarot," Bailey said. "Or the way Hilary Bienville died. I think our killer is driven by rage and the motivation is sexual. The implications of the baton down Devereaux's throat are hard to ignore."

"The mayor's office and the chamber of commerce say our tourism has dropped probably fifty percent," Helen said. "The mayor asked me this morning about our 'progress.' I didn't tell him Smiley is back. Are you sure you saw him, Dave?"

"What kind of question is that?" I said.

"Frenchie Lautrec was in my office this morning. He says you beat the crap out of him."

"Why's he telling you that now?" I said.

"He's dumping in his pants."

"Why?" I said.

"He's not big on sharing."

"We gave him a uniform and a badge and power over defenseless people," I said. "He's a coward. That's why he's afraid. Not because of me."

"You don't look like you had a lot of sleep last night," she said.

"Thanks for telling me," I said. "What if Bailey and I go down to Cameron Parish?"

"Have at it," she replied.

BAILEY CHECKED OUT a cruiser and lit it up, and we were at the motel in less than two hours. The sky was lidded with rain clouds, lead-colored, the wind blowing out of the south, the waves filled with yellow sand and seaweed and swelling over a dock that resembled a torn spinal cord. The motel owner took us to Tillinger's room. The lock had been jimmied, and the interior of the room was crisscrossed with footprints, probably from cops at the scene. The owner pushed open the bathroom door. He was a small, nervous man who wore a tie and a white shirt and stank of cigarettes smoked in a closed room.

"You can see the two holes in the curtain," he said. "The bullets hit the wall by the window. They left the shower running. It almost ran my tank empty."

"What kind of vehicle did your guest drive?" I said.

"A truck like a painter or plumber uses. Full of dents."

"Where is it?" Bailey said.

"The cops come back and towed it off," he said. "They say this guy broke out of a prison hospital. He killed his family."

I showed him a picture of Tillinger.

"That's him," the owner said. "Who's gonna pay for all this?"

"All what?" Bailey said.

"The holes in the wall. The rug. The shower curtain. The door. My water bill."

"How long was our guy with you?" I asked.

"Two weeks and three days. This is the state's fault."

"What is?" I said.

"The guy running loose. Vandalizing people's property. The three guests that checked out when they saw cops all over the place."

"We'll look around a bit and let you know when we leave," I said.

"Look at that lock," he said, glaring at the doorjamb as he walked out. "Don't mess up this room any more than it is."

"You got it," I said.

He slammed the door.

"What a happy guy," Bailey said.

I pushed the door snug with the jamb and wedged a chair under the knob. "He's going to be even unhappier."

"What are you doing?"

"Tillinger was in the room for over two weeks. He left behind everything he owns."

"The Cameron deputies or cops from Texas probably bagged it," she said.

"They bagged what they saw. Tillinger has outsmarted all of us at every turn."

The desk and closet and chest of drawers were empty except for a Gideon's Bible in the desk drawer. A copy of *Time* magazine and a soiled shirt lay on the floor in the bathroom. I pulled the sheets and blanket and bedspread off the bed and upended the mattress against the wall. Nothing. I stood on the bed and unscrewed the vent high on the wall and reached inside. When I removed my hand, it was covered with cobwebs and dust. I climbed back down and ran the pages of the Bible against my thumb. They were heavily annotated with a ballpoint. The ink did not look old.

"What are you looking for, Dave?"

"Tillinger has his own frame of reference. He thinks he's more intelligent and insightful than other people. He may be a religious fanatic, but he also wants to be onstage. That kind of guy always keeps a diary or a collection of drawings or notes about the world. He's like all megalomaniacs; he wants to scratch his name on history."

"Maybe we should talk to the Cameron sheriff."

"We'll be fooling around here for two days," I said.

I rolled up the mattress and felt along the edges. Then I saw a slit in the side and a rectangular lump under the case. I worked my hand deep inside, but the object had slid to the center. I pulled my arm free and opened my pocketknife and ripped open the case and tore it loose from the stuffing. A notebook with thick cardboard covers lay among the stuffing.

I clicked the light switch, but the power was off. I had the feeling the owner had hit the circuit breaker to make our job harder. I went to the window and opened the notebook and held it to the light. The handwriting was cramped, like Tillinger's mind, a place that I suspected was filled with images generated by biblical accounts of genocide and divine wrath. The first page read: "The Story of Hugo Jefferson Tillinger and His Search for Justice and the Killer of Lucinda Arceneaux." The narrative was rambling, much of it dedicated to his trial and conviction and removal to death row. There appeared to be water stains on the page that contained his account of the house fire and the death of his family. I think the emotion was real. Then the narrative took a turn, with several entries written in red ballpoint rather than blue.

Here's the first:

> Found the jackpot in the old records of Charity Hospital in Lafayette. Desmond Cormier was brought there when he was one day out of the womb. The man who brought him was named

Ennis Patout. Patout wouldn't admit to being the father. He said the mother was Corina Cormier and came from the Chitimacha Indian Reservation. She left the baby in the back of a semi in Opelousas and went wherever her kind go.

The second entry in red:

The Cormier grandparents ran a little store but have been dead many years. Looks like Desmond dumped his folks and went to Hollywood. Wonder if he knew Charlie Manson's crowd. Wonder if he ever kept his joystick in his pants. The whole place is deserving of a firestorm, if you ask me.

These words were written by the same man who wanted a Hollywood documentary made about his life.

He had made notations about Antoine Butterworth and Lou Wexler and several actors I had not met, as well as Joe Molinari, the victim hanged in a shrimp net; he also mentioned the names of the dirty cops, Frenchie Lautrec and Axel Devereaux. But there was no question about the person at the center of his investigation: The emphasis was on Desmond Cormier. I had no idea why. Maybe Tillinger was simply a celebriphile. Or a potential assassin. Desmond was everything Tillinger was not. There was another consideration I couldn't ignore: Tillinger had known Lucinda Arceneaux well, and the rest of us had not known her at all.

The notebook ended with these words, again in red ballpoint:

There's an Ennis Patout in Opelousas. Maybe this is the father of Desmond Cormier. Or maybe he's the son of the father. I think time is running out for me. I think the men from Huntsville are going to find me and take me back and fill my veins with poison and drive the light from my eyes. I've got news for them. If they want to take me alive, they'd better bring a lunch. "The day is coming, burning like a furnace, and all the arrogant and every evildoer will be chaff and the day that is coming will set them ablaze." Malachi 4:1.

I closed the book. The western sun was blue and red and strung with clouds that looked like industrial smoke as it descended into the Gulf.

"Are you too tired to go to Opelousas?" I said.

"What's in Opelousas?"

"The past."

"Let's go," Bailey said.

I could see the fatigue in her face, a deadness in her eyes. Neither of us had mentioned my leaving her house yesterday after she had probably spent half the day preparing for my arrival.

"We've done enough for today," I said. "I'll buy you dinner."

"I'd better go home."

"Sure," I said.

"Let's keep it professional from here on out," she said. "Is that okay?"

I felt a crack spread across my heart.

"No problem," I said.

Chapter Twenty-Two

THE NEXT MORNING I found Ennis Patout's name in the Opelousas phone directory. I checked out a cruiser, and Bailey and I drove to St. Landry Parish. The morning was clear and cool, the grass in the neutral ground mowed and sparkling with dew. As we neared Opelousas, I looked across the seat at her and said, "A good night's sleep is the cure for lots of things, isn't it?"

She smiled and didn't reply.

I turned off at the exit and drove to an old two-story soot-stained stucco building on the two-lane to Baton Rouge. It had been a car dealership during the Depression and was now a wrecker service and repair shop for diesel trucks. The gas pumps in front were out of order and rusted. I had called Patout before we left New Iberia; when I'd identified myself, he'd hung up. A black man in a filthy white jumpsuit was working on an engine in the shop.

"Is Mr. Patout here?" I said.

"Upstairs. What you want?"

I opened my badge holder. "I called earlier. Ask him to come down."

"He ain't gonna like it."

"Why's that?"

"Mr. Ennis don't need a reason." He went up a wooden staircase inside the shop and came back down. "He'll be down in a minute. He's got to take his heart medicine."

A moment later, a towering man emerged from the doorway that led to the stairs. He had the same wide-set pale blue eyes as Desmond, and the same long upper lip and the same muscularity, but that was where the similarity ended. His face made me think of a broken pumpkin. The eyes were out of alignment, the blank stare like a slap. There was a repressed ferocity in his stance. His hands were grimed and hung at his sides. His jumpsuit was dirtier than the black man's. From five feet away he had an odor like a barrel of old shrimp.

"I'm Detective Robicheaux," I said. "This is Detective Ribbons. I called you from New Iberia."

He didn't look at Bailey. "I know who you are." Even though he had a French name, he had a deep-throated Mississippi or North Louisiana accent.

"We're looking for an escaped convict named Hugo Tillinger," I said. "We have reason to believe he might try to contact you."

"Never heard of him."

"He's heard of *you,*" Bailey said. "Your name and city of residence were in his notebook."

"Tillinger, you say?" he said.

"Yes," I said. "He was convicted of burning his family to death."

"What's he want with me?"

There are many ruses police can use legally in interrogating a witness or suspect, and one of the most effective is to indicate you posses knowledge that in reality you don't. "I think he wants to talk to you about your son, Desmond Cormier."

"Who says I got a son?"

"It's a matter of record," I said. "You took the baby to Charity Hospital in Lafayette many years ago. You probably saved his life. You never see Desmond? He's a famous man."

"I know what you're trying to do," he said. "This is about her, ain't it? She's back telling lies."

"Could be," I said, with no clue about the reference. "Why not give us your perception of the situation and put it to rest?"

"She's a drunk and a whore," he said. "I was good to her when nobody else was. She slept with everything that wore pants. I caught her a bunch of times, but I never hit her."

"We're talking about Corina Cormier, right?" I said.

"Who's it sound like?"

"Where can we find her?"

"I wouldn't know." He was looking at Bailey now. "If she's alive, she's probably a hag. The man that slept with her had to tie a board across his ass so he didn't fall in, and that was forty years back."

"You need to dial down the language, Mr. Patout," I said.

"Don't you lecture me, boy," he said. "In fact, it's time for you to git. I got work to do."

"Git?" I said.

"This is St. Landry Parish. You got no authority here. Come back with a warrant or stay the hell away from me. That means you drag your sorry asses out of here."

There are times you hold your ground, and there are times you walk away. In this instance we were off our turf. There was another factor involved. Patout was not the kind you took down easily. He was the kind you sometimes ended up killing.

His hands still hung at his sides, curled like an ape's, the nails half-mooned with dirt and grease. "Why you staring at me?"

I could feel my old enemy flickering to life like a flame working its way up a cornstalk in late summer. "See you down the road," I said.

I winked at him. It was a poor mask for our defeat at the hands of an ignorant and obviously violent man. We got back into the cruiser and drove away.

"SEE YOU DOWN the road?" Bailey said.

I didn't reply. One mile down the road, she said, "Turn around."

"What for?" I replied.

"Either you turn around or I'll get out and walk."

"Bad idea."

"Then stop the car."

The flasher was already on. I U-turned in the middle of the two-lane and drove back to Patout's wrecker service. Bailey and I got out at the same time. Patout was inside the shop, under a truck hood. He lifted his head. "What now?"

"You see this?" Bailey said.

"Your badge?" he said.

"It's not just a badge. It's a symbol of honor and integrity. You *will* respect it. You will not use profanity in speaking to an officer of the law, and you will not tell him or her what you will and will not do. And you will never again disrespect anyone from our parish who carries this badge. That starts with calling an adult 'boy.' "

His eyes shifted on mine. "She for real?"

"Why don't you man up and apologize?" I said.

"All right," he said.

"All right, what?" I said.

"I apologize. You come at me hard. I ain't up to it. I got a bad heart and a bad temper. Don't pay me no mind. How's Desmond doing?"

"Go ask him," Bailey said.

"I doubt he'd want that."

"Give it a try," Bailey said.

"I've thought about it," he said. He stared at the concrete floor, his eyes empty, his emotions, whatever they were, as dead as wet ash. "What's done is done. There ain't no changing it. He was a good little boy. I always miss that little boy. Cain't get him out of my head sometimes."

AFTER LUNCH I talked to Helen in her office.

"So Hugo Tillinger is running around naked without his truck, and Smiley could be anywhere, and y'all's interview with Desmond Cormier's father was a dead end?"

"I don't see it that way," I said. "Tillinger is a smart guy. If he's digging around in Desmond's family, it's for a reason."

Helen was standing by the window. "Come here."

I walked behind her desk and stood next to her.

"Look across the bayou," she said. "Those people picnicking under the shelters and children flying kites on the baseball diamond have no idea what the world is really like. Can you imagine showing any of them a photograph of Axel Devereaux with the baton shoved down his throat? Or Hilary Bienville torn apart? Or what some of Smiley's victims looked like?"

"You're preaching to the choir," I said.

"You're not hearing me. I'm saying a black flag has its purpose."

"It's not a good one, either," I said.

"This from you? Stop it."

"It's a mistake to create a mystique about these murders," I said.

"They're just regular meat and potatoes?"

"I'm saying they're about money."

"That's what you want to believe. You know better."

I looked at my watch. "I'd better get on it. Anything else?"

"You and Bailey getting along?"

"Why wouldn't we?"

"You deserve a good life, bwana."

"Could you translate that for me?"

Her gaze dropped to my chest and arms. I was wearing a white dress shirt and a tie.

"You have too much starch in your shirts," she said. "You ought to switch your laundry service. Loosen up. Go with the flow."

"Adios," I said.

HELEN WAS BEING invasive about my sex life in part because hers was so outrageous, but I was glad she had changed the subject from a discussion that no cop likes. Here's the truth about the profession I have served most of my adult life: There are uncomfortable moments for almost all cops. The struggles are similar to those of the mystic with doubt about God's existence; the lover who looks into the eyes of a companion after orgasm and sees only disinterest and an uncoupling of the spirit; or the humanist who watches a neighbor whip a child savagely in the yard. If a cop is on the job long enough, he will see things he never discusses with anyone, not unless he is afflicted with the same psychological disorders that define the sociopaths he locks up. The moment I'm describing, the one that happens in the middle of the night, when the booze and weed and pills aren't working anymore, is the realization that real evil is not simply a product of environmental factors. It may be a disembodied presence floating from place to place, seeking to drop its tentacles into whatever host it can find.

What are its origins? I don't know. Charles Manson and his kind are harlequins and poseurs. Anyone who wants to check out the collective nature of evil can take a photo tour of Hitler's extermination camps and decide whether William Blake's tiger is out there or not.

LATER THAT SAME day, Smiley Wimple was sitting in a Morgan City Laundromat, reading a Wonder Woman comic, when two men came in the front door. He had not seen them before, but he knew their kind. Their tight suits had a liquid shine; they wore hairstyles and sideburns that were thirty years out of fashion; they stank of pomade and deodorant and made Smiley think of walking chemical factories. They always had cigarettes either in their mouths or cupped in their hands, as though they were fire dragons, the inventors of flame, a fiery force that caused people to melt like wax from their heat. Their eyes ate up the scenery and the people in it. Their meters were always running, tick-tick, tick-tick, tick-tick.

The two men walked straight to Smiley's chair. He was wearing a safari hat and Ray-Bans. He peered over the top of the comic like a smiling angel-food cake. "Hi, hi," he said.

"Come with us," one of the men said. His black mustache had gray hair and tiny pieces of food in it.

"I was taught not to talk to strangers, even though they might be nice."

"That's us. Nice," the same man said. When he grinned, the skin around his mouth looked shriveled, like it was rubber or it wouldn't work right.

"My friends call me Smiley, although my real name is Chester."

"Yeah, we know that," the same man said. "My name is Jerry Gee. You don't remember us from Miami?"

"I'm from New Or-yuns."

"Great city," Jerry Gee said. "They got, what-do-you-call-'em, beignets that melt in your mouth. The broads the same way. Whatcha reading?"

The clothes in the dryers were spinning and falling, buttons clicking against metal, cloth toppling across the glass, like living creatures inside a bathysphere that had broken from its cable. The air smelled baked and clean and comfortable, like a womb Smiley didn't want to leave. He dropped his eyes to his comic. Wonder Woman was deflecting bullets with her magic bracelets.

"Hey, you hearing me?" Jerry Gee said.

"I'm reading about Wonder Woman."

"Yeah? She's a chunk, huh?" Jerry Gee said.

"Don't be disrespectful of her," Smiley said.

"Yeah, I know what you mean. I dig her, too," Jerry Gee said. His dark hair glistened with oil, one strand hanging through an eyebrow, an impish working-class kid out of a 1930s Bowery Boys film. "There's a fat envelope for you in our car. It's from a mutual friend."

"Then we can have some lunch," the second man said. He was taller than the other man and wore his shirt lapels outside his suit, exposing his chest hair. There were rings on his fingers inset with stones, more like brass knuckles than jewelry. "My name is Marco. Like Marco Polo. After we have lunch, we'll come back and help you fold your clothes."

Smiley rolled his comic and sat with his hands clamped between his thighs. "I have to go wee-wee."

"We'll go with you. To watch the bathroom door," Jerry Gee said. He leaned down. "This place is full of cannibals, man. You ought to find a better part of town."

Smiley squeezed his penis. "I'm going to wet myself."

"Go. By all means," Jerry Gee said, stepping back.

The men followed Smiley to the restroom and waited outside.

Marco combed his hair in a mirror, squatting to get a better view of himself, patting his hair with his free hand. Jerry Gee hit the door with his fist. "Roll up your wiener. There's people waiting here."

The two men laughed without sound.

"I'm going poop," Smiley replied through the door.

"You can take the trash can with you," Marco said.

Smiley opened the door. A piece of toilet paper was stuck to his shoe. Marco glanced back into the Laundromat, then shoved Smiley into the alley. "Get in the Buick. We're gonna have a talk."

"No, you made fun of me."

Jerry Gee opened the rear door of the Buick. Marco hooked one finger in Smiley's mouth and slung him inside and climbed in after him. Jerry Gee got behind the wheel, locked the doors, and started the engine. In seconds they were on the four-lane, ascending a bridge that overlooked the Atchafalaya River and miles of flooded woods where frightened egrets lifted into the air like snowflakes blowing in a violent wind.

JERRY GEE DROVE along a levee and parked in a grove of persimmons by a bay. Through the tree trunks, Smiley saw the sunlight blazing on the water and a half-sunken shrimp boat circled by alligator gars that rolled like sea serpents. Jerry Gee got out and opened the back door. He pulled Smiley onto the ground, which was covered with damp yellow leaves that were spotted with black mold. Jerry Gee scooped up a handful and stuffed them into Smiley's mouth. Smiley gagged and tried to crawl away. Jerry Gee kicked him between the buttocks, then stood on his spine.

"This is the preview. Don't make us look at the main feature. You had a job to do, but you didn't do it. You were supposed to call in with what you learned or clip the guy."

Smiley sat up, hiccupping, his eyes cups of grease and dirt. Marco leaned down and slapped him across the ear. "You deaf? Answer the man!"

Smiley stared at the movements of the gars, the waves washing through the pilothouse of the sunken boat, the persimmons on the ground that were crawling with ants.

"What's it take?" Marco said. "You want us to hurt you? I mean really hurt you? I got tools in the trunk you ain't gonna like."

"Get him up," Jerry Gee said.

Marco picked up Smiley and began dusting him off.

"Against the car," Jerry Gee said.

Marco held his hands out palms up, as though to say *What?*

"Do it," Jerry Gee said.

Marco shoved Smiley over the fender and pushed his face down on the hood, flattening it sideways against the metal, twisting Smiley's mouth out of shape.

Jerry Gee picked up a broken tree branch. "I heard you had a bad time in an orphanage and you ended up queer-bait on the streets. So how about a trip down Memory Lane? Get in touch with the origins of your problem?"

Jerry Gee nodded at Marco. Marco stared back and mouthed, *What the fuck?*

"Take his pants down," Jerry Gee said.

They were elastic-waisted and slid easily over the knees. Even though the weather was warm, Smiley's buttocks and thighs prickled.

"Last chance, Smiley," Jerry Gee said, teasing Smiley's butt with the points of the branch.

"Only my friends call me Smiley. You're not my friend."

"You caused all this," Jerry Gee said. "So shut up."

Smiley felt a pain like a handsaw piercing his rectum and viscera and climbing up his spine and out his mouth.

When he woke up, he was lying on the ground. The two men were looking down at him; framed against the sun, their faces were lost in shadow.

"You all right, little buddy?" Marco said.

Smiley didn't answer.

"You gonna be a good boy?" Jerry Gee said.

"Yes," Smiley said.

"What'd you get for us?" Jerry Gee said.

"The bad man from Texas on my recorder."

"Why didn't you just say that?"

"Because he doesn't know anything about anything. I didn't want anybody mad at me."

"You should have popped him," Jerry Gee said.

"He didn't kill his family. Someone told me a big fib."

"You're a righteous dude," Marco said, lifting him to his feet. "Clean yourself up and get in the car. We'll buy you an ice cream on the way back to your car. Hey, act like a man and stop crying."

Smiley's eyes were swimming. Inside the bronze glaze on the water, he saw a metal shield rise to the surface like a great bubble of air released from the ancient world. A woman clad in a red and gold bodice and metallic-blue shorts sprinkled with stars waded to the shore, a magic rope coiled on her belt. She smiled at him, her eyes filled with the lights of love and pity.

THE MEN TOOK him back to the Laundromat and folded his laundry for him and put it into a basket. Marco set the basket in the back of Smiley's car and got in the front, and Jerry Gee followed them down the highway to the business district of a small town that had been killed by Walmart. The sun had just set. The buildings and streets were deserted, the store signs removed, the walls pocked with rusted spikes. The entire neighborhood seemed leached of color, even the sky, like a cardboard movie set. A few cars were parked behind an old two-story building that once was a dry goods store. Smiley and the men ascended wood stairs in back and went inside. There was a rumbling sound below.

"You rent a room above a bowling alley?" Marco said.

Smiley sat on the bed and stared into space. "I pretend they're toy soldiers. They all fall down and get up again."

"You're a special kind of guy, all right," Jerry Gee said. "Where's the recorder?"

"I'll get it." Smiley reached toward the nightstand.

"Whoa," Marco said. He pulled out the drawer and removed the recorder. He clicked it on and listened. "That's Tillinger?"

"I told you, didn't I?" Smiley said.

"Yeah, you did," Marco said. "You want an aspirin or something?"

"You hurt me inside. You're not my friend. Don't pretend."

"We're sorry," Marco said. "You shouldn't have jerked us around. We're just taking orders here."

Jerry Gee took the recorder from Marco and held it to his ear and listened while he gazed down at the street. He clicked it off. "I'm taking this back to Miami."

"It's mine."

"Not anymore it isn't. Answer me something, will you?"

"What?" Smiley said.

"They say you use deer urine. Like when you're on the job. That's for real?"

"It hides the human smell," Smiley said.

"The people you're about to clip aren't deer or elks," Jerry Gee said.

"There's no difference. We're all animals."

"You know this area pretty good?" Jerry Gee said.

Smiley was still on the bed, the Wonder Woman comic by his thigh. He didn't answer.

"Where do we go for a good pump?" Jerry Gee said.

"You mean to do something with bad women?" Smiley said.

"In this case, bad is good."

"Back in Morgan City."

"Will you take whatever you're sucking on out of your mouth? Where in Morgan City?"

"I'm not sucking on anything." Smiley gave him the name of a bar and the name of the motel next door.

"I'm not gonna get a nail there?" Jerry Gee asked.

"A what?" Smiley said.

Jerry Gee rubbed his hand on top of Smiley's head, then patted it for extra measure. "You're a cute little guy. Keep using that deer urine. The right broad is waiting for you out there."

AFTER THEY WERE gone, Smiley bathed in a claw-footed tub down the hall and dressed in clean underwear and an unpressed khaki shirt and green cargo pants and pink tennis shoes with Mickey Mouse's face embossed on the rubber toes. He snugged a baseball cap on his head and walked painfully down the stairs and got into his car and drove to the storage shed he rented on the edge of town. Inside were his survival gear, a box of passports and driver's licenses, a suitcase filled with clothes, his stamp and coin collection, boxes of comics that he read over and over and did not think of as collectibles, a scoped 1903 Springfield, a Taser, half a dozen pistols, a Browning automatic rifle, an M107 sniper rifle, an AK-47, the classic British commando knife, flash grenades, and a box that contained a weapon he had tested but never used on the job.

He unlocked the box and reached inside and hooked the thick straps of the unit in his hands and dragged it free. His face and hands were tingling like chimes blowing in a tree or the music of an ice cream truck. In minutes he was on his way to Morgan City, the night sky clearing, the stars shining as brightly as they did on Wonder Woman's short pants.

He passed a boatyard and a series of docks and a ramshackle nightclub. Next door was a motel that advertised porn and hourly rates. Smiley drove back and forth in the parking lot of the club, then circled the motel, but he saw no sign of the two men or their midnight-blue Buick. He drove to the motel entrance and went inside. A man about thirty, with a mustache and sideburns as shiny as black grease and pipe-cleaner stems for arms, wearing a vinyl vest with no shirt, sat behind the counter, working a crossword puzzle.

"Hi, hi. Can I have a room for thirty minutes?" Smiley said.

"Thirty minutes?" the clerk said. He looked beyond Smiley out into the dark. "You with somebody?"

"I have to poop."

"You're putting me on."

"I have to go poop real bad."

"Go to the club next door."

"People wee-wee on the seat."

"You need to get out of here, man."

Smiley kept the back of his head to the surveillance camera on the wall. "You don't have to get nasty."

The clerk set down his pencil. "Want me to walk you to your car?"

"Have my friends Marco and Jerry Gee been here?"

"We don't give out the names of our guests. What does it take for you to get the message? Out!"

"Maybe I'll come back later. I like crossword puzzles."

"That's it," the clerk said, and got off his stool.

"You are bad. You'll see what happens to bad people," Smiley said. The bell above the door tinkled as he went out.

HE PARKED BEHIND some Dumpsters, with a view of both the club and the motel. At 12:17 a.m. the Buick pulled into the parking lot, and Marco and Jerry Gee went inside the club, flipping away their cigarettes, Jerry Gee's against the wall. At 1:48 they came out the front door with two women. One was thick-bodied and wearing a shiny black skirt. The other was a rail, dressed like a cowgirl, unsteady on her feet, her jeans hanging on her hips. The four of them got into the Buick and drove to the front of the motel. Marco went inside, then came back out and got behind the wheel and drove the four of them to the rear of the building. None of the nearby rooms were occupied. Jerry Gee and the woman in the black skirt went into one room, Marco and the cowgirl into the one next door.

For the next twenty minutes Smiley sat motionlessly behind the wheel, his eyes half closed, his face as insentient as wax. He got out of the car and walked across the parking lot and squatted down by the back of the Buick and eased the tip of his stiletto into the air valve and watched the tire settle on the rim.

At 3:18 a.m. Jerry Gee stepped out of his room, flexing his neck and shoulders, his coat on, the thick-bodied woman now wearing only panties and a bra behind him. She looked like she was cursing at him. Then she closed the door. A moment later Marco came out of the other room. The cowgirl looked at him briefly through the curtain, then closed it. While Smiley watched from his car, Marco and Jerry got into the Buick and started to back out. The steel rim of the flattened tire sliced through the rubber and crunched on the concrete.

Smiley pulled a .22 semi-auto from under the seat and got out and circled around the far side of the motel. He entered the front door and came back out moments later, wiping something off his cheek with his shoulder. He circled back to the Dumpsters and unlocked his trunk and dropped the semi-auto on the mat and worked the straps of his newly acquired weapon over his arms and shoulders. The brace and propane tanks fitted comfortably against his back. The wand and igniter were simply designed and as weightless as aluminum; the hand-grip trigger was a pleasure to squeeze. He walked softly across the parking lot as Marco and Jerry Gee were spinning off the nuts on the tire.

"Hi, hi," Smiley said.

Both of them were on their haunches. They looked at the object in Smiley's hands and on his back, and their faces drained.

"Get in your car," Smiley said.

"Jesus Christ," Marco said. He slipped sideways and had to right himself on the concrete.

"You have made me very mad."

"Look, anything you want," Jerry Gee said.

"I want you in your car," Smiley said, gritting his teeth.

"We still got the broads inside," Jerry Gee said. "We got liquor. You want a drink? We can talk this out."

Smiley lifted the tip of the wand.

"Okay, you got it, man," Jerry Gee said. "What we did earlier today was all business. We take orders just like you. It wasn't personal. Okay, okay, okay. We're getting in the car. We'll drive somewhere. Right?"

"Get in both on the same side, passenger door," Smiley said.

"Sure," Marco said. "Remember what I told you? You're a righteous dude. It was me said that."

"You told me to act like a man. I don't look like a man?"

"You're a good guy," Marco said. "I was telling Jerry that. I was telling the girls. Come on, you can meet them. They're good girls."

"Get in the car and leave the doors open. Then start the engine."

"Sure," Marco said. "Don't point that thing. This isn't happening here. You're having some fun. I can understand that. Take it easy."

"I'll count backward from three," Smiley said.

"Okay, we're on it," Marco said. "We all work for the same guys. We got to keep that in mind."

"Three," Smiley said.

"I hear you," Marco said. He worked his way across the seat, followed by Jerry Gee. Both of them stared at Smiley, waiting for approval, unable to look directly at the wand of the flamethrower.

"Roll down the windows," Smiley said.

"All four? What are we doing here?"

Smiley didn't reply.

"Okay, we're on it," Jerry Gee said, fumbling at a window button. "You want your recorder back? It's in the glove box."

The faces of the men looked like colorless prunes twisted out of shape. Their eyes were filled with a level of helplessness they probably had never experienced.

"Close the doors. Don't touch the gearshift," Smiley said.

The men eased the doors shut. Jerry Gee lifted his eyes to Smiley. "Please, man. I got a family. I ain't a bad—"

Smiley stepped backward into the darkness, ten feet, twenty feet, almost thirty feet. The wind was cool, out of the south, smelling of salt and rain. He tightened his finger inside the trigger guard. The stream of flame arced through the Buick's window and turned the interior into a firestorm, curling over the roof, blowing the windshield onto the hood. When he released the trigger, the dashboard was bubbling, and Marco and Jerry Gee sat amid the receding flames like shriveled mannequins powdered with white ash.

The thick-bodied woman opened the door of her room and stared in disbelief.

"Run," Smiley said.

"Sir?"

"It might explode. Get the other bad woman and run. You have been very bad. Don't do these kinds of things anymore."

"I won't."

"My friends call me Smiley. You can call me Smiley, too. What's your name?"

"Dora."

"It's nice to meet you, Miss Dora. Tell the other lady what I said. You should not keep company with bad men or go to bad places."

"You're not going to come back and hurt me, are you?"

"I don't hurt good people. I'm sure inside you are a very nice person."

She eased the door shut and gently set the bolt. Smiley walked to his vehicle, placed the flamethrower into the trunk, and drove away. The neon sign in front said VACANCY. The office light was on. No one seemed to be at the desk. The motel and its semi-tropical ambiance had become a still life—orderly, tranquil, each thing in its proper place, washed clean as though a mystical rain had fallen.

In less than forty-five minutes, Smiley was back in his rented room, sound asleep, his comic on the pillow next to him, the cover tilted so Wonder Woman could watch over him.

Chapter Twenty-Three

I GOT THE CALL from the sheriff in St. Mary Parish at four-fifteen a.m. "We got two guys fried outside a hot-pillow joint," he said. "I think it's your boy, that crazy pissant who was killing people about eighteen months back."

"Wimple?"

"A security camera in the parking lot of a nightclub caught him. About five-three, propane tanks on his back, looks like he fell in a bag of flour? How many people match that description?"

"He had a flamethrower?"

"Come down if you want. I got to get on it. We cain't find the night clerk."

I called Bailey Ribbons and picked her up fifteen minutes later.

MORE THAN A dozen squad cars, ambulances, and fire trucks were parked at the crime scene, flashers ripping or blinking in the sunrise. The ground and asphalt and motel and nightclub were damp with humidity and partially in shadow, the air the color of a bruise, an odor like old fruit wafting on the breeze. The two victims were in the front seat of a Buick pockmarked with paint blisters, heads on their chests as though they had tired of the show and gone to sleep.

"The drip line from the flamethrower doesn't go back much more than twenty-five feet," the sheriff said. He was a huge man, about six and a half feet, over fifty, his stomach still flat. He was originally from Amarillo and once was a Texas Ranger. "If the gas tank had blown, it might have taken that little asswipe with it."

"I think Smiley Wimple would have liked that," I said.

"Say again?"

"He would have made a great pilot in the Japanese air force," I replied.

The sheriff looked into space. He was from another generation. "We found the clerk."

We followed him to the office. There was a doorway behind the counter. I looked up at the surveillance camera.

"Somebody already dumped it," the sheriff said. He went through the doorway, then looked back at me. "You coming?"

The living area had a small kitchen and a table and one chair and a small bed. A harsh lightbulb hung from the ceiling. Porn magazines were on the table and stacked on a wall shelf. Both doors of a cabinet under the sink were open. A bare-chested thin man wearing a vinyl vest was inside the cabinet, so packed under the pipes that he was almost a ball. As far as I could tell, there were three entry wounds in his face and one in the throat and one in the mouth. No visible exit wounds.

"The shooter picked up his brass, but I figure it was a twenty-two, maybe hollow points," the sheriff said. "You reckon this kid was trying to hide?"

Bailey touched a can of Ajax on the floor with her shoe. "No, he was put in there. Wimple wanted to humiliate him. He was probably locked in a small space when he was a child, so he visits the same fear on anyone who mocks him."

"I've got a hooker in the back of my cruiser," the sheriff said. "Her name is Dora Thibodaux. The Buick was parked right in front of her room. The room was rented by a guy named Jerry Gemoats, the same man the Buick is registered to."

"Can we talk to the woman?" I said.

He handed me a key. "I put her on a D-ring. I don't think you'll get anything. Her teeth are rattling."

Bailey and I walked to the sheriff's cruiser. The windows were down. Dora Thibodaux was handcuffed by one wrist to a steel ring on the floor of the back seat, her shoulder at an awkward angle. Her eyeliner had run and her hair was a tangle of snakes. Two Band-Aids were affixed end to end along a vein inside her left forearm. Her face was out of round from either hangover or withdrawal.

I gave Bailey the handcuff key. She got in the other side and unlocked the woman's wrist. "I'm Detective Ribbons, Ms. Thibodaux. This is Detective Robicheaux. We're homicide detectives in Iberia Parish. We're investigating the deaths of the two men in the Buick, nothing else. Understand?"

"I didn't see nothing," Thibodaux replied.

I leaned down to the window. "We're not asking you to describe what you didn't see, Miss Dora. We already know who killed the two men. His name is Chester Wimple. Sometimes he calls himself Smiley." I saw the recognition in her eyes. "He told you his nickname?"

"I ain't saying nothing, me."

"Smiley doesn't give everyone permission to use his nickname," I said. "It's a compliment."

She raised her face, her eyes on mine.

"You think Smiley might hurt you?" I said.

"No."

"A guy who hosed down two people with a flamethrower wouldn't do that?"

"I know somet'ing about men. He said I was a nice person."

"Your friend in the next room, she took off on you?"

"She ain't no good. Ain't no loss."

"Why didn't you leave?"

"Seymour knows me."

"Who's Seymour?"

"The night clerk. He would have given y'all my name and I'd be in worse trouble than I am. Where's he at?"

"We're interested in the two guys in the Buick," I said. "Did they tell you their names?"

She shook her head.

"They used their first names to each other," I said. "Don't lie to us, Miss Dora."

"They're dagos out of Miami. You know what that means."

"You're not afraid of Smiley, but you're afraid of the two dead guys?" I said.

"Their kind ain't ever dead."

"Others like them are coming?"

"Sure, what you t'ink? They work for the Mob. They said they was gonna pop a guy. They said they was gonna do it for the state of Texas. I tole them they was full of it."

"Because you didn't want to believe they would do that?" I said.

"I ain't t'ought it t'rew."

"You want something to eat?"

"No," she replied. "I'm starting to get sick."

"You saw Smiley's face, Miss Dora," I said.

"If he was gonna hurt me, he would have already done it."

"He's not a predictable man."

"You lying, you. You know it, too." She rubbed at her nose with the back of her wrist.

"Stay with Detective Ribbons," I said.

I walked to the sheriff, then returned to the cruiser. The sun was above the trees now. I could see a dredge boat chugging down a canal surrounded by a sea of grass that had turned brown from saline intrusion. I leaned down to Dora's window. "How much money do you have?"

"Nothing."

"You didn't make the john pay up front?"

"Not wit' them kind."

I put a five-dollar bill into her shirt pocket. "You're free to go. Get something to eat."

"Ain't I lucky?" she said, squeezing past me. Her body smelled of nicotine and rut and booze. She looked back at me, then took the bill from her pocket and scrunched it in her palm and threw it in the wind.

AT NOON, I went to Clete Purcel's office on Main Street. The waiting room was empty, littered with cigarette butts and candy wrappers and orange rinds and a splayed sandwich with a half-moon bite taken out of it. Clete was sitting at the spool table under the beach umbrella on the concrete pad behind the office, reading the *Advocate* and drinking a bottle of Mexican beer and sucking on a salted lime. His green eyes were dulled over, as if smoke from a dirty fire were trapped inside them.

"Leaving the dock early?" I said.

"I thought about it."

"Something happen?"

He flattened the wrinkles on the front page of the newspaper with his hand. "That little creep is killing people again."

"The two guys who got it were probably hit men."

"Hit men are sane. This shit-for-brains starts gunfights in crowded casinos."

That was how Clete's former girlfriend had died, although the round had not come from Smiley's weapon.

"He could have taken out a witness," I said. "He didn't. She's a hooker named Dora Thibodaux. Know her?"

"Works out of a dump south of Morgan City?"

"She laid one of the hit men. His name was Jerry Gemoats."

Clete scraped up the newspaper and stuffed it into a trash can under the table. "Who cares?"

"The hooker seemed to think well of Wimple."

"I bet he loved his mother, too. What was the name of the hit man again?"

"Jerry Gemoats."

Clete straightened his back. "He was the go-to mechanic for any hits out of Miami. Somebody with serious money sent him here. Who was the other hitter?"

"We don't know. The car they died in was registered to Gemoats."

Clete went into his office and came back with a file folder. He dropped it onto the glass table and opened it. He tilted the beer to his mouth and chugged half the bottle, the foam sliding down the inside of the neck. I swallowed and tried to hide the knot in my throat, the sense of longing I could not get rid of. "You got a soda?"

"In the icebox."

I went inside and came back out with a can of orange-tasting carbonated water I could barely drink. The sun was like an acetylene torch on the bayou. "What's in the folder?"

"I checked with some shylocks in Vegas and Tampa. Except they don't call themselves shylocks anymore. They're 'lending institutions.' I'm not making this up. This fat fuck in Tampa probably has ten million on the street and went to the fifth grade. The vig is four points a week."

"Can you get to the point?"

He gave me a look. "Everybody I talked to said Desmond Cormier is up to his eyes in debt. Kind of like Francis Ford Coppola when he made *Apocalypse Now,* except he didn't borrow from people who do collections with chain saws. Maybe Wimple and Gemoats and the other gash hound were here to protect Cormier. The Mob can bleed Cormier for the rest of his life; plus, they love being around actors."

"Wimple was supposed to take out Tillinger and didn't, so somebody sicced the two hitters on him?"

"That'd be my bet," Clete said.

But I was not thinking about Miami button men or Smiley Wimple or the daily immersion into a sewer that constituted my livelihood. Clete followed my gaze to the sweating green bottle of Mexican beer on the table.

"Can I make an observation?" he said.

"No."

"You're falling in love with a young woman, and you think it's wrong. Stop pretending you're a monk. It's going to get you drunk again."

"Butt out, Cletus."

"I know your thoughts before you have them. You think you have to marry every woman you sleep with. Except this time she's too young. So instead of being human, you're going to do a number on your own head and get back on the dirty boogie. In the meantime, you don't let the young woman have a vote. Maybe she knows what she's doing. Who died and made you God?" He drained the bottle, his throat working, and dropped it loudly into the trash can. "You're peeling my face off."

"I wonder why."

"Search me. I think you're too sensitive."

I LEFT THE OFFICE early that afternoon and drove to Bella Delahoussaye's house. Through the houses I could see Bayou Teche and the elephant ears that undulated in the current at high tide. I was holding a bouquet of yellow roses and a music box with chocolates inside. Bella was wearing tight jeans and a pullover when she answered the door. She tilted her head. "Look at Santa Claus."

I stepped inside and handed her the roses and set the music box on the couch. " 'Jolie Blon' is on it."

"You come to court me, baby?"

"You're an extraordinary woman."

"Come here."

I stepped closer to her. She worked her sandals off by pushing one foot against the other. She stood on top of my shoes and put her arms around me and pressed the entirety of her body against mine, her face buried in my neck, her hair soft and freshly washed and air-blown and swelling against my cheek. I squeezed her in a way I had not squeezed a woman since the death of my wife.

She stepped back and touched my face. "But you ain't here to win my heart away, are you?"

"I'd like to. But you're right."

"You got a comb?"

I removed it from my back pocket and handed it to her. As a beautician might, she stroked my hair back over my head, along the sides, and through the white patch I'd carried since childhood. "I knowed when I first met you, you had the blues. You ain't got to explain anything. Sometime down the track, you need a place to park your hips, you know where I'm at."

"That's a line from Bessie Smith."

"You was born for the blues, Dave. Take care of yourself out there."

The Maltese cross glinted at her throat. She picked up my hand and kissed the back of it and pressed it on her breast, then released it and flattened her hand on my heart. Her eyes seemed to reach inside my mind. If I ever saw death in a woman's eyes, it was at that moment. But I did not know if I was looking at my reflection or hers or that of someone else I knew. She opened the door and remained standing in it as I walked to my truck. It was Indian summer, the evening sky porcelain blue, the sunlight like a cool burn. When I looked back at her cottage, the door was shut, the curtains closed. Bella Delahoussaye was the personification of Old Louisiana. I felt as though an icicle had pierced my heart.

I DROVE TO BAILEY Ribbons's home on Loreauville Road and parked in front and walked up on the gallery and tapped on the screen door. When she came to the door, she was wearing a bathrobe, a towel wrapped around her head. "What's going on?"

"I've got two tickets to Marcia Ball's performance at the Evangeline Theater tonight."

"Do I have time to dress?"

"It doesn't start until eight."

"Come in."

She left me in the living room and went into the back of the house. I didn't take a seat. I stared at nothing, the blood beating in my wrists. I could hear her opening and closing drawers. She came back in the hallway, still in her robe, her hair wet on her shoulders. "What's the real reason you're here, Dave?"

"I've never been good at self-inventory."

"Let me give you mine. I went into law enforcement because I got fired from my teaching job."

"For what?"

"I changed a black girl's grade."

"Why did you change her grade?"

"So she wouldn't be expelled."

"That sounds terrible," I said.

She stared at me, her eyes round and unblinking, a flush on her throat. "Are we going to the concert?"

"Anyone who turns down tickets to a Marcia Ball performance has a serious spiritual disorder."

"I'll be just a minute," she said.

THE CONCERT WAS wonderful. The buffet, the formal dress, the smell of the mixed drinks, the gaiety of small-town people who are overjoyed when a famous artist visits them, the location of the concert in the old Evangeline Theater, where I saw *My Darling Clementine* with my mother in 1946, seemed proof that the past is always with us, in the best way, if one will only reach out and dip his hand into it.

Afterward, I drove Bailey home in my truck. She seemed to sit closer to me than she usually did, but I couldn't be sure. The light was burning on the gallery, the shadows of the camellias and hibiscus waving on the grass. I parked on the edge of the light and cut the engine. The magnolia tree on the far end of the gallery was in late bloom, the fragrance overwhelming. Bailey sat very still, looking straight ahead. I could hear the engine's heat ticking under the hood.

"Dave?" she said.

"Yes?"

"Do you have regrets? Or rather, do you take them on easily?"

"There are several people I regret not killing."

"You have a sensitive conscience and a tender heart. Those are not always virtues."

"I'll try to be as mean-spirited as I can."

I saw a grin at the side of her mouth. "I'm weak."

"About what?"

"Need. You're a widower. You're vulnerable."

"Wrong."

She turned toward me. The tips of her dark brown hair were aglow in the moonlight. Her mouth looked like a flower about to open.

"Oh, Dave," she said.

"Oh, Dave what?"

"Just oh, Dave."

I got out of the truck and walked around the front of it. I opened her door. When she stepped out, I pulled her against me and kissed her shoulder and neck and hair and eyes. Then we walked up the steps inside, closing the door behind us, going straight down the hallway into the bedroom, leaving the light off. It felt strange being in an intimate situation with a woman other than my wife. I turned my back while she undressed.

"Dave?" she said.

The back of my neck was burning. "You have to excuse me. I'm awkward about a lot of things."

"Turn around," she said.

The moonlight fell on her through the side window. Her body had the smoothness and radiance of a Renaissance painting. "Are you going to make me feel really dumb?"

"No," I said. I took off my shirt, trousers, and socks, and we got into bed, each on a side and reaching for the other. Then I pressed her back on the pillow and kissed her on the mouth and on her eyes and on the tops of her breasts. I kissed her thighs and stomach and put her nipples into my mouth and felt her nails in my hair and her breath on my forehead and her legs widening to receive me, then I was deep inside her, the welcoming grace of her thighs embracing mine, her moans and the wet cadence of her body like the iambic beat of a rhyming couplet.

Behind the redness in my eyelids I saw a pink cave filled with gossamer fans, a wave rotating through it, sliding over heart-shaped coral covered with underwater moss that was as soft as felt, deeper and deeper, as though I were dropping through the center of the earth, then I felt my loins dissolve and the light go out of my eyes and my heart twist with such violence that I thought it would burst.

Then I was standing in a place I had seen at a distance but never stood upon. I was at the entrance of a canyon that had turned pink and then magenta, streaked with shadows as the evening sun moved across it. It was the most beautiful place I had ever seen, as though I were standing on the lip of Creation or its terminus. A woman was standing next to me. She stepped closer and enveloped me in her cloak and lay back on a bare rug atop a pine bough, and I laid my head on her breast and the two of us rose into the sun, and I closed my eyes and felt my seed go deep inside her, and I put my face between her breasts and kissed the salt on her skin and heard her heart pumping as though it were about to break.

I rose sweaty and hot from Bailey, already longing to enter her again, and for the first time in my life saw what it all meant and realized that I would never allow death to hold claim on me again, and that Bailey Ribbons had perhaps saved me from myself.

Chapter Twenty-Four

I WENT HOME THAT night and left at sunrise and drove down to Cypremort Point, where Desmond Cormier maintained his beautiful home on the tip of the peninsula, where all of this started with the body of Lucinda Arceneaux floating on a wood cross, the chop sliding across her sightless blue eyes.

Why dwell upon the image? Answer: Any homicide cop can deal with sadism or bestiality or wholesale murder when the victims are part of the culture that took their lives. But when the victims are female teenage hitchhikers on their way to New Orleans to see a concert, a young couple forced into the trunk of their own car that was set on fire by two Oklahoma psychopaths, a little boy who was anally raped before he was killed, a mother with her two daughters who trusted a boatman on vacation and were raped and tied to cinder blocks and dropped one at a time into the ocean with their mouths taped, each having to watch the fate of the other, when you see these things up close and personal, you never free yourself from them, and that's why cops pop pills and spend a lot of time at the watercooler in the morning.

These things are not generic in nature or manufactured incidents found in lurid crime novels. They all happened, and they were all the work of evil men. You can drink, smoke weed, melt your brains with downers or whites on the half-shell, or transfer to vice and become a sex addict and flush your self-respect down the drain. None of it helps. You're stuck unto the grave, in your sleep and during the waking day. And that's when you start having thoughts about summary justice—more specifically, thoughts about loading up with pumpkin balls and double-aught bucks and painting the walls.

The wind was blowing hard, straightening the palm fronds on the sides of the road, driving the waves against the blocks of broken concrete that had been dropped into the shallows to prevent the erosion of the bank. Up ahead I saw Antoine Butterworth jogging along the road in a sweatshirt and orange running shorts, his skin the metallic tone of a new penny. A cabin cruiser close in to the shore seemed to be pacing him. A man in shades and the blue coat and white trousers and white hat of a yachtsman was standing on the bow. He yelled something to Butterworth through his cupped hands, then waved goodbye.

The cabin cruiser motored away, twin exhaust pipes gurgling. I pulled abreast of Butterworth and rolled down the passenger window. "Want a lift?"

"I'm pretty sweaty," he replied, not slowing.

"Suit yourself."

I drove on to Desmond's place and parked by his porte cochere and got out. My coat was whipping in the wind, sand and seaweed rilling in waves that burst against the shore and filled the air with spray and the smell of salt. Butterworth ran up the drive and picked up a towel that hung on an outdoor shower, then wiped his armpits and the insides of his thighs. "Where's your lovely lass?"

"I didn't get that," I said. "Must be the wind."

"I said 'lass.' Detective Ribbons."

"I'll tell her you asked about her."

"I hope you're not here for me."

"Is Desmond home?"

"Fixing breakfast. Will you join us?"

"Who was the guy on the boat?"

"A tarpon fisherman out of Tampa. Why?"

"No reason. A fine-looking boat."

"You're always a man of mystery," he said.

I wondered how he had lived as long as he had. I went up the wooden steps and knocked on the front door. Desmond answered shirtless and in a pair of cargo pants, staring expectantly over my shoulder. "Hi, Dave. Bailey's not with you?"

THIS STORY STARTED with Desmond, and as I stood in his living room, I believed it would end with Desmond. I must make a confession here. Like many, I was drawn to Desmond for reasons hard to admit. He was one of us, born poor, hardly able to speak English the first day he got on the school bus, rejected for either his race or his heritage or his culture, forbidden to speak French on the school grounds. But unlike the rest of us, he had a vision, one greater than he or the world in which he was born, and he painted it as big as a sunset on the Mojave Desert.

When Ben Jonson said Shakespeare belonged to the ages, I think he was also talking about people like Desmond. Des was staring at me with a spatula in his hand, quizzical, the framed still shots from *My Darling Clementine* behind him. "You're looking at me in a peculiar fashion, Dave."

"Didn't mean to. I need to talk to you about a few things. Finances, mostly."

"No more gloom and doom. It's too fine a day. Say, how did you like the concert last night?"

"I didn't see you there," I said.

"I was in the back. Saw you with Bailey. You two aren't an item, are you?"

"How about minding your own business?"

"Sorry. I have the highest respect for you both."

Desmond was a good director but not a good actor. He was breathing through his mouth, his jaw hooked, his profile like a Roman gladiator's, his eyes pieces of stone.

"You don't approve of my being with her?" I asked.

"I don't impose my way on others," he said.

"Right. That's why you're a film director," I said.

"Let's have some breakfast. Or at least have coffee. I really admire and like you, Dave. Why won't you accept that?"

I guess his charm was another reason we envied Desmond. He wore the world like a loose cloak and could dine with paupers or kings and accept insult and acclaim with a diffidence that unsettled both his admirers and detractors. I never knew another man, either rich or poor, who achieved his degree of personal freedom.

"How about it? Some eggs and bacon?" he said.

"If you can answer a question or two," I said.

"I'll give it my best."

I followed him into the kitchen. Butterworth was on the deck, performing some kind of ridiculous martial arts exercise.

"Evidently you're in serious debt," I said.

"Hollywood runs on other people's money," he replied.

"You owe major amounts to some bad guys."

"Money is money. It's not good or bad. The issue is how you use it."

"Your big creditors are out of Jersey and Florida."

"Walt Whitman is buried in one state and Marjorie Rawlins in the other."

"Pull your head out of your ass," I said.

"Would you like two strips of bacon or three?"

I was determined not to let him shine me on. I went into his bathroom to wash my hands. There was a hypodermic in an open felt case on the lavatory. I went back into the kitchen. "I hope the needle belongs to Butterworth."

"It doesn't belong to me, if that's what you're asking."

"A juju woman told me I was wearing a ball and chain. She's probably right. But I think you're in the same club, Des."

"You know your real problem, Dave? You smear your guilt on anyone you can."

Then I said something I had not intended to say. "Bailey and I interviewed your father."

His face tightened like the skin on a shrunken head. His knuckles were white on the handle of the spatula. "Say that again?"

"His name is Ennis Patout. He owns a wrecker service outside Opelousas."

He resumed scraping eggs out of the skillet. "I never had a father. Someone may say he's my father, but he's not. Are we clear on that?"

"He seemed to have remorse about your childhood. He said you were a good little boy."

"You'd better get out of my life, Dave."

"My father was a drunk and a barroom fighter and an adulterer. But he wasn't capable of being anything else. Accept people for what they are."

Desmond turned off the stove, then pulled open the sliding doors that gave onto the deck. The wind was whistling, the waves bursting on the shoreline. "Come in, Antoine. Dave is heading back to New Iberia. Help me eat this lovely breakfast."

He was a foot from my face. I tried to hold his stare, but it was hard. His eyes seemed sightless, like none I had seen except in the faces of the dead. There was no twitch in his mouth or cheek or flutter in his throat or sign that he possessed any emotion other than hatred of the world and specifically me.

"You scare me, Des."

"I'm glad. Now get out of my house."

THAT EVENING, FALL was in the air, and I wanted to rid myself of stories about the evil that men do and the duplicitous enterprises that govern much of our daily lives. Piled leaves were burning in the gutters along East Main, the wind puffing them alight and scudding serpentine lines of fire along the asphalt. I could smell the cold autumnal odor of gas and pine needles and ponded water and lichen on stone and candles burning inside carved pumpkins. Alafair and Bailey and I ate a fine dinner on the redwood picnic table in the backyard, then went to a late movie and came home and ate bowls of ice cream and blackberries in the living room. I had almost forgotten how wonderful the life of family could be.

After Bailey was gone, Alafair said, "You and Bailey seem to be hitting it off pretty well these days."

"That's a fact."

She smiled with her eyes. I looked through the window at the sparks spiraling off the ashes of a leaf fire. "She's a nice lady," I added.

"No one could argue with that," she said. She punched me on the arm.

THE NEXT DAY was Friday. At 9:17 a.m. my desk phone rang. I don't know how, but I knew who it was, in the same way you know when you've stepped on chewing gum or when it's the knock of a paranoid neighbor who believes your cat is deliberately spraying his vegetable garden.

"Robicheaux," I answered.

"Guess who," the voice said.

"You need to go somewhere else, Mr. Tillinger," I said.

"Thought you'd be glad to hear from me."

"Those two killers in Cameron Parish almost put you out of business. Maybe it's a good time for you to visit Nebraska or Antarctica."

"If I read the newspaper right, they might be the two guys that got fried by a flamethrower. What's that tell you?"

"It doesn't tell me anything," I replied.

"I got the Man Upstairs on my side."

"You know the will and mind of God?"

"I wouldn't put it that way."

"Why are you calling me?" I said.

"Bet you've already forgotten Travis Lebeau."

"He was dragged to death on asphalt. That's a hard image to forget."

"Lebeau was in the Aryan Brotherhood, and the Aryan Brotherhood was providing the skanks that dirty cop was pimping for. Those AB boys thought they were going to be players. Didn't work out too good, did it? For the dirty cop, either."

"Axel Devereaux?"

"The one who got a baton shoved down his windpipe."

"I've got a theory about you, Mr. Tillinger. You want to be in the movies, even if it costs you your life."

"Miss Lucinda knew something that got her killed, Mr. Robicheaux." His voice had changed, like that of a man who had spent a lifetime hiding who he really was. "I talked with Desmond Cormier's father."

"You did *what*?"

"I followed you and the woman to Ennis Patout's wrecker service in Opelousas."

"You've been following Detective Ribbons and me?"

"Free country."

"Not for you it isn't," I said.

"You want to hear what Patout told me?"

I could hear my breath against the phone receiver. I wanted to hang up on him but knew I couldn't. "Yes."

"He didn't say anything except to threaten me."

"I think you have some kind of cerebral damage, partner."

"Try this. I checked birth records in the courthouses hereabouts. Patout had a daughter twenty-five years ago."

"You said 'had.'"

"That old boy didn't let race get in his way, either," Tillinger said. "Starting to put it together? See you around."

THE BLOOD VEINS in my head were dilating. I went down to Bailey's office. She was out of the building. I checked out a cruiser and headed for Opelousas. I tried to piece together all the random bits of information that showed a possible motive or pattern in the murders of Lucinda Arceneaux, Joe Molinari, Travis Lebeau, Axel Devereaux, and Hilary Bienville. Each was, in some fashion, ritualistic. Perhaps the tarot and the Maltese cross were involved. So were cruelty and rage. But as soon as I linked one homicide to a second or third, my logic would fall apart.

Lucinda Arceneaux had been injected and perhaps died without knowing she was being murdered. Yet the killer, if he was the same man, had beaten Hilary Bienville without mercy. Why her? She was a harmless uneducated woman trying to raise a child by herself and each night allowing her body to be penetrated and degraded and smeared with the fluids of unshaved men who stank of alcohol and dried sweat and filling station grease. Don't let anyone tell you prostitution is a victimless crime. The men who strike women are moral and physical cowards. Every street cop, every detective, sees violence against women with regularity, more today than in past decades. For the misogynist, women like Hilary Bienville are plump fruit waiting to be picked. My mother was the victim of men like the killer of Hilary Bienville. They appear in my dreams, their bodies naked and sweaty, their hands like the claws on crabs.

What's the point? Hilary Bienville had gone to Clete for help. She told him she was involved with a white man who had gotten inside her head and seemed to have total power over her. But she had also said something that didn't fit with the details of the homicide. Just outside Opelousas, I hit the speed dial on my cell phone.

Clete answered on the first ring. "Talk to me, big mon."

"Remember when you told me about Hilary Bienville visiting you at the motor court?"

"Yeah, she said she had a john who liked her to massage his back while he messed with her head. A white guy."

"But he told her something about herself. Something that got her even more confused."

Up ahead I saw the city limits sign and a deep-green grove of slash pines on the swale.

"He called her the Queen of Cups," Clete said. "He also called her a chalice. He said she was chosen."

"But the guy who killed her stuck a Christmas-tree star on her forehead."

"I'm not getting the connection."

"The Suit of Cups in the tarot represents love," I said. "The chalice can also mean fertility and rebirth. Bailey thinks the star represents the Suit of Pentacles."

"I still don't get it," he said.

"Pentacles has to do with prosperity. The killer was showing contempt. Hilary was a prostitute. She didn't measure up."

"I think you're getting too deep into this guy's head. You did that with the BTK guy. Bad mistake."

"How else do you explain the symbols our guy is obviously using?"

"The day you figure out these guys is the day you eat your gun."

"Quit it."

"I have a funny feeling sometimes," he said.

"About what?"

"That we're all dead and don't know it."

I took the cell phone from my ear and looked at it and then put it back.

"My exit is just ahead," I said. "Catch you down the track."

I folded the phone and dropped it on the seat before he could say anything else.

As I GOT out of the cruiser at Ennis Patout's wrecker service, I could see him playing checkers with his mechanic on top of an oil can inside the bay. He was eating a sandwich with one hand, his gaze fixed on the game, dirty fingers pressed deep into the bread. The black man looked directly at me and shook his head in a cautionary fashion.

"Hello, Mr. Patout," I said. "I'll make it quick."

Patout moved a checker with one finger. "Not quick enough."

"Hugo Tillinger came to see you?"

"Yes, sir, he did."

"What'd he have to say?"

"Nothing. I run him off."

"Did you have a daughter, Mr. Patout?"

He put down his sandwich, his eyes still on the checkerboard. His neck was as corded as a cypress stump. "You stay out of my life."

"The mother of your daughter was not the mother of Desmond Cormier?" I said.

"Louis, call up the chief of police and tell him to send an officer out here."

"Yes, suh," the black man said. He rose from his chair and went inside the office.

"You fathered a daughter with a woman of color?" I said.

Patout's eyes had the lopsided look of two egg yolks in a skillet. "What if I did?"

"I'm not judging you, sir. I need your help."

He propped his big hands on his knees and stared at a wall hung with old tires and fan belts and drop cloths and a child's bicycle that was rusted and missing one wheel. "It was twenty-five years back. The colored girl didn't want a white man's baby. At least she sure as hell didn't want mine. I went to Corina."

"Corina is Desmond's mother?"

"She said, 'Milk through the wrong fence, carry the pail home by your own self.' She was drunk and throwing things. Maybe clap got to her brain."

"If she didn't want Desmond, why would she want to raise another woman's child?"

"I thought maybe we could get back together. Shows you the kind of fool I was." He pointed at the bicycle on the wall. "I bought that for Desmond and tried to give it to his grandparents. They told me to begone. Anyone ever say that to you?"

"No, sir," I replied. "Mr. Patout, there's something missing from your account. Why did Desmond's mother bear you such hostility? Why would the grandparents be angry with you when you were trying to do the right thing? The same with the black woman who had your child."

"You got to ask them."

"Did you force yourself on the black woman?"

He folded his hands, then squeezed one hand with the other. "A man has needs."

"You raped her?"

"I didn't think of it that way."

"And you did the same with Desmond's mother?"

"That's what she told others. But it was a goddamn lie." He took a blue bandana out of his overalls and blew his nose on it. "I don't want to talk no more."

"What happened to your little girl?"

"Church people took her."

"What happened to the mother?"

"Killed herself."

He stared at his steel-toed shoes, his fingers spread like banana peels on his thighs. I pulled the mechanic's chair close to him and sat down. "You owned up. Over the years you did what you could. Tell the Man on High you're sorry, then fuck the rest of it."

"I'd appreciate it if you'd leave," he said, the words deep in his throat.

"Who are the church people, Mr. Patout?"

"I heard she ended up with a colored preacher and his wife in Cade, just outside New Iberia."

"What's the name of the preacher?"

"I never got his name."

"You've been forthcoming. Don't ruin it by lying."

"Arceneaux. Her name was Lucinda Arceneaux."

He raised his eyes to mine. If there's a hell, I believe I could have reached out and touched its heat on his cheek.

Chapter Twenty-Five

THE NEXT DAY was Saturday. I woke in the blueness of the dawn to a sound that I thought came from a dream. In the dream, Negro convicts of years ago were laying track on a railroad line outside Angola Farm. They were wearing ankle chains and driving steel spikes through the rails into the railroad bed, their hammers ringing in three-four time.

I sat up and looked out the back window. Lou Wexler, stripped to the waist, his shirt hanging on a camellia bush, was tossing horseshoes at a steel spike he had obviously driven into the ground without asking. I put on my khakis and a sweatshirt and went outside. "Do you invite yourself into everyone's backyard at six in the morning, or are we just lucky?"

"Sorry," he said. "I'm supposed to pick up Alafair at six-fifteen and I arrived a little early. She didn't tell you?"

"No."

"We're having breakfast at Victor's."

"What does that have to do with waking up other people? I don't want a horseshoe pit in my yard, either."

"Felicitously noted, sir."

"Felicitously?"

He turned his head sideways, grinning. "We're filming a plane crash at Lake Martin later in the day. Exciting stuff. Why not come out?"

"Thank you. All booked up."

"At heart I think you're one of us."

"Say again?"

He offered me a stick of gum. I shook my head. He stuck one into his mouth as though we had all the time in the world. He seemed to wear sensuality like a uniform. His body had the same smooth tone and flat stomach and small nipples as Desmond's; his armpits were shaved, his upper arms swollen like those of a gymnast. Mon Tee Coon and Snuggs stared down at us from an oak limb overhead.

"You said I'm like one of you."

"Oh," he said. "You obviously love movies. The same with Mr. Purcel. We're not a bad lot. Give us a chance. We're making this area rich."

"I don't see that."

"We blew the budget out the window. One hundred and twenty million dollars, and the meter is still running. Desmond is broke. By the way, on the subject of Des, you sure got to him."

"In what way?" I said.

"Something to do with his background, I guess. Des is full of secrets. I don't probe them."

"Any discussion I had with him was about a series of homicides. Nothing else."

"I'm sure that's the case, Mr. Robicheaux. Sir, it's not my intention to offend. The culture I live in is garish and abrasive by nature. We spend our time diddling each other to keep our minds off other things."

"What would those others things be?"

"Growing old. Watching our looks dissolve. Pretending we can reclaim our youth. Is there any fool like an old fool, sir?" he said.

"Who are you talking about, podna?"

"Me. Who else?" He picked up a horseshoe and flipped it thirty feet onto the steel pin, his movements as fluid as water. "Bingo! Is Alafair up?"

THIRTY MINUTES AFTER they were gone, the phone rang on the kitchen counter. I looked at the caller ID. The caller's number was blocked, but I answered anyway. "Dave Robicheaux. Who is this?"

"I hope I didn't wake you up," a mewing voice said.

"Smiley?"

"I'm glad you called me that. Because that's what all my friends call me."

"I saw what you did to those guys in Morgan City. You're a piece of work."

"I watched you."

"Say again?"

"I watched you through binoculars. You and the pretty lady you work with. I can read lips. Y'all were very nice to the lady who sells herself."

I felt dizzy. I pulled up a chair and sat down. "Let me explain something to you. You're a hired assassin. I'm a sheriff's detective. People like me put people like you in institutions. Sometimes we send them to the injection table. People like you don't call up people like me to pass the time of day."

"You don't have to get smart-alecky about it."

"Those two guys were hitters out of Florida, right?"

"Now they're not anything."

"Why'd you kill them?"

"They did mean things to me." I could hear his breath increasing. "One of them used a stick."

"That makes you a target now, doesn't it?"

"No."

"You fry two mobbed-up guys and you're not a target?"

"The bad people who come after me are the target. They need to be protected from me, Detective Robicheaux."

"You're one in a million, Smiley." I looked at my watch. Trying to trace his call was a waste of time. He used an ingenious relay system and seemed to know an enormous amount about technology. The same with ordnance and ballistics. "Why'd you call?"

"Tell Mr. Purcel I'm sorry about the detective lady who died at the casino in New Or-yuns."

"She didn't 'die.' She was killed."

"By somebody else's bullet. It was not from my gun."

"You started a gun battle in a public place. Other people paid the price."

"You're talking bad to me. You stop it."

"That's because you're starting to make me mad, Smiley."

"My tummy hurts. You're upsetting me"

"I don't mean to. An evil man broke up my family when I was a kid. I went to Vietnam and got even. Understand what I'm saying?"

"You killed people?"

I felt my throat closing. "To be honest, I don't feel like talking about it."

"They were soldiers?" he said.

"Most of them. Maybe—"

"Maybe what?" he said.

"I killed people accidentally. Or I gave orders that led to the death of IPs."

"Death of what?"

"Innocent People."

I could hear him breathing against the receiver. In my mind's eye, I saw a face with tiny nostrils and eyes that were unreadable and a mouth searching for a teat.

"You still with me?" I said.

"Then you're not much different from me."

"Wrong, Smiley."

"Are you saying I'm not your friend anymore?"

"No, sir. I didn't say that at all."

He was silent, as though sifting through his thoughts or rebuilding his fortifications. "I'll be close by. Maybe we can work together."

"That's not going to happen."

"Owie," he said.

"What happened?"

"A man just stepped on my foot. He mashed my toe. Hey, come here, you!"

"No, Smiley. Don't do that. Leave other people alone. Did you hear me? If you want to be my friend, you can't hurt other people anymore."

"Fooled you," he said. "Bye-bye. You're a nice man."

I wanted to smash the phone.

I HOOKED MY BOAT trailer onto my truck and drove to Clete's cottage at the motor court. An old problem had come back to me, one that I used to treat with four fingers of Jack and a beer back. I felt as though someone had extinguished a hot cigarette on my eyelids. It's part of the pucker syndrome. Haven't heard of it? It's a level of anxiety you'd eat glass to get rid of. Think about a column of men going down a night trail, rain clicking on their steel pots. The trail is sown with 105 duds or toe poppers or bouncing Betties. You feel as though your skin is being peeled from the bone by a pair of pliers. You wait for the *klatch* under a man's boot or the *ping* of a trip wire, and you fear your insides will turn to water and your sphincter to jelly. To up the ante, Sir Charles blindly fires a grenade with a captured blooker into the jungle, showering dirt and water on the canopy of trees. Your rectum has constricted to the size of a pencil head. That's the pucker syndrome.

Clete was washing his Caddy in front of his cottage. He squeezed out the sponge and dropped it into a bucket. "You look a little wired."

"You got a Dr Pepper?"

"Inside."

I got one out of his icebox and came back out. I told him about Smiley's call.

"Blow it off," he said. "Wimple is on third base and knows it."

"He doesn't bother me. He only kills people from his own culture."

"So what's the problem, noble mon?"

"The guy who killed Lucinda Arceneaux will try to outdo himself."

"You got the blue meanies, big mon. They go away."

"With a fifth of vodka, they do."

He looked at my boat trailer. "Want to entertain the fish?"

• • •

WE PUT THE boat in at Henderson Levee and shoved off. It was sac-a-lait season, the weather cool and sunny, the sky the same hard blue you see in Montana that time of year. On one flooded island, the swamp maples had turned red and the leaves on the cypress looked exactly like green lace transforming into gold, all of it infused with a glow that seemed to radiate from inside the tree. I eased the anchor down into the silt and felt the stern swing us tight in the current, then hooked a shiner on the end of my line and lobbed the line and bobber and baited hook into a cove ringed with water hyacinths.

Clete was chugging a bottle of Japanese beer, the sunlight dancing inside it.

"Where'd you get that?" I asked.

"A Fujiyama mama I met in the Quarter. She told me she was here with a television crew, except she was staying in a dump off Airline Highway."

I didn't say anything. I knew more was coming.

"I was in pretty bad shape when I left in the morning. She gave me a box of Japanese booze. I told her I'd pay her for it. She said, 'You already pay.' When I got home, I discovered my wallet was empty."

"When are you going to grow up?"

"What's the big deal? It's all rock and roll."

I had given up trying to argue with Clete. He was unteachable and incapable of change, and probably the only man I ever knew whose innate goodness was so intense, he could walk through evil and not be blighted by it.

"Dave, here's the long and short of it," he said. He flung a Rapala in a high arc and watched it splash, then began retrieving it past the tip of the island, the lure swimming like a wounded minnow. "We're different in a way you won't admit. I grew up in a rathole in the Irish Channel. I joined the Crotch to get out of New Orleans. You grew up in a world of sugarcane fields and thousands of ducks flying over and people going to the *fais do-do*. That world has pretty much slid down the pipe."

"I think I figured that out, Clete."

"You still don't get it. You see the oak trees getting cut down, the marsh disappearing, the trash in the water and the ditches, the politicians chugging pud for anybody with a checkbook, the 'I don't give a fuck' attitude. But you keep waiting on something to happen that will be so bad, people will see the error of their ways and start doing things differently. Like a big AA meeting. You said it yourself: The Great Whore of Babylon doesn't go to meetings."

"You're saying I want the equivalent of a hydrogen bomb to be dropped on the state I love?"

"That comes close."

"Thanks for the insight."

"No problemo, big mon."

I could have gone on and quietly mocked his logic, but I was the one who had spoken disingenuously. I knew the real reason Clete had ended up in the sack with an Asian woman. The love of his life was a beautiful Vietnamese girl who lived on a sampan at the edge of the South China Sea. She was murdered by the Vietcong because she slept with a good-hearted jarhead whose father had beaten him almost every day of his life with a razor strop.

"What are you thinking about?" Clete said.

"Nothing."

"I didn't mean all that stuff about everything ending. It's never the last waltz. Not unless you want it to be."

I wasn't listening. Through the flooded trees, I saw a glint like a reflection off a telescope or maybe a scoped rifle. Then it was gone.

"You see something?" Clete asked.

"Yeah. You got your binoculars?"

"My opera glasses." He took them out of his tackle box and handed them to me. "What is it?"

I focused the glasses and moved them back and forth across the willows and tupelos and gum trees. "Maybe a guy."

"What do you mean, maybe?"

Through a clear spot I could see a rotting oil platform, egrets, and a stray pelican flying low across the water, then a man standing in an outboard in the shallows, wearing a windbreaker and a slouch hat, his face shadowed. He had the butt of a rifle propped on his hip. The rifle was scoped.

I started the engine. "Pull the anchor. There's a guy inside the trees with a scoped bolt-action."

"Isn't it deer season?"

"Not with regular firearms."

Clete pulled the anchor and clunked it into the bow. We headed around the island. The outboard was gone, but we could hear its drone across the water, perhaps from a channel that led into another bay. I cut our engine. Now the only sound was the chop against the hull.

"You see his face?" Clete said.

"No."

"Is it still alligator season?"

"Yeah, it is."

"So don't worry about it," Clete said. "Right?"

"This is a fishing area, not a target range."

"So it was a jerkoff who has his gun mixed up with his dork."

But we both knew better. Nobody hunts gators with scoped rifles, and no person of goodwill looks through the scope at another individual. I restarted the engine and we headed home, the wind in our faces, ten degrees colder now, like a slow burn on the skin.

I SHOWERED AND WENT to Bailey's house, hoping we could have a late dinner. She had gone shopping in Lafayette and told me she expected to be home by eight.

It was almost nine. I called her cell phone twice and went directly to voicemail. I sat on the gallery and waited. Then I began to go places in my head I probably shouldn't have. Or at least that's what I felt at the time.

I could not explain away the presence of the man with the bolt-action rifle on the flooded island. Clete and I had enemies. Every cop does. But few of them seek revenge. I witnessed the electrocution of two murderers I helped convict, partly out of duty, partly at their request. Neither of them bore me enmity. None of my past experience as a detective in New Orleans or New Iberia had been any help in solving the series of murders connected with the tarot or the Maltese cross. What was the motivation? That was the big one. The old saw money wasn't working.

How about someone who had declared war on something much larger than he was, a misanthrope with the vision of Captain Ahab in his pursuit of the white whale? The kind of man who wanted to destroy beauty and goodness whenever he found it? That brought to mind the image of a man firing out of a resort window in Las Vegas.

Or maybe he was the kind of man who hated others so much he would kill their friends or loved ones so the real target would suffer daily for the rest of his or her life. I thought again of the damage done to the body of Hilary Bienville.

I called Bailey a third time. No answer. I called Alafair at the house.

"Hi, Dave," she said.

"You okay, Alfie?"

"Don't call me that dumb name."

"Are you okay?"

"Sure. What's going on?"

"I'm just checking."

"Where are you?"

"In front of Bailey's house. I don't know where she is. She said she would be back from Lafayette by eight."

"You know how the traffic is."

"What did you do today?"

"We quit the shoot early and I played tennis with Des at Red's."

"When did you start hanging out with Desmond?"

"He's in the dumps. They're going broke. Lou is and so is Antoine. They borrowed against their homes and their video business. Dave, I know you're not sympathetic, but how many people would risk everything they own to create an epic film that will probably bomb?"

"I saw a guy with a scoped rifle at Henderson Swamp. I think he was looking at me and Clete through the scope."

"Why didn't you say that?"

"I don't know who it was. Maybe it was just a guy."

"Maybe it was Smiley Wimple," she said.

"Smiley doesn't have a beef with either Clete or me. So that means for now we don't trust anyone. Got it?"

"That's a little broad."

"Did you hear me?"

"Copy that. Where are you going now?"

"I'm not sure," I said.

But I was lying.

Chapter Twenty-Six

THE BLUES CLUB on the bayou was packed, bodies pressed one against the other, people shouting in order to hold an ordinary conversation, the band blowing the joint down with Clifton Chenier's "Ay-Te Te Fee." I squeezed my way to the bar. Lloyd, the indignant black bartender with the small head, waited silently for me to order.

"Bella Delahoussaye!" I shouted.

"What?" he shouted back.

"Where's Bella?"

He looked at the bandstand. "She ain't here!"

"Where is she?"

"Running late! Like always!" he shouted. "What you want, man?"

"Half a barbecue chicken, double dirty rice, and a diet Dr Pepper!"

Ten minutes passed. Still no Bella. The bartender brought my food on a paper plate with a napkin and a plastic fork and knife. The noise was getting louder. My head was coming off.

"Where's the Dr Pepper?" I shouted.

"I tole you, this ain't a soda fountain!" the bartender replied. He walked away. A big man who looked familiar sat down next to me.

"Watch my food, will you?" I said.

I worked my way outside and checked the parking lot. I didn't have Bella's phone number and had no way to contact her except to call the city police in St. Martinville and ask the dispatcher to send a car to her cottage. I didn't think Bella would appreciate the gesture. I went back inside and sat down. I could see Sean McClain sitting at a table below the bandstand. He was with several other young people and drinking a beer from a bottle.

"Find what you were looking for?" the man next to me said.

I looked at him. His face was as generic and uninteresting as a shingle. "I know you?"

"You came into my former place of employment in St. Martinville."

I had to think. "Harvey?"

"You got a good memory."

"You never heard of Evangeline. You called me 'asshole' and 'fuckball.' "

"I was having an off night. You were acting weird on top of it. Sorry about the asshole and fuckball references. You come here often?"

"No," I said. "I'm waiting on Bella Delahoussaye."

"The black gal with the magical fingers?"

"Pardon?" I said.

"The way she plays guitar. She's got magic."

I started eating. I tried to catch the bartender's eye.

"What'd you think I meant?" Harvey asked.

"Nothing," I replied.

He saw me trying to get the bartender's attention. "What do you need?"

"My drink."

"The bartender here's got an attitude." He tapped his knuckles on the bar.

"He's all right," I said. "Let him alone."

The front door opened and a clutch of people came in. In the center was a slender ebony-skinned woman wearing an African head wrap and a sleeveless turquoise and gold dashiki, her body clicking with beads and chains and bracelets. I got up and clamped my hand onto Harvey's shoulder. "You're on guard duty again."

The woman was not Bella. I stopped by Sean McClain's table. He stood up to shake hands. His friends smiled. "I didn't know you hung out here, Dave."

"Not really. Just tonight," I said.

"Everything okay?"

"Sure."

"Want to join us?" he said.

"Thanks," I said. "Nice seeing y'all."

I went back to the bar. A soda cup filled to the brim had been placed next to my plate. "Where'd that come from?"

"I told him to get on it. He said he didn't have Dr Pepper. I asked him if he had Coca-Cola. Between you and me, I think the guy's got a racial problem. Better eat up."

"You paid for the Coke?"

"Big deal."

I looked at the doorway. No Bella. I could feel a sensation like a guitar string tightening around my head. I filled a fork with chicken and dirty rice. It was cold and tasted like confetti. I lifted the cup to my lips and tilted back my head. I felt the Coca-Cola and crushed ice slide over my tongue and down my throat. But something else was in the cup. What had I done? Did I not recognize the smell, the golden glow inside the barrel the whiskey was aged in, the cool fire that lit my loins and caused me to close my eyes with release and surrender, as though a treacherous lover had returned from long ago for another go-round between the sheets?

I set the cup down on the bar, harder than I should have, perhaps more in pretense than in alarm.

"You dig Jack, right?" Harvey said. "He didn't have Dr Pepper. So I told the guy to give you Coke and Jack. What's with you?"

"Everything."

"Tell you what, I'm outta here. Keep a good thought. Buy yourself a condo in Crazy Town. I also take back my apology for calling you asshole and fuckball."

He spun off the stool and walked away in the crowd. My left hand was on the cup. I felt its coldness seeping into my fingers. For a drunk, a moment like this produces the same sensation as coitus interruptus. I raised the cup, then put it down again. I had never wanted to drink so badly in my life, even when I was on the grog full-time and would wake with a thirst so great I would have committed a serious crime to quench it.

I got off the stool and worked my way through the crowd onto the porch and then into the parking lot. In the distance I could see the lights of the sugar mill, the smoke from the stacks an electrified white against a black sky. I wanted to be on a cane wagon in the year 1945, safe with my parents, far removed from the metabolic addiction that had been my undoing since I was sixteen. I heard someone walk on the gravel behind me.

"You have trouble with that guy, Dave?" Sean said.

"It was a misunderstanding."

"You don't look right."

"I'm off my feed. I'm okay."

"You want me to drive you home?"

"I think Bella Delahoussaye is in danger."

"The lady in the band?"

"I think she may be a target of the guy who killed Lucinda Arceneaux."

"Oh, man," he said. "Bring your truck around. I'll tell my friends."

It's funny how a simple kid like Sean McClain can make you proud to be an American.

IT BEGAN TO rain as we rolled into the black district of St. Martinville. The streets were wet and shiny, the streetlamps oily inside the mist. Up ahead I could see yellow pools of lightning in the clouds high above the town square.

"I got to ask you something," Sean said. "Hit me upside the head, if you want."

"What is it?"

"Was you drinking back there at the club?"

"I took a swig out of a drink I didn't order."

He stared through the wipers on the windshield. A streetlight cast shadows that looked like rainwater on his face.

"You don't believe me?" I said.

"It's kind of like saying you didn't know what the food was on your plate." He looked at me to see how I would take it, then looked away.

"You carrying?" I asked.

"On my ankle. I didn't mean no offense."

"I know that, Sean. You're a good guy."

Yes, he was, and I wished I had not brought him along. Think back on your life. How many major decisions did you actually make? Or better put, how many decisions did you make that at the time seemed inconsequential but down the track had enormous influence on either you or others?

I pulled to the curb in front of Bella's cottage. A solitary lamp shone behind a window curtain. Her roof gutters were clogged with pine needles and Spanish moss and spilling over on the walls and windows. I heard Sean unstrap the Velcro holster on his ankle.

"Stick it in the back of your belt," I said.

"Think I'm a hothead?"

I cut the engine. "In the right circumstances, everyone's a hothead."

We got out in the rain. I had put on a hat. The rain ticked on the brim and blew in my face. Sean wiped his eyes. "Want me to head around back?"

"Stay behind me."

"Somebody give you a tip on this, Dave?"

"No. No one. It's just a feeling."

"Say that again?"

I walked ahead of him. I had clipped my nine-millimeter on my belt. I tapped on the screen door and waited. There was no movement inside the house. Through the curtains I could see a lamp on a table by one end of the couch. I thought I could make out a shadowy figure at the far end, but I couldn't be sure. The buildings on both side of Bella's cottage were dark, the thick banana plants under her eaves impossible to see through. A bolt of lightning popped on the bayou, illuminating the yard like a flashbulb: The banana plants were as yellow as old teeth and streaked with black mold. Then the yard was dark again. I opened the screen and knocked hard on the inside door.

"I'm going around back," Sean said.

"No," I said.

"Barricaded suspect."

"No," I repeated.

"That's the protocol."

I reached for his arm. "Give it a minute. Don't do anything you don't need to do."

He pulled away from me. "You're wrong on this, Dave. I'm going around back."

How do you convince a kid in the middle of an electrical storm that an unannounced nocturnal police visit to a neighborhood, particularly a black one, produces fear, and that fear gets people killed?

He looked over his shoulder to assure me. "I got this covered." He stepped into the middle of the yard, his hand tucked around the butt of the hideaway resting inside the back of his belt, the rain beading on his face. The clouds flared again, and a man who had been hiding in the banana plants bolted for the street. It made no sense. If the man feared us, why didn't he run for the alley? Then I remembered that access to the alley was sealed off by a wood fence between Bella's cottage and the neighbor's house.

"Police officer! Halt!" Sean said. He pulled his piece from his belt and pointed it in front of him with both hands. It was a .22 semi-auto.

"Hold on, Sean!"

"Son of a bitch has a gun."

"Let him go, let him go, let him go."

"The motherfucker has a gun. I saw it."

"Lower your weapon!" I shouted at Sean.

The figure turned in the middle of the street; I don't know why. Maybe he was trying to surrender. But he held his right arm straight out in front of him. Perhaps he was trying to show that he had a gun and was going to set it down. How do you put yourself inside the head of an armed faceless man who can park a pill in the middle of your face with a cat's-whisker pull on the trigger?

"Drop it! You hear me? Drop it!" Sean shouted. "Don't think about it! Do it! Do it! Do it!"

I saw the man's wrist start to turn downward. Maybe he was going to set his weapon slowly on asphalt so it wouldn't discharge. I had my badge out and was holding it so it reflected the streetlamp. I felt the situation begin to correct itself. "Just lower your weapon slowly and set it down and step away from it. We'll all go home safe."

I thought I saw the man's knees start to bend. I thought I saw a smile of recognition on his face. But I also saw the barrel of the Luger tilt upward as he started to squat down.

Sean starting shooting, pop-pop-pop-pop, four or five or maybe seven rounds, I couldn't count them. The bolt on his .22 semi-auto locked open on an empty chamber.

The man with the Luger went straight down like a puppet released from its strings.

"Fuck!" Sean said.

I stepped off the curb. A car was coming down the street, its headlights sweeping across us. Hugo Tillinger was on his back, wearing a suit coat over a T-shirt, his face unshaved. His body looked like a broken question mark. There were two entry wounds in his throat, one in his chest, and one above his ear. His hand fluttered at his throat. A large red bubble issued from his mouth. The Luger lay by his side. I pushed it away with my foot and squatted down, my knees aching.

"Where's Bella?" I said.

His eyes closed and opened.

"Answer me. What did you do to her?"

He shook his head. His teeth were red. A guttural word was trying to climb out of his voice box.

Sean was standing beside me. "Dave, I didn't want to do it."

I pulled him away from Tillinger. "Now's not the time for it."

"I begged him to drop it. I never drew down on anybody."

"Put your piece away."

"Yes, sir."

"There's an emergency kit behind my front seat. Get the reflectors and the flashlight and flares and light up the street. The first-aid kit is under the seat. I'm going inside."

"Dave, I didn't want to. You know that, right? He's gonna make it, isn't he?"

"Listen to me. He dealt it. It was a righteous shoot," I said. "I saw him raise the gun. You identified yourself and told him to drop his weapon. He refused the command. Your life was in danger. Say that last part back to me."

"My life was in danger?"

"Say it again."

"My life was in danger."

"End of story. You copy?"

"Yes, sir."

"Get a bandage on his throat."

I got out my cell and called in the ambulance request and the shots-fired as I walked around to Bella's back door. I draped a handkerchief over my hand and, with my thumb and one finger, turned the knob. The door was unlocked. Gas was hissing from the burners and oven. I clicked on my penlight. Bella's acoustic guitar was on the floor, the sound box stomped into kindling, the neck broken in half, the bridge and strings a rat's nest. A candle in a red votive was flickering in an open cupboard. I pinched out the candle, turned off the gas, and broke out the windows with a skillet.

I walked into the living room and picked up the lamp on the table by the couch and held it above my head, sending the shadows back into the walls. Bella was sitting on the far end of the couch, her hands in her lap, her wrists fastened with ligatures, each of her eyes X-ed with tape. Her head rested on her shoulder as though she had dozed off on a streetcar in New Orleans at the end of the day. Except this was not New Orleans and she was not on a streetcar and her neck had been broken and a long-stemmed brass chalice with a rose in it had been fitted into her hands.

I called Bailey on my cell phone. "Need you in St. Martinville, two blocks south of the square. Bella Delahoussaye has been murdered. Sean McClain put at least four rounds in Hugo Tillinger."

"How did this happen? I mean, about Sean."

"I'll tell you when you get here."

"Tillinger is the perp?" she said.

"I don't know. The gas was on. A candle was burning ten feet away."

"You think he did burn his family to death and was doing a repeat?"

"That's why I need you up here."

"You okay?"

"The killer put her in ligatures, taped her eyes so she looks like a cartoon character, and broke her neck."

Bailey arrived twenty minutes later. The medics were loading Tillinger in the back of their unit. Bailey came up the steps, wearing khakis and half-topped boots and a kerchief tied on her head, her badge hanging from a cord around her neck. The St. Martin detectives had already been through the cottage. The coroner was out of town. Bailey pulled on her latex and squatted down so she could look directly into Bella's face. She stood up and lifted the hair off the back of Bella's neck.

"No contusions or bruising except for one abrasion on the left side, like a necklace or chain was torn off it," she said. "I think whoever killed her hooked one arm around her head and snapped the vertebrae. He either has military training or has done it before."

"The last time I saw her, she was wearing a Maltese cross," I said.

"Like Hilary Bienville?"

"Yes."

"Who killed her, if it wasn't Tillinger? There was no one else around, correct?"

"No one we saw."

"So why was he here?"

I shook my head.

"What happened with Sean?" she said.

"Later."

Two St. Martin detectives in suits were standing in the doorway.

One was smoking a cigarette. At my request, they had waited to remove the body.

"Say, if you guys have a Ziploc, I'll bag the chalice and the rose for you guys," Bailey said.

The detective who was smoking flipped his cigarette into the yard. "There on the front seat of the cruiser. Knock yourself out."

"Thanks. Oh, flag your cigarette butts, will you?" she said. "I'd hate for the guys at the lab to get your DNA mixed up with a homicidal maniac's. You guys didn't use the toilet, did you?"

They stared at her as they would a space creature. I put a Ziploc in her hand. She removed the chalice and the rose from Bella's fingers and slipped it inside.

"He made her the Queen of Cups," she said. "Hilary Bienville didn't meet the standard, so he substituted this poor lady for his sacrificial offering."

"What does the rose mean?" I said.

"A Freudian would probably say it's sexual. But nobody listens to Freud anymore. What's in the rest of the house?"

"He destroyed her guitar in the kitchen."

"Any sign of forced entry?"

"No."

"So he probably knew her. He taped her eyes because he's a coward. He used X's to degrade her. He bears animus toward the arts or music or creativity. He left the gas on and a candle burning so the house would blow up."

"What are you saying?"

"I think this has Tillinger's stamp on it," she said.

"Because Tillinger tore heavy-metal posters off his daughter's wall?"

"Because the state of Texas believes he burned up his family."

"Earlier today Clete and I saw a guy with a rifle in a boat. He was looking at us through a telescopic sight."

Her eyes roved over my face. "Want me to take it from here?"

"You think I'm imagining things?"

She put her arm in mine. "Walk with me."

We went into the kitchen together. The wind was blowing through the windows I had broken, the linoleum shiny with glass. "How well did you know the woman?"

"Well enough."

"You won't hurt my feelings."

"She was an artwork, a Creole Venus rising from the sea with a guitar hanging around her neck."

"I smelled alcohol on Sean."

"He's a one-beer kid. It wasn't a factor."

"I also smell it on you."

"I picked up a drink by mistake."

She ran her hand down my arm and wrist and squeezed my hand and pressed her forehead against my shoulder. "If Tillinger didn't do this, we'll find the guy who did and gut him from his liver to his lights and hang him on a fence post. I promise you."

THE AMBULANCE DROVE away with Tillinger. The plainclothes who'd flipped his cigarette in the yard was Jody Dubisson. He wore sideburns and had hair that looked like a black plastic wig, and chewed gum constantly and probably had something wrong with his wiring, but he wasn't a bad guy. "The perp was trying to tell me something. I put my notebook and a felt-tip in his hand."

"We don't know he's the perp," I said.

"Yeah, Spider-Man probably did it. Want to take a look?"

I opened the cover of the notebook. Tillinger had scrawled "AB" and "PRO" and "UNC" and "JAIL" on the first page.

"Mean anything to you?" Dubisson said.

" 'AB' could stand for Aryan Brotherhood. The rest of it could mean anything."

He handed me two sticks of gum. "One for you and one for the kid." He raised his eyes to mine. "Get me?"

"Alcohol wasn't a factor in the shooting."

"Did I say it was? You look like shit."

"It's part of my mystique."

"Your what?" he asked.

"Did you know Bella?"

"Saw her a couple of times on the street. She was a juju woman or something?"

I looked at the sky. It was roiling with black clouds. "I like to think she's with the stars."

"You're a funny guy, Robicheaux."

I put my finger on the first page of his notebook. "Can I have that?"

"You can copy it. This is our collar."

Chapter Twenty-Seven

AT 10:17 ON Monday morning, Helen came down to my office. "I just got off the phone with the authorities in Texas. Guess what?"

"They're no longer in a hurry to get Tillinger back," I said.

"How'd you know?"

"His medical care could run into millions."

She pulled up a chair. "Go over everything again."

I did as she said. Helen was a good cop, in my experience second only to Clete Purcel, and not someone you took over the hurdles. But I didn't want Sean McClain hurt worse than he already was.

"You left a bar and went to Delahoussaye's house because you had a feeling?" she said.

"That's correct."

"You know how that will sound to others?"

"That's their problem."

"Sean McClain had been drinking at the club?"

"He wasn't impaired."

"How about you?"

"I picked up a cup I shouldn't have," I said.

Her jaw tightened.

"Here's the long and short of the shooting," I said. "Tillinger pointed his weapon at us. Sean told him to drop it over and over."

"Tillinger pointed his gun *at* you or in your direction?"

"That's too fine a distinction," I said.

"I think you're holding back on me."

She was right. Tillinger probably had thought I was in his corner. He was probably going to lower the weapon and place it on the asphalt. There may have even been a smile on his face. Then Sean had started firing. Maybe if he had waited two seconds more, the Luger would have been on the asphalt and Tillinger would have had his hands in the air.

"I wish I hadn't taken Sean with me," I said. "If it's on anybody, it's on me."

"It's an imperfect world, bwana. But we're stuck with it."

"Anything else?"

"St. Martin Parish thinks this is open and shut," she said.

"Based on what?"

"Tillinger was at the scene with a gun in his hand. That might be a clue."

"Were there prints on the chalice?" I asked.

"No."

"Did Tillinger have gloves on his person?"

"Jody Dubisson says he's still looking," she said.

"This is a crock and you know it," I said.

"Simple people like straight lines."

"I think Tillinger was carrying the Luger to protect Bella, not to take her life."

"How would Tillinger know the killer was headed to her place?"

"Maybe Tillinger was following him. He probably would have made a good cop. Helen, Tillinger is a human being. The guy we're dealing with doesn't have a category."

My notebook was open on the desk blotter. She looked at the copy I had made of Tillinger's attempt to identify the killer. "What do you make of that?"

"I think the Aryan Brotherhood is a player," I said. "Maybe there's a link between them and our jail scandal. Maybe 'UNC' means 'University of North Carolina' or 'uncle.' Maybe 'PRO' means 'producer.' You can go into meltdown thinking about all this."

"Let's go back to our jail scandal," she said. "What's the link between it and the murder of Lucinda Arceneaux?"

I shook my head, my eyes neutral.

"Don't give me that," she said. "I know you, Dave."

"I don't have any answers," I said. "I wish I did."

She waited a long time before she spoke again. "Any word from Iberia General?"

"The neurologist said the inside of Tillinger's head is egg batter."

She looked at the pad again. "I'd like to kick Sean McClain in the butt."

"He's a good kid."

"But he messed up royally." She paused. I knew she wanted to say more, all of it bad.

"I messed up, too," I said.

She scratched her forearm, her face empty. Then she got up and stood behind my chair. I never knew what Helen would do when she was behind me. Sometimes her silence scared me. As I've said, several people lived inside her, some dangerous, some adventurous, some erotic and almost predatory. People talk about coming out of the closet. Helen had a warehouse the size of a city block to come out of. She gripped my shoulders, sinking her fingers into the tendons. I could smell the freshness in her clothes, almost feel the heat in her body.

"There are two people in this world who know every thought you have, Pops," she said. "One of them is Clete Purcel. Guess who the other is?"

"No idea," I replied.

"What's Bailey think?"

"Our guy is a trophy killer in reverse. Or maybe he has boxes of panties and bras and wallets. He'll keep doing it until we burn his kite."

She drew a fingernail across my neck. "Go out on your own and I'll have your head in a basket."

"I'll look forward to it," I said.

I WASN'T DOING WELL with Bella's death. I went to a noon meeting, owned up to an accidental slip—although I wasn't sure it was entirely accidental and said so—and dropped by St. Edward's Church, and I still wasn't doing well. I went back to the department and talked with Bailey, who was getting nowhere on the forensics with the St. Martin authorities, primarily because there weren't any; then I called Clete Purcel and told him everything and arranged to meet him in Red Lerille's Health and Racquet Club at five-thirty p.m.

When I walked into the gym, Clete was hitting the heavy bag, whamming it on the chain with sky-blue bag gloves, wearing baggy knee-length red Everlasts and a sleeveless gray LSU jersey soggy with sweat. He smelled like an elephant in rut.

"Big mon," he said, steadying the bag.

"You got something for me?" I said.

"A kid named Spider Dupree. He did a three-bit in Soledad. The AB made him give back his ink. They did a few other things to him, too. Let me hit the shower."

"Think you need it?"

"I shower if I need it or not."

Twenty minutes later, I met him at the juice bar. His hair was neatly combed, his face glowing and youthful, his slacks and shirt pressed. For just a moment, in the soft pastel lighting, he looked like the cop I walked a beat with in the Quarter, when both of us were sure we would never die. We ordered two fruit drinks, a sprig of mint stuck in the shaved ice.

I looked around. "Where's your man?"

"We're meeting him at a biker joint at seven." Clete wiped at a nostril with one knuckle. "Dave, I got to have some assurances on this."

"On what?"

"What you're thinking about. It's like you got a bee buzzing behind your eyes. You're on lock and load, noble mon."

"I don't know where you get these ideas," I said.

"If you haven't noticed, every emotion you have is on your face."

"Will you stop it?"

He looked around. No one was within earshot. "Here's the real problem. The guy who killed Bella doesn't need motivation. He does it for kicks. You knew his kind in Nam. They weren't abused as children. Their mothers didn't strap them on the pot. They came out of the womb perverse and meaner than a bucket of goat piss on a radiator."

"So?" I said.

"So you start thinking up crazy things about Arabs and Russian oligarchs and corrupt politicians. These political cocksuckers—and Louisiana and Jersey and Florida are full of them—they don't waste their time killing people. They're too busy robbing the rest of us blind. Face it. We've got that killer in Kansas on our hands, what's-his-name, BTK. You can't outthink him because there's nothing there to outthink. The guy loves power and pain and watching the light die in his victim's eyes."

"That wasn't the case with Bella."

"Because she was older and smarter and read him for the piece of shit he is."

You didn't slide one by Clete Purcel. "Why'd this kid have to give his ink back?" I said.

"Ask him."

THE BIKER BAR was on the north side of Lafayette. Like most biker bars, it could have served as a laboratory dedicated to the study of misogyny, atavism, and contradiction. A Confederate battle flag was tacked by the corners to the ceiling, puffing in the breeze from an electric fan. The Reich service flag was nailed to one wall; on another wall was a black flag with two white lightning bolts. I always thought the greatest irony of the patrons was in their dress. They affected the roles of Visigoths and iconoclasts but simultaneously seemed to seek uniformity and anonymity. They dressed alike, looked alike, and spoke in the same guttural voice, as though all of them gargled with muriatic acid. The swagger and the way they hid their features inside their facial hair reminded me of actors who were terrified someone would catch on to who they really were.

This does not mean they weren't dangerous. They were ferocious in groups and found in each other the strength they didn't own themselves, and their leaders were not only intelligent but disarming and impressive when need be. No matter the occasion or the environment, messing with them was a mistake.

Spider Dupree was probably twenty-five at the outside, his shoulder-length red hair washed and blow-dried. He wore zoot pants high on his hips and an oversize white long-sleeve shirt with silver thread in it and pearl snap buttons on the pockets and cuffs. The skin below his left eye had been disfigured. A biker bar seemed a strange environment for a kid who obviously had been forced to give back his ink.

Clete introduced me. Spider Dupree's handshake was as light as air, his eyes like misaligned black stones at the bottom of a fish bowl.

"You probably wonder why I'm doing this," he said. "I joined a church and got clean. That also means I got to stay on the square."

"Sure," I said. Trying to return his gaze was impossible. His eyes seemed to watch separate screens at the same time. "Good to know you, Spider."

He touched one of the scars that dripped from his eye. "My story is on my face. I got no secrets. These guys here treat me all right. Let's go over in the booth. You want a beer or anything?"

Before I could reply, Clete said, "Give me a Miller and give Dave a Coca-Cola with some cherries and a lime slice. Right, Dave?"

I didn't answer.

We waited for Spider to come to the booth with the drinks. "You told me you took a hit of Jack," Clete said. "So I jumped the gun."

"Forget it. What'd Spider go down for?"

"Rolling gays in the Castro District."

"Three years?" I said.

"He beat the hell out of them with a blackjack, mostly in the mouth. You could say he has a little bit of a denial problem. He was fresh meat as soon as he went into gen pop."

Dupree sat down next to Clete. It was hard not to be distracted by the scars below his left eye. They resembled a pink, segmented worm someone had stepped on. He wiped at them with his wrist and grinned with half his mouth. "They make my eye water, although that don't make sense."

"Tell Dave why the AB wanted their ink back."

"I took down four guys to earn my teardrops. Two in the shower, one in the yard, one in the block. Then they told me I had to come across for maybe half a dozen swinging dicks. They used a screwdriver. I would have been killed if I hadn't gotten transferred to Atascadero."

I let my eyes slip off his. I couldn't imagine what his childhood must have been like. "Yesterday's box score."

"I lit up one guy in lockdown. That sound like somebody who should pull a train?"

I looked at Clete.

"You were stand-up, Spider," Clete said. "Nobody is holding anything against you. Right, Dave?"

"Right," I said.

There was a warm light in Spider's eyes that reminded me of a nineteen-year-old door gunner I once knew, a mindless kid who had no idea how his rhetoric unnerved other people.

"About this guy who got suffocated in the Iberia Parish prison?" Clete said. "Two guards sat on him?"

Spider seemed to come out of a trance. "Yeah, he was AB. But deaf and a nutcase. He started fighting with the hacks and they sat on him. He was a hump for a cop named Devereaux."

" 'Hump' like a boyfriend?" I said.

"No, he worked for the cop."

"Pimping?" I said.

"Cooze, coke, and crank. Now it's cheese and oxy. I don't like to talk about this too much."

"Why not come clean?" I asked.

"That's the point: I *am* clean. Trips down memory lane don't do a lot for my serenity."

"We totally dig what you're saying," Clete said. "You're doing a solid for us, Spider. We won't forget it."

"The guy who got smothered cooked his head when he rode with a couple of motorcycle clubs on the West Coast."

"Tell Dave about the tats," Clete said.

"Around one ankle. A chain of crosses."

"Like big fat ones?" Clete said.

"Yeah," Spider said.

"The Maltese cross?" I said.

"The what?"

"I remember the man who died in the jail," I said. "His name was Frank Dubois. That's who you're talking about?"

"Yeah, he had a coat of arms tattooed on his back. He could speak Latin or ancient Greek or some shit. He knew sign language, too."

"Did he know Lucinda Arceneaux?" I asked.

"I don't know who that is," he answered.

"Are any Hollywood guys involved in this?" I asked.

"One, for sure."

"Who?" I said.

"A guy who likes to hang girls up on coat hooks," he said. "Least that's what I heard. He's got a funny name."

"Antoine Butterworth?" I said.

"Rings a bell," he replied. "I got to get back to work. That's eight-fifty on the drinks. The tip is on me. If you're gonna hang around, don't get too intimate with the clientele. There's a lot of abnormal people around these days."

WE WENT OUTSIDE to Clete's Caddy. It was parked behind the club by a stand of trees strung with dead vines. The wind had turned cold; yellow and black leaves were tumbling through the parking lot and floating in pools of rainwater greasy with oil. The bikers' motorcycles were parked in straight lines, the wheels at the same angle, the bodies wiped down and shining in the moonlight.

Clete put an unlit cigarette in his mouth. His porkpie hat was slanted on his forehead. I removed the cigarette from his mouth and flipped it into the water. He watched it floating in the pool. "You think Butterworth is our guy?" he asked.

"We've run him six ways from breakfast," I said. "He likes playing the bad boy. I get the feeling he wants to be knocked around."

"How's he different from those guys inside?" he said, looking at the club. "Just because they're imitation Hells Angels doesn't mean they don't kill people."

"Let's get out of here. It's depressing."

"Why do they bother you?"

"Who?"

"Bikers," he said.

"It's not bikers. It's these kinds of bikers. If they had their way, we'd be living in the American Reich."

But he was no longer listening. "There's a guy you're not thinking about, Dave."

"Oh yeah?"

Clete put another cigarette into his mouth. This time he lit it. The smoke came out of his mouth like a piece of cotton. "A guy you keep pretending isn't dirty."

I zipped up my windbreaker and buttoned the collar. I took the second cigarette from his mouth and dropped it into the water. "Stop playing games with me, Clete."

"Who's standing in the middle of all this and doesn't get touched?" he said. "Who's got a reason to do you some serious injury? In this case by degrading and then killing Bella Delahoussaye?"

"I know where you're going. Get off it."

"Who has an obsession with John Ford's work and Henry Fonda and Wyatt Earp and Clementine Carter and the actress who played her and the woman here in New Iberia who looks just like the actress?"

"It's not Desmond. That's crazy."

"You're sleeping with Bailey Ribbons, Dave. In Desmond Cormier's mind, you stole his dream. Wake the fuck up."

ON TUESDAY MORNING, a nurse called me from Iberia General. "Hello, Mr. Robicheaux. I hope I'm not bothering you."

"Not at all," I said. I looked at my watch.

"I know how busy you are," she said.

"What could I help you with?"

"I almost didn't call. It's about your friend. Please don't take this the wrong way. He seems like a good person."

"I'm sorry, ma'am. I'm not quite connecting here."

"Oh, you know, that cuddly little fellow."

"Cuddly?"

"He brought a box of Ding Dongs and a comic book and a teddy bear to Mr. Tillinger's room. I had to explain to him that Mr. Tillinger is comatose and perhaps will never be otherwise. But he shouldn't have come into the ward at five a.m. I wondered if you could speak to him. Without hurting his feelings."

I sat forward in my chair. "He didn't give his name?"

"It slips my mind. I'm glad I'm retiring this year. He has a lisp."

"Wimple?"

"Sorry, that wasn't it. Oh, wait a minute. It was a nickname. How silly of me. He said his friends call him Smiley. He said you were his friend."

"I didn't catch your name."

"Alice Mouton."

"Miss Alice, I don't wish to upset you, but the man we're talking about is a psychopath. If you see him or if he contacts you again, do not indicate that you know his identity. Call us. Are you following me on this?"

The line was silent.

"Miss Alice?"

"Yes."

"You did everything correctly. You're not at risk. His enemies are usually people who have harmed children."

"What do you want me to do with the things he left for Mr. Tillinger?"

"Is there any receipt with them, a label that shows their origins?"

"Not that I see."

"I'll pick them up. In the meantime, leave them with Mr. Tillinger."

"That's where they are now. The man tucked the teddy bear under Mr. Tillinger's arm."

ONE HOUR LATER, I got the call I knew was coming. "Mr. Robicheaux?"

"I hear you visited Mr. Tillinger, Smiley," I said.

"The lady told you?"

"Nobody had to tell me. Everybody knows when you're in town."

"Are you making fun of me?"

"Not me."

"That deputy named Sean shot an innocent man."

"You've got it wrong."

"Some colored people saw it from their car."

"Tillinger was armed. He was pointing a German Luger at both me and the deputy."

"But you didn't shoot. The deputy did. That means you knew Mr. Tillinger wasn't going to shoot."

He had me again. "Don't go near my colleague."

"I go where I want."

"Not in this instance."

"I am very angry. Mr. Tillinger was brave. He told the truth about his family. He stood up to me under very difficult circumstances. Y'all have committed an evil act, Mr. Robicheaux."

"It's Detective Robicheaux. But I want you to call me Dave. You know what Witness Protection is?"

"Don't try to trick me."

"You could be of great value to us. But you've got to disengage from settling scores on your own. Things aren't always what they seem. None of us is God."

The phone line was silent.

"Don't hang up on me, Smiley," I said. "The young deputy who shot Mr. Tillinger made a mistake. You've made mistakes, haven't you?"

"Yes."

"Sean is a good kid. He's feeling a lot of guilt right now. He needs a friend, not an enemy. I bet Mr. Tillinger would tell you that. Right or wrong?"

"Maybe."

"We've got a deal?"

"About the deputy?"

"Yes, the deputy."

"All right," he said.

I was sweating and my heart was pounding. I got up from my desk, the phone in my hand. I felt as though I had stepped into a vortex. Down below I could see the bayou and a pirogue spinning emptily in the center of the current.

"You still with me?" I said.

"We're on the same side now?"

"You bet."

"But you know there's a difference between us, don't you?"

"I don't know how to respond to that."

"I don't have restraints. I do things other people have seen only in their dreams. And I don't feel bad about that at all."

Chapter Twenty-Eight

THAT EVENING I went home in a funk. I felt powerless. We had no viable suspects in the series of murders that had begun with Lucinda Arceneaux; a deranged man like Smiley Wimple was making calls to me that I couldn't trace; and outsiders and sybarites like Antoine Butterworth were wiping their feet on us.

Alafair had already fixed supper and was putting it on the table when I walked into the kitchen. She was wearing a white dress and makeup.

"Where are you going tonight?" I asked.

"Lou and I are seeing *Kiss of Death* with Richard Widmark at UL."

"Wexler again?" I said.

"Give it a break, Dave."

"I just think he's too old for you."

Talk about feeding one to the batter.

"Do you realize how absurd that sounds, coming from you?" she said.

Rain was pelting the trees in the yard, the sky running with ink. I opened the screen door and let Snuggs and Mon Tee Coon inside, mud and all. "I majored in being ridiculous."

"I'm glad you're going out with Bailey," she said.

That was my daughter.

"You're a good guy, Alf."

"Lou thinks *Kiss of Death* is too strong for me," she said.

"When Tommy Udo pushes the old woman in the wheelchair down the staircase?"

"Lou didn't know I came from El Salvador. When I told him what happened in my village, he got upset. He's very protective."

"I might come in late tonight," I said.

"You're seeing Bailey?"

"No."

She waited for me to go on. But I didn't. Her face clouded.

"I'm putting in some overtime," I said.

"Are you and Clete up to something?"

"This has nothing to do with Clete."

"That's like one side of the coin saying it has nothing to do with the other side."

"Watch out for Tommy Udo," I said.

I DROVE DOWN TO Cypremort Point. The sky was sealed with black clouds except for a band of cold light along the horizon. The tide was coming in, the waves dented with rain and thudding as heavy as lead against the shore. Up ahead, Desmond's house glistened against the sky. I parked on the road and walked up the steps in the wind and rain. I had no plan in mind. I could not even say why I was there, except that Clete Purcel had planted the seeds of doubt in my mind about Desmond Cormier.

In his work, Desmond was fascinated by light and shadow. But was that a result of his artistic compulsion or an externalization of a struggle within him? His physical energies and appetites were enormous, his latent anger sometimes flickering alight in the recesses of his eyes, as though the child in him would have its way. Even his goodness was like a child's, brightening a room one moment, gone the next. His unknowability and mercurial behavior and insularity caused awe and fear in others. If he had an artistic antecedent, it was Leonardo, chipping away at a block of marble, releasing a statue that could be either a Madonna or a gargoyle.

I walked onto the deck, more voyeur than visitor, but I no longer cared about protocol or decorum. I felt soul-sick at what had been done to Bella Delahoussaye. I remembered many years before when

I saw Joan Baez perform "The Night They Drove Old Dixie Down" at Ole Miss, and the chill her words sent through me when she sang "Just take what you need and leave the rest / But they should never have taken the very best."

And that's what Bella was—the very best.

Through the sliding glass doors I could see the glittering beam of a movie projector and the images in a black-and-white film dancing on a screen pulled down from the ceiling. Desmond was lying on his side on the couch, his head propped on his elbow, wearing only slacks and sandals without socks, his torso as smooth and firm and flawless as water running over stone.

Amid the sounds of the waves and wind I heard the sound track of the film, then saw the scene taking place on the screen. Henry Fonda and Ward Bond and Victor Mature were walking toward the O.K. Corral in Tombstone, Arizona, in the early-morning hours of October 26, 1881. In minutes, Doc Holliday, played by Mature, would be coughing a bloody spray into a handkerchief, and Wyatt would step into history, and he and Clementine Carter would stand inside a frame of film that would capture mortality more than any I had ever seen.

I walked back to my truck and got inside but did not start the engine. It was hard for me to think of Desmond as a suspect in a chain of homicides. But I've interviewed men in lockdown units who look no different from you and me and make you feel that the system has made a terrible mistake. The worst of the worst often seem the most harmless. Most of them have the facial expressions you see in a bowl of oatmeal. In Montana I knew a twenty-one-year-old kid who killed two people before he got to prison, then killed or helped kill five more during a riot. He had to be awakened from a sound sleep the afternoon of his execution.

The wind was buffeting my truck and straightening the palm fronds in Desmond's yard and pushing waves onto the blocks of concrete that shored up the bank at the tip of the point. The waves were full of seaweed and ropy with froth, sucking the sand inch by inch from beneath the concrete blocks, undoing our best attempt at avoiding the inevitable. I thought about Lucinda Arceneaux and the white boat on which she may have been held captive before her death, and the person or persons who murdered her, and I wondered if human nature and our susceptibility to evil would ever change, or if we would continue in our war against the earth until we dissolved all our landmass and our structures and ourselves and returned the planet to the watery blue orb it once was.

But I knew what was really on my mind. Desmond may not have been a killer, but he knew people who were. A participant in the massacre at Pinkville, a gunbull who put one of the bodies in the levee at Angola, a Mississippi nightclub owner who buried a civil rights worker alive—they're always there, hovering on the edge of our vision. We just don't admit it. Factor in the culture of New Jersey, Florida, southern Louisiana, and Hollywood. Smiley Wimple comes off looking good.

I pulled my hat over my eyes and decided I would sit there until dawn if I had to. Why? I don't know. Maybe I had questions about Desmond I didn't wish to admit. He was obviously drawn to Bailey Ribbons, even obsessed with her, but he seemed to live a celibate life. I wondered if he was gay, or bisexual, or sexually involved with Antoine Butterworth, whom he constantly defended. Or if he was an intravenous addict. I had seen a syringe on his lavatory. I had also seen the tattoo of a Maltese cross on his ankle. I didn't want to believe it, but Desmond was dirty, I just didn't know to what degree.

He came out the front door of his house, wearing a slicker and a slouch hat and western boots. I was no more than thirty yards away and was sure he saw me. But he didn't seem to. He opened his garage door with a remote control and got into a metallic-green pickup with an extended cab and drove past me, his profile silhouetted by the dash light, his self-absorption of a kind I always associated with pathological behavior.

As he drove away, his headlights tunneled through the rain. I waited until he was a quarter mile down the road, then followed him to a back-road cemetery outside New Iberia. I turned down a dirt road in the opposite direction, parked behind an empty shack, and cut my engine and lights and walked along a ditch strewn with litter. The rain had quit and the moon was up, and through a canebrake I could see Desmond among a cluster of crypts that were cracked and half sunk in the ground. The original occupants of the cemetery had been people of mixed blood who segregated themselves from both whites and full-blood African-Americans and, in death, perpetuated the system that had oppressed them. Fog as tangible as wet cotton was puffing out of the coulee and clinging to the ground and trees and a piked iron fence that had been knocked askew by farm machinery. I saw Desmond lay a long-stemmed rose on a crypt that was as dazzling and white and incongruous in the setting as a block of snow. I had no doubt who was inside it. I had seen a photo in *The Daily Iberian* of the funeral service conducted for Lucinda Arceneaux.

Then Desmond did something I didn't expect, since, to my knowledge, he was not a religious man. He knelt on one knee, his head bowed, one hand on the crypt. The fact that he knelt was not what bothered me. It was the way he did it. He seemed to affect the ritual of the Templar knight acknowledging both his liege lord and his fanatical mission. When he rose, it was with the poise of a man at peace with an agenda that would soak Europe and the Holy Land with blood for three hundred years.

He got into his truck and drove away. I followed him to the highway. I didn't know where he was going, but the image of Doc Holliday and the Earp boys walking toward the O.K. Corral was hard to get out of my mind.

DESMOND DROVE STRAIGHT through New Iberia and up the old two-lane to the little settlement of Cade, where Lucinda Arceneaux's father lived and maintained his small church and where, a short distance away, Frenchie Lautrec's flat-topped home sat.

Desmond cut his headlights and rolled slowly to a stop in front of Lautrec's house. A streetlight burned on the power pole at the corner of the property. He got out of his truck and opened the door to the extended cab, then pulled a scoped rifle from the back seat and closed the door. He twisted the sling around his left forearm and cupped the stock with his right hand and went through Frenchie's front door without ever slowing down, most of the jamb exploding into the living room.

No sound came from inside the house. I removed my 1911-model army .45 from under the seat and slipped off the holster and took off my hat and hung my badge from my neck and jumped across a rain ditch and went through the yard and into the house, pulling back the slide of the .45, easing a round into the chamber. At almost the same moment, the lights went on at the back of the house.

"Dave Robicheaux, Desmond!" I shouted. "Put your rifle on the floor."

No answer.

"You're my friend, Des! But drop your weapon or I'll blow you out of your socks!"

Then I smelled an odor that lived in my dreams, one that went back to a tropical country in the monsoon season when bodies floated loose from improvised graves and declared war on the living.

Desmond came out of the kitchen, trying to clear his throat and doing a poor job of it, a handkerchief held to his mouth, his rifle pointed at the floor. I pulled the rifle from his hand and dropped it. "What's back there?"

He coughed and spat in a wastebasket. "See for yourself."

I went inside the bedroom. The body was hanging from an electrical cord tied to a ceiling beam that someone had exposed by ripping out the Sheetrock. The cord was probably taken from a ceramic lamp that had been smashed on the floor. The back of the victim was turned toward me, the wrists wrapped behind with electrical tape and the roll still hanging from the skin, the body stretched as lean as an exclamation mark. A chair lay on its side against one wall. One loafer was on the floor, one on a foot. I cupped my hand over my nose and mouth and walked to the other side of the body and looked up into the face of Frenchie Lautrec. A cloth canary protruded from his mouth.

This was the same man I had detested, even the way his face

looked, like a bleached football with a trimmed goatee and mustache glued on it. I had not only torn him apart with my bare hands, I had jammed the broken parts of his camera down his throat. He was a pimp, a predator, a misogynist, a degenerate, a sadist, and a cop on a pad, but no one could look at his face now and not feel sorry for him. His neck was not broken. He had gone out the hard way. His eyes were open and contained an expression like a lost child's.

I went outside and punched in a 911 on my cell. Desmond was standing a few feet away on the lawn, like a casual spectator. "What's the cloth canary mean?"

"It's Sicilian for 'Death to snitches.' "

"The Mob got him?"

"The canary was in an ornamental birdcage in the living room. I saw it when I was here before. The Mob didn't do this, and you know it."

"I don't know anything," he said.

"Why did you come here, Des?"

"I heard he might know something about Lucinda Arceneaux's death."

"Lucinda was your half sister, you lying son of a bitch. I followed you to her grave. Less than an hour ago."

His face drained. "You have no right."

"I thought you were stand-up, but you're a bum," I said. "Somebody you know killed her, and one way or another, you've been covering for him. I think it's because you didn't want to interrupt the flow of money into your picture."

"That's not true."

"Go sit in your truck until the meat wagon gets here. I don't want to be around you."

I don't think I ever saw greater shame in a man's face. I knew I would later regret the harshness of my words, but at the moment I did not, I suspect because I still wanted to believe George Orwell's admonition that people are always better than we think they are.

• • •

After the paramedics and three cruisers and a fire truck and Bailey and Cormac Watts had arrived, I told Desmond to get out of his pickup and lean against the fender.

"What are you doing?" he said.

"You're under arrest."

"What for?"

"I'll let you know." I ran my hands under his armpits and down his sides and inside his legs and over his ankles. Then I hooked him up and led him to the back of a cruiser.

"This is bogus," he said. "Quit acting like a jerk. I can sue you for this."

"You've been gone from Louisiana too long," I replied.

I put him in the cruiser and shut the door. I looked back at Lautrec's house. All the lights were on. Through a side window I could see Cormac walking around Lautrec's body, studying it.

I followed the cruiser to the parish prison and locked Desmond in a part of the jail that was particularly spartan and depressing—in fact, it was little more than a narrow corridor between two rows of barred cells that resembled zoo cages, all of them empty.

"Why are you taking out your anger on *me*?" he said.

When you place someone in custody, you don't answer questions, nor do you negotiate. If you do it right, the routine is a bit like the army: You speak in terms of rank and principle and always in the third person, never the second. I scratched at my face as though I had not heard the question. "A bondsman will be available in the morning. Any inmate at the jail is entitled to at least one phone call."

"Come on, Dave," he said. "What's going on?"

I threw the protocol away. "You knelt at your sister's crypt."

"I don't understand what you're saying."

"Your posture made me think of a Crusader knight."

"My *posture*?" he said. "You talk like you're out of your mind."

"You've got a Maltese cross tattooed on your ankle."

"From my biker days."

"My ass."

He leaned his forehead between two bars, his eyes downcast. I could hear a toilet flushing in another part of the building. "Those things you said back there?"

"What about them?" I said.

"You meant them? I'm a bum?"

"I think you don't let your right hand know what your left is doing."

"You don't understand, Dave. Production money comes from all kinds of places. The studio doesn't back up an armored truck on your lawn and dump it on the grass. Some of it is casino money out of Jersey. Some of it is from a group building nuclear reactors. There might be a little Russian or Saudi money involved. It's a consortium."

"So?"

"I don't know how all these killings happened. The Jersey guys were worried about their investment. Maybe they're involved."

"The Mob is a bunch of tarot fans? When did you discover Lucinda Arceneaux was your half sister?"

"Just a little while back," he replied, his eyes on mine.

"How far back?"

"A few weeks, maybe."

"Who told you?"

"My old man. Ennis Patout."

"A few weeks, huh?"

"Yes," he said. He blinked and let out his breath without seeming to, his expression benign.

"Lesson in lying, Des," I said. "Don't try to control your mannerisms. People who tell the truth are bored by what they're saying and show it."

"You know why it's so hard to talk to you, Dave? It's because you cloak yourself in AA bromides and try to pass them off as the wisdom of the ages."

"Who paid for your half sister's crypt? Her father is a preacher with a few dozen poor people in his congregation. I bet you spent five grand on the crypt and at least half that on the coffin."

"All right, I paid for it," he said. "I didn't want to acknowledge my father or the world in which I grew up. I hate my father, and I hate what he did to my mother."

"Your mother dumped you, bub. Get your facts straight."

"If these bars weren't between us, I'd break your jaw, old man or not."

"You looked the other way when your sister was murdered," I said. "Who's got the problem?"

He tried to grab my shirt. I walked down the corridor, my footsteps ringing like hammers inside a submarine.

IT WAS ALMOST three in the morning as I drove down East Main. My eyes felt seared, like there was sand in them, as though I had looked into the pure white fire of an arc welder's rod touching metal. My throat was dry, a pressure band forming on the right side of my head, my heart constricting whenever I took a deep breath.

Why the agitation? Why my unrelieved anger toward Desmond? I was entering a dry drunk. But this one was different. I had taken a hit of Jack at the blues club, and booze stays in the metabolism for as long as thirty days. For an alcoholic, having thirty days of the enemy at work in the heart and blood and brain while not being allowed to drink could probably be compared with practicing celibacy for the same amount of time in a harem.

I knew bars that closed their doors to the public at two a.m. but continued to serve their friends until dawn, and casinos that kept the tap flowing twenty-four hours a day, seven days a week, as long as you stayed at the tables or the machines. If you want to get slop-bucket-deep in an alcoholic culture, there is no better place than the state of Louisiana. It's a drunkard's dream, a twenty-four-hour chemically induced orgasm, a slide down a rainbow that lands you with a soft bump in the Baths of Caracalla. Think I'm exaggerating? Ask any souse highballing out of Texas into Lake Charles.

I passed my house and turned at the Shadows and drove around the block to St. Peter Street and circled back to East Main, then parked in front of the old Burke home and walked down to the bayou and sat under a live oak on the water's edge. I had sat under the same tree with my father, Big Aldous Robicheaux, on V-J Day in 1945. There were still slave cabins on the bayou, although they had been turned into corn and grain cribs for the carriage horses that some people still used to go to church on Sunday morning. I had never been fishing. My father bought a cane pole with a wooden bobber and a hook and a lead weight for twenty-five cents from a man of color. The weight was a perforated .36-caliber pistol ball that the colored man had found on a battle site farther down the bayou. I will never forget swinging the bobber and the lead ball and the baited hook into the current, then watching the line come taut and the backs of the alligator gars rolling on the edge of lily pads when the bobber disturbed them.

My father could not read or write and barely spoke English, but he understood the natural world and the culture of Bayou Teche. To us, the bayou was not simply a tidal stream that knitted together what we call Acadiana; it was part of a biblical epic and, because of its mists and fog-shrouded swamps, a magical place inhabited by lamias and leprechauns and medieval tricksters and voodoo women and the spirits of Confederate soldiers and cannibalistic Atakapa Indians. It was a grand place to grow up. The day I threw my line into the water, I knew I would never leave Bayou Teche, in part because of the event that occurred as a result of my father buying the cane pole from a colored man.

The bobber had been carved from a piece of balsa wood and drilled with a hole into which a shaved stick was inserted to secure the line. I saw the bobber tremble once, then plunge straight down into the silt. I jerked the pole so hard, I broke it in half, and the line and bobber and lead bullet and hook and worm and a big green-gold goggle-eyed perch went flying into a tree limb above us. My father went to the Burke house and borrowed a garden rake and combed the fish out of the tree for me. I still suspect this may be the only time in history that a fish has been caught in a live oak tree with a garden rake.

That postage stamp of a moment has always remained with me as a reminder of the innocent world in which I grew up. Or at least the innocent world in which we chose to live, perhaps to our regret. When I sat under the tree at three in the morning, an old man watching a barge and tug working its way upstream, I knew that I no longer had to reclaim the past, that the past was still with me, inextricably part of my soul and who I was; I could step through a hole in the dimension and be with my father and mother again, and I didn't have to drink or mourn the dead or live on a cross for my misdeeds; I was set free, and the past and the future and the present were at the ends of my fingertips, filled with promise and goodness, and I didn't have to submit to time or fate or even mortality. The party is a grand one and infinite in nature and like the music of the spheres thunderous in its presence, and I realized finally that the invitation to it comes with the sunrise and a clear eye and a good heart and the knowledge that we're already inside eternity and need not fear any longer.

I drove home and went inside just as the wind came up again and the clouds closed over the moon and white hail began pinging and bouncing on the roof. In minutes I was asleep and had to be shaken awake at dawn by Alafair so I could shower and shave and go to work.

Chapter Twenty-Nine

CORMAC WATTS WAS the best coroner we ever had, more cop than pathologist. I always liked him. He was gay and imaginative and happy and, like many gay people, at peace with the world even though the world had often not been kind to him. If he had any professional fault, it was his tendency to extrapolate an encyclopedic amount of information from a fingernail paring, which sometimes did not help his credibility. He called me at the office on Wednesday afternoon. "Ready for the breakdown on Frenchie Lautrec?"

"I thought death by strangulation was death by strangulation," I said.

"That's the cause of death, all right. But we've got some issues."

"I can't tell you how much I hate that word, Cormac. I rank it with 'awesome' and 'amazing.' "

"You want to hear what I've got or not?"

The truth was, I didn't want to hear it. The sun was shining while the rain was falling, and there was a huge rainbow that dipped out of the clouds into the middle of City Park.

"Yes, please tell me about Lautrec's corpse," I said.

"I think he faked his own murder."

"His wrists were taped behind him."

"Think back," Cormac said. "When you found him, the roll was barely wrapped around the left wrist. He could have gotten loose."

"Not if he was unconscious."

"His blood was clean. There are no injection marks on the body. No fresh bruises or abrasions from somebody lifting him up. He kicked the chair into the wall."

"How do you know?"

"His right loafer was on the floor. Part of a toenail was inside the sock. He was right-handed. He kicked the chair with his right foot and chipped the nail."

"That could have happened if someone else kicked it out from under him," I said.

"Nope, the weight would have been going away from him. It's unlikely the blow would have broken the nail."

I rubbed my temples. "Lautrec had no feelings about anything or anyone except himself. I don't see him as a suicide."

"About ten days ago I saw him in my insurance agent's office. He was there with his daughter."

"I didn't know he had one."

"She lives in Biloxi. My agent said Lautrec bought a life insurance policy. My agent wanted to sell me one, too."

"Can we stay on the subject, Cormac?"

"Lautrec could be a menacing presence. My agent was about to have a coronary. I don't think he wanted to insure Lautrec."

"Why not?"

"Because Lautrec got his way or he made other people miserable?"

"I'll give your insurance agent a ring," I said. "Anything else?"

"Lautrec had a Maltese cross tattooed inside his calf."

"That bothers me," I said.

"You think we're dealing with a cult?"

"I don't know. I don't understand any of this."

I called Cormac's insurance agent. Lautrec had bought a three-hundred-thousand-dollar policy that did not cover suicide. His daughter was the beneficiary.

I WENT INTO HELEN'S office. She was just about to go home. I told her everything I had just learned. She sat back down. "You buy Lautrec offing himself?"

"Maybe he was scared."

"The only thing Lautrec feared was not getting laid."

"Cormac is adamant," I said.

"How about prints on the Sheetrock torn out of the ceiling?"

"None."

Helen looked tired, older. "You know where this is going, don't you?"

"Yep, pin-the-tail-on-the-donkey time."

IN ANY GIVEN situation, the majority of people believe whatever they need to: Up is down, black is white, dog shit tastes good with mashed potatoes. This is how the collective response to an unsolved series of killings works: Shock and anger are followed by fear and the purchase of weapons and security systems, arrest of a scapegoat, rumors that the killer's wealthy family has quietly committed him, or sometimes the mind-numbing statement by the investigators that the evidence they could not find proves the homicides are not related and that a serial killer is not at large in the community.

What does an intelligent investigator do? He doesn't listen to any of it. The detail that stuck with me from my conversation with Cormac was the Maltese cross on Lautrec's calf. I used the word "collective" regarding the response to killings. For me, the word is always a pejorative. My father spoke a form of English that was hardly a language, but in Cajun French he could speak insightfully. My favorite of his sayings was "Did you ever see a mob rush across town to do a good deed?"

My feelings were stronger than his. Hobnailed boots in unison never bode well for anyone, and the further down the food chain you get, the more heinous the agenda. The Maltese cross meant Lautrec was on board. But with what? He was neither a leader nor a follower; he was an opportunist, a walking gland, a genetic throwback trying to lure a primitive woman in animal skins away from the fire and into the darkness of the cave. What would frighten him so much that he would bail off a chair and swing back and forth on an electrical cord and not pull his wrists loose from the tape that barely restrained them?

Of course, there was another possibility. Maybe he was guilty. I believed then and I believe now that he was one of those made different in the womb. He enjoyed cruelty and visiting it upon women he couldn't control. I suspected he was capable of inflicting the kind of damage that had been done to Hilary Bienville before she died. Or he could have been a secondary participant in the attack. He had worked in the parish prison during the previous administration, when inmates were badly abused. Once again, I had no answers. I heard the cops who nailed the Hillside Stranglers never had answers either. Or the ones who nailed BTK in Kansas or the Night Stalker in Los Angeles.

I went down to Bailey's office, but she had left for the day. I drove to her house. The sun had gone out of the sky, and the rainbow arcing into City Park had evaporated, replaced by smoke from the sugar mill that drifted onto the trees and grass like black lint.

BAILEY WAS IN the backyard, playing with her calico cat, who had the male name of Maxwell Gato. She picked up Maxwell and bounced Maxwell's rump in her palm and handed her to me. Maxwell was a longhair and must have had twenty pounds of fat on her. I bounced her up and down also. The cat closed her eyes. I could feel her purring.

"What's going on, sailor?" Bailey said.

"Sailor?"

"You don't like that?"

"That's what my wife Bootsie used to call me. Did you eat?"

"No. How about I fix us something? Then we might mess around. How's that?"

"That's pretty nice."

But I was hiding my feelings. I didn't feel right about Bailey. She was an aging man's wet dream. Beautiful, intelligent, loving, and full of laughter in bed. Pardon me if my remarks are too personal or if they violate good taste. She smelled like flowers and the ocean when she made love, and she moaned like one of Homer's Sirens. In the last heart-twisting moment, I felt an electric current inside her that seemed to take control of both of us. Her body and mouth and hands and ragged breath and even her nails hooked in my back became a gift, a prayer rather than an erotic act, a moment so intense I wanted to die inside it and never leave. When I rose from her, I felt unworthy of what had just happened in my life.

I watched her at the stove. Her thick brown hair was piled on her head, spiked with two long wooden pins, the kind that women wore during the Victorian era. I had not noticed earlier that her stove was refashioned from one manufactured to burn wood. It had claw feet, and the porcelain was painted with green tendrils, as it would have been in an earlier time.

"Will you quit staring at me?" she said.

"Sorry."

"Do I remind you of someone else? The wife you lost?"

"You remind me of everything that's good."

"No, I can see it in your eyes when you think I'm not looking. I'm someone else to you."

"I don't believe that time is sequential," I said. "I believe the world belongs to the dead as well as the unborn. I've seen Confederate soldiers in the mist at Spanish Lake. I've wanted to join them."

"Did you just say what I think you did?"

"I think I stole you from another time. I'm sure that's what Desmond thinks. I fear someone may take revenge on me by hurting you or Clete or Alafair."

"You're talking about Desmond? He's in jail."

"For breaking and entering. It won't stick."

"I can take care of myself. You get these crazy ideas out of your head. You also need to forget about Confederates in the mist."

"They're there. I've talked with them. I put my hand through a drummer boy's shoulder. He was killed at Shiloh."

Her eyes were empty; I wondered if she was deciding whether to ignore me or to disengage from our relationship. She let in Maxwell Gato, then lifted her up and kissed the top of her head and put her in my arms. "The world belongs to the living, Dave. These things you're telling me have nothing to do with reality. What's really on your mind is our relationship. You think you're too old for me, and you think you're doing something morally wrong."

"That's not true," I lied.

"You're in better shape than men who are thirty-five. You're honest and kind and brave. You think I care about your age?"

"A few years down the road you will."

"Let me worry about that. What did you mean when you said you stole me out of another time?"

"I think there're doors in the dimensions." Maxwell Gato began pushing her back feet into my arm so I would play with her. I gently tugged her tail and bounced her up and down. "I've always thought normalcy was overrated."

Bailey was wearing moccasins. She took Maxwell Gato from me and set her on the floor, then stood on tiptoe and kissed me on the mouth and folded her arms behind my neck. "Do you love me, Dave?"

"Of course."

"Like a daughter? Because that's the way you're talking to me."

"I love you because you're one of the best people I've ever known, and one of the most beautiful."

She stood on my shoes and buried her head in my neck, her body shaking.

"Are you all right?" I said.

"I'm always all right. Just hold me."

"Tell me what's wrong."

"Hold me. Tighter. Please."

An hour later, she got up from the bed and showered and came back into the bedroom, a towel wrapped around her, her body damp and warm and glowing. She lay down next to me, then cupped her body into mine and held my hand with both of hers and told me what she said she had never told anyone, at least not in detail.

AT AGE SEVENTEEN, one year into her widowhood, she had a summer job as a ticket taker for a carnival and rodeo and Wild West show that was headquartered in Louisiana and traveled through the Great American Desert. In the fairgrounds of a small city in Utah rimmed with red cliffs and a green river flanged by cottonwoods, she was tearing tickets at the entrance when she saw three young men sitting on the back of a flatbed truck. They were sweaty and sunbrowned, with physiques as lean as lizards. They wore beat-up black cowboy hats and tight Wranglers and cowboy boots stippled with hay and manure. They grinned as though they knew her; they were drinking soda pop and eating handfuls of pork rinds from a bag. The tallest one pulled a bottle from a cooler and dropped off the flatbed and approached her.

"Want a Coca-Cola, darlin'?" he said. "*Ice*-cold."

"No, thank you," she said.

There was a shine in his eyes. He was shaved, his black hair trimmed, his face fine-boned and tanned and unwrinkled. "Bet you don't remember me."

"You don't look familiar."

"I knew Boyd. Your husband. I drove with him a couple of times. In Baton Rouge."

She waited for him to offer his sympathies. Instead, he grinned. "I'm glad I run into you. I owed Boyd some money. Eighty dollars, to be exact. My name is Randy Armstrong. When I was driving, they called me the Bogalusa Flash."

"That's where you're from?"

He seemed not to hear her. He took out his wallet. "Sorry about what happened. It's part of the reason I gave up stock car driving. I've got thirty dollars here. I'll have the rest tomorrow."

"That's very nice of you." She took the money from his hand, her fingers touching his palm.

The next morning she went about her chores, feeding animals, serving food under the tent where the roustabouts and the operators of the rides ate. In two days they would be loading the animals onto a train and the carnival rides on trucks and heading for Grand Junction. Randy and his two friends were at one of the tables. He winked at her. "Payday today," he said. "I ain't forgot."

She shared a small round-cornered aluminum trailer with an Indian woman named Greta who sold jewelry and T-shirts and smoked two packs of cigarettes a day and drank half a bottle of cough syrup every night before going to sleep. That evening Bailey served the tables under the tent, then sat down and ate by herself and watched the sun set on the cliffs and the green river and the cottonwoods, the air filled with the music from the carousel and the shouts of teenagers on the rides, the evening sky turquoise and printed with the lights of the Ferris wheel and the Kamikaze.

She saw no sign of Randy and his friends. Not until late the next night, when the lights were clicking off on the rides and the game booths, and the roustabouts were starting to take down the Kamikaze. Randy tapped on her trailer door and removed his hat when she opened it. He handed her a fifty-dollar bill. "I didn't get my check cashed till today. Let's get a taco before they give it to the hogs. I ain't kidding. A pig farmer buys all this slop they been feeding people at five dollars a plate."

"If it's slop, why do you eat it?" she said.

"It's finger-licking-good slop."

She went with him to the taco stand, and he got two plates free from the concession operator, and they sat on a wood bench and ate the tacos.

"Ever been to Grand Junction?" he said.

"No," she replied.

"I know the hot spots. Dancing and all." He grinned with innocent self-satisfaction. "Eat up. I got to check on them two boys I live with. Then we'll take a walk up in them cliffs, catch the last of the sunset."

They went to his trailer, a big one that had curtains on the windows and an air cooler on top. His friends were sitting in folding chairs outside, enjoying the breeze.

"I got to get something," Randy said.

"What?" she said.

"An ice-cold root beer." He stepped inside, then motioned her in as though wanting to share a secret. He closed the door behind her. "I got some chocolate cake in here that'll break your heart, if them two out there ain't ate it all."

"We'd better be going if we're going to see the sun set," she said.

He took the cake out of the refrigerator. The shelves were almost empty except for a bottle of bulk wine. The cake was small and had not been cut. He sliced it in half and pared off a thick chunk and put it on a paper plate with a plastic fork and handed the plate to her. "Give it a try. They got twelve-step programs for people that take just one bite. I got to wash my hands." He held them up as though that proved what he planned to do.

She put a small piece on the fork and eased it onto her tongue. It *was* good. Minutes later, she heard the toilet flush and the faucet squeaking. He came out of the bathroom wiping his hands on a paper towel. "I'm ready for a chunk of that my own self. But first—" He opened the refrigerator again and lifted out the bottle of bulk wine. "I have one glass a night. Just one. To prove I control it, that it don't control me."

"You had a problem with it?" she said.

"Not no more. I'm my own man, not like them sobriety people always whining about it, know what I mean?"

"Not quite," she said.

He looked at her empty plate. "You munched it down. Want some more?"

"No, thank you. Could I use your bathroom?"

"You betcha. I just douched it with a little air freshener."

"Pardon?"

"Don't pay me no mind."

She stepped inside the narrow confines of the bathroom. After she relieved herself, she tried to rise from the toilet seat and seemed to melt inside. She felt as though the tendons in the backs of her knees had been severed. Her hands and arms and vocal cords were useless. Spittle ran in a string off the corner of her lip.

Randy opened the door. "You all right, little lady? Here, get up. That's it. Walk with me. That's right, baby. Everything is gonna be all right. Lie down on my bed and let me get your shoes off. Relax, the Bogalusa Flash is on the job."

Through a haze, she saw his two friends appear behind him. He shoved them back out the door. "Wait your turn," he said.

SHE WOKE AT dawn, rolled up in a ball by her trailer, shivering in the dew. She pulled herself up on her knees. The strap of her hand-tooled leather purse was tangled around her neck. Her clothes and skin and hair stank of the wine she remembered someone forcing over her teeth and down her throat. She stumbled into the trailer and got sick in the bathroom.

"What happened to you?" said Greta, the woman she lived with.

Bailey sat in a chair and wiped her face with a washcloth, then opened her purse and took out her wallet. The thirty loose bills Randy had given her earlier and the fifty-dollar bill he had given her later were gone. She pulled aside the curtain on the back window and gazed at the empty spot where Randy's trailer and diesel truck had been parked. "I think I need to go to a hospital."

"Hospital?" Greta said. " 'Cause you got drunk?"

A dog with mange was defecating in the bare spot. After it scratched dirt over its feces, it limped away, one of its back legs obviously injured.

"That's what they'll say, won't they? That I got drunk."

"We're carnival people, girl. It ain't an easy life."

HER HEAD LAY sideways on the pillow, her eyes looking into mine.

"What's the rest?" I asked.

"The show went to Grand Junction that same day," she said. "Randy and his friends weren't there."

"You didn't call the cops?"

"Seventeen, drenched in wine, smelling of vomit? That would have given Bubba and Joe Bob a good laugh."

"What happened down the track?"

"It was August, the end of the season. We were up by the Indian res in western Montana, at the foot of the Mission Mountains. I remember ice in a waterfall high up on the mountain. The ice looked like teeth."

"Those guys showed up?"

"They were already there. Greta parked us about a hundred yards from them. I had almost made my peace with what they did."

"Greta didn't give you any advice?"

"She was a Lakota. She said, 'The way of the world ain't the way of Wakan Tanka.' That meant you were on your own."

"What happened to those guys, Bailey?"

Her eyes went past me to a photo on the wall. In it were her grandfather with his crew in front of a B-17. "I ended up serving them at the table under the tent. Outside, Randy said, 'Glad you put it behind you, little lady. Truth is, Boyd owed me eighty dollars, not the other way around. I guess I figured Boyd still owed me. Sorry about that.' "

"What'd you say to him?"

"Nothing. I went back to the trailer and cried."

I sat on the side of the bed. I was in my skivvies. Maxwell Gato jumped on the bed and got between us and flipped on her back. I picked her up and set her on the floor. "You did something, Bailey. What was it?"

"It happened that night," Bailey said. "The rides and fairways had all shut down. I went to their trailer and knocked. I don't know why. Maybe I wanted them to hurt me so somebody would call the police and arrest them. Or maybe I simply wanted them to look me in the face. If I'd had a gun, I would have scared them. There was no sound inside. I think they were stoned. It's funny how I felt. I wasn't thinking about them. I kept an empty spot in my head, like I didn't want to know what I was planning to do. Snow was blowing off the tops of the mountains in the moonlight, and I thought about how beautiful the earth was."

She sat on the side of the bed and took her shirt off the bedpost and began putting it on.

"Tell me what happened," I said.

She buttoned her shirt slowly, staring at the wall as though it were a movie screen. Her back was cold when I touched it. "I don't want to do this to you, Dave."

"You're not doing anything to me."

"There was an orange crate full of butcher paper by a Dumpster not far away, and a five-gallon can of diesel in the back of their pickup truck. I put the crate under the propane tank on the trailer and poured the diesel on it and set it on fire."

I stared at her. She had been right. I wasn't ready for it. "Tell me the rest."

"The fire was very fast. I could feel the heat on my skin, even while I was running away. They died. All of them. I didn't see them die, but I heard them. I put my fingers in my ears."

"This didn't happen from a burning propane tank."

"The trailer was a meth lab."

"Nobody questioned you?"

"No one had reason to. I started to tell Greta. She put her hand over my mouth. So now you know."

There are moments when you realize that our greatest vanity lies in the belief that we have control of our lives and that reason holds sway in human affairs. Hugo Tillinger was probably wrongly convicted for the arson murder of his family and now lay in a coma, put there by a young deputy consumed by guilt. My homicide partner had burned three men to death, and no one knew about it except me and an Indian woman who was probably dead. As Stephen Crane suggested long ago, most of us are adverbs, never nouns, not even the pitiful degenerates who gang-raped a trusting seventeen-year-old girl.

"Those guys dealt it," I said. "You didn't intend to kill them. I think they got what they deserved. That's it."

"That's it?"

"They wrote their fate before they ever met you. How many lives did they destroy with meth? How many other girls would they have raped? Don't stack the time of evil people, Bailey."

She sat down next to me and rested her head on my shoulder. "Have I made a burden for you?"

"Want to know the truth? When guys like that buy it, I'm glad."

"Don't say that."

"My mother and my second wife died at the hands of guys like that. I say fuck all of them."

I felt her body jerk with the coarseness of my language. "I'm sorry," I said. But my words were gibberish. There are images you never get out of your head, and we both knew it.

Chapter Thirty

THURSDAY HAD BEEN a long day for Clete. He had to pry a bail skip out of a chimney in Abbeville. The skip's hysterical girlfriend tore Clete's new sport coat with a butcher knife. A disbarred lawyer stuck him with a bad check for a two-month investigation, and his Caddy got towed from a yellow zone. That evening he ate downtown and took a walk onto the drawbridge by Burke Street. He leaned on the rail and looked down at the long bronze ribbon of Bayou Teche unspooling beneath his feet, its banks lined with live oaks and lily pads. It seemed to dip off the edge of the earth.

He could see the fireflies in the trees and smell gas on the wind, and he felt a sense of mortality that was as cold and damp as the grave. The light was shrinking on the horizon, and an island of dead leaves was floating under the bridge, undulating with the current. He had a package of cigarettes in his pocket and wanted to light one up. He tore up the package and dropped the pieces down a sewer drain.

It was almost dark when he got back to the motor court. He parked the Caddy in the cul-de-sac and went inside his cottage and turned on the television, not caring which channel came on. He cracked a Budweiser and was tempted to pour a shot in it but instead sat down in his stuffed chair and tried to concentrate on the television and forget the morbid sensations that had flooded him on the drawbridge. Then he realized he was watching Ingmar Bergman's *The Seventh Seal*.

He turned off the set, returned his unfinished beer to the refrigerator, chain-locked the door, showered, and put on his pajamas. The time was 9:17. The rest of the world might have its troubles, but

Clete Purcel was going to bed early, safe and sound in his cottage that was always squared away and meticulously clean. If he was lucky, he would sleep through the night without dreaming and rise to a better day, one in which he did not feel the pull of the earth.

An hour later, deep inside his sleep, he felt a squeeze on his wrist. He opened his eyes in the blackness. His right hand jerked tight against a handcuff that was hooked to the bed frame. Four feet away, a diminutive man with the complexion and muscle tone of liquid soap was seated in a chair, illuminated by the glow of the bathroom night-light.

"Hi, hi," the man said. "Guess who came to see you."

Clete pinched his eyes and waited for them to adjust. "How'd you get in?"

"The cleaning lady left the door open," the man said. "I've been under your bed since this afternoon. Your carpet is smelly."

The man wore pink tennis shoes and tight shorts and a boxlike white hat with a starched brim and had a smile that made Clete think of red licorice. A small semi-automatic rested on his thigh.

"You hooked me up with my own cuffs," Clete said. "Pretty impressive."

"I could have done something else to you. I have the chemicals to do it."

"Listen, Wimple—"

"No! No! No! It is rude to call people by their last names. Do. Not. Do. That."

"Sorry," Clete said. "Let me start over. Listen. Guy. Who. Burns. People. Alive. With. A. Flamethrower, what the fuck are you doing in my cottage?"

"The people I used to work for are after me."

"Just because you lit up a couple of their guys? I'm shocked."

"They violated me. With a tree branch."

"How about unhooking me and we'll talk about it? You want some ice cream? That's a big favorite of yours, right?"

"Don't try to trick me."

"You know my daughter is Gretchen Horowitz, don't you?"

"She kills for hire."

"That's what she *did,* past tense. She's a documentary filmmaker now. But don't get her pissed off, know what I mean?"

"You mean, don't hurt you?"

"What I'm saying to you is don't fuck with the wrong people, Smiley whatever-the-fuck-your-last-name-is."

"I didn't give you permission to call me Smiley."

"Then shove it up your ass."

"The deputy who shot my friend Hugo Tillinger is named Sean McClain."

"Tillinger is your friend?"

"Why did the deputy kill him?"

"Tillinger pointed a Luger at McClain. At Dave Robicheaux, too. Dave's on the square. You know that. I'm going to turn on my side, okay?"

"I took the gun from under your mattress."

"I'm still going to turn on my side. Look, you got a rotten deal as a child. I can relate to that. But you're coming down on the wrong people. *Diggez-vous* on that, noble mon?"

"Dig what?"

"Sean McClain is a good kid. He's going through a bad time over what happened. Like you said, the Mob is your problem. They're assholes, not interesting guys who look like Marlon Brando and James Caan. What do you know about the Jersey crowd?"

"They lent a lot of money to a movie company here."

"You hear anything about Russians?"

"They're building atomic reactors. They launder money in a place called Malta."

"How do you know this shit?"

"I hear people in Miami and New Or-yuns talk."

"Unhook me. I'll give you a free pass. You got my word."

"Do you want to be my friend?"

"I think you're a righteous dude. Everybody has a few character defects."

"You know what I'll do if you lie, don't you?"

"I got a sense of your potential when you poured Drano down Tony Nemo's throat."

Smiley got up and stuck the semi-auto into his pants pocket. His stomach was pouched over his waistband. He leaned down, pausing long enough to search Clete's eyes. He popped the manacle with Clete's key and stepped back.

Clete pushed himself up in bed, his hands in full view. "What'd you do with my piece?"

"Your thirty-eight?"

"Yeah, my thirty-eight."

"You'll find it when you go wee-wee."

"You dropped my thirty-eight in the bowl?"

"I flushed first."

"Can I dress?"

"No."

"This is getting to be a drag. Will you tell me what you want and get out of my life?"

"I want to hire you to cover my back. I'll be your friend."

"I appreciate the compliment, but you've killed too many people. I think you enjoy it. That's not a good sign."

"The people I killed hurt children."

"I don't think that one will wash, Wimple. Sorry. Smiley."

"If they didn't hurt children, they protected people who did. Are you calling me a liar?"

"Look, you did me a solid once. You took out a former gunbull who was two seconds from snuffing my wick. But you started a gunfight that killed a female detective. She was my lady for a while. That one won't go away."

"It was an accident."

"Tell her that."

Smiley's teeth looked like rows of tiny white pearls, the gums barely holding them in place. His nostrils were slits. "In or out?"

"Out," Clete replied, his eyes flat. He waited, his mouth dry.

"You're making me mad," Smiley said.

"You don't have to tell me."

Smiley stood up from the chair. "Sometimes I do bad things when I get mad."

"Really?"

"Don't make fun of me."

"I didn't. You took on the Mob. Nobody has ever done that. You've probably got them dumping in their drawers. But don't let them take you alive. You copy on that? Go out smoking."

A gust of rain and wind swept across the roof; lightning that made no sound bloomed around the edges of the curtains.

"Will you try to follow me?" Smiley said.

"No."

"I know what you're thinking."

"No, you do not know what I'm thinking," Clete said.

"We're alike."

"Time to beat feet, podjo."

"We're two of a kind. I like you. I want you to be my friend."

"You're getting weird on me, little mon. Are you hearing me? Hello, Mars."

"Little mon?"

"Take it as a compliment."

"I'll be in touch. So will she."

"Who is 'she'?"

"Wonder Woman. She looks over me."

Clete sat on the edge of the bed, his hands cupped on his knees. He stared at the floor. "I've really enjoyed this. But I'm going in the bathroom now."

"You took care of an orphan boy."

"You can't win on the game you pitched last week," Clete said.

Clete continued to gaze at the floor, his head bowed. He heard the door open and felt the rain rush inside, then heard the door close. He got up from the bed and looked through the curtains. The driveway was black and shiny and empty. He went into the bathroom and retrieved his snub-nose from the toilet bowl and washed it, then dried it and oiled it and put it into its holster and lay back down and stared at the ceiling and listened to rain pattering on the roof, his eyelids stitched to his forehead.

HE WAS AT my back door early the next morning. Alafair and I were at the breakfast table. This was an old routine with Clete. At sunset he would begin deconstructing the world and himself, then at sunrise be at my door, forlorn and stinking of rut and weed and beer sweat and in need of my absolution, as though I had any such power.

I pushed open the screen. "I don't hear any sirens."

He brushed past me. "That's not funny. Hi, Alafair."

"Hi, yourself, big guy," she replied.

"About to take off for the set?"

"Not for a while," she said.

Clete's eyes were wandering all over the kitchen. Snuggs and Mon Tee Coon were eating out of their bowls on top of a newspaper, their muddy tracks strung behind them. "I was just passing by," he said.

I grinned at him. "Tell me what you did."

"I didn't do anything."

"That's why your BP is about two hundred or so," I said.

"Can I be honest here?" he said, glancing at Alafair.

"Get the marbles out of your mouth, will you, Clete?" I said.

"It's what I didn't do. Wimple was in my cottage last night. He was not only in it last night, he waited for me under the bed all afternoon."

For some reason Snuggs stopped eating and looked up at him.

"He hooked you up or something?" I said.

"How'd you know?"

"Because it's the kind of stuff Smiley does. Did you call it in?"

"I let him slide."

"You're kidding?"

"I gave him my word."

"I don't believe this," I said.

"The enemy of my enemy is my friend."

"Until you get a shiv between your shoulder blades."

"Wimple finds people we can't get close to," he said. "There's nothing about the Mob he doesn't know. He's like a worm inside a corpse."

Alafair put down the toast she was eating. "Thanks, Clete."

"Can I have a cup of coffee?" he said. "I got the shakes. Wimple creeped me out. It's like talking to a giant slug."

"You know I have to report this to Helen."

"Do anything you want. What's better, getting to the bottom of Lucinda Arceneaux's death or putting a guy in a cage who's got a triple-A battery for a brain?"

"Helen might have you picked up, Clete."

"For what, not getting myself killed? Wimple said there's Jersey and Russian money going to a movie company hereabouts. He said the money gets laundered in Malta."

"Malta as in Maltese cross?" I said.

"Yeah, the kind that's been showing up on dead people."

"How does a piece of stamped metal or a tattoo on a dead person connect with money laundering?" I asked.

"Let me turn it around on you. If the Maltese cross isn't a signal about money, then what does it represent? Some guy's fascination with the prizes in a box of Cracker Jack?"

I picked up Snuggs and cuddled him in my arm. I wiped his feet with a paper towel.

"Did you hear me, Dave?" Clete said.

"Yeah, I did. I've got no answers. But if Smiley caps somebody else—maybe Sean McClain—you'll never forgive yourself."

He looked like I'd punched him in the stomach.

HELEN WAS FURIOUS when I told her of Clete's contact with Smiley.

"What was he supposed to do?" I said. "Run outside and catch one in the face?"

"Clete didn't call it in."

"What good would that have done? Smiley has never been in custody anywhere. Plus, I think the department discounts anything Clete says."

Her fists were knotted on her desk pad. I thought I had her.

"Hugo Tillinger died at seven-thirty this morning," she said.

I felt my heart drop.

"Iberia General called a half hour ago," she said. "You know what this means for Sean McClain?"

I WENT BACK TO my office and dipped into my file cabinet and laid out all my notes and manila folders and photographs and medical reports and printouts from the state police and FBI on the series of homicides that had begun with the death of Lucinda Arceneaux. I was convinced the killer was insane, obsessed, imperious, and wired in to a frame of reference no one else would comprehend. But others were involved, if only tangentially. Corrupt or sadistic personnel in the department were players, and members of the Aryan Brotherhood, and the Mob, and film people who weren't bothered by blood money, and Russian or Saudi wheeler-dealers, and possibly a bank that laundered money in Malta.

Maybe such an aggregate of causality seems improbable for a series of crimes in a disappearing wetlands area on the southern rim of our country. But the truth always lies in the microcosm. Wars of enormous importance and consequence are usually fought in places no one cares about. The faces of the players change, but not the issue. You go to the center of the vortex and soon discover you have already been there. It's a matter of seeing the details.

In this instance the key had to be in the tarot. Lucinda Arceneaux was the crucified Christ. The walking cane through the heart of Joe Molinari represented the Suit of Wands; the net in which he was suspended suggested the Hanged Man. The sequined star pasted on the forehead of Hilary Bienville was the Suit of Pentacles. The chalice the killer had fitted into the dead hand of Bella Delahoussaye was symbolic of the Suit of Cups.

What was *not* in the photographs?

Answer: The Suit of Swords. But what if there were bodies out there we hadn't found? I couldn't think my way through the material I was looking at.

The term "conspiracy theory" has become a term of contempt, I suspect because many of the electorate cannot accept that sometimes more evil exists at the top of society than at the bottom. One by one I looked at the photographs of the victims. It was a somber moment. That the photographs had been taken at all seemed heartless, an invasion of the victim's suffering and despair and vulnerability. They were the kind of photographs that defense lawyers never want a jury to see. The image that hurt me most was of Bella Delahoussaye.

I wanted to believe Bella spat in her tormentor's face. I wanted to believe she humiliated him for the worm he was. But I knew Bella was better than that. She probably treated him with pity, which drove him into an even greater rage.

I closed her folder and propped my elbows on my desk blotter and lowered my forehead on my hands and asked my Higher Power to go back in time and be with Bella in her last minutes. Then I felt a level of anger that was so great and violent and dangerous in its intensity that it caused half of my face to go dead. I hoped no one passing in the hallway looked through my window.

Chapter Thirty-One

SATURDAY MORNING WAS perfect. The sunrise was striped with pink and purple clouds, the live oaks a deep green after the rain, the bayou high above the banks, the lily pads and elephant ears rolling with the current. It was a study in the mercurial nature of light and shadow and the way they form and re-create the external world second by second with no more guidance than a puff of wind. I believed it was akin to the obsession of Desmond Cormier with John Ford's films and the Manichean dualism of light and darkness. I believed I was looking into the center of the Great Mystery right there in my backyard.

But my lighthearted mood did not last long. Later, as I was raking leaves in the front yard, I saw Antoine Butterworth's Subaru coming up East Main, past the library and city hall and the grotto devoted to Jesus' mother. I turned my back to the street, gathering up an armload of leaves to stuff in a barrel, hoping that Butterworth would drive on by.

I heard his wheels turn into my driveway and bounce with the dip. The top of his Subaru was down. He cut his engine and got out, dressed in pleated white slacks and a golf shirt and sandals, with a pale blue silk bandana tied around his neck, the way a rogue Errol Flynn might wear it. He held a manila envelope in one hand.

"Normally, I'd take this to your supervisor," he said. "But since she's not in on Saturday, I thought you wouldn't mind my dropping by. What a snug little place you have here."

"What is it, Butterworth?"

"Actually, I was made privy to this material by Lou Wexler, busy little shit that he is."

"You're not a Brit. Why do you try to talk like one?"

"You don't think Lou is a little shit? Oh, I forgot, he's dating your daughter."

"She's not dating him, bub."

"That would be news to Lou."

I began raking again, the tines biting into the dirt.

"He did some checking on your partner, Detective Ribbons," Butterworth said. "Want to hear the results?"

My hands were tingling. I raked harder, a bead of sweat running down my nose.

"Not curious at all?" he said. "My, my."

I stopped, the rake propped in my hand. "Say it."

"Bailey was a bad little girl and was playing with matches."

I held my eyes on his. How could either Wexler or Butterworth know about the arson deaths of the three rapists on an Indian reservation in western Montana? According to Bailey, she had never told anyone what she had done except me and the Indian woman with whom she lived.

"Cat got your tongue?" he said.

"I'm off the clock now," I said. "I'm also on my own property."

"Meaning?"

"You might be having your next meal through a glass straw."

"I'll leave this private investigator's report for you to read at your leisure. Ta-ta."

"Why would Wexler be interested in the background of Detective Ribbons?"

"It's not Wexler. Outside of posing in front of a mirror, his chief interest in life is lessons in classical Latin, if you get my drift. Put it this way—he loves to shoot films in Thailand. Desmond told him to check out your partner."

"Why her?"

"You and she are hurting Des financially. That said, by extension, you're hurting Lou and me."

"Get off my property."

"Not interested in the tykes who got burned in a schoolhouse fire?"

Then I realized he wasn't talking about the death of the rapists. My stomach felt sick, my face sweaty and cold in the wind. "Where'd this happen?"

"In Holy Cross, in the Lower Ninth Ward. None of the children died. But a certain little girl was in a lot of trouble for a while. The welfare worker said she was 'disturbed.' Broken home, alcoholic mother, poverty, all that Little Match Girl routine, no pun intended."

I went back to raking, my hands dry and stiff on the rake handle, my eyes out of focus.

"No clever remarks?" he said.

"I think you're full of it."

"Just going to let it roll off your back?"

I didn't look up. "What's the worst thing that ever happened to you?"

"Let's see. Three things, actually. I took a couple of AK rounds that probably had feces on them. One of my wives gave me the clap. And spending time in this place."

I took the manila envelope from his hands, walked him to his vehicle, and slammed him into the seat hard enough to jar his teeth. Then I tore his envelope into pieces and sprinkled them on his head.

"Keep being the great example you are," I said. "We know you can do it."

Then I got into my truck, drove around his Subaru—scraping the fender with my bumper—and headed up Loreauville Road to Bailey's cottage, my heart the size and density of a cantaloupe.

SHE WASN'T HOME. I got on my cell phone and called Frank Rizzo, an old friend and former arson investigator who had served five years as a superintendent with the New Orleans Fire Department. "Bailey Ribbons?" he said. "Yeah, that clangs bells. You say a schoolhouse in Holy Cross?"

"Yeah, in the Lower Ninth."

"Can you give me a date?"

"No." I hated to tell him I had torn up the document that contained the information we needed.

"I'll get on it. You need it right away? It's the weekend."

"I'd appreciate it."

Two hours later, he called back. "It was twenty-one years ago, after school. Some Girl Scouts were holding a meeting there. One of them said she had learned how to make a fire with flint and kindling. But she couldn't get the fire started. The other girls lost interest and went outside. A few minutes later, the curtains were burning."

"Who was doing the demonstration with the flint and kindling?"

"Bailey Ribbons. She was thirteen."

"So it was an accident?" I said.

"This is where it gets sticky. She denied starting the fire. There was a hot plate in the room. She claimed one of the other girls had left it on and a coat had fallen off a wall hook on top of the coil. Except there were match heads in the kindling. It was obvious she wanted to impress the other girls and had set up the demonstration before she got there."

"What was the conclusion on the report?"

"Maybe the coat did fall on the hot plate. A social worker and the school counselor said the girl had problems. The mother was a drunk, the father gone. The mother and daughter lived on food stamps and church charity. We gave the girl a lecture and dropped it. It was a judgment call, the kind you want to forget."

I could hear a sound in my ears like wind blowing in a seashell. "Why did you want to forget it?"

"When you train as an arson investigator, you try to learn what goes on in the head of a firebug. It's about power and control. That little girl had every warning sign on her. Has this woman done something I should know about?"

I felt my throat tighten. "Her jacket is clean. A guy was trying to spread some dirt on her."

"You doing a background check for the department?"

"Something like that," I said.

"Glad to hear everything worked out."

"Yeah," I said meaninglessly.

"It can go the other way sometimes."

"Pardon?"

"You know, you err on the side of compassion. Then ten years down the line, you find out the person you let go fried a bunch of people."

After I hung up, my knees were so weak I had to sit down.

THAT EVENING A squall blew through the parish, knocking down branches on power lines and flooding the storm sewers and gutters on East Main. I had no idea where Bailey was. I wondered if I had been played, or if I was dealing with a sociopath or a pyromaniac. But that's the nature of gossip and lies or half-truths or incomplete information. Suspicion begins with a fine crack and grows into a chasm. I fed Snuggs and Mon Tee Coon in the kitchen and tried to take comfort in their company.

"How are you guys doing?" I said.

I got a tail swish from Mon Tee Coon.

"Let me make a confession to you," I said. "I think the world would be a better place if we turned it over to you and the rest of us got off the planet."

They continued eating, noncommittal. I heard Alafair pull into the drive and get out and run through the puddles into the house. She got a towel out of the bathroom and came into the kitchen, wiping her face. "All the traffic lights are knocked out. What a mess."

"Where've you been?"

"Playing handball at Red Lerille's with Lou."

"Earlier today Antoine Butterworth was here with some dirt on Bailey Ribbons."

"Dave, I don't want to hear any more about Antoine. He's weird. What else is new? End of subject."

"This isn't about Butterworth. He says he got his information from Lou Wexler."

"No, this isn't adding up. What would Lou know about Bailey Ribbons? Why would he have any interest in her?"

"Evidently, Wexler hired a PI as part of his scut work for Desmond Cormier."

"Lou does not do scut work. He's a producer and a writer. He's bankrupted himself out of his loyalty to Desmond. You may not know this, but when Des finishes the picture, he may well have produced one of the greatest films ever made. And the only way he can finish it is to beg, borrow, and steal every nickel he can. Maybe you don't agree with that, but give him and Lou some credit."

I took the towel from her hand and wiped her hair with it. "You want me to fix you something to eat?"

"No." Her eyes remained on mine. "This isn't about Antoine or Lou, is it?"

"No."

"What did the PI dig up on Bailey?"

"She may have accidentally started a fire in a schoolhouse when she was thirteen."

"That's it?"

"She'd put some matchheads inside some kindling she wanted to light with a flint."

Alafair went to the icebox and took a pitcher of tea from the tray, her eyes neutral and impossible to read. She had graduated with honors from Reed and had finished Stanford Law at the top of her class. She had an IQ that only two people in a million have.

"What's the rest of it?" she asked.

I shook my head.

"Don't play games with me, Dave."

"I'm not sure who Bailey is."

"She's got a history? Something to do with fire?"

"I'd better not say any more."

She set the pitcher of tea on the table and turned toward me. "Oh, Dave, what have you gotten yourself into?"

• • •

ONE HOUR LATER, the sky had grown darker, the rain heavier, blowing in sheets on the bayou. The phone rang on the kitchen counter. I looked at the caller ID before I picked up. "Is that you, Sean?"

"Remember when we went fishing and you said you'd have my back?" he said.

"Sure." The truth was, I didn't remember. But that didn't matter. "What's up, podna?"

"I'm a little snaky today and probably not seeing things right. Some of Hugo Tillinger's church friends was taking his body back to Texas, so I went over to the funeral home and hung around. I wasn't in uniform."

Wrong move, I thought. But I didn't say it.

"One guy asked if I was a relative or friend. I told him I was just paying my respects. I guess you could call that lying."

"You were in a difficult situation," I said. I rubbed my forehead and sat down in a chair. I knew where we were going, and I wanted to get out of it as fast as I could. I started to speak again but didn't get the chance.

"So the guy asks me where I knew Tillinger from. I told the guy I shot him."

"Listen to me, Sean—"

"He didn't say a word. He just stared at me with his eyes misting over. I never had anybody look at me like that."

"You're an honorable man. That's why you went to the funeral home. Nobody has the right to condemn you. That man wasn't there when Tillinger pointed a Luger at us."

"I wanted to explain it to him."

"There're situations for which no words are adequate. This was one of them. I'm sure that fellow respects you for coming to the funeral home."

I heard him take a breath. "I didn't mean to pester you," he said.

Through the window I could see lightning flickering on the oak trees in the yard, the door on Tripod's empty hutch swinging in the wind. "I'd better go now," I said.

"What I just told you ain't the only reason I called. I could have dropped a guy tonight. I called you because I don't know if I'm going crazy or not."

"Could have dropped whom?"

"Somebody out by my barn. I called him out and he took off running."

"Clear this up for me, Sean, and get it right. You say you could have dropped him. You drew down on him, you had him in your sights, what?"

"Lightning flashed and I saw somebody inside the barn. His skin looked real white. I think he had a rifle. I cain't be sure. I had my piece out, but I didn't raise it. He run out the back of the barn into the pecan trees."

"Did you call it in?"

"No, sir."

"Why not?"

"I don't want people to think I'm losing it."

"Will you be there for the next fifteen minutes?"

SEAN RENTED A paintless termite-eaten farmhouse with a wide gallery and a peaked tin roof down by Avery Island. All the lights were on in the house when I pulled into his dirt yard and went up the steps with a raincoat over my head. He opened the door.

"Hate to be an inconvenience and general pain in the butt," he said. "Want some coffee? It's already made."

"No, thanks."

He was wearing a white T-shirt and starched jeans and flip-flops. Leaning by the door was a scoped rifle with a sling. A holstered revolver and gun belt hung on the back of a chair in the dining room.

"Miss Bailey get aholt of you?" he said.

"No, I've been looking for her."

"That's funny. She was just here."

"What for?"

"She thought this Smiley guy might want to do me in 'cause of Tillinger being his friend or something."

"That's a possibility. You think you saw Smiley Wimple?"

"I ain't sure."

"You weren't in the service, were you?"

"No, sir." He waited. "How come you ask me that?"

"You've got your whole environment lit up. You'd make a great silhouette on a window shade."

"I don't study on things like that."

"On what things?"

"Dying. I figure everybody has a time. Till it comes, I say don't study on it."

"Let's take a look at your barn."

He put on a raincoat with a hood, and we went out into the rain and walked under an oak tree and crossed a clear spot and entered the dry barn. He closed the door behind us and pulled the chain on a solitary lightbulb. Fresh shoe marks were stenciled in the dirt, though not to the extent that I could tell their size.

"Were you in here?"

"No, sir."

"You stood outside?"

"Yes, sir."

"And the guy ran from here to that pecan grove?"

"Like I said."

"Your clothes didn't get wet?"

"They was sopping. That's why I put on dry ones."

"I was just wondering. I thought you might have secret powers."

"You did, huh?"

It was too late to take back the wisecrack. "What else did Bailey have to say?"

"I don't remember."

"Sean—"

"To heck with you, Dave. I'm sorry to have bothered you."

He pulled the chain on the light and walked back to his house, the rain glistening on his raincoat, his profile as sharp as snipped tin.

• • •

I DIDN'T SLEEP THAT night. Early Sunday morning I drove to Clete's motor court and banged on his door. The rain was still falling, a thick white fog rolling on the bayou, the air cold, like snow on your skin. Clete answered the door in his pajamas. "Have you gone nuts?"

"Thanks for the kind words," I said, brushing past him.

He shut the door. "You had trouble with Bailey Ribbons?"

"Why do you think that?"

"You're a mess with women."

"I'm a mess?"

"Yeah, without my guidance, you'd really be in trouble," he said. "What's the haps with Bailey?"

"I've got to have your sacred oath."

At first he didn't answer. He put on a bathrobe and fluffy blue slippers. Then he said, "Don't be talking to me like that, big mon. You either trust me or you don't."

I told him about the men who raped Bailey, and the fire she set under the propane tank on their trailer, and how all three men died, and the trouble she had in Holy Cross when she was thirteen. Then I told him about my visit the previous night to Sean McClain's place.

"McClain couldn't recognize Smiley Wimple?" Clete said. "Wimple looks like an albino caterpillar that glows in the dark."

"Yeah, I wondered the same thing."

"Sean McClain bothers you for some reason?"

"He's been around too many murder scenes," I said. "That's what I keep thinking. Same with Bailey. I don't know who she is."

Clete started a pot of coffee on his small gas stove. He opened his icebox and took out a box of glazed doughnuts and tossed it to me. "You know what you're always telling me, right?"

"No."

"People are what they do, not what they say, not what they think, not what they pretend to be."

"That's not reassuring. Bailey killed three people. That's what she did. With fire."

"These guys were running a meth lab. They deserved what they got. Besides, she told you about it. Would she get on the square like that if she were jacking you around?"

"Why is it that everything you say has something in it about genitalia?"

He removed the coffeepot from the stove and set it and two cups on the table. "Dave, there's an explanation for what you're experiencing. The guy we're after is waging war against this entire community. He wants us at each other's throats. Don't fall into his trap."

"How do you know this?"

"I don't. It's just a thought. But nothing else makes sense."

We were both quiet. I took a bite out of a doughnut.

"I've got a worse scenario, one I can't get out of my head sometimes," Clete said. "I wake up with it in the middle of the night. Some mornings, too. That's when it really gets bad."

"What does?"

"The dream. I dream we're all dead. We fucked up while we were alive and now we're stacking time in a place where there're no answers, only questions that drive you crazy. I went to a shrink about it."

"What did he say?"

"Nothing. I didn't give him a chance. He was one of the people in the dream. Enjoy the day we get, Streak. Being dead is a pile of shit."

Chapter Thirty-Two

THAT MORNING, I went to Mass at St. Edward's, and that evening I attended an AA meeting at the Solomon House, across the street from old New Iberia High. When I left the meeting, the stars were bright against a black sky, and a warm breeze was blowing through the live oaks in front of the old school building. It was a fine evening, the kind that assures you a better day is coming.

Sean McClain was leaning against my pickup in uniform, his head on his chest, the brim of his hat pulled down over his eyes.

"What's happenin'?" I said.

"Didn't mean to get in your face last night," he replied.

"You didn't."

"I been studying on a few things. I don't know if they're he'pful or not."

"You figured out who was in your barn?"

"Probably that little rodent nobody can catch."

"Wimple?"

"Whatever," he said.

"Let me set your mind at ease on that," I said. "If that were Smiley Wimple, we probably wouldn't be having this conversation."

"I'd be dead?"

"Probably."

"I been thinking about various clues on these murders," he said.

"Clues?"

"There haven't been many. Not from the day we seen that poor lady floating on the cross."

"I'm not following you, Sean."

"The clue we didn't give much mind to is that green tennis shoe me and you found on the beach. Size seven."

"It's not much of a clue, Sean."

"Y'all run a DNA on it, though, right?"

"Yeah, it belonged to Lucinda Arceneaux."

"If she was wearing one, she was wearing two."

"That's right," I said, my attention slipping away.

"One of the people who called in the 911 said there was a scream from a lighted cabin cruiser."

"You got it."

"Why not search every cabin cruiser on Cypremort Point?" he said.

"Search warrants aren't that broad, Sean."

He picked up a pebble from the curb and flung it at the street. "Well, I was just trying to come up with something. Sorry I ain't much he'p."

But Sean had opened a door in my head. A green tennis shoe with blue stripes. It didn't go with the purple dress Lucinda Arceneaux had died in.

"Why you got that look on your face?" Sean said.

"Because I just realized how stupid I've been."

I WOULDN'T CALL IT an epistemological breakthrough, but it was a beginning. Monday morning I went to our evidence locker and found Lucinda Arceneaux's purple dress. I also retrieved the green tennis shoe with blue stripes that Sean and I had found. I signed for both the shoe and the dress, then drove to St. Martinville and got a plainclothes to let me in Bella Delahoussaye's house. In her closet I found almost the same purple dress on a hanger, except it had been sprayed with sequins. She had been wearing it the first time I saw her at the blues club on the bayou.

I drove to the little settlement of Cade and the trailer home of Arceneaux's father, located on cinder blocks behind his clapboard church. The bottle tree next to the church tinkled in the wind. When the reverend opened the door, he looked ten years older than he had at the time of his daughter's death. I was holding the dress and the tennis shoe inside a paper bag.

"Can I help you?" he said.

"I'm Dave Robicheaux, Reverend. I wondered if I could talk with you a few minutes."

"You're who?"

"Detective Robicheaux. I was assigned the investigation into your daughter's death."

"Oh, yes, suh. I remember now," he said, pushing open the door. His hand was quivering on his cane, his eyes jittering.

I stepped inside. "I need you to look at this dress." I pulled it from the bag. Sand and salt were still in the folds.

"Why you want me to look at it?"

"Lucinda was wearing this when she died. Have you seen it before?"

"I don't remember her wearing a dress like that. But I cain't be sure, suh."

"I see."

"What else you got in there?"

"A tennis shoe. Do you recognize it as hers?"

He took it from my hand. The wet shine in his eyes was immediate.

"She was wearing tennis shoes like these the last time you saw her?" I said.

"Yes, suh. When she left for the airport."

"Sir, why don't you sit down? Here, let me help you."

"No, I'm all right. Can I have her shoe?"

"We have to keep it a while. I'll make sure it's returned to you."

"That dress couldn't be hers," he said.

"Why not?"

"She always called her green and blue shoes her 'little girl' shoes. She wore them with jeans. She always dressed tasteful."

"What do you know about Desmond Cormier?"

"He paid for her burial. He's a nice man."

"You ever hear of a man named Antoine Butterworth?"

"No, suh."

"Did Lucinda talk about Mr. Cormier?"

"I never axed her much about those Hollywood people. She said most of them were no different from anybody else. How'd she get that dress on? They took her clothes off when she was dead? Who would want to degrade her like that? I don't understand. How come this was done to her?"

His voice broke. He couldn't finish.

I silently made a vow that one day I would have an answer to that question, and I would put a mark on the perpetrator that he would carry to the grave, if not beyond.

TUESDAY MORNING, WE got a search warrant on the entirety of Desmond's house at Cypremort Point. It was a hard sell. Previously, we had been granted a search warrant on the part of the house considered the living area of Antoine Butterworth. The district attorney had to convince the judge that Desmond was a viable suspect in the death of Lucinda Arceneaux. The truth was otherwise. Desmond was a walking contradiction: a Leonardo, a humanist, a man who had the body of a Greek god, a man who would hang from the skid of a helicopter and then bully one of his subordinates. The DA got lost in his own vagueness and asked the judge if I could speak.

"Since you don't seem to be informed about your own investigation, I would be happy to hear from Detective Robicheaux," the judge said. He was a Medal of Honor recipient and had thick snow-white hair and was probably too old for the bench, but his patrician manners and soft plantation dialect were such a fond reminder of an earlier, more genteel culture that we didn't want to lose him. "Good morning, Detective Robicheaux. What is it you have to say, suh?"

"Desmond Cormier has been elusive and uncooperative since the beginning of our investigation, Your Honor," I said. "Through a telescope on Mr. Cormier's deck, I saw the deceased, Lucinda Arceneaux, tied to a cross floating in Weeks Bay. I asked Mr. Cormier to look through the telescope and tell me what he saw. He denied seeing anything. The deputy with me, Sean McClain, looked through the telescope and saw the same thing I had."

"The body?" the judge said.

"Yes, Your Honor."

"I don't know if that's enough to grant you a warrant, Detective."

"Mr. Cormier also broke in to the home of Deputy Frenchie Lautrec after Lautrec took his life or was killed by others. Lautrec had a tattoo of a Maltese cross on one leg. Desmond Cormier has one, too. I've seen it. We have reason to believe that Lautrec may have been involved both with prostitution and the series of the murders in our area. I believe Mr. Cormier may have been an associate of Deputy Lautrec."

I had overreached the boundaries of probability and even the boundaries of truth, but by this time, I didn't care about either.

"I am deeply disturbed by the implications in this investigation and the paucity of evidence it has produced," the judge said. I absolutely loved his diction. "Your warrant is granted. I recommend you conduct your search in such a way that there will be no evidentiary problems when the person or persons who committed these crimes is brought into court. We are all sickened and saddened by what has occurred in our community. Good luck to you, gentlemen."

One hour later, Sean McClain, Bailey, and I began ripping apart Desmond's house.

DESMOND WAS FURIOUS. He paced up and down in his living room. He was wearing cargo pants and sandals and an LSU football jersey cut off at the armpits. He watched us dump his shelves, lift armfuls of clothes from his closets, shake drawers upside down on the beds, clean out the kitchen cabinets, tip over furniture, and pull the trays out of the Sub-Zero refrigerator and freezer. His pale blue eyes looked psychotic, as though they had been clipped from a magazine and pasted on his face.

I think Desmond was bothered most by Bailey's coldness as he watched her casually destroying the symmetry and order of his household. But the worst had yet to come. She took down the framed still shots excerpted from *My Darling Clementine.* She lifted each of them off its wall hook and pulled the cardboard backing loose from the steel frame, then dropped each onto the couch as she might a bit of trash.

"What are you looking for?" he said. "How could my framed pictures have anything to do with a murder investigation? You of all people, Bailey, you know better. Damn you, woman."

"Please address me as Detective Ribbons. In answer to your question, we'll look at whatever we need to."

He started to pick up the frames and photos and squares of cardboard.

"Leave those where they are," she said.

"A pox on all of you, Dave," he said. "You motherfucker."

"You jerked us around, Des," I said. "You brought this on yourself."

"How so?"

"You're involved with a cult or a fetish or some kind of medieval romance that only lunatics could have invented," I said. "You've been covering your ass or somebody else's from the jump. Maybe if you stopped lying to people who are on your side, we wouldn't have to tear your house apart."

"Why don't you start arresting Freemasons? Or guys with Gothic tats? You're a fraud, Dave. You settled for mediocrity in your own life, and you resent anyone who went away and succeeded and then returned home and reminded you of your failure."

I was in the midst of pulling the stuffing out of his couch. I straightened up and got rid of a crick in my back. "I've got news for you, Des. Some of us stayed here and fought the good fight while others left and joined the snobs who think their shit doesn't stink."

His left eye shrank into a pool of vitriol, one so intense that I wondered if I knew the real Desmond Cormier.

We went downstairs under the house where he parked his vehicles. He stayed right behind us, his hands knotting and unknotting. There was a huge pile of junk in one corner. It started at the floor and climbed to the ceiling and looked water-stained and moldy at the base.

"What's that?" I said.

"The detritus of Hurricane Rita when my house was flooded. The trash my guests leave behind."

Three more deputies in uniform pulled in. "Just in time," I said to them. "Get your latex on, fellows."

"You enjoying this, Dave?" Desmond said.

"No, I'm not. I always thought you represented everything that's good in us. I thought you were a great artist and director, one for the ages."

He looked like someone had struck a kitchen match on his stomach lining. Behind him, Sean McClain pulled a black gym bag from the pile and shook out a towel, a Ziploc bag with a bar of soap in it, a sweatshirt, a spray can of men's deodorant, a pair of Levi's, and a flowery blouse. Then he shook the bag again. A tennis shoe fell out.

"Better take a look at this, Dave," Sean said.

"What do you have?"

Sean hooked his finger inside the shoe and lifted it from the pile. The shoe was lime green with blue stripes. "Size seven. Just like the one we found in the surf."

I looked at Desmond. "What do you have to say?"

"I don't know whose bag that is, and I never saw that shoe. Lucinda Arceneaux wore one like it?"

"Sell your doodah to somebody else," I said.

"Am I under arrest?"

"It doesn't work like that," I said. "But if I were you, I wouldn't plan any trips."

"So you're finished here?" he said.

Bailey stepped close to him, her eyes burning into his face. "Do yourself a favor. Stop acting like a twit and own up. You're an embarrassment."

His face twitched at the insult. I didn't know Des was still that vulnerable.

"Let's get back to work," I said. "Lay everything out on the lawn."

• • •

That afternoon, Lucinda Arceneaux's father identified the flowery blouse as his daughter's. He was unsure about the Levi's, but the size matched the clothes still hanging in her closet. There was no doubt the tennis shoe was hers. At four that afternoon I told Helen about everything I had.

"Okay, I'll talk to the DA's office in the morning," she said.

"Why not get an arrest warrant today? Don't give Desmond a chance to blow Dodge."

"We'll see what the prosecutor says. I don't think the clothes and shoe will be enough. The gym bag could belong to Butterworth."

"Butterworth is not our guy. Or at least not our primary guy."

"Why?"

"He wears his vices too openly. He's a showboat."

"Why your certainty about Desmond Cormier?"

"The killer is an iconoclast."

"A what?"

"A breaker of images and totems. But our guy is also infatuated with them."

"Sorry, that sounds like the kind of stuff Bailey comes up with."

"What does it take?" I asked. "Desmond has been playing us from the day we pulled Lucinda Arceneaux out of the water."

"But playing us about what? Most of his denial has to do with the source of his money. That doesn't make him a killer. Besides, Lucinda Arceneaux was his half sister, for God's sake."

"The issues are one and the same. The homicide is connected to money."

"We don't know that," she said.

"Speak for yourself."

"Cool out, Pops. We're going to nail him, but right now I'm not sure for what."

"Great choice of a verb."

"I love you, bwana, but sometimes I think I committed an unpardonable sin in a former life, and you were put here to give me a second chance."

"What if Desmond is our guy and he does it again?"

"I have a hard time thinking of him as a serial killer."

"Our guy is not a serial killer. There's a method to his madness."

She didn't answer; she obviously had given up the argument.

"What if he's protecting the murderer and the murderer kills someone else?" I said. "Maybe another young woman like Lucinda Arceneaux?"

"You just made sure I won't sleep tonight," she replied.

THE NEXT DAY, we went to work on the origins of the bag. It had come from an online vendor in California that had gone out of business five years ago. There were latents on the deodorant can, but they weren't in the system. Bailey came into my office. "I just got a call from Butterworth."

"He called *you*? You didn't call him first?"

"He said he wants to come in."

"With an attorney?"

"No. He said he wants to clear the air."

In any investigation a cop looks for what we call "the weak sister." I believed we had just found ours. "Call him back. Tell him we'll meet him in City Park at noon."

"Not here?"

"We want him to feel comfortable, as though he's among friends."

"Sounds a little deceitful."

"These guys invented deceit."

"Okay," she said. "Want to get together this evening?"

"Sure."

"Because that's not the impression I've been having."

"You shouldn't think that way, Bailey."

"You don't think less of me because of what I told you about my past?"

"No," I replied, trying to keep my face empty.

"See you at six?"

"Looking forward to it," I said.

After she was gone, I could feel my heart racing, but I didn't know why.

WE MET BUTTERWORTH with a box of fried chicken and crawfish at one of the picnic shelters in the park. He parked his Subaru under an oak and got out. He wore white slacks and a lavender long-sleeve silk shirt that twisted with light on his spare frame; his tan was even deeper than when I had seen him last. He put a Nicorette on his tongue.

"Sit down," I said. "Have some of Louisiana's best fried food. It has enough cholesterol to clog a sewer drain."

"Very good of you. Thank you."

"What did you want to tell us, Mr. Butterworth?" Bailey said.

"Of a concern or two I have. Our enterprise—or rather, the film culture—is a diverse one. Our common denominator is a desire for money and power and celebrity. I suspect you have determined that by now."

"The same could apply to many groups of people," Bailey said.

"Our production company is independent of the studios, which stay alive only through the computerized adaptation of comic books. In other words, we find production money in unlikely sources."

His faux accent and manner were already starting to wear. "We're conscious of that, Mr. Butterworth," I said. "What's the point, sir?"

"We take money from Hong Kong, Russians, Saudis, and some people in New Jersey."

"And you launder money for some of them?" Bailey said.

I tried to give her a cautionary look.

"Use any term for it you wish," Butterworth said. He fished in his shirt pocket as though looking for a cigarette. "I want you to understand my position. I don't kill people. I saw enough of that in Africa."

"You make and sell war games for teenagers," Bailey said.

"I can't deny that," he said. "I also buy Treasury bonds, and if you haven't noticed, the United States government is the biggest weapons manufacturer in the world."

"Come on, Mr. Butterworth," I said. "Let's get to it."

"A number of people from the Mafia have shown up in our lives. Why is that? They want an immediate return on their money. Second, a nasty little worm of a man with a ridiculous name evidently roasted a couple of their lads."

"Smiley Wimple?" I said.

"Yes, that naughty boy."

"You called him a worm of a man," I said. "You've seen him?"

"He was on the bloody set, eating an Eskimo Pie."

"How'd you know the guy was Wimple?" I said.

"I've seen him before. He was killing people here three years ago. He seems to have a fondness for the area."

I didn't know if I believed him or not, and frankly, I didn't care. Butterworth had a circuitous way of spreading confusion without offering any information of value.

"Here's what I think, Mr. Butterworth," I said. "You plan to give us nothing. In the meantime you're strapping on a parachute so you can bail out of the plane before it crashes."

"Desmond's film will be one of the greatest ever put on the American screen," he said. "I've led a rather worthless life, but I take great satisfaction in the knowledge that I had something to do with a creation of that magnitude. Des has only a short run ahead of him. I hope he can finish his film."

"Say again?" I replied.

"He's on the spike. Don't ask me what goes into his veins, because I don't know. Whatever it is, it's a cocktail from hell."

Our table was spangled with sunshine, the moss waving overhead, the wind cool off Bayou Teche. The petals of the camellia bushes were scattered on the grass like drops of blood. As a cop, you hear everything that human beings are capable of doing. That doesn't mean you get used to it. Evil has a smell like copper coins on a hot stove, like offal burning on a winter day, like a gangrenous-soaked bandage at a battalion aid station in a tropical country. It violates your glands and your senses. Its odor stays in your dreams, and you never fail to recognize it in your waking day. I swore I smelled it on Butterworth's skin.

"No comment?" Butterworth said.

"You're diming your friend and doing it without shame," I said. "It's a bit embarrassing to witness."

He looked at Bailey. "He's obsessed with you."

"Who is?" she said.

"Desmond," Butterworth said. "Be careful. A great artist is just this side of mad. If you doubt me, thumb through the bios of those who torment themselves for months trying to paint a starry night or the likeness of God. Desmond uses chemicals not to escape reality but to find it. How insane can one man be?"

Chapter Thirty-Three

I PICKED UP BAILEY at six o'clock. Or tried to pick her up. She came to the front door in a gingham dress. I was wearing a suede sport coat and freshly pressed slacks and a light blue shirt and a plum-colored necktie. "Ready?"

"Where are we going?" she said, as though surprised.

"Dinner and a movie."

"I already fixed something."

"Then a film?"

"Whatever you like. Are you turning into a monk?"

"If so, I'm not aware of it."

"Come in, Dave. We need to talk."

I didn't want to come in or to talk. If someone had pointed a gun at me and asked me to state my honest feelings about Bailey, I wouldn't have known what to say. My obsession with her was probably as great as Desmond's. Maybe I was trying to reclaim my youth; maybe I wanted to be her protector. It was hard for me to separate her from the image of Cathy Downs standing by the road while Henry Fonda tells her that one day he may return to Tombstone, although he knows full well that his business with the Clantons is not over and he will never be back.

Yes, it was hard for me to separate Bailey from Clementine Carter, until I thought about the three men Bailey had set on fire.

I stepped inside and closed the door behind me. She had set the dining room table and lit a candelabra in the center. "You're looking at me that way again. It makes me very uncomfortable," she said.

"That's a pretty dress. You look beautiful in it. You're beautiful in anything, Bailey."

"I wish I hadn't told you about what I did in Montana. You think I should resign my job?"

"For what purpose?"

"Maybe I should report myself to the authorities in Montana."

I could feel my heart thudding, my stomach churning. "This is the reality. The case was closed years ago. In the eyes of the law, three meth dealers blew themselves up. Probably all three had records as dealers and predators. Their deaths were marked off as good riddance. If you reopen the case, you will be involved with the courts for two or three years and then probably be given probation. Everybody involved with the case will secretly wish you stayed in Louisiana. In the meantime you will be financially destitute and ruined professionally. What good would come out of it?"

"I'd sleep again," she said.

I had tried. But I couldn't even convince myself. And I had not addressed the arson investigation at the school in Holy Cross, even though I had discussed it with Clete, for which I felt another layer of guilt.

"Desmond hired a PI to dig up dirt on you," I said. "Or rather, he got Lou Wexler to hire the PI who dug up your past."

"Pardon?"

"You were part of an arson investigation when you were thirteen. The fire was at a Girl Scout meeting in Holy Cross."

"Yes, it was an accident."

"I talked to a retired fire department superintendent," I said. "He believed they cut you some slack because of the problems in your home."

"You're saying I'm a firebug?"

"No," I said. But the word stuck in my throat.

"So what *am* I?"

"Someone who had a hard young life. Like a lot of us."

"What do we do now? Make love? Eat dinner? Pretend nothing has happened?"

"I'm not sure."

She went to the dining room table and pinched out the candles one at a time. "There. Good night, sweet prince. May flights of angels sing thee to thy rest."

I stared at her dumbly. She avoided my eyes. I think she was on the edge of crying. I went outside and got into my truck and drove home in the last of the sunset. I don't think I ever felt more alone.

THAT SAME EVENING, Alafair and Clete went to Red Lerille's Health and Racquet Club in Lafayette. Alafair played tennis with a friend under the lights in the outdoor courts, then joined Clete inside, where he was slowly curling and lowering a hundred-pound barbell, his upper arms swelling into muskmelons. Then she realized Lou Wexler was in the free-weight room also, forty feet away, dead-lifting three hundred pounds, his back and thighs knotted as tight as iron. He released the bar, bouncing the plates on the platform.

"Hey, you," he said.

"Hey," she replied. "I thought you had to go back to Los Angeles to work out something with the union."

"Got it done on the phone," he said. "Des wants to keep me close by. He seems to go from one mess to the next."

"I'd rather not talk about Des."

"Right-o. I saw the big fellow over there, what's-his-name, Purcel. You're here with him?"

"Y'all haven't met formally?" she said.

"No, just a nod or two. I saw him at Monument Valley, I think. When he visited the set. No need to bother him."

"You two would hit it off."

"You know me, Alafair, I'm a bit private."

She gestured for Clete to come over anyway. "This is Lou Wexler, Clete. He's a producer and writer on our film."

"Glad to know you," Clete said, extending his hand.

"Likewise," Wexler said. He didn't take Clete's hand. His attention had shifted to a man in a black-and-white jumpsuit wearing yellow workout gloves who had just walked in and begun pumping twenty-pound dumbbells. The man in the jumpsuit stiff-armed the dumbbells straight out in front of him, twisting them rapidly back and forth, the veins in his neck cording. His head was shaped like a lightbulb, with several strands of hair combed across the crown.

Alafair followed Wexler's line of sight to the man in the jumpsuit. "Who's that?"

"One of the happy little fellows who was indicted in the Iberia Parish prison scandal."

"That's Tee Boy Ladrine," Clete said. "He was a guard at the jail. He was found not guilty."

"How could anybody work there and not know what was going on?" Wexler said.

"I know what you mean," Clete said. "He was tight with Frenchie Lautrec, the guy who hanged himself. But Tee Boy rents his brain by the week. On a good day he can tie his shoes without a diagram."

"What does intelligence have to do with pretending he didn't know a man was suffocated in there?" Wexler said.

"You don't have to tell me, noble mon."

"Noble what?"

"I was saying jail sucks," Clete said. "I've been in a number of them, and not as a visitor."

"Tell me, Mr. Purcel, would you stand by while some poor fellow has the air crushed out of his lungs?" Wexler asked.

"Probably not."

"That's the only point I was making. A decent fellow acts decently. I just don't think it's a good idea to let a bugger in a jumpsuit come into a fine club like this."

Clete's gaze focused on nothing. "I'd better grab a shower and one of those health drinks."

Alafair put her hand on Clete's upper arm. It felt as hard as a fire hydrant. "We'll have a drink together. Right, Lou?"

"Of course. Let me hit the shower, too. What a fine evening.

Shouldn't get fired up over a cretin who probably never heard a shot fired in anger."

They walked toward the locker rooms, and Alafair thought Wexler's absorption with the former jail guard was over. Then Wexler veered off course as though he had tripped. He collided solidly into Ladrine, knocking him into the mirror above the dumbbell racks.

"Sorry, there," Wexler said. "Must be some soap on the floor. Are you all right? You look like someone shoved a baton up your ass. Order up at the bar. I have a tab. The name is Wexler."

Then he continued on his way. Alafair's face was burning.

"The guy is from overseas," Clete said to Ladrine. "I think he took a round in the head from ISIS or something."

"Oh yeah?" Ladrine said. His eyes were tiny coals.

"The next time I see you at Bojangles', the drinks are on me," Clete said.

Twenty minutes later, Clete and Alafair and Wexler met at the juice bar. Just as their drinks arrived, Ladrine walked by, unshowered, still wearing his jumpsuit, a gym bag hanging from his hand.

"Excuse me a moment," Wexler said. He caught up with Ladrine. "Apologies again, fellow. It's chaps such as you who keep the darkies in their place. You're a genuine testimony to the superiority of the white race." He sank his fingers into Ladrine's arm and slapped him three times between the shoulder blades, hard, putting his weight into it, leaving Ladrine stupified.

Wexler came back to the bar and chugged half his tropical drink, blowing out his breath. "I wonder who he voted for."

"Have you lost your mind?" Alafair said.

"Just having a little fun," Wexler said. "I'm sure he took it as such." Clete had remained silent. Wexler caught it. "You want to say something to me?"

"You're quite a guy," Clete said. "I thought his lungs were going to come out of his mouth."

"No, I'm not quite a guy," Wexler said. "Desmond is the man, the champion of us all, and about to go to hell in a basket. He belongs at

Roncevaux and yet won't heed the call. I guess that's why I love and pity him so."

Alafair looked at Wexler as though she had never seen him before.

EARLY THE NEXT morning, Clete called and asked me to meet him at Victor's, where he ate almost every day.

"What's going on?" I said.

"I just want to have breakfast with you."

I knew better. Clete never did anything in a whimsical way or without a purpose.

He was waiting for me at the door of the cafeteria, wearing a dark blue suit and a dark tie, his shoes shined. He wasn't wearing his porkpie hat, which, by anyone's standards, was a tacky anachronism. We got into the serving line, and he began stacking his tray with scrambled eggs, sausage patties, bacon, hash browns with a saucer of milk gravy on the side, toast dripping with butter, grits, orange juice, coffee and cream.

"Sure you got enough?" I said.

"I've been cutting back on sugar and the deep-fried stuff. Can you tell?"

"Yeah, I think so," I said.

We found a table in the corner and started eating. I wondered how long it would take for him to get to the subject at hand, whatever it was.

"Why the suit?" I asked finally.

"I'm going over to East Texas. There's a service for Hugo Tillinger." He stared innocuously at the door as though he had said nothing of consequence.

"You don't owe Tillinger anything, Clete."

"If I'd called in a 911 when he jumped off the top of that freight train, maybe a lot of this stuff wouldn't have happened. Later I had a chance to bust him, and I didn't do that either."

"He wasn't a player. Lose the sackcloth and ashes. And leave those people in Texas alone."

"Think so?"

Once again I had become his priest. "Yeah, over the gunnels with the doodah." But I was bothered by Tillinger's death, too. I thought he got a raw shake all the way around. I tried to change the subject. "Did you and Alafair have a good time at Red Lerille's last night?"

"She didn't tell you about the run-in with Tee Boy Ladrine?"

"The jail guard who got fired?"

"Yeah, Lou Wexler deliberately plows into him, then apologizes by pounding on his back until the guy can't breathe."

"Wexler has a beef with him or something?"

"Something about civil rights and how the inmates got treated in the jail. He got a little sensitive with me."

"You?"

"So I tell him he's quite a guy, and he starts talking about Desmond Cormier and Roncevaux and how much he loves and pities Cormier."

"Alafair didn't tell me any of this."

"Wexler's gay?"

"I don't know. He seems attracted to Alafair."

"What's this stuff about Roncevaux?"

"It's high up in the Pyrenees. A battle took place there in the eighth century. *The Song of Roland* is a celebration of it."

"So what do medieval guys clanking around like bags of beer cans have to do with Hollywood?"

"It's a little more complex than that."

"Speak slowly and I'll try to catch on. Use flash cards if you have to."

"Clete, I was trying to—"

"Forget it," he said.

"There are people who believe that the legends of King Arthur and the search for the Holy Grail and the horns blowing along the road to Roncevaux make it all worthwhile."

"Make *what* worthwhile?"

"Being born. Dying. That kind of thing."

Clete pointed a finger at me. “I don’t want to hear that again. I’ve got enough crazy people in my life already.”

Other diners were starting to look at us. Clete bent in to his food. Then he wiped his mouth and said, “This stuff is sick, Dave. The deaths of the women, the subhuman cruelty. I can’t sleep. It’s like coming back from Nam. It’s like I’ve got tiger shit in my brain.”

“We’ll catch whoever is responsible, Clete. It’s a matter of time.”

“What about Alafair?” he said.

“What about her?”

“Somebody was stalking us with a scoped rifle at Henderson Swamp. Maybe the same guy was at Sean McClain’s house. If he can’t clip one of us, maybe he’ll find another target, one whose loss you’ll never survive.”

“That’s not going to happen,” I said, my face flushing.

“You know the future?”

“Knock it off.”

“Our guy won’t stop until we tear up his ticket. I’m going to do it, Streak. I’m going to paint the landscape with that cocksucker.”

The tables around us had gone quiet. I stared at my plate, my ears ringing, wondering where Alafair was at the moment.

WHEN I GOT back on the sidewalk, I called her on my cell. “Hey,” I said.

“Hey, yourself.”

“I’m just checking in on you, Baby Squanto.”

That was her nickname when she was little. She had a whole collection of Baby Squanto Indian books. “I’m at the set, down by Morgan City. We’re shooting some of the last scenes.”

“What time will you be home?”

“Probably by seven. What’s going on?”

“Nothing. Clete told me about Lou Wexler getting into it with the guy at Red’s.”

“Lou doesn’t like white men who knock women or minority people around.”

"A man who cares for a woman doesn't get into a confrontation in front of her," I said.

"Lou is a good person, Dave. How about laying off the people I work with? Just for one day."

"I didn't know I was that bad."

"I'm going to give you a recorder for your birthday."

"See you this evening."

I closed my phone. Clete came out of the cafeteria and crossed the street and got into his Caddy in the alley, where it was parked. He drove away without waving. I wanted to believe he hadn't seen me. I watched the taillights of the Caddy disappear in the traffic, headed west, toward Lafayette and I-10. I felt even older than my years but did not know why.

CLETE DROVE FOR three hours to a brick church in the piney woods of East Texas. Behind it, headstones trailed like scattered teeth down a slope to a lake spiked with dead trees, the banks churned with the hoof prints of Angus that had the red scours. The foundation in the church was cracked, the broken panes in the stained glass replaced with cardboard. Clete parked his Caddy and got out. The trees in the distance were bright green, the light harsh. There was a rawness in the wind that chilled his bones.

The post-burial service, which Clete had indicated he would not attend, had just started. He knew none of the people there. They seemed to be simple people, out of yesteryear, with work-worn hands and faces, the kind of people who didn't quarrel with their lot and accepted death as they would a shadow moving across a meadow, subsuming whatever was in its path. There was an innocence and shyness about them, like that of children, and he wanted to tell them that but didn't know how.

The grave had been filled in, the humped dirt partly covered by a roll of artificial grass. A tall man in black, his hair hanging over his ears, read from the Book of Psalms. Then the service was over, and the mourners drifted off to a table loaded with food in the shade of the church. Clete's head was cold, and he wished he had brought his hat. He caught up with the man in black. "Sir?"

The man kept walking. On the far side of the lake, Clete thought he saw a white boxlike truck pull into a grove of pine trees.

"Reverend?" Clete said.

The man in black turned around. His face was chiseled, shrunken in the coldness of the wind. One wing of his starched collar was bent up in a point, like a shark's tooth. "People here'bouts call me Preacher."

"My name is Clete Purcel. I'd like to ask you a question about Mr. Tillinger. I'm a private investigator. My question is rather direct and maybe offensive."

"Go ahead and ask it."

"Did Mr. Tillinger kill his wife and daughter?"

"No, I do not think that. Hugo would never harm his family. But he had associates who are another matter. Men who do the devil's work."

"Sir?" Clete said.

"They sell arms in Africa. I visited Hugo before his escape. He wanted to come clean on his life and get shut of the wrongful things he did."

"Do you know the names of these guys selling weapons?"

"No, sir."

"Would anybody else here know?"

"We have nothing to do with those kinds of people. Would you like to have something to eat with us?"

"Yes, I would," Clete replied. "Thank you."

He walked with Preacher to the picnic tables in the shade. The white truck was still parked among the pines on the far side of the lake; the folding door on the passenger side was open. Clete thought he saw the sun glint on a pair of binoculars. A jolly fat woman handed him a ham-and-onion sandwich. "You look like you're fixing to fall down, you poor little thing. You better eat up."

"Y'all have ice cream trucks hereabouts?" he asked.

"Like anywhere else, I guess," she said "You don't want my sandwich?"

"Yes, ma'am, I want it," he said, biting into the bread.

"Hang around. I got more," she said. She smiled broadly.

"Got to go to work."

"I bet you were a deep-sea diver in the service," she said, still beaming.

He tried to smile at her with his eyes and say nothing, but his energies were used up. "I always liked ham-and-onion sandwiches. Dinner on the ground and that sort of thing."

The woman continued to smile at him. She looked massive, her skin windburned, her eyes playful. He gazed at the white truck. It couldn't be Wimple, could it? Was he losing it? The woman was laughing at a joke someone had told, then looking at Clete. She squeezed his shoulder. "Don't be so solemn. We all get to the same place. I call it the Gingerbread House."

Had she just said that? Her mouth was moving, but no sound was coming out. The preacher was looking at him, too, his hand like a claw around his Bible. Clete left the table and walked toward his Caddy. It seemed too early for the sun to be setting, as though nature had conspired to steal part of the day from him. The white truck was still in the trees. He found a musty sweater in the Caddy's trunk and put it on under his suit coat; his skin felt dry and cold and raw when he touched it. He drove away from the graveyard, the mourners shrinking inside his rearview mirror.

HE TURNED ONTO a dirt road and tried to access the far side of the lake but ended up on a cattle guard in front of a locked gate. He got out on the shoulder and scanned the trees with his binoculars. The truck was nowhere in sight. He threw his binoculars onto the passenger seat and drove five miles on a county road, then turned east on the interstate. Just as he crossed the Louisiana line, he thought he saw the white truck behind him.

The heater in the Caddy wasn't working. He couldn't remember when he had felt so cold or when his hands had felt so dry and chapped on the wheel. He pulled into a truck stop and had a waitress fill his thermos with black coffee.

"You got some aspirin?" he said.

She glanced at the counters that were stocked with snacks and over-the-counter curatives. "Right behind you."

"I think I'm about to fall down."

"Stay here."

She left the counter, then returned with two aspirins on a napkin. She was tall and dark-haired and middle-aged and seemed out of place and too old for her job. A globe and anchor were tattooed on the inside of her forearm. "You don't look too good, gunny."

"How'd you know I was in the Crotch?" he asked.

"I can tell."

"Can you do something else for me?" he said.

"Depends."

"Would you look over my shoulder at the gas pumps and tell me if you see an ice cream truck out there?"

"One isn't there now."

"Now?"

"I saw an ice cream truck after you came in. It left."

He put a ten-dollar bill on the counter and checked into the motel behind the truck stop. As he walked toward his room, he felt as though his feet were stepping into holes in the floor. He chain-locked the door and fell onto the bed and pulled a pillow over his head. Behind his eyelids he saw artillery rounds mushrooming in a rain forest, scribbling trails of smoke on the night sky like giant spider legs. A navy corpsman was holding a thumb on Clete's carotid, his hand shiny with gore, struggling to get a compress on it with the other. The corpsman's face looked made of bone under his steel pot.

Chapter Thirty-Four

SMILEY DID NOT measure time in terms of clocks or calendars. Time was a series of sensations, like bubbles rising from a caldron, without meaning or predictability. A therapist had told him he'd been raised in an environment where cruelty was masked as love, and the consequence would remain with him like a stone bruise on the soul for the rest of his life.

He associated sleep with a brief respite from the world, followed by a wet bed in the morning and a belt across his buttocks. Breakfast was a bowl of porridge and a glass of cold milk unless he was assigned to the punishment chair. As a runaway, he learned that the streets of Mexico City were shady and cool in the day and cold at night, and the male and female prostitutes in front of the cantinas were not his friends. He also learned that the hands and lips and genitalia that moved over his body were a testimony to his status in the world—namely, that Smiley Wimple was food, and the scabs and rags and stench on his body and the lice nits in his hair would never be a deterrent to the class of men who preyed upon him.

Two nights ago he had boosted an ice cream truck from inside the corporate creamery in Lafayette, and yesterday he had driven it to a playground in the little town of Sunset and handed out boxes of Popsicles and Eskimo Pies and ice cream sandwiches to a throng of black children. He did the same in back-of-town Lake Charles and a poor neighborhood in Baton Rouge. He changed license plates twice, although there was apparently no need. A sheriff's deputy in West Baton Rouge Parish bought a frozen sundae from him.

Early this morning he had driven to New Iberia to try to get rid of his growing obsession with Clete Purcel. Why did this man bother him? Smiley wasn't sure. Smiley trusted children and some people of color but few white adults, including himself, the latter in large part because he had been taught he was worthless.

So he kept his contact with others minimal. When he had a problem, he did what addicts and alcoholics call a geographic: He went somewhere else. That was why he liked airplanes. An airplane was an armored womb that not only protected him but was detached from the earth and all its troubles.

Regarding his line of work, he had no illusions. The people he worked for paid well and gave him Disney World tickets but laughed at him behind his back, at least until someone told them of his capabilities. In fact, Smiley had made a mental note long ago to get to know some of them better after he retired and could afford to do a freebie or two.

Then why the obsession with the man named Purcel?

The answer lay in the man's eyes. There was a calmness in them, a lack of either fear or hostility, a green glow that was unreadable but seemed to absorb everything and nothing. The pale smoothness around the sockets was like a baby's. Most of the people Smiley knew had scales around their eyes.

Maybe he needed to prove himself wrong about Clete Purcel. The people he had trusted usually turned out to be traitors, which meant they had to be punished. This man was different. He was a violent man capable of great kindness, a protector not only of abused children and women but people who had no voice or power and were used and discarded. He could have been the male companion of Wonder Woman. The two of them could have married and been Smiley's parents. That thought filled him with a sensation like sinking in a bathtub of warm water.

He had followed the Caddy into East Texas and watched the graveyard service through the binoculars, then followed the Caddy back into Louisiana, even into the truck stop, where the man named Purcel had bought a thermos of coffee.

That was when Smiley, in his preoccupation with Purcel, got careless and picked up a tail of his own.

He recognized the vehicle from Miami's Little Havana, a silver Camaro with oversize rear tires and a grille shaped like the mouth of a sea creature and mufflers that throbbed on the asphalt. The owner was Jaime O'Banion, a psychotic button man from New Orleans whom Tony Nemo used to call "half-spick, half-Mick, and half-anything-else-that-don't-use-rubbers."

Of course, Smiley had taken Tony Nemo off the board with a container of Drano and had always wanted to do the same for Jaime O'Banion. Word was Jaime had done a whole family with a bomb in Mexico City, children included. Jaime presented another problem. He was the only button man in the business who was so dangerous and good at his craft that he got away with hits inside Miami, which had been an open city since the days of Lansky and Trafficante. Worse, Jaime obviously knew Smiley was following Clete Purcel, and he may have seen Purcel check into the motel behind the truck stop.

Smiley had made a mess of things, as when he had messed in his underwear at the orphanage. He could almost hear the whistle of the belt. After sunset, he abandoned the ice cream truck and boosted a vintage pickup from behind a bar. He threw a backpack loaded with the tools of his trade onto the passenger seat and headed for the motel, wondering if his own time had come.

CLETE COULD NOT explain the affliction that had spread through his body since the afternoon. It had begun with violent spasms he associated with food poisoning, an aggregate of intestinal pain worse than his wounds in Vietnam, coupled with the fever and chills that went with the malaria he had picked up in El Sal. He was curled in a ball under the bedcovers in the motel, his teeth clicking, the buzz of nonexistent mosquitoes in his ears, when he realized he was not alone.

A lamp burned on a table by the wall. A shadowy figure was

pouring soup out of a can into a pot by a hot plate. Clete tried to raise himself and fell back on the pillow. "What are you doing here?"

"A bad man knows where you are," Smiley said. "His name is Jaime O'Banion. You know him?"

Yes, Clete thought, but he was too weak to say the word. The night chain on the door had been snipped in half, the electric lock probably opened with a key card from a compliant desk clerk. Clete closed his eyes and breathed slowly in and out, his forehead sweating, cold as ice water.

"I need to get you away from here," Smiley said.

"No," Clete said.

"Yes. Do not argue."

"Don't talk to me that way," Clete said.

Smiley didn't reply. Clete could smell the soup heating in the pan; then he heard Smiley take the pan off the hot plate and pour it into the cup of an army-surplus mess kit. Smiley pulled up a chair next to the bed and filled a spoon with the soup.

"Eat."

"No."

"If you don't eat, your liver will be hurt."

"It's already a football."

"Open."

Clete got up on one elbow and took the spoon out of Smiley's hand and drank the soup off the spoon. He fell back on the pillow. "Where's O'Banion?"

"He's gone now. But he'll be back about an hour after the bars close."

Clete didn't try to answer. Smiley knew the culture: The pavement princesses and the truckers on the prowl and anyone hooking up late would be doing the dirty bop by three a.m.

"Have some more," Smiley said. He held out the aluminum cup so Clete could dip the soup from it. Clete dropped the spoon onto the rug. Smiley washed it in the sink. Clete reached for the drawer of the nightstand.

"What are you doing?" Smiley said.

"My piece is in there."

"Not now, it isn't."

Clete lay back on the pillow, his arm over his eyes. "You need to go. I'll call 911 for an ambulance."

"He's close by. He may be in the next room."

"I'd rather be dead than have whatever is inside me."

The room was quiet a long time. The pain was like glass twisting inside him. Then, when he thought he could stand it no longer, a strange transformation happened in his metabolism. The pincers that seemed to be tearing his intestines apart turned to snowmelt flooding his body. His head sagged as though his spinal cord has been severed; he felt himself drifting into a dark, safe place beneath the earth. Someone cupped his forehead, taking his temperature, and then the same person folded Clete's .38 in his hand and placed his hand and weapon on his chest as though arranging a corpse in a coffin. Clete heard the door open and click shut, then he fell asleep.

When he woke, the room was completely dark, and his throat was so dry he couldn't swallow. He fumbled for his cell phone and hit the speed dial. *Come on, Streak, answer your phone.*

"Clete?" a voice said.

"Yeah," he rasped. "Mayday."

"What?"

"I feel like I died. Remember when I told you we might be living among dead people?"

"Are you drunk?"

"Smiley Wimple was here. He said Jaime O'Banion is here, too. Don't call the locals."

"Why not?"

"They hate my guts. They'll put me in the can. Or worse."

"Where are you?"

Clete said the name of the truck stop and town and passed out again, the cell phone bouncing on the carpet.

• • •

SMILEY WAS NOT equipped to understand a phrase like "intimations of mortality." But he understood its smell. The smell was in the ditches behind the cantinas where the prostitutes poured their buckets at sunrise, and in the slums where the poor raked rotting food with their bare hands from a smoldering garbage dump, and under a bridge outside Torreón where the narco-gangsters hung their trophies from wire loops and left them for bats to eat.

Smiley never thought about what lay on the other side of death, but he knew one thing for sure—people killed other people all the time. They just did it in a different way. With bombs from an airplane. With drones or rockets. That way the images were reduced to a neat and tidy satellite video, one that had no sound.

Smiley was not one to argue. Nor did he brood upon the ways human beings conducted themselves. The issue for those at the bottom of the pile was simple: Don't be drawn in by lies, and don't let others use you. The only people who dismissed the importance of power were those who possessed it or those who liked their roles as human poodles.

The only true friend he ever had was a girl a little older than he in the orphanage. She loved him and washed his body in the morning and hid his wet sheets so he wouldn't be punished, and sometimes read poetry to him. He understood little of the meaning, but occasionally a line stuck with him that somehow defined a central mystery in his life. He remembered one line in particular. It came at the end of what she called a sonnet, one written by a young man named John Keats: *On the shore / Of the wide world I stand alone, and think / Till love and fame to nothingness do sink.*

Did that mean we were on our own, and that love and fame were of no value, and that neither the earth nor the crowd provided reward or succor? Did our only victory lie in survival, in solitude, far from the distant crowd? Or was the poet saying it was better to be the giver of death than its recipient?

Smiley chose to believe the latter. But now he was undoing his own ethos, helping the man named Purcel instead of taking care of business first, which in this instance meant dealing with Jaime

O'Banion, known as the cruelest and smartest mechanic on the East Coast. The choice of O'Banion as the hitter meant the Mob was going to make an object lesson of Smiley, old-style, the way they did Tommy Fig in the Irish Channel years ago when they freeze-wrapped his parts and strung them from a wood-bladed ceiling fan in his own butcher shop.

Smiley's problem with O'Banion wasn't simply professional. They had run into each other at Disney World and at the track in Hialeah and also at the Jazz Festival in New Orleans. O'Banion wore white suits and silk shirts and tight vests and two-tone shoes and a Panama hat, and he had a coarse Irish face that reminded Smiley of a twisted squash. Sometimes a prostitute was glued to his arm. An entourage of sycophants usually followed him. O'Banion called Smiley *gusano* (worm) to his face; he once said to his friends as Smiley walked by, "Here comes queer-bait. Grab your cocks, boys."

The sycophants snickered openly, safe in O'Banion's presence.

Now Smiley was parked behind a truck stop in a stolen pickup, the stars bright, dawn one hour away, wondering how O'Banion would make his play. He reached inside his tool bag and retrieved a long-barreled, silenced, .22-magnum semi-auto, one of two that he had custom-made. He loved to touch the barrel and trace his fingertips up and down the coldness of the steel, his eyes closed, his wee-wee stiffening inside his pants. He could hear himself breathing inside the truck cab, his heart slipping into overdrive. He set down the pistol until his arousal went away, then swallowed and cupped his mouth, longing for the release his work gave him.

O'Banion would be coming soon. But where and how? The truck stop and motel employed servicepeople who came and went at odd hours. O'Banion was a legend when it came to disguises and deception. Wearing surgical garb, he had walked into an OR in Tampa and popped a confidential informant on the operating table. In horn-rimmed glasses and a tweed suit and a wig that fit his head like a football helmet, he'd followed a Mississippi judge into the men's room of the county courthouse, exchanged pleasantries with him at the urinal, then, on his way out, casually blown the judge's brains all over the mirror. He also used disposable backup, usually junkies and black gangsters who thought they were about to make the big score and ended up in a Dumpster.

Smiley took a breath. What was the smart thing to do? Easy answer. Let Purcel worry about himself and catch O'Banion down the road with one of his women on his arm, out in public. Yes, stipple his vest with tiny red flowers and look into O'Banion's eyes while he did it.

Yes, yes, yes.

Smiley twisted the key in the ignition and felt the pickup's engine jump to life. He saw a black man enter the side door of the motel, pulling a laundry cart behind him. A woman with a vacuum followed. A man in a delivery uniform was smoking a cigarette in front of the main entrance; he flipped it in a high arc and went inside the building. A couple got out of a cab, laughing, walking unsteadily, and also went inside.

Smiley cut the engine, his head pounding. It wasn't fair. He was being given a choice between abandoning his entire ethos or abandoning Purcel. The only person whose advice he had ever sought and depended upon was the girl in the orphanage in Mexico. But he had killed her and her lover, and now he had only the voice of Wonder Woman to guide him.

What should I do?

Use your imagination, she said.

Go inside?

Pretend you have my magic bracelets and golden lariat.

Those are for women.

Don't make sexist remarks.

I'm sorry.

I was teasing. I love you, Smiley. I'll always be with you. These are evil people. You know what we do with evil people, don't you?

I DIDN'T LIKE NOT calling on the locals to help Clete. But I also trusted his intuition. He was the bane of the Mob, cops who extorted freebies from hookers, racists, misogynists, people who abused animals, slumlords, and child molesters. I knew insurance executives who probably would have him killed if they could get away with it. Clete was a one-man wrecking ball with steel spikes. He'd obliterated a mobster's home with an earth grader on Lake Pontchartrain, thrown two pimps off a three-story roof through a pecan tree, dropped a Teamster out of a hotel window into a dry swimming pool, poured sand or sugar or both into the fuel tanks of a plane loaded with wiseguys, lodged the head of a New Orleans vice cop in a toilet bowl, taken out his flopper in the parking lot of the Southern Yacht Club and hosed down the upholstery in the car of Bobby Earl (Louisiana's most infamous racist) where Bobby was about to get it on with his new socialite girlfriend.

The stories were endless. He was the bravest and most generous man I ever knew, and the most self-destructive. His most valued possession was his code of honor, and he would die rather than compromise it, and for that reason I never argued with him when he put principle ahead of safety.

I clamped an emergency light onto the roof of my pickup and kept the accelerator to the floor until I reached the truck stop and motel forty miles from the Texas line. The stars had started to fade, the darkness draining from the sky in the east. Outside the headlights, I could see the slash pines along the highway, puffing in a balmy breeze that should have marked the beginning of another fine day.

Up ahead, emergency vehicles were pulling into the truck stop, all of them lit up like kaleidoscopes. I saw a fat woman in a bathrobe wailing as she ran from the motel, her eyes as big as half dollars, her hands raised to the heavens.

Chapter Thirty-Five

THE SECURITY CAMERA on the second floor of the motel showed a man wearing gloves and a mask getting on a chair and extending a spray can toward the lens. The mask was made of hard plastic, shiny purplish white, and cast to imitate a weeping spirit in a Greek tragedy. Nothing came out of the spray can. The man shook it and tried again. Still nothing. He looked over his shoulder. No one else was in the hallway. He dropped the spray can into a trash receptacle just as the elevator door opened and a couple who appeared drunk got out. A woman with a vacuum entered the hallway from the fire exit.

There were now four people inside the lens of the camera. The man who had disposed of the can did not take off his mask. The woman with the vacuum removed a small pistol from a pocket in her dress and let it hang from her hand. She was thick-bodied and muscular and had blond hair that hung like dirty string in her face. She hunched her shoulders as though asking a question. The man in the mask pointed at a room a few feet away.

The woman stared at the security camera. The man in the mask pointed again at the room, obviously agitated. The woman's companion had a lean discolored face, and scar tissue in his eyebrows, and the lithe flat-chested physique of a prizefighter. He also seemed to be staring at the camera. He spoke in sign language to the man in the mask. The woman with the vacuum was short and plump and dark-skinned, perhaps Hispanic. She, too, looked at the camera, then went to the trash receptacle and retrieved the spray can. Her breasts were visibly rising and falling. None of the four people spoke. The man in the mask began to speak in sign language that, later, a police technician would translate as "I'll shoot it when we leave."

CLETE LAY ASLEEP on his stomach in his skivvies, his face flat against the mattress, his arm hanging over the edge, his knuckles touching his piece on the floor. He was dreaming about the Asian woman who died at the hands of the Vietcong because she had taken a shanty Irish grunt into her heart. He never remembered her in an impure fashion or even what others would call an erotic one; instead, she remained with him as a spiritual immersion into the damp flowers he saw in his mind when he entered her, subsumed by the sweetness of her breath and the protective grace of her thighs and the way she pressed his face between her breasts and combed the back of his head with her nails after she came.

But his dreams about her always ended with terror. He saw the automatic weapons blaze from jungle blackness high up on the shore, and the rounds dance across the water, ripping into the sides of the sampan. She had been on top of him when the AK round struck her between the shoulder blades and exited from her chest. She'd fallen forward, dead, her hair tangled across his face.

Now Clete sat up in bed, his hands covering his eyes as though he could shield them from the screen inside his head. He beat his fists on the mattress at the irreversible nature of his loss, and stamped one foot on the carpet. It was the red-black rage he had never been able to leave in Vietnam, the one that sought a victim who had no idea of the danger he had just tapped into.

Clete washed his face in the bathroom and lay back down. In minutes he drifted off in a haze that was as warm and pink as morphine; he hoped the sun was about to rise on a new day, one that contained the gifts of both heaven and earth.

• • •

SMILEY'S FAVORITE LINE from a song was one by Hank Williams: *I'll never get out of this world alive.* That was the way to think. Why fret yourself over what you can't change?

This time the situation was different. He was making choices that were not part of the program. Wonder Woman told him what to do and when to do it. But when he strayed from the program, her voice turned to static, then disappeared in the wind. That meant one thing: He was on his own. For Smiley, being alone guaranteed a return to his childhood status in Mexico City and a predatory world other people couldn't imagine in their worst nightmares.

The personality that lived within him at the orphanage had been a victim, a pathetic child who took control of his life by burning himself with cigarettes. Wonder Woman freed him and gave him license to kill and a libidinous joy in the work he did, cleansing the earth of cruel men who had no right to the air they breathed. That was how Smiley saw it.

The only restrictions in the program had to do with conflicts about the targets and self-interest. He didn't do hits for money alone; the target had to deserve his fate. Occasionally, Smiley worked pro bono. Why not? A Jewish friend of his once told him that a good deed by a Cossack was still a good deed. Smiley couldn't quite figure out what that meant, but he knew it had something to do with the importance of good deeds.

The second restriction—putting himself at risk on behalf of others—could become an ethical quagmire. A button man in Key West who claimed he had killed forty-five men and seven women had told Smiley, "You got a lot of talent, kid. You'll probably go a long way. Don't screw it up."

Years later, he saw the killer on a television interview inside a maximum-security federal prison. The man's eyes had the brightness of obsidian, his face the color and expression of cardboard. When asked if he ever felt remorse over the people he'd killed, he said, "I didn't know none of them." When the journalist asked about the damage he had done to the victims' families, the killer said, "I didn't know none of them either."

Smiley could not fathom the man's thinking. How could not knowing somebody make killing acceptable? Was Smiley made different in the womb, like the button man? Or was he the sword of justice? If the latter was true, he had to give up all thoughts of himself. That could be a rough go.

There was still time to leave Purcel to his own fate. *Don't screw it up.* Those words may have come from the mouth of a man who stank of salami and red wine and hair tonic, but they were hard to argue with.

Smiley felt like someone had hammered a nail between his eyes. He drove the stolen pickup in a wide circle around the back of the motel. Eighteen-wheelers were passing on the four-lane, headed for Big D or Little Rock or Baton Rouge or New Orleans. All Smiley had to do was join them. Then he would be back inside the program, safe, taking care of himself again, having a little fun once in a while.

Just when he thought he had established a moment of serenity in his head, Wonder Woman's words came back like a slap.

You know what we do with evil people, don't you?

A DOOR FAR DOWN the hall on the motel's second floor opened, and a man pulling a suitcase on wheels came out and walked to the elevator. The four people standing by the security camera walked in separate directions, as though returning to their rooms or duties. The man in the mask stepped inside the fire exit, then returned when the elevator closed. The blond woman got a step ladder from a broom closet and tried to unload the camera but had no success. Six minutes had elapsed since the four people had assembled.

They approached the door that the man in the mask had pointed at. Then the elevator cables rattled and the wall shook as the elevator stopped on the second floor; the doors slid open. The four people in the hallway stood frozen on either side of the targeted room. No one exited the elevator. The dark-skinned woman who may have been Hispanic walked toward the elevator door, dragging her vacuum behind her. She turned to the others and shook her head. The man in the mask slipped a key card through the lock on the targeted room. The lock made a dry clicking sound. The man in the mask leaned against the door, prepared to burst into the room, his weapon cocked.

SMILEY DID NOT like enclosure, in part because of the closets he'd been locked in at the orphanage. Nor did he like the smell of wet towels and washcloths and sheets and pillowcases soiled with BO and people's coupling. But any port in a storm, even though it was a smelly one. In each hand he held a custom-made .22 Magnum semi-auto. His heart was dilated with adrenaline, his wee-wee swelling, an odor as heavy as the ocean rising into his nostrils, like birth, like Creation itself.

This would be his finest hour.

FOR WHATEVER REASON, caution or anger at the man in the mask or simply a desire to do things differently than the others, the blond woman did not accept the inspection of the elevator and walked toward it. The man in the mask paused, his hand on the room's doorknob. Inside the elevator was a laundry cart filled to the top with dirty linen and towels. The blond woman stared at it for a long moment, perhaps noting the bulge in the canvas on one side.

The hands of a man whose body resembled an overgrown white caterpillar rose from the piled linen, each hand gripping a blue-black semi-auto. The first round hit the blond woman in the center of the forehead. She went straight down on her knees, jarring the wig off her head and revealing the face of Jaime O'Banion.

Smiley sprang from the laundry cart into the hallway, casually firing a second shot into O'Banion's mouth.

The man in the mask went out the fire exit. Smiley shot the dark-skinned woman and the man who looked like a prizefighter before they had any idea what was happening to them. Then he opened the fire exit and looked down the stairs. He heard an outside door open and then slam shut. He went back to O'Banion's body. He couldn't believe it: O'Banion was alive, his face twitching like a bowl of tapioca. At least his nerve endings were alive. Maybe he could receive messages.

"You still in there, Jaime?" Smiley said. "Better grab your cock. Queer-bait is back in town."

Smiley fired five rounds into O'Banion's face, *zip-zip-zip-zip-zip,* just like that. Smiley straightened up, a stitch in his side. *Owie,* he thought. He bent his body back and forth like a bowling pin rocking.

He didn't gather up his brass; nor did he try to destroy the security camera. He limped back into the elevator, straightening his back, trying to get the stitch out of his side. He closed the doors and rode down to the first floor and walked over to the restaurant, his tool bag on his arm, wincing with each step. He ordered toast and coffee from a nice waitress who had a globe and anchor tattooed on the inside of her forearm. She didn't write down the order.

"Did I do something wrong?" he asked.

Her eyes drifted away. "You're leaking."

Smiley put a hand under his jacket, feeling for the place the stitch had been. He looked at his palm, then bit his lip, thinking. He wadded up a handkerchief and pressed it inside his shirt. "Could I have a fried pie to go? With a scoop of ice cream in one of those cold bags?"

Chapter Thirty-Six

A PLAINCLOTHES DETECTIVE BANGED on Clete's door with the flat of his fist. A uniformed deputy sheriff stood behind him. Clete opened the door in his skivvies. He looked at the paramedics bagging up the bodies on the floor. "Help you?"

"Yeah," the detective said. He stared at Clete, recognition swimming into his eyes. "Are you Clete Purcel?"

"What do you want?"

"What do I want? What the fuck are you doing here?"

The detective was big and wore a gray suit and spit-shined needle-nosed cowboy boots, a gold badge on his belt.

"I was sleeping," Clete said. "Until you beat on the door."

"What are you doing *here,* in this part of Louisiana?"

"Passing through to New Iberia. I'm a PI. I'm on a case."

The detective raised his hand for the paramedics to stop their work. He unzipped two bags, already on the gurneys. "Step out here."

"I'm not dressed."

"Nobody is interested in your dick. You know any of these people?"

Clete stepped into the hallway. His gaze moved across the faces of the three gunshot victims, lingering for less than a second on the face of Jaime O'Banion.

"No, I don't know any of these people," he said.

"You're a liar," the detective said.

"I used to be a homicide cop at NOPD," Clete said. "A dog-fuck on your own turf is no fun. But that's your grief, not mine. So how about eighty-sixing the insults?"

"Get your clothes on."

"Search my room. Check my piece. I'm not your guy. You know it."

The detective put a cigarette into his mouth but didn't light it. "You'll like our facilities. After two or three days, the baloney sandwiches start to grow on you."

"Fuck you."

"What did you say?"

"You're queering your own investigation," Clete said.

"The guy's an asshole," the deputy said. "How about we let it slide?"

"Hook him up," the plainclothes said.

"In his shorts?"

"Throw a blanket over him. Take him down the back stairs. Maybe he won't trip."

I PARKED MY PICKUP and hung my badge around my neck. To circumvent the emergency vehicles and personnel, I cut through the restaurant and went out the exit, headed for the motel. A waitress was smoking a cigarette by the back door. She had a sweater over her shoulders. Clete was being marched toward a squad car, his wrists cuffed behind him. Someone had draped a blanket on his head. His boxer shorts and bare legs were exposed.

"Detective Dave Robicheaux, Iberia Sheriff's Department," I said. "Wait up."

A plainclothes looked at me. His eyes were as hard as agate. "Problem?"

"Yeah," I said. "This man belongs in a hospital. I'm here to pick him up."

"There're three stiffs in the meat wagon. One looks like he was drug facedown a fire escape. His name is Jaime O'Banion. Your friend says he never saw him before."

"That's why you hooked up Clete Purcel?"

"Interfere with this investigation and you can join him."

On the edge of my vision, I saw a waitress, her arms folded across her chest. She dropped her cigarette into a butt can and approached us. "Couldn't help listening in, Stan," she said to the plainclothes. "If you're busting my friend there, you got the wrong fellow."

"Don't give me a hard time, Flo," he said.

"Trying to save you from making a mistake, Stan. You can check my time card," she replied. "I punched in at six-fifteen. Before that, I was in my friend's room from midnight until six-ten."

"This guy killed a federal witness."

"Cut it out, Stan. He was in the Crotch. In Vietnam."

"Are you sure about the times, Flo?"

"Do you think I enjoy talking about this in public?"

The plainclothes turned to the deputy. "Unhook him." He pointed his finger at Clete. "Have a nice day."

Clete pulled the blanket around him. He smiled at the plainclothes. "Hey."

"Hey, what?" the plainclothes said.

"Next time I'm in town, I'll drop by. We'll have coffee. I really dig this place. It's the prototype for Shitsville. When you're here, you know you can't go any lower. There's got to be a kind of serenity in that."

I stepped in front of the plainclothes, interdicting his line of sight. "Thanks for your courtesy, Detective."

His eyes lit on mine. "Get him out of here."

"That's a done deal," I said.

I watched him and the deputy walk away. I had known his kind all my life—mean to the bone, a walking penis, angry from the day he came out of the womb. He'd get even down the track, perhaps with a stun gun or a baton or a sap, on the body of an unsuspecting victim who would have no idea why he was being abused, and the rest of us would pay the tab, as always.

When I turned around, the waitress was gone.

"You were shacked up last night?" I said.

"Are you kidding?" Clete said. "My stomach was a septic tank."

"What's the story on the woman?"

"I don't know. I got to check her out. You see the way she walks? Cute ta-tas, narrow waist, big smooth rump." He pulled on himself under the blanket. "My plunger just woke up."

"Stop that."

"Everything is copacetic. Hold all my calls. I'll be right back." He walked through the fire trucks and ambulances and squad cars and emergency personnel and spectators to the motel entrance and went inside, his blanket flapping at his heels, like a misplaced prophet who had stumbled into the twenty-first century. But that was Clete Purcel.

Ten minutes later he was back, his hair wet-combed, his loafers buffed, his tie on, and his suit coat buttoned.

"I've got my flasher on my pickup," I said. "Stay on my bumper."

"I've got to talk with the lady first. What was her name? Flo?"

"It's time to go, Clete."

"When a woman wants you to know something, she lets you see her thoughts. You didn't know that?"

"You see her thoughts?"

"Come with me. I'll tell her you're on the square."

What was the best way to have a conversation with Clete Purcel? You said nothing, and you didn't try to understand what he said. You grabbed a noun and a verb here and there and went with it.

I followed him inside. Flo was behind the counter. No one else was within earshot.

"What'd you want to tell us, Miss Flo?" Clete said.

She looked in my direction.

"Dave is my podjo from NOPD, back when we were the Bobbsey Twins from Homicide," Clete said.

"There was a little guy in here," she said. "He had a red mouth, like he was wearing lipstick. He was bleeding under his jacket. Talked with a lisp."

"He give you a name?" Clete said.

"No. He asked for a fried pie and a scoop of ice cream to go. Know anybody like that?"

I placed my business card on the counter. "Call me if you see him again, Miss Flo."

She pushed the card back at me. "Nope."

"Nope, what?" I said.

"I don't borrow trouble," she replied.

"Perfectly understandable," Clete said. He took a ballpoint from his pocket and began clicking it. "You dig movies? I live for movies. I love people who love movies." He pulled a paper napkin from the dispenser and slid it and the pen toward her. She wrote a number on it. He stuck the napkin in his pocket. "Why didn't you dime the guy?"

"Every girl has a soft spot." She held his eyes.

Clete blushed. I couldn't believe it.

THE NEXT DAY, Helen called the detective who had hooked up Clete, and he emailed her the video from the security camera at the motel. She and Bailey and I watched it in her office. Bailey said little and didn't look in my direction. Even though I was watching Smiley Wimple sling blood on the walls, I couldn't get my mind off Bailey Ribbons. What a fool I was, I thought. I longed to touch her, to hold her, to smell her skin and hair, to be inside her. To be honest, I don't see how any man on earth can live without a woman. Women are the perfect creation. I don't care who hears that. Even before I hit puberty, they lived nightly in my dreams, and I have the feeling they'll live with me in the grave.

"You with us, Dave?" Helen said.

"Sure."

"What do you think?"

"About what?"

She froze the screen. "About what you just watched, for Christ's sake."

"O'Banion's ticket got punched. So did the woman and the guy who has a face like a speedbag. Who are they?"

"We don't know yet," she said. "Boy, you're a ball of sunshine."

"The issue is the guy in the mask," I said.

"Duh," she said.

"He's an amateur," I said.

"Amateur how?" Bailey said.

"He messed up with the spray can," I said. "Rather than admit he messed up, he tried to hide the can and let the others be identified. Eventually, they would have given him up."

"Maybe they weren't going to be alive much longer," Bailey said.

"Maybe," I said.

"What's with the sign language?" she asked.

"That and lip reading are invaluable in prison," I said.

"So the guy in the mask doesn't care about loyalties?" Bailey said. "Somebody with no feelings? A hard case, a real piece of shit?"

"You don't have to use that language," I said.

Helen was looking at both of us now. "What is this?"

"Just making an observation," Bailey said.

"Whatever is going on with you two, leave it at the door," Helen said.

The room was quiet.

Bailey coughed under her breath. "Everyone is sure that's Wimple who climbed out of the laundry cart?"

"He left his brass," Helen said. "The prints on them are his."

"I thought he was a pro," Bailey said. "Why wouldn't he pick up his casings?"

"He was wounded," I said.

They both looked at me. "Where'd you get this information?" Helen said.

"A friend of Clete's," I said. "A waitress."

"Why didn't she tell the investigator at the scene?" Helen said.

"Because the investigator is a troglodyte," I replied.

"How bad is Wimple hurt?" Helen said.

"From what the waitress said, he was bleeding from his side."

"I don't get any of this," Helen said. "Wimple is a psychopath, but he's protecting Clete? And Jaime O'Banion was taking orders from an amateur who cost him his life?"

"That about sums it up," I said.

"And?" she said.

"The guy in the mask is not a noun," I said.

"I'm not in the mood, Dave," she said.

"Read it like you want," I said. "Nothing we do is going to change what's happening."

Helen looked at Bailey. "Do you have any idea what he's saying?"

Bailey shook her head. But I saw it in her eyes. She knew exactly what I was saying, and I knew at that moment that neither of us would ever be able to separate entirely from the other, no matter how great our differences.

"Let me know if I can help you with anything else, Helen," I said.

I got up and walked down the corridor to my office. I knew it was probably a self-indulgent act and stupid on top, but I didn't care. I stood at my window and gazed at the Teche. It was high and yellow and running fast, a cluster of red swamp-maple leaves spinning in the current and disappearing around a corner as though dropping into infinity. I wondered if I wasn't watching a message, one requiring us to acknowledge not only the lunar influences on the tide but the place to which we all must go.

Chapter Thirty-Seven

FIVE MINUTES LATER, Bailey came through my door without knocking. "You just walk out? On the case? On you and me? On everything?"

"I wouldn't put it that way," I said.

"Oh, really?"

"I'm not right for you, Bailey. I was deceiving you and myself."

"Why don't you let me be the judge of that?"

I looked at the bayou again. The light was gold in the trees along the bank, the grass a pale green, the camellia bushes swelling in the wind. The surface of the water seemed to shrivel like old skin. When I turned around, she was six inches from my face. "I want to pound you with my fists," she said.

"I don't blame you."

"Are you having a psychotic break?"

"You knew what I was talking about with Helen."

"About the guy in the mask not being a noun?"

"Yes."

"You're saying he's a symbol? Something we turned loose on ourselves? So what?"

"I know who he is. I just can't prove it. I can almost see him in my mind."

"I think you're slipping your mooring," she said.

"I'm a detail or two away."

"If you knew who our guy was, we wouldn't be having this conversation." I didn't answer. She looked into my eyes. "Don't you dare, Dave."

"Clete feels the same way."

"I don't care what you feel. Neither one of you is an executioner."

I left her standing there and walked out of my own office.

"You hear me?" she called down the hallway.

I kept walking, down the stairs, through the foyer, and out the rear exit and into the brightness and the cold of the day and the tannic odor of late autumn on the wind.

THAT NIGHT, ALAFAIR came in late. I was reading under a lamp in the living room. Snuggs and Mon Tee Coon were curled up with each other on the rug.

"I called you a couple of times," I said. "Where were you?"

"With Desmond and some of the crew," she replied. "We have to go back to Arizona and reshoot a couple of scenes."

"Now is not a good time to be around Desmond."

"I work for him."

"Smiley Wimple is in the vicinity. He's badly wounded. I think he's going to paint the walls before he goes out."

"What does that have to do with Desmond?"

"Everything."

"You're fixated, Dave. You don't see it."

"Fixated on what?"

"The destruction of the world you grew up in."

"I'm supposed to ignore it?"

"You're also fixated on Bailey Ribbons," she said.

"She has nothing to do with this."

"You got yourself into a relationship that you feel is wrong. You see her as a symbol rather than as a woman. You feel guilty about loving all the things you love. How fucked up is that?"

"Don't use that language in our house."

"Sorry, I'll go across the street and send you semaphores through the window."

I put down the book I was reading and went into the kitchen.

Snuggs and Mon Tee Coon followed me, probably thinking they would get a snack.

"I didn't mean it, Dave," Alafair said from the doorway.

"What was that about semaphores?"

"Nothing. I was just grabbing a word out of nowhere."

"Do you work with anyone who knows sign language?"

"I've never seen anyone on the set use it."

"The guy who almost killed Clete knows sign language. He was using it to communicate with Jaime O'Banion at the motel."

"Why are you coming down on Desmond?"

"Because he's dirty. Because he lies. Just like all the people who prey on us."

"You'll never change," she said.

I spread newspaper on the floor and opened a can of sardines and put it down for Snuggs and Mon Tee Coon.

"Answer my question, Dave. In what way is Desmond dirty?"

She was leaning against the doorframe, her black hair auraed with lights from the streetlamps on Main, her weight slouched on one foot, her jeans hanging low on her lips. It was hard to believe that this tall beautiful woman was the little Salvadoran girl I'd pulled from an air bubble trapped inside a sunken airplane off Southwest Pass.

"Take care of yourself, Baby Squanto," I said. "Don't let this collection of motherfuckers fool you."

"You make me want to weep," she replied.

THE NEXT DAY was Saturday. I woke at four and fed the animals on the back steps, then drove in the coldness of the dawn to Clete's motor court. I tapped lightly on the door. The oak trees were ticking with water in the darkness, the bayou swirling through the cattails and canebrakes along the bank. Clete opened the door in a strap undershirt and boxer shorts that went almost to his knees.

"Most noble mon," he said, his eyes full of sleep.

I stepped inside and closed the door behind me. He sat down in a stuffed chair, a blanket humped over his shoulders. A crack of light from the bathroom fell on his face. His cheeks were unshaved, his hair hanging on his forehead like a little boy's. He tried to act attentive, then his head sank on his chest. I felt sorry for waking him and burdening him with my troubles; however, I knew no one else I could go to. I may have seemed the secular priest in his life, but the truth was otherwise. Yes, Clete was the trickster from medieval folklore, Sancho Panza with a badge, but these attributes were cosmetic and had little to do with the true nature of the man. Clete Purcel was the egalitarian knight, the real deal, his armor rusted, his sword unsheathed, his loyalties unfailing, with a heart as big as the world.

"They're going to get away with it," I said.

"Who's 'they'?"

"Desmond Cormier and his entourage. They're going back to Arizona and shutting down the circus while we lick our wounds."

"I'm not copying, big mon. I need coffee and massive nutrients."

"Stay where you are."

I started a pot of chicory coffee and got out a skillet and loaded it with six eggs, eight strips of bacon, and a ring of buttered biscuits.

"Fix some for yourself, too," he said.

"I did."

"Oh."

I broke two more eggs into the skillet, then set the table. I could feel his eyes on me.

"You're thinking about doing it under a black flag?" he said.

"Call it what you want."

"I can live with black flags," he said. "You can't."

"The friends of Tillinger you met at the graveyard service told you he was mixed up in arms sales?"

"That's what the preacher said. He visited Tillinger in jail."

"That means he didn't come here just to see Lucinda Arceneaux," I said.

"Hard to say," Clete replied. "The preacher said Tillinger wanted to get clean of his past."

"Okay, think about it. We've got all kinds of information that doesn't seem to connect with itself. Russians building nuclear reactors, money laundering in Malta, greaseballs out of Miami, Nicky Scarfo's old crowd in Jersey. So what's the common denominator?"

"Desmond Cormier doesn't care where he gets his money," Clete said. "What's unusual about that? Casino owners and marijuana growers pay millions in taxes. The IRS doesn't want that kind of money?"

"Except the issue is not the money," I said. "The issue is about a guy who hates this area and hates the people in it and most of all hates women who are a challenge to him."

Clete looked into space as though seeing the bodies of Bella Delahoussaye and Hilary Bienville. He came to the table and sat down but didn't touch his food. "No, it goes deeper than that. The guy put a rose and a chalice in Bella's hands?"

"That's right."

"How's that fit with the guy who hates this area?"

"He was offering a sacrifice."

"To what?"

"To himself, although he doesn't know that."

"And the only real evidence y'all have is the black gym bag from Cormier's garage?"

"Yeah, with Lucinda Arceneaux's shoe and blouse inside."

"And Cormier still says he doesn't know who owns the bag?"

"Yep."

Clete started eating, his eyes lidless. "He's got a Maltese cross tattooed on his ankle?"

I nodded.

"There's another possibility in all this, Dave. You're not going to like it."

"What?"

"Smiley Wimple. This guy kills people like other people change their socks."

"Wrong guy," I said.

"A guy who fries people with a flamethrower is the wrong guy?"

"He covered your back a couple of times, and now you feel guilty about it," I said.

"You think Cormier is really behind all this?"

"I can't get him out of my head," I said.

Clete pushed away his plate and drank from his coffee. "How do you want to play it?"

"Dust 'em or bust 'em. The choice is theirs."

"But that's not what you're thinking about, is it?" he said.

"Who wants to get to the barn wearing a drip bag?"

In the distance, somewhere beyond the watery rim of the place where I had been born, I thought I heard horns echoing off canyon walls. Or maybe that was just my grandiose disguise for what we in AA call self-will run riot.

SMILEY HAD USED a pair of sterilized tweezers to remove the .25-caliber piece of lead that one of the bad people at the motel had parked in his side. He had also packed the wound with gauze and medicine he had stolen from a pharmacy. The blood had coagulated and no longer leaked through the bandage, but he could see the inflammation around the edges of the tape, and when he touched it, it was as tender as an infected boil.

There was a doctor in Houston and another in New Orleans, both addicts, with malevolent eyes and fingers that were dirty and invasive. Smiley had almost shot one of them for the way he looked at Smiley's wee-wee. In fact, if Smiley made it out of this one, he might visit the good doctor again, this time with a can of Liquid-Plumr.

The pain pills he had stolen allowed him to sleep and to walk without a limp and, most important, to think clearly. What was there to think about? Getting the people who were responsible for his pain, who had sent Jaime O'Banion after him, who had caused the killing of the innocent colored women and who wanted to kill his friend the fat man named Clete Purcel.

The movie people were part of it. They had to be. O'Banion must have been paid with Jersey or Miami money, the same source used by the movie people.

Outside an Opelousas bar, Smiley had boosted a Ford-150 pickup that a pair of rednecks had left the key in. The dash panel was like a spaceship's. He loved diving into it and smelling the leather and feeling the power of the engine and the deep-throated rumble of the exhaust. If Smiley straightened out a few people in the next day or so, he could be on his way to Mexico with about thirty thousand in cash that he kept in a backpack, leaving behind his weapons and all the hateful people he had worked for. He'd check into a hospital, maybe in Monterrey, and watch the evening sun turn into a blue melt over the hills while he ate a bucket of ice cream with a spoon that had a head the size of a silver dollar.

On Saturday morning he drove to the movie set outside Morgan City and was told that the film company was shutting down and holding a wrap party at City Park in New Iberia. Everyone was invited as a thank-you and tribute to the city. He checked into a motel on the four-lane south of town, then showered and dressed in a white suit with a glittering blue vest and suede boots and a plum-colored tie and a planter's straw hat that rested on his ears, his pain in containment. There was only one problem. A flicker was going on behind his eyes, as though someone were clicking a light switch on and off inside his head.

At the park, children were playing on the swings and seesaws and the jungle gym, running through the picnic shelters and the tables loaded with food and drinks. Where did all the children come from? He saw flowers, too, or swirls of color inside the deep greenness of the grass where there should have been no flowers or swirls of color. It was the end of autumn or even the beginning of winter, wasn't it? Some of the children looked Hispanic, with elongated eyes and badly cropped hair. He was sure he knew them from years ago. Some had died at the orphanage, one of them so small and emaciated that his body was removed in a pillowcase.

The earth seemed to be moving under his feet. He sat down at a picnic table under one of the shelters and waited for his dizziness to pass. It didn't. A Cajun band was playing a song he had heard over and over since he came to Acadiana.

Jolie blonde, regardez donc t'as fait,
Tu m'as quitte pour t'en aller,
Pour t'en aller avec an autre, qui, que moi,
Quel expoir et quell avenir, mais moi, je vais avoir?

Even though he spoke Spanish, Smiley could not understand the Acadian dialect. But somehow he knew the song was about loss. The musicians were sunbrowned and lean, the kind of Cajun men for whom privation had been a way of life during the days of the oligarchy. They played most of their songs with joy, but not this one. The cast in their eyes was funereal. Smiley felt a spasm in his side as though a lance had pierced it.

Two little girls were staring at him. They were wearing pinafores and had flowers in their hair. Their eyes seemed unnaturally sunken. "You all right, mister?" one of them said.

"I have a tummyache," he said. "My name is Smiley. What's yours?"

"I'm Felicity," one said. She had red hair and was covered with freckles. "This is Perpetua. Your face don't have no color, Smiley."

He slipped his hand into his coat pocket and took out a twenty-dollar bill. "There's an ice cream truck by the street. Can you get me a Buster Bar and whatever y'all want?"

They walked away, looking back at him strangely. What bothered him about the girls? Their dresses were clean, but their skin looked powdered with dust. He felt the ground shift again and wondered if he was losing his mind. The oaks shook, and leaves as thin as gold scrapings filtered through the limbs and bands of sunlight. He reached down and picked up a handful of leaves. They fell apart and sifted and then disappeared between his fingers. For a moment he thought he saw Wonder Woman at the edge of his vision, her gold lariat dripping from her belt, her magic bracelets and her star-spangled bosom bathed in cold sunshine.

He knew there was a term for the affliction he had. What was it?

Peritonitis? A septic intrusion working its way through his entrails, boring a hole in his stomach. He felt his colon constrict; his eyes went out of focus.

Help me, he said to Wonder Woman.

But she was lost in the crowd, maybe gone from the park entirely. His heart sank at the thought of being alone. He saw the little girls coming toward him. The girl with the freckles was carrying a cold bag. She put it in his palm. "Your Buster Bar and change are in the bag."

"Where are yours?"

"We don't need any. We're here to take you home."

"Home?" he said.

"We're dead, Smiley," the other girl said. "We've been that way a long time."

He rose from the table, backing away from them. Then he turned and plunged into the crowd, past the platform where the Cajun band was playing "Allons à Lafayette."

He continued walking through the trees to the other side of the park, deep into a clump of oaks where there were no tables or picnic shelters and the grass was uncut and strung with paper cups and napkins and plates blown from the recreational areas. It was cold in the shade. Or was he losing blood, causing his body temperature to drop? He saw a Subaru convertible parked farther down the slope, the top and windows up, the shadows of the trees black on the windows. He saw a black woman moving around in the back seat, as though trying to position herself on her knees and not finding adequate space.

Then he realized what he was watching.

The images filled him with embarrassment and shame; they were part of the unclean thoughts he'd been taught not to have. The man was spread-eagled, his shirt unbuttoned, his trousers down, his bronzed muscle-corded abdomen exposed. The woman's head moved up and down above his body. The man's eyes were closed, his face suffused with pleasure.

Smiley wanted to run away. But he recognized the man: He was one of the movie people. The men always looked the same—their bodies hard, their hair bleached at the tips, the sun's warmth trapped inside their skin, their teeth perfect, their eyes sparkling as they stared into the faces of ordinary people, never blinking.

No one else was around. Smiley pulled his small .22 semi-auto from his pants pocket and clicked off the safety. He curled his left hand inside the Subaru's door handle. Neither the woman nor the man heard him ease the door open. Then the woman stopped what she was doing and turned around and held both of her hands in front of her face, her bottom lip quivering.

"No," she said. "Please, suh. Please, please."

Smiley pulled the trigger. The firing pin snapped on a dead round. The man came to life, his eyes opening, his teeth shiny with saliva.

Chapter Thirty-Eight

CLETE HAD TO pick up a bail skip in St. Martinville at nine a.m. I left him at the motor court and drove to Desmond's home on Cypremort Point. My cut-down twelve-gauge was wrapped in a blanket behind the seat. I had no plan in mind. However, that statement is one I have always distrusted in other people, and I distrust it even more when I think it or say it myself. The unconscious always knows what the person is doing or planning. The agenda is to find the situation and the rationale that will allow the individual to commit deeds that are unconscionable.

No matter how you cut it, I was back to the short form of the Serenity Prayer, known in AA and other recovery groups as Fuck It. I cannot praise the nuances of Fuck It enough, but you already know the drill. I ached to get back on that old-time rock and roll, this time not with the flak juice but with double-aught bucks and pumpkin balls at point-blank range.

Don't mistake this for a paean to the gun culture. It's my admission of the madness that has defined most of my adult life.

No one was home. A gardener was raking the yard. He said Mr. Cormier was at a picnic in New Iberia.

"How about Mr. Butterworth?" I said.

"I don't have no truck wit' Mr. Butterworth's goings or comings, suh," he said, his eyes downcast.

I drove back home and left the shotgun behind the seat and went inside. I heard Alafair clicking on her keyboard in her bedroom. I stood in the doorway until she reached a stopping place. Snuggs was sleeping inside her manuscript basket, his thick tail hanging through the wire. I didn't know where Mon Tee Coon was. Alafair's hands were still for a long time, as though she were coming out of a trance.

"Hey, Squanto," I said.

"Sorry, Dave. I didn't see you there."

"Is that your new book?"

"Yeah, it's called *The Wife.*"

I looked through the window and across the bayou. "Is that the movie crew over there?"

"The whole city is invited."

"You're not going?"

"I took your advice. I'm getting loose from Des and his crowd. I'm not going to Arizona for the reshoot either. Des is leaving in the morning."

"What changed your attitude?"

She rubbed her forehead and took a breath. "I love Hollywood, I don't care what people say about it. But Des isn't Hollywood, Dave. He's Leonardo da Vinci working for Cesare Borgia, except he won't admit it."

"He's laundering money?"

"Probably."

"Where's Wexler in all this?"

"We're just friends."

"No man is just a woman's friend."

She jiggled her fingers at me. "Bye, Dave."

I went into the kitchen and fixed a sandwich and ate it, drinking simultaneously from the milk carton. I could not remember ever drinking from a milk carton or any container I shared with someone else. There was something loose in my head. Or, better said, like wet paper tearing or wires shorting out or images moving behind a curtain you know you're not supposed to touch.

I opened the back door to let in Mon Tee Coon, muddy feet included, then walked out in the yard and gazed across the Teche at the celebrants in the park. I had a feeling in my chest that is hard to describe. It was similar to the recurrent nightmare I had as a child when my mother ran off with the man named Mack and my father stayed drunk and bloodied his fists on any man foolish enough to come within an arm's reach. In the dream, the sky turned to a sheet of carbon paper, then the sun descended over the earth's rim and time stopped forever, with no transition into a heavenly kingdom or purpose or meaning of any kind. Without knowing it, I had found the quintessence of death, with no ability to explain it to others.

I heard Alafair open the screen door behind me. "I forgot to tell you, the deputy at the evidence locker called," she said.

"What about?" I asked.

"He just said call him."

The deputy who oversaw our evidence storage was a kindly old man named Ben Theriot. No one was sure of his age, and his eyes were very bad and his memory not much better, but no one had the heart to force him into retirement.

"How you doin', Mr. Ben?" I said when I got him on the line.

"Maybe not too good, Dave. 'Member that gym bag you brought in?"

"The one from Desmond Cormier's place?"

"Yes, suh, that one. I was cleaning the top shelves and I knocked it off. A li'l mint-like t'ing fell out. It must have been wedged in the lining. I ain't seen it at first and I stepped on it."

"What is it, exactly?"

"A Nicorette."

I remembered interviewing Antoine Butterworth in City Park and Butterworth putting a Nicorette on his tongue. "Put it in a Ziploc and we'll see what the lab can do for us Monday."

"Dave, I hate to tell you this, but I wasn't t'inking too good. I just put some lotion on my hands 'cause I got dry skin, and I picked up the mint and dropped it back in the bag."

I pinched my eyes with my fingers and tried not to react. "Don't worry about it. The information you've given me is helpful on its own."

"You ain't just saying that?"

"Use some tweezers to put the mint in a Ziploc and we'll be fine."

"T'ank you," he said.

Maybe we had just blown the first solid evidence we had in the murder of Lucinda Arceneaux, but what do you say to people who are doing their best when their best is not enough? Besides, I didn't need any more evidence. I had come to believe that if you threw a rock at Desmond or Butterworth or anyone in their vicinity, you would probably hit a guilty man.

There was nothing lighthearted about my sentiment. I could feel a weight the size of a brick in my chest.

"Where you going, Dave?" Alafair said.

"Are Butterworth and Desmond in the park?"

"Everyone is."

I nodded. "Nice day for it, huh?"

"For what?"

I smiled and shrugged, then went into the backyard and threw pecans at a tree trunk. When I heard her clicking on the keyboard again, I walked down the driveway, got into my truck, and headed up Loreauville Road for Bailey Ribbons's cottage.

I DIDN'T TRY TO tell her why I was there, because I wasn't sure myself. I don't mean to be too personal, but long ago I made my troth with the Man Upstairs and asked that my sacrifice be acceptable in His sight. I never looked back, even when I fucked my life with a garden rake. I knew the score: You were in the club or you weren't. For a drunk, loss of sobriety quickly becomes loss of everything you value and love and respect, including your soul and then your life. When you're sober, you roll the dice with the sunrise. That's a victory in itself and not one to be taken lightly. It's glorious to just be part of the action. But control remains an illusion.

Bailey didn't know what to make of me. It's funny how she reminded me of a prim girl who had walked out of a frontier schoolhouse. "You came to your senses?" she said. "You gave up the old-man routine?"

"No, I'm still old. But I owe you a debt."

"What debt?"

"You shared your life with me, kiddo."

"Call me that again and I'll slap your face."

I put my hand on her shoulder. "I'll always love you. I'll be there for you any time you need me."

"God, you're nuts."

"Probably."

"Dave, there's something in your eyes that's really troubling."

"What?"

"You're going to do something that's not you."

"I've never found out who I am," I said. "I don't think anyone does. That's the biggest joke of all."

We were standing in front of her cottage. The wind was blowing her dress against her legs. Her mouth was the color of a bruised plum. I wanted to kiss her, but I knew if I did, I wouldn't leave. So I told her again I loved the name Bailey Ribbons, and I drove away.

I MADE A STOP at St. Edward's Church and, before I left, stuck a thick fold of bills into the poor box. Then I headed for City Park, a clock ticking in my head. I knew how the day would end. Or maybe "day" was the wrong term. I was no longer registering the passage of time in minutes or hours or days or weeks or months. I knew I had entered a new season in my life, one that had nothing to do with rotations of the earth. It's the season when you accept your fate and give up fear and worry and end your lover's quarrel with the world and follow the foot tracks of hominids into a place that is perhaps already at the tips of your fingers. When that happens to you, you'll know it, and if you're wise, you will not try to explain it to others, any more than you would try to explain light to a man born without sight.

As chance would have it, my moment of peace after leaving the church would be intruded upon by the ebb and flow that reduce tragedy to melodrama and a grander vision of the human story to procedural squalor. This came in the form of my cell phone vibrating on the truck seat.

I picked it up, my eyes on the road. "Robicheaux."

"Where are you, Pops?" Helen said.

"Just coming out of St. Edward's."

"Get over to the park. I've already sent the bus. I'm not sure what's going on. Sean McClain is already there. From what he says, Wimple may have done a curtain call."

"He killed somebody?"

"It sounds too weird for belief. We ROA at the park."

"Copy that."

I drove down East Main, past my house and the Shadows, and rumbled across the steel grid of the drawbridge over the Teche, then entered the urban forest we call City Park. If anything was amiss, I couldn't see it. The celebrants were going at it, the band playing, long lines at the beer kegs and the hard-liquor tables. I drove along the asphalt path toward the far end of the park, then saw an ambulance backed into the trees, its flashers blinking. A cruiser was next to it, its door open, and Sean McClain was standing in the shadows, talking into his mic. I pulled in behind him. A black Subaru convertible with California tags was parked in a dry swale piled with dead leaves and strewn with air vines. The medics were jerking a gurney out of the ambulance.

"What do you have, Sean?" I asked.

"Looks like that old boy run out of luck. I mean if that's him."

I walked through the leaves to the lip of the swale. Both front doors of the Subaru were open, the passenger seat shoved hard against the dashboard. Smiley Wimple, wearing a white suit, was curled in a ball on the ground. His eyes were open and sightless. There was a bloody hole in his suit, just above his heart. He seemed strangely at peace. A small blue-black semi-auto rested in his right palm.

Other emergency vehicles were turning off Parkview Drive, winding their way past the old National Guard Armory.

"What happened?" I said.

"A black woman, name unknown, called in the 911," Sean said. He took a notebook out of his shirt pocket. "This is what I got from the dispatcher."

"Go on."

"The black woman said, 'There's a little-bitty man been killed in the park. He didn't have to do it.' "

"'*He* didn't have to do it'?"

"Yes, sir."

"No idea who 'he' is?"

"No, sir. Have you and me seen this car before? Maybe at Cypremort Point?"

"That's exactly where we saw it. It belongs to Antoine Butterworth."

I put on latex and looked in the back seat of the Subaru. There was a dime bag of weed on the floor and a .22 casing on the seat. I straightened up and closed the door just as Helen's cruiser pulled in. She got out and looked at Smiley's body. She was wearing navy blue slacks and a starched white shirt and her gold shield and service belt. "That's Wimple?"

"Afraid so."

Her eyes lifted to mine, flat and all business. "A great loss to the world? That's what you're about to say?"

"If I grew up like he did, I probably wouldn't be any different. I can't figure out how the shooter got the drop on him."

Helen put on latex and squatted down and used a ballpoint to ease the semi-auto from Smiley's hand. She dropped the magazine and pulled back the slide. A round was in the chamber, an indentation where the firing pin had struck it. She tapped the round loose and caught it in her palm. It was unfired. The firing pin had hit upon a dead round. She stood up and bagged the gun and magazine and loose round.

"How do you read it?" she said.

"According to Sean, the 911 caller said, 'He didn't have to do it.'

There's no brass on the ground. Wimple didn't get off a shot. The shooter had a choice. He decided to pop Wimple. At least that's what the 911 caller seemed to be saying."

"You ran the tags?"

"I don't have to. That's Butterworth's car."

"Why would he arbitrarily kill Wimple?"

"Maybe he was scared shitless. Or maybe he did it for fun."

"Any lawyer would get him off on self-defense. Why would he flee the scene?"

"He's probably heard stories about the bridal suite at Angola."

"I don't buy that," Helen said. "Wimple had a reason for targeting Butterworth. He killed only two types of people: child abusers and people who tried to hurt him. Butterworth is not a child abuser. So something else is involved. Maybe Butterworth is our guy after all."

"That, or he's *one* of our guys."

"Who do you think the woman might be?"

"Someone poor and desperate and willing to do anything for a few dollars."

The wind blew through the trees, scattering the leaves and straightening the air vines, and I saw something I hadn't seen before. I squatted down next to Smiley's body again. Broken daisies and crushed buttercups and rose petals were with the leaves. I picked them up in my hand and stared at them. Even in the shade they were as bright as splashes of paint from a brush. There were no flowers of this kind growing anywhere near the crime scene. I looked into Smiley's face. There was a wet glimmer sealed in one eye, more like an expression of warmth than sorrow.

"What are you looking at?" Helen said.

"These flowers. I don't know how they got here."

"What flowers?"

"These." I lifted my hand.

"Those are leaves."

I stood up and looked at the shafts of sunlight shining through the canopy. I brushed off my fingers. I looked at her and then at my hands. "I haven't had much sleep the last couple of nights."

"Don't go weird on me, bwana. Let's get whatever we can to the lab."

The paramedics placed Smiley into a body bag and pulled the zipper over his chin and nose and eyes and the crown of his head, then dropped him onto the gurney and trundled him into the ambulance, the bag shaking as though it were filled with porridge.

Chapter Thirty-Nine

Two hours later, I was at Clete's motor court. He sat silently in a chair by the window, his profile silhouetted against the window shade, while I told him everything that had happened in the park.

"I never believed Wimple would get capped by an amateur," he said.

"He probably had a box of old ammunition and got careless after he was wounded at the motel."

"Thanks for reminding me," he said.

"It's not your fault."

"I didn't say it was. What's the plan?"

"There's an APB on Butterworth."

"That's not what I asked."

"We take him down and give him his alternatives. We stop screwing around. I don't believe there's just one guy anymore. Cormier could have stopped all this a long time ago."

"I'll take it a step further," Clete said. "From what I know, or what you've told me, I think Cormier and the rest of them are on the spike and their heads glow in the dark. Maybe the bunch of them are into S and M. I hear Cormier has a pole you could fly the flag on."

As always, I was awed by the images Clete picked out of the air. "I wouldn't know," I said.

More important, I didn't want to believe that the shy redbone boy whom I had always admired was capable of allowing a murderer and a sadist to thrive in our midst. By the same token, I had no doubt there was a cruel element in his personality, one that was like a candle guttering and flaring alight again.

"I feel like we've passed over something," Clete said.

"That's the way every investigation goes," I said.

"This is different. This ritual stuff, the tarot, posing the victims, yeah, that's all real. But there's something we missed, something real simple." He waited for me to speak. "Come in, Houston," he said.

"I saw some crushed flowers by Wimple's body. There were no flowers anywhere around the crime scene. I picked them up in my hand and tried to show them to Helen and they turned into leaves."

He lifted his shoulder holster from the back of a chair and slipped his arm through it. "We've got enough problems, noble mon."

"I interviewed three people at the picnic who said they saw a man answering Wimple's description talking to two little girls who were wearing flowers in their hair and around their necks. No one knew who they were or where they came from."

"Drop it."

"It was you telling me we may be living in a necropolis. How cheerful a thought is that?"

"That's why I never listen to myself," he replied.

"I went by St. Edward's this afternoon. I think I might be headed for the barn. You know the feeling. Don't tell me you don't."

"If you go down, so do I. So fuck that."

Clete removed his .38 snub from his holster, flicked out the cylinder from the frame, and dumped the rounds into the wastebasket. He took a fresh box of shells from the kitchen cabinet and began dropping them one at a time into the chambers, his eyes clear, his face untroubled. "Who do you think the little girls were?"

"A woman said she heard one of them say her name was Felicity and her friend's was Perpetua."

He nodded as though the names meant something to him, but I was sure they didn't. They were the names of two women who died in a Roman arena in the early third century.

"Wimple looked at peace. I think—"

"Yeah?" he said.

"I hope Smiley is in a good place. Let's take a ride."

Ten minutes later, my cell phone vibrated and I answered the strangest phone call I have ever received.

THE CALLER ID said *Caller Unknown,* but there was no mistaking the voice.

"Detective Robicheaux?"

"Butterworth?"

"Yes," he said. The word had a knot in it as tight as a wet rope.

"Where are you, sir?" I asked.

"That's not important."

"Do you want to tell me something?"

"Yes."

"About Smiley Wimple?"

"Yes."

"There's an echo. Are you on a speakerphone?" I said.

"Yes."

"It would be better if you came in on your own. Bring a lawyer. The shooting looks like self-defense to us."

"No. I'll be going away."

"Not a good idea," I said. Clete and I were still in his cottage; he was looking at me from across the room.

"I've had many problems over the years," Butterworth said. "I ruined my reputation in Hollywood. Desmond has been a good soul to me. But he's about to bid his origins adieu, and perhaps the love of his life. That's all I have to say."

"Where are you, sir?"

"What difference does it make?"

For just a moment I thought I heard wind rushing and waves breaking. "Don't sign off, partner. Did you kill Lucinda Arceneaux?"

There was no answer.

"Are you hearing me? Get on the square, Mr. Butterworth. You're an intelligent, educated man. Don't buy in to self-pity."

"You're quite the fellow. It's been good knowing you, Detective Robicheaux."

"What are you saying?"

"Nothing. Nothing at all. That's all any of it is. Nothing. Someday you'll read between the lines."

He broke the connection. Clete stared at me. The strap of his shoulder holster was pinched against his shirt. "What was that about?"

"I don't know how to read it. I wish I had it on tape."

"Got any idea where he was calling from?"

"Waves and wind in the background."

"Cypremort Point?" he said.

THE TIDE WAS in, and the clouds in the west had turned to gold, and the waves were curling and exploding on the blocks of concrete at the base of Desmond's property. The garage doors below the house were open. No vehicles were inside. I cut the engine, and Clete and I walked up the two flights of wooden steps to the entrance. The door was slightly ajar. I tapped it with my fingertips. It drifted back on the hinges.

"Iberia Sheriff's Department!" I called.

There was no answer. I went inside with Clete behind me, his snub-nose in his right hand. The sliding door to the deck was open, the room redolent with salt spray.

"Man," Clete said, wincing.

Butterworth had slipped from a stuffed leather chair and was sitting on the floor, his head twisted to one side. There was an entry hole under his chin and a .22 semi-auto inches from his hand. The bullet had obviously traveled through the roof of his mouth and embedded or bounced around in the brainpan. One eye had eight-balled. The drip from the entry wound ran like a snake inside his silk shirt.

I started toward him. Clete clenched his fist in the air, the infantryman's sign to stop. He went into all the rooms of the house and came back out. "Clear."

I called Helen on my cell phone. "Send the bus to Desmond Cormier's place. We've got another one."

"Desmond?" she said.

"Butterworth. It looks like he capped himself. With a twenty-two auto. I have a feeling we'll match the casing with the one in the back of his Subaru."

"What are you doing there?"

"Butterworth called me. He wouldn't tell me where he was. I thought he might be here."

"Who's with you?"

"Clete."

"You took him out there and not Ribbons?"

"Affirmative. Out." I shut my phone.

"Trouble?" Clete said.

"Always. You see anything wrong here?"

"About Butterworth? Hard to tell. He was the kind of guy who's hell on his victim but can't take the heat himself."

"His Subaru is in the pound. How'd he get here?" I said.

"Maybe in a cab. Run the tape backward. Lucinda Arceneaux died of a heroin injection between the toes. Who uses needles like that except a junkie? You found Butterworth's works during a search, right?"

"Desmond might be an intravenous user, too," I said.

Clete was wearing his porkpie hat. He took it off and spun it on his finger. "Helen is pissed because I'm here?"

"Forget it. I'm probably winding down with the department anyway."

"I'd better blow."

"You're not going anywhere." I looked around the living room. The sun had started its descent into the bay. The light was shining in the hallway on the framed still photos. "Earlier you said we'd missed something."

"Yeah, three women have been killed. What do they have in common?"

"Bella Delahoussaye was a singer," I replied. "Hilary Bienville was a part-time hooker. Lucinda Arceneaux wanted to get innocent people off death row. All of them were black."

"They all had qualities," he said. "The guy who killed them hated and desired them. How about the guy in the shrimp net? What was his name?"

"Joe Molinari," I said.

"He's the one who doesn't fit."

Clete went out onto the deck. The wind was blowing hard, spotting his Hawaiian shirt with raindrops. He started back inside, then stopped and looked down at something in the track of the sliding door. He dug it out with the tip of his ballpoint and picked it up between his fingers. "Take a look."

"A tooth?"

"Part of one," he said. "There's blood on it."

"Maybe the round knocked it out of Butterworth's mouth."

"Maybe," he said. "Think we're getting played?"

"Before Butterworth hung up on me, he praised Desmond."

"Like he was being forced to?"

"I'm not sure. He was obviously distraught. The last thing he said was 'Someday you'll read between the lines.'"

"Got any idea where Cormier is?" Clete said.

"No, but when we find him, he'll appear shocked and indignant and dismayed."

"Congratulations," he said. "I think you're finally catching on to this guy."

I turned in a circle to look at the room again. Butterworth's tenor sax was propped against the couch; the mouthpiece lay on the couch's arm. A large vintage Stromberg-Carlson record player stood against one wall, its top open, its console lit. I looked at the LP on the spindle. It was a recording of Norman Granz's *Jazz at the Philharmonic,* which included Flip Phillips, the legendary tenor sax man Desmond had told me Butterworth admired.

"You give me too much credit," I said to Clete. "I haven't caught on to squat."

• • •

I HAD NO IDEA where to start looking for Desmond. Bailey showed up with the ambulance and Cormac the coroner and the forensic team. Clete stayed down by the water, his back to the house.

"No idea where Des is, huh?" Bailey said.

"Des?"

"Don't take your anger out on me, Dave."

"No, I don't know where he is."

"He's a moody, sentimental guy," she said.

"What's that mean?"

"I hear the whole crew is headed back to Monument Valley in the morning," she said. "I think he'll sell his house and we'll never see him again."

I had to give it to her. She was always ahead of the game. I wondered what things would have been like if I had met her fifty years ago. "Will you take over here?"

"Where are you going?"

"To find Desmond."

"Take Clete Purcel with you. Helen is on her way."

I looked into the magical light that lived in her eyes, and I knew I would never get over her, no matter what she might have done in her younger years. "See you later."

"I said Desmond was sentimental. That doesn't mean I trust him. Watch your ass, Dave."

"Don't use that kind of language," I said. I even tried to smile. But I couldn't believe I'd said that, and in that moment I knew I was fixated on the image of Clementine Carter as much as Desmond was, and that I would have a secret longing for both Clementine and Bailey the rest of my life and I would share it with no one.

I WENT OUTSIDE INTO the wind and picked up Clete and headed north up the two-lane. I told him of my conversation with Bailey about Desmond.

"So where do you think he is?" Clete said.

"At Lucinda Arceneaux's crypt or his birthplace."

"You're buying in to that crap again?" he said.

"Buying in to what crap?"

"Cormier as the great artist. Great artists bully and degrade people on the set. Because that's what he did, right?"

We drove in silence. The sun hung as bright as a bronze shield over the bay. Pelicans were plummeting from the sky like dive-bombers, their wings tucked back, disappearing under the water, then rising again with baitfish pouched inside their beaks.

"I got to say something," Clete said.

"Go ahead."

"I want to believe Butterworth isn't a suicide and our guy is still out there. I want to believe that because I planned to blow up his shit. No, worse than that. I want to take him down in pieces."

"So?"

"So, nothing. You talked to Butterworth before he did the Big Exit. If someone was holding a gun on him, he could have sent you a signal any number of ways."

"Maybe it was that statement about reading between the lines."

"Titty babies who beat up hookers like to sound profound. The truth is, they're titty babies who beat up hookers, usually small ones."

"He was listening to a recording of *Jazz at the Philharmonic* and maybe playing along with it. He might have stopped to clean his mouthpiece. Why would he suddenly call me up and commit suicide?"

"Suicide isn't a rational act. I knew mercenaries in El Sal. They were all looking for the boneyard. They just didn't know it. You know what I think?"

"No."

"Butterworth and Cormier had some kind of complicated relationship going on. I also think we'll never know. We'll never know what it is either."

Maybe he was right; maybe not. I didn't care. I had always believed in Desmond in the same way I'd believed in Bella Delahoussaye. They came from the Louisiana I loved, and I loved Louisiana in the same way you love a religion. You don't care if your obsession is rational, and you're not bothered that your love is partly erotic. The Great Whore of Babylon is a commanding mistress. Once she widens her thighs and takes you inside her, she never lets go.

"Forget the crypt," Clete said. "Go to the res."

"Why the res?"

"The casino is there, and probably some of the scum-suckers out of Jersey who have been backing Desmond's films. Maybe they brought their skanks and he can get his knob polished before he continues his life as a great artist."

Chapter Forty

We found Desmond Cormier in the late afternoon on the piece of hardscrabble land where his grandparents had run a general store; now the land was pocked with sinkholes and overgrown with persimmon trees and palmettos and swamp maples cobwebbed with air vines and storm trash blown out of the Atchafalaya Basin. Desmond was standing by a Humvee, staring at the shadows near an inlet that had turned red in the sunset. Behind us, I could see the glow of the casino in the distance.

I think the images he saw were not the ones I described. I believed he was looking into the past at the skinny twelve-year-old boy who roped cinder blocks to each end of a broomstick under a white sun and began creating a body that would put the fear of God into the bullies who tormented him on the school bus. I suspect he wondered about the fate of the bullies who taunted him and shoved him onto the gravel. Some were probably dead, some stacking time in Angola, some cleaning floors with mops and pails. If he ran into them, they probably would not connect him with the boy they had mocked. One thing I was sure of: If Desmond did meet them, he would treat them with kindness.

That's why he angered me. He had the capacity to do enormous good in the world. But he handed out his gifts one coin at a time, and never with anonymity, unless you counted his payment for Lucinda Arceneaux's crypt.

His talent had received global recognition, but his faith in his creativity was not enough to make him forswear the illegal money that powered his artistic enterprises. And enterprises they were.

Without the sweaty multitudes and the satisfaction they demanded for the price of a theater ticket, Desmond probably would have been running an independent company filming lizards in the Texas Panhandle.

I parked on the faint outline of the dirt track that traversed the property, and asked Clete to stay in the truck.

"You got it," he replied, and tilted his porkpie hat down on his eyes.

I walked up behind Desmond. He showed no awareness of my presence, even though I knew he heard me.

"What's the haps?" I said.

He grinned in the same way he could light up a room when he was a kid. "How's it going, Dave?"

"Hard to say, things have been moving so fast. It looks like Antoine Butterworth killed Smiley Wimple, then popped himself."

"Whoa."

"You haven't heard?"

"What was that about Antoine popping himself?"

"He called me from your house, then parked one under his chin. That's what it looks like."

"I don't believe that."

"If it's any consolation, he praised your name before he pulled the plug."

Desmond was facing me now, his sleeves rolled, his forearms pumped and vascular. "Don't be cynical, Dave. Antoine is my friend."

"Your 'friend' may have arbitrarily murdered Smiley Wimple."

"What do you mean, 'arbitrarily'?"

"That's what the only witness says. Wimple's gun misfired, and Butterworth didn't have to kill him, although a prosecutor would never be able to prove that."

Desmond rubbed at his nose. "You're not jerking me around? Antoine's dead?"

"Unless he's been resurrected."

"Where is he?"

"Probably on a slab."

"You're a callous man."

"He told me someday I would be able to read between the lines. Have any idea what he meant?"

"No."

"Where does your money come from?" I asked.

"Half a dozen sources, all of them legitimate."

"You might have a Maltese cross tattooed on your ankle, but you'll never be Geoffrey Chaucer's good knight," I said. "I don't care how many showers you take, you've still got shit on your nose."

He turned his face to the wind, his hair lifting, his wide-set eyes devoid of light, his expression as meaningless as a cake pan, his torso a piece of sculpted stone inside his shirt. Had he swung on me, I wouldn't have been surprised.

"He suffered?" he said.

"Butterworth? Maybe. He was listening to a *Jazz at the Philharmonic* concert before he signed off."

"That sounds like him. He loves Flip Phillips."

"The man I talked to was sweating ball bearings."

"He was an artist," he said. "In his way, a dreamer."

"When he wasn't hanging up working girls on coat hooks. You're going to Arizona tomorrow?"

"At sunrise."

"Make all the pictures you want," I said. "I'm going to get you." I walked away.

"You think you can hurt me?" he called to my back. "After what's happened here? That's what you think?"

I got into the truck and started the engine. Clete had been drowsing. "Hey! What's going on with Cormier?" he asked.

"He was shocked and indignant," I replied.

We drove back to the two-lane and headed home, an orange sun dissolving into the wetlands, threaded with smoke from stubble fires.

• • •

EARLY SUNDAY MORNING, Cormac the coroner called me at home. "I couldn't sleep last night."

"What's the problem?" I said.

"I'll probably have to declare Butterworth's death a suicide, but it bothers me."

"Why?"

"The broken tooth your friend Purcel found in the door track. The bullet went in behind the jaw and traveled upward through the tongue and the palate in a clean line. It's possible the bullet deflected off the tooth, except I don't see the evidence."

"Call it like you see it," I said.

"Here's my other problem: I talked to the prosecutor last night. I think everyone wants to shut the book on this one."

"Wimple and Butterworth get bagged and tagged, and everyone goes home happy?"

"People are people," he said. "What's your opinion?"

"Desmond Cormier knows the truth, but he's never going to tell us."

"His half sister was murdered. What the hell is wrong with this guy?"

"Money and power," I said. "You know a stronger drug?"

"How about getting up in the morning with a clear conscience?" he replied. "You talked with Butterworth before he went out. You believed he capped himself?"

"I think maybe someone was setting up Cormier, and I think he's too dumb to know it."

I FIXED A BOWL of Grape-Nuts and milk and blackberries and ate it on the back steps. I also brought a bowl of cat food for Snuggs and Mon Tee Coon. The trees were dripping with humidity, the bayou high and swollen with mud, the flooded elephant ears along the bank beaded with drops of water that slid like quicksilver off the surface. I heard a vehicle pull into the driveway, then footsteps coming around the side of the house.

"Hope I ain't disturbing your Sunday morning," Sean said. He was in uniform, his cheeks bright with aftershave, his gun belt polished, the creases in his trousers as sharp as knife blades.

"Get yourself a cup of coffee off the stove. Alafair is still asleep. Give me a refill, too." I handed him my cup.

He went inside and came back out with a filled cup in each hand. He sat down beside me and looked at Snuggs and Mon Tee Coon. He had a small mouth, like a girl's, and eyes like a child's. "I went out to the airport this morning."

"What for?"

"To watch them movie people take off. They were happy, like all the things that happened here don't mean anything."

"I'm not following you."

"I killed a man. I'll have him in my dreams the rest of my life. None of this would have happened if it hadn't been for these people."

"Blame other people, and you'll never have peace."

"That's what you told yourself in Vietnam?"

"I wasn't that smart."

"Dave, I'd give anything if I hadn't shot Tillinger. It's eating me up."

"I don't think Tillinger would hold it against you, Sean. He made a choice—the wrong one. Wherever he is, I think he knows that and forgives you for it."

"You don't dream about the men you killed?"

"Sometimes."

"What do you do about it?"

"Not drink."

He put down his coffee cup and rubbed one hand on top of the other. "I feel like I ain't no better than them deputies that suffocated the deaf man at the jail."

"You're nothing like those deputies."

"That's a sad story, you know? I heard the deaf man was trying to make sign language when he died."

I looked at my watch. "I'm going to Mass at St. Edward's. Want to go?"

"Thanks for the coffee. I appreciate you listening to me."

"Run that by me again about the deaf man and sign language?"

AFTER HE WAS gone, I went to St. Edward's. When I returned, a note was on the refrigerator door. It said: *Went to Café Sydnie Mae for brunch. See you this afternoon.*

I looked out the side window. Alafair's car was still in the porte cochere. I called her cell phone. The call went straight to voicemail. I called the Café Sydnie Mae in Breaux Bridge. She wasn't there. It was 11:14 a.m.

I went to the office and opened my file drawer and took out every folder I had on the series of homicides that had begun with the murder of Lucinda Arceneaux. I also accessed every bit of electronic information I could find on Frank Dubois, the deaf man who had been suffocated in the Iberia Parish jail. He had one of those rap sheets that was full of contradictions, like a puzzle box shaken up and dropped on the floor. He grew up in New Orleans, on the edge of the Garden District, and attended Tulane University for three years in the 1960s, but was arrested twice for possession; then he cruised on out to sunny CA and got hooked up with the Mongols. He had half a dozen narcotics-related arrests in San Bernardino, Bakersfield, and Oakland, and ended up spending a year in Atascadero. A prison psychologist had noted in the margin of his sheet: *I.Q. above 160, symptoms of borderline personality disorder. Antisocial, narcissistic, and fears isolation and physical restraint. Potentially dangerous.*

I went through my notes on all the victims. Joe Molinari still perplexed me more than the others. Why did our killer want to murder such a harmless man? His jobs took him nowhere, and his employers were of no substance and rarely kept records. Except one: Molinari had been a janitor for two years at the Iberia Parish courthouse.

This may sound strange to an outsider, but the patronage culture in Louisiana is systemic, from the most humble kind of work to the governor's office. Procedure, honorable conduct, attention to the rules, acuity, experience, and skill have secondary value at best. You cannot get a state job cleaning a toilet unless you know someone. For a man like Molinari—who did asbestos teardowns—a steady paycheck, decent hours, health insurance, social security, and unemployment coverage were a gift from God.

So who got him the job? I called Helen and asked.

"I remember him working at the courthouse," she said. "He kept to himself."

"No friends?"

"He used to eat lunch with a deputy by the cemetery."

"Which deputy?"

There was a long silence.

"Helen?"

"One of the guys who suffocated the inmate at the jail. Son of a bitch."

I could hear the receiver humming in my ear. "You can't be expected to remember information from twenty-five years ago."

"No, no, I screwed up. The deputy was his cousin. He probably put in a word for Molinari and got him the job. Maybe Molinari's death is connected to the scandal at the jail."

"Could be," I said.

"Dave, I had my head up my ass. I pulled your badge when I should have pulled my own. The deaf man, what was his name?"

"Frank Dubois," I said.

"Where was he from?"

"New Orleans. He went to Tulane. A former AB kid named Spider Dupree said that Dubois had a coat of arms tattooed on his back and spoke Latin or Greek."

"Dave, I need to apologize to you. I acted like a real bitch."

"You may be lots of things, but that's not one of them," I said.

"That's why I love you, Pops."

I called Bailey and told her what I'd learned.

"You think Molinari was payback for the suffocation death?" she said.

"Yeah, I do."

"So who's the tie-in with Molinari?"

"I don't know. Maybe one of our movie friends."

"I need to tell you something," she said. "Desmond called me last night."

"You don't have to tell me anything, Bailey."

"He asked me to go to Arizona with him. I told him no."

"Bailey—"

"I don't know if it's over between us or not," she said.

"It was wrong from the jump. Not on your part. Mine. I took advantage of the situation."

"I'm a victim?" she said. "I'm too young and inexperienced to know what I'm doing?"

"Got to go, Bailey."

"Every time we talk, I feel like someone extracted my heart."

I eased the phone down in the cradle and stood at the window, looking down at the Teche and the sunlight flashing as brightly as daggers on the current.

I CALLED DESMOND CORMIER'S home number. There was no answer. I called Sean McClain on his cell phone. "This morning at the airport, who'd you see get on the plane?"

"There was two planes," Sean said.

"Okay, who'd you see get on?"

"I don't know their names."

"You saw Desmond Cormier?"

"No, sir."

"How about Lou Wexler?"

"I don't know who that is. What's wrong?"

"I don't know where Alafair is."

"You think—"

"Yeah, that's exactly what I think, and it scares the hell out of me."

"What do you want me to do?"

"Go back to the airport and find out who was on those planes."

"Maybe Alafair will show up, Dave. Don't get too worried."

"Do you remember what Hilary Bienville's body looked like?" I asked.

I WENT FROM HOUSE to house up and down East Main, asking my neighbors if they had seen Alafair leave our simple shotgun home. I mention its simplicity at this point in my story to indicate the contrast I felt between the loveliness of the morning, the leaves blowing along the sidewalks, the flowers blooming in the gardens, the massive live oaks spangled with light and shadow, all of these gifts set in juxtaposition to the violence and cruelty that had fallen upon us like a scourge and now seemed to have cast their net over my daughter.

I walked past the Steamboat House, which sat like a dry-docked ornate paddle wheeler in an ambience of Victorian and antebellum splendor that often belied the realities of slavery and, later, the terrorism of the White League during Reconstruction. Farther down the street, an elderly lady was on her hands and knees, weeding the garden in the old Burke home, a pair of steel-frame spectacles on her nose. She looked up at me and smiled. "How do you do, Mr. Robicheaux?"

"Just fine," I said. "Alafair went somewhere with a friend while I was at Mass. I wondered if you might have seen her."

"I didn't see her, but I did see an unusual car stop in front of your home," she replied, still on her hands and knees. "I've seen it before."

"Unusual in what way?"

"I think the name is Italian."

"A Lamborghini?"

"I'm not much on the names of cars."

"What color was it?"

"Definitely cherry-red. No question about that."

Wexler.

"Have I upset you?" she asked.

"You've been very helpful," I said, the backs of my legs shaking. "Thank you."

I hurried away, my stomach sick.

Chapter Forty-One

I CALLED ALAFAIR'S CELL phone again, and again it went straight to voicemail. I called Sean.

"Yo, Dave," he said.

"What's your twenty?"

"Just coming back from the airport. Couldn't find anybody who knew anything positive. One guy said he thought he saw Cormier get on a private plane, but he wasn't sure."

"Lou Wexler rents a place in St. Martinville, but I don't know where. He drives a cherry-red Lamborghini. Go to the St. Martin Sheriff's Department and find out. We ROA there."

"You can probably beat me there."

"I'm picking up Clete Purcel."

"What's the deal on Wexler?"

"I don't know. I missed something on him. Something Clete told me. Or maybe Alafair told me. I can't remember."

"Copy that," he said. "Out."

I got into my truck and drove past the Shadows, then swung over to St. Peter's Street and headed for Clete's motor court. On Sundays, Clete usually washed or waxed his convertible and barbecued a pork roast or a chicken on the grill under the oaks by the bayou. If the weather was warm, he wore his knee-length Everlast boxing trunks and LSU or Tulane or Raging Cajuns sweatshirt, his upper arms the circumference of a fully pressurized fire hose. With luck, his metabolism would be free of the toxins that had impaired much of his life.

This morning, however, none of the foresaid applied. He was walking up and down in front of his cottage, cell phone to his ear, wearing a Hawaiian shirt outside his slacks; his shoes were shined, his hair wet-combed. He looked thinner, twenty years younger, wired to the eyes. I stopped the truck and got out, the engine still running. "What's going on?"

"I was just calling you. Where's Alafair?"

"Maybe with Lou Wexler."

He looked into space, then back at me. "Wexler?"

"Yes."

"I thought maybe—"

"What?"

"I'm confused. I saw Cormier drive by early this morning."

"Are you sure?"

"How many guys around here have an expression like a skillet and look carved out of rock? I thought maybe he went to your house."

I rarely saw fear in the face of Clete Purcel. He pinched his mouth.

"What is it?" I said.

"I just got a call from Alafair."

"You talked to her?"

"No. There was just a little hiccup of a voice, like she'd butt-dialed and was talking to somebody else and clicked off again. At least, that's what I thought I was hearing."

"You're not making sense, Cletus."

"I think maybe she was saying 'Help.' "

I felt a hole open in the bottom of my stomach. "Was Desmond driving a Lamborghini?"

"No, he was in a Humvee, same one he was driving at the res."

"The lady who lives in the old Burke home saw a cherry-red Lamborghini stop at my house."

"It was Wexler?"

"There's no other Lamborghini around here. Just a minute." I called Helen at home. No one answered. I called Bailey Ribbons. "I think either Lou Wexler or Desmond Cormier has got his hands on Alafair," I said.

"That doesn't sound right," she said. "Des is probably in Arizona now."

"He's not. Clete saw him a short while ago."

"I don't understand," she said.

"It's not difficult. Desmond Cormier is a liar."

"You don't have to talk that way," she said.

I hung up.

"What do you want to do?" Clete said.

"We're supposed to ROA with Sean McClain in St. Martinville."

"I need my piece."

"Get it," I said.

"What have you got in the truck?"

"Don't worry about it," I said.

WE DROVE UP the two-lane toward St. Martinville, through the tunnel of oaks on the north side of New Iberia. Perhaps it was the season or perhaps not, but the light was wrong. It was brittle, flickering, harsh on the eyes, suggestive of a cruel presence in the natural world. We passed the two-story frame house with a faux-pillared gallery that had been built by a free man of color before the War Between the States. According to legend, he had worn elegant clothes and spoken Parisian French and had his land and wealth stolen from him by carpetbaggers after the war. To this day, no one has ever succeeded in painting the building a brilliant white: within a short time, the paint is quickly dulled by dust from the cane fields or smoke from stubble fires, as though the structure itself bears the legacy of a man who betrayed his race and sought to become what he was not at the expense of his brethren and ultimately himself.

As I stared through the windshield, the two-lane unspooling before me, I knew something was terribly wrong in the external structure of the day, in the rules that supposedly govern mortality and the laws of physics. Dust devils were churning inside the uncut cane, troweling rooster tails seventy feet into the air, although the temperature was dropping and the wind was cold enough to dry and crack the skin. By the side of the road was a watermelon and strawberry stand with wooden tables under a live oak hung with Spanish moss. There had not been a fruit stand on that road for decades; plus, we never saw melons and strawberries after August, unless they were imported and on sale at an expensive grocery in Lafayette.

Then I saw two middle-aged people holding hands by the roadside. The man was huge and wore strap overalls and a tin hard hat slanted on his head. He grinned and gave me the thumbs-up sign. The woman wore a wash-faded print dress and a red hibiscus flower in her hair; she was also smiling, like someone welcoming a visitor at an entryway.

The man and woman were my mother and father. Behind them, I saw Smiley Wimple with two little girls dressed in white and hung with chains of flowers. The wound in Smiley's side glowed with an eye-watering radiance.

My truck shot past them, blowing newspaper and dust all over the road.

"Watch where you're going!" Clete said.

"You saw that?" I said.

"Saw what?"

I looked in the rearview mirror. The newspaper had settled on the asphalt. There was nothing on either side of the highway except pastureland and cane fields. "Did you see those people?"

"What people?"

"Don't shine me on," I said.

"I didn't see anything. What the hell are you talking about?"

I stared at him, then had to correct the wheel to keep from going off the shoulder. "I'm not going to jack you around. I just saw my parents. I saw Smiley, too. With two little girls."

"Pull over."

"No."

"This isn't Nam, Streak. You roger that, noble mon? We got no medevac. In the next fifteen minutes we may have to kick some serious ass. You stop talking bullshit."

"I know what I saw. Don't give me a bad time about it either."

"Okay," he replied. "Okay. We can't blow it. These guys are going to kill Alafair."

"Guys?"

"The sick fucks are working together."

"For what purpose?"

"It's about the jail. It's a war on this whole fucking area." He looked straight ahead, rigid in the seat, his fists clenched like small hams on his knees, his face as tight as latex stretched on his skull, his chest rising and falling.

"You're losing it, Clete."

"This from the guy who just saw his dead parents?"

His right hand was twitching on his thigh.

YOU KNOW HOW death is. It can be a strange companion. Its smell is like no other in the world. I remember an ARVN graves unit digging up the bodies of villagers who had been buried alive along a streambed deep in the heart of Indian country. The stench broke through the soil and reminded me of the whores pouring their waste buckets into the privies behind the cribs on Railroad Avenue, back when I threw the newspaper in New Iberia's old red-light district. The putrescence of the odor, however, doesn't compare to the image of the flesh when it's exposed by a shovel. It's marbled with whitish-yellow boils and fissures in the skin that look like centipedes, and the eyes resemble fish scale and are either half-lidded or as bulging and black and white as an eight ball.

If a person is interested in the kind of war scene my patrol stumbled upon, I can add a few details to satisfy his curiosity. If our hypothetical observer had been there, he would have seen the bodies being rolled into tarps, and the hands of the dead that were little more than bones held together by a hank of skin; he would have also noticed that the fingernails were broken and impacted with dirt; that night our observer would have had a very stiff drink and tried to convince himself that Dachau and Nanking were a historical perversion and not a manifestation of the worm that lives in the human unconscious.

These are certainly not good images to reflect upon, but I like to offer them for the purview of those who love wars as long as they don't have to participate in one. That said, the ubiquity of the worm does not manifest itself only on battlefields. It can take on an invisibility that is more insidious than the footage I can never rinse from my dreams. You don't smell it or see it, but in your sleep, you see it grow in size and nestle on your chest and squeeze the air from your lungs. You spend the rest of the night with the light on or a drink in your hand or your hand clasped on a holy medal, and you pray on your knees for the dawn to come. After the sun breaks on the horizon, you may see figures standing in the shade of a building, or in an alleyway, or among wind-thrashed trees, and you'll quickly realize the bell you hear tolling in the distance is one that no one else can either hear or see.

That's when you know you've taken up residence in a very special place you cannot tell others about, lest you frighten them or embarrass yourself. You've seen the great reality and have accepted it for what it is, and in so doing, you have been set free. But by anyone's measure, the dues you pay are not for everyone. Psychiatrists call it a Garden of Gethsemane experience. It's a motherfucker, and you never want to have it twice.

I'm saying I no longer worry about death, at least my own. But the thought of losing my daughter was more than I could bear. There is no human experience worse than losing one's child, and to lose a child at the hands of evil men causes a level of emotional pain that has no peer. Anyone who says otherwise is a liar. That is why I never argue with those who want to see the murderers of their children receive the ultimate penalty, although I do not believe in capital punishment.

We crossed the St. Martinville city limits and rode through the black district, past Bella Delahoussaye's cottage, and stopped in front of the sheriff's department. Sean McClain was standing outside his cruiser, waiting for us.

I parked and got out of the truck. "What do you have?"

"Wexler's address up the bayou," he replied. "A deputy said he saw the Lamborghini go through the square early this morning. He remembered it because it was in his brother-in-law's repair shop for a couple of days."

"That's why Wexler was driving Butterworth's Subaru in the park," I said. "Is there a deputy sitting on Wexler's place?"

"I told them not to do nothing till you got here."

"Give me the address. Follow us but stay a block behind."

"What about the St. Martin deputies?" Sean said.

I shook my head.

"Is that smart?" he said.

I looked at him without speaking.

"It's your show," he said.

WE PULLED INTO a shady lot on the Teche, just outside the city limits. The house was a large, weathered gingerbread affair, the wide, railed gallery overgrown with banana fronds, the rain gutters full of leaves and moss, the tin roof streaked with rust. The chimney was cracked, a broken lightning rod hanging from the bricks. There were no vehicles in the yard or garage. I got out and banged on the door, then circled the house. My caution about the St. Martin Parish authorities was unnecessary; no one was home. I splintered the front door out the jamb and went inside.

Every room was immaculate and squared away. I began pulling clothes off hangers and raking shelves onto the floor.

"What are you doing?" Clete said.

"Finding whatever I can."

"We don't know that Wexler has Alafair. Cormier is out there somewhere."

"It's Wexler. She was here. I can feel it."

Clete looked at me strangely.

"It's something a father knows," I said.

Sean McClain was still outside. Through the open front door, I saw Bailey Ribbons pull into the lot in a cruiser. She got out and walked into the living room. "Helen says we'll have the whole department on this, Dave. What do you have so far?"

"We found out from a St. Martin deputy that Wexler's Lamborghini was in the shop. He'd probably borrowed Butterworth's Subaru when Wimple accosted him."

"You dumped his closets and shelves?" she said.

"I'm just getting started."

"Maybe dial it down a little bit? We don't want to lose something in the shuffle."

She was right. I was in overdrive. "Check the kitchen. I'm going in the attic."

I pulled down the drop door in the bedroom ceiling and climbed up the steps. I shone a penlight around the attic walls. A heavy trunk, a wardrobe box, and a handwoven basket-like baby carriage were in one corner. The wardrobe box was stuffed with historical costumes that smelled of mothballs. The baby carriage was filled with bandanas, women's shoes, empty purses and wallets, and old Polaroids of third-world women in bars and cafés. All the women were smiling. The trunk was unlocked. I lifted the top. It was packed with video games, the kind that award the shooters or drivers points for the victims they rack up.

I dumped the trunk and wardrobe box, then the baby carriage. As the purses and wallets and women's clothing and photos spilled on the floor, I saw the one object I did not want to find, one that sucked the air from my chest.

I picked it out of the pile and went down the ladder and eased the drop door back into the ceiling, then went into the kitchen. Bailey was sitting at the table. "What is it?"

I set the box on the table. "The tarot."

"Shit," Clete said behind me.

I sat down and put the deck in Bailey's hand. "See if there's anything significant about the deck. Missing cards or whatever."

She began separating the suits, then stopped and set one card aside. It was a card called the Empress. It was also disfigured. She resumed sorting the deck and put four other cards with the Empress.

"The Queen of Cups, the Queen of Pentacles, the Hanged Man, the Ten of Wands, the Empress, the Ace of Wands, and the Fool all have X's cut on them," she said. "The Queen of Cups is Bella Delahoussaye. The Queen of Pentacles is Hilary Bienville. The Hanged Man and the Ten of Wands could be Joe Molinari. The Fool might be Antoine Butterworth. The Empress is Lucinda Arceneaux. The Ace of Swords is for sure Axel Devereaux."

"You're sure about this?" Clete said.

"No," she replied. "That's all guesswork."

"Why is Lucinda Arceneaux the Empress and not Hilary or Bella?" I said.

"The Empress is the earth mother, the patroness of charity and kindness."

"Why are you so certain about the Ace of Swords for Axel Devereaux?" I said.

"The Ace of Swords means raw power," she said. "In reverse, it can mean loss and hatred and self-destruction. Devereaux had a baton shoved down his throat. The killer put a fool's cap on him to ridicule him in death."

"Why two cards for Molinari?" I said.

"Good question. My guess is Wexler thinks of him as both a sacrificial and a mediocre personality. Molinari was related to one of the guards in the jail?"

"Yes," I said. But she already knew that. She was holding something back; I was afraid to find out what.

"The High Priestess is missing from the deck," she said.

"What's the High Priestess?" I said.

"She sits at the entrance to Solomon's Temple. She holds the Book of Wisdom in her hand and is identified with purity and intellectualism."

I felt my heart slowing, as though it no longer had the power to pump blood. "You think the High Priestess is Alafair?"

Bailey visibly tried not to swallow. "Who else would it be? Maybe he saved her out. There's something else I want you to see."

I coughed into my hand. "What?"

"This." The letters *B* and *S* had been scratched into the table's surface. "They're fresh, maybe cut with a fork. They mean anything to you other than 'bullshit'?"

I was having trouble breathing. "They're a message to me from Alafair. I think they stand for 'Baby Squanto.' "

I went outside and across the gallery and out into the yard. The sky was an unnatural blue, shiny, hard to look at. Bailey followed me. "Everything we're doing now is based on speculation," she said.

"I think everything you said is correct," I said. "Don't try to put a good hat on it."

"That's not what I'm talking about," she said. "The guy we're dealing with is a ritualist. What looks crazy to us makes complete sense to him. He's going to come back to the place he started. The challenge is to put yourself in the head of a lunatic."

"Say that again?"

"Ritualists often seek symmetry. People with severe psychological disorders have trouble drawing a tree or making a circle. Our guy will try to come full circle."

"With the cross out on the water?" I said.

"Or something like it."

"Do you have any idea how many square miles of water you're talking about?" I said.

"That's about as good as it gets, Dave," she replied. "I'm sorry to say all these things. Maybe I'm dead wrong."

I looked back at the house. The sun was higher in the sky. The shadows had dropped down into the trees. The house looked cold and empty and drab in the bright light.

"It all seems too easy," I said.

"What does?" she said.

"The baby carriage filled with trophies from his crimes. The boxed cards with X's cut on them."

"He's a trophy killer," she said.

Clete was talking to Sean by the gallery while Sean stared at his feet as though being berated. Clete walked toward me. "Can you give us a minute, Miss Bailey?" he said.

"No, I cannot," she said. "Where do you get off with that attitude?"

"I was just wondering about McClain," he said.

"What about him?" she said.

"He told me he might be going out to Hollywood. That Cormier might be casting him."

"What does that have to do with anything?" she said. "He's a kid."

"I thought he was North Lousiana's answer to the Lone Ranger," Clete said.

"What did you tell him?" I asked.

"That he shouldn't be palling around with a guy who might be aiding and abetting a murderer," Clete said.

I stared at Sean in the sunlight. He wore a department hat that made his face look gray and dusty under the brim, as if he had been working all day in a field. He tried to smile at me, but his lip seemed to catch on a bottom tooth.

"You sure that kid's not hinky?" Clete said.

My cell phone vibrated in my pocket. It was Lou Wexler.

Chapter Forty-Two

"I'M GLAD I caught you," he said.

My hand was trembling on the phone. "Where are you, Mr. Wexler?"

"Trying to find Alafair. Lose the formality. We're on the same side."

"Alafair is not with you?"

"Desmond has her. Stop listening to that man's lies."

"We're at your house in St. Martinville. I saw the tarot. I saw your trophies in the attic."

"What trophies?"

"The wallets and purses and shoes and bandanas."

"Those are props from a film we made about a serial killer." He gave me the title and named the actors and the directors. My head was throbbing. I couldn't process his words.

"I don't know anything about a tarot," he went on. "If you found it in my house, Des put it there. He's been salting the mineshaft. Isn't that the term for it?"

"How do you account for the shooting in City Park?"

"You've got me on that one. My Lamborghini was in the shop, so I borrowed Antoine's Subaru. I was having a go of it with a local lady when this nasty little sod walked up on me and tried to put out my wick. So I clicked off his switch. I shouldn't have run. I was going to turn myself in today. I have an attorney. You can check out my story."

"Tell me where you are."

"I'm not quite sure about my safety at this point."

"You think we're going to kill you in custody?"

"I've seen the way you and your Falstaffian friend do business, sir. The other problem is I don't think you have a bloody clue what's been going on in your own life."

"Repeat that?"

"I don't like to be the bearer of bad news, but your homicide partner is not what she seems. She set fire to a school as a child, and she fried some fellows at a fairgrounds up in Montana."

"How do you know this?"

"I knew her in New Orleans. I was sticking it to her long before you did. Sorry to tell you, she's not Clementine Carter, as Des is always saying. What a fucking joke. I'll be back with you later. Or maybe not."

He broke the connection. I folded the phone in my hand and tried to keep my face empty.

"That was Wexler?" Bailey said.

"Yes," I replied.

"What did he say?"

"That except for shooting Wimple, he's an innocent man."

"Do you believe him?"

"Did you know him in New Orleans?"

"No."

"Never saw him before you came to the Iberia Sheriff's Department."

"No. Is that what he told you?"

"We need to get a net over Desmond Cormier," I said.

"Cormier has Alafair?"

"I'm not sure about anything."

She looked at me in dismay. I walked toward my truck. I have long had problems with vertigo, the kind caused by a tightening of blood vessels in the brain. I could feel the ground caving under my feet. Then I felt Clete fitting his hand inside my upper arm. He opened the driver's door and steadied me so I could step inside.

"I'm all right," I said.

"What did that cocksucker say?"

"He knows things about Bailey that would be impossible for him to know, unless he'd had a relationship with her. He says the stuff from the attic are movie props. He knows nothing about a tarot deck."

"What else?"

"Alafair may already be dead. Or maybe Cormier has her. I just don't know."

"Don't say that about her being dead. You hear me, Streak? Don't even think it. I'm going to get these guys. I promise you."

He looked like he was drowning.

BAILEY AND OUR departmental pilot and I took the pontoon plane over the wetlands south of New Iberia. It might have seemed a waste of time to others, but we had nothing else to go on. I had no idea where Desmond Cormier might be. Wexler knew Bailey's history, which gave plausibility to the other things he'd said. Possibly he had worked as a companion killer with Desmond. That I've spoken of Desmond's physiognomy several times probably says more about me than Desmond. The prenatal alcoholic influence stamped on his features was undeniable, the inner reality one I had never wanted to accept.

As the plane dipped and turned and glided over the swamps and marshlands that were shrinking daily, I wondered what to look for. Maybe a white cabin cruiser couched in a green harbor. A cherry-red Lamborghini. A houseboat or a duck camp where Alafair had set a fire as a mayday signal. These thoughts were the product of desperation, and they led me to worse thoughts, namely, that I might see Alafair costumed and floating out to sea, closing the circle for the killer, as Bailey had predicted.

I had thought my days in the Garden of Gethsemane were over and my ticket had been punched, and that I belonged to the club of those who were inured to the worst the world could offer. But as I looked at the miles and miles of salt grass and flooded gum trees and milky-green curtains of algae that floated atop the bays, I knew that

I was powerless over my situation, and the last remnant of my family had perhaps been subsumed by the evil forces I have fought against all my life, most of it in vain.

WHAT DOES THE expression "hell on earth" mean? In my experience, it usually has to do with our own handiwork. Freight cars clicking down the tracks on their way to Buchenwald. A nineteen-year-old peasant girl set alight while tied to a stake in Rouen, France. The slaughter of fifty million buffalo to starve the American Indian into submission.

Or a child who survived a massacre in an El Salvadoran village and grew into an attorney and a novelist, only to be kidnapped by a fellow countryman and perhaps locked in a car trunk, hog-tied, eyes and mouth wrapped with tape. That image lived like a scream inside my head.

WE LANDED OFF Cypremort Point and taxied across the water to a dock where Clete Purcel was waiting for us. He was wearing a windbreaker and khakis and lace-up canvas-and-rubber hunting boots, his hair blowing in the wind. He looked at Bailey, then back at me. "I got a tip."

I waited, the wind cupping in my ears.

"From the black gal who was chugging pole for Wexler when he popped Wimple in City Park," he said.

"We don't need the detail," Bailey said.

"Do you want to hear me out or not?" he replied.

"What did she say?" Bailey asked.

"She turns tricks out of a couple of motels in Lafayette," he said. "She does specialties for geeks. She says Wexler is a regular. She had dinner one time with Cormier."

"Dinner?" I said.

"Yeah, she knows him pretty good. She says he's weird."

"What does she know about Alafair?" I said.

"I'm trying to get to that," he said. "She says Wexler and Cormier brought her to a duck camp. Cormier went off on his own while she took care of Wexler. She says Wexler told her there were drowned Nazi sailors about half a mile from shore. She thought he was making fun of her." He kept his eyes on me.

"You know a place like that?" Bailey said.

"I'm not sure," Clete replied.

I knew exactly where the place was, and so did Clete. In the early days of World War II, German U-boats lay in wait for the oil tankers that sailed from the refineries in Baton Rouge. In New Iberia, we could see the glow of the tankers burning at night, just beyond the southern horizon. In the fall of '42, a German sub had been depth-charged from the air and sunk in sixty feet of water. All these years it had been sailing, as far out as the edge of the continental shelf, but it always came back to the place where it had been sunk.

"Where's the black woman now?" Bailey said.

"I talked to her on her cell," Clete said. "She's not going to come anywhere near us."

Bailey had come to the dock in a police cruiser, and I had my truck. Clete's Caddy was parked by a boat ramp.

"I'm going to head back to town," I said to Bailey. "I'll call you from my house."

"We need the black woman," she said. "What's her name?"

"I can't give it to you," Clete said.

"You're about to get yourself in some serious trouble," she said.

"What's new?" he replied.

She walked away, her back stiff with anger, the wind blowing hard enough to show her scalp. I didn't like deceiving Bailey, but I no longer trusted her, or Sean McClain, or several other colleagues who had ties to Axel Devereaux.

"I brought my AR-15," Clete said.

"You're sure the hooker isn't jacking us?"

"I'm like you," he said. "Not sure of anything. Let's rock."

• • •

IT WAS ALMOST dusk when we arrived at the southern end of Terrebonne Parish and parked on the levee. We walked down the slope into water over our ankles. I had put on a canvas coat and a hat to keep the tree limbs out of my eyes, and had stuffed one pocket with double-aught bucks and pumpkin rounds, and slung my cut-down pump from my shoulder. I had a flashlight in my other coat pocket, and a spare magazine for Clete's AR-15. He had taken it off a drug mule he'd busted as a bail skip on Interstate 10. It was outfitted with a bump-fire stock and fired as fast as a machine gun.

The sandspits were blanketed with egrets that rose clattering in the canopy while we tried to work our way silently through the sloughs and over logs and piles of organic debris that squished under our feet and smelled like fish roe.

Air vines hung in our faces, and a bull gator slithered on its belly into a deep black pool six feet from us, and cottonmouths that had not gone into hibernation were coiled on cypress limbs just above the waterline. Behind us, out on the Gulf of Mexico, the sun was a giant dull-red orb that seemed to give no heat. Clete was ahead of me, his shoulders humped, his rifle in a sling position, a thirty-round magazine inserted in the well. He cocked his left arm, his fist clenched, signaling me to stop. Through the flooded trees and the late sunlight dancing on the water, I could see a dry mound and a cabin built of untreated pine that had turned black from lichen and water settlement and lack of sunlight. Wind chimes tinkled on the gallery, and smoke rose in the twilight from an ancient chimney and flattened in the trees. I could smell either crabs or crawfish boiling in a pot. The scene could have been lifted from 1942, just before a United States Coast Guard plane came in low over the water and dropped a single charge and broke the back of a Nazi sub.

In back of the cabin were a privy and a stump that served as a butcher block with an ax embedded in it, the nearby ground scattered with turkey and chicken feathers; a boat shed containing a pirogue that hung on wires from the ceiling; and an unmaintained levee overgrown with willow saplings and palmettos. Through the trees, I could see a white cabin cruiser in a cove, rising and falling with the incoming tide. Clete eased down into a squat and scooped mud with his left hand and rubbed it on his face, around his eyes, and on the back of his neck. He looked over his shoulder at me and pointed to the left, indicating that I should flank the cabin.

I shook my head. I didn't know why. For the second time that day, I didn't trust what I was looking at. The silence, the lack of motion, and the rigidity of the cabin seemed to contain an intensity on the brink of tearing itself apart. I had only one precedent for the feeling. Imagine a village surrounded by rice fields, a fat harvest moon above the hooches, water buffalo snuffing in a pen, villagers nowhere in sight, a shiny strand of wire stretched across the trail leading into the ville.

What do you do?

Light it up, Loot, whispers a sweaty black kid from West Memphis, Arkansas, his hands knuckling on his blooker, his breath rife with fear. *Light the motherfucker up.*

Clete gestured at me again. We were both on one knee now. I pointed two fingers at my eyes, then pointed at the front of the cabin. The sun was almost gone, the hummock sliding deeper into shadow. The cabin door was open. I could see a fire burning inside a woodstove, like liquid yellow-red lines sketched against the surrounding blackness. I also thought I saw the shapes of two figures, both motionless, but I couldn't be sure. Even though we were on the cusp of winter, the air was dense with humidity, as though the environment itself were sweating. I pushed the moisture out of my eyes with the heel of my hand and tried to see clearly through the door. But as with anything you stare at too long in poor light, I could not determine where reality ended and fear and fantasy began.

Charlie's in there. Ain't no time to be kind to animals. Time to bring the nape, Loot.

But that was what someone wanted us to do. That's what the bad guys always want us to do. I could hear the chop slapping against the hull of the cabin cruiser, a gator rolling in a channel and probably ripping through tangles of water hyacinths, flinging mud and water into the trees. I picked up a dirt clog and flung it to the left of the cabin.

Nothing.

Clete began working to the right. I can't tell you how I knew something was wrong. Maybe it was Clete's determination to mete out summary justice regardless of the attrition. Or maybe I remembered all the times he and I had gone in under a black flag and later had to deal with the specters that ask you why.

Or maybe my angle of vision was better than his. I knew there were two silhouettes beyond the doorway. One was larger than the other. The smaller figure wore a hat. Both figures were as still as the oil paint on a canvas.

I wished we had brought Bailey and backup. I tossed a piece of dirt at Clete, trying to get his attention. He kept moving in a crouch to the right, past the cabin door, then into the shadows of the trees, easing down into grass that was three feet high. I had to make a decision. I couldn't communicate with Clete. I had no way of knowing whether he had seen the two figures. I also had no idea who they were. What if the cabin cruiser was not Wexler's or Desmond's but the property of a recreational fisherman who had decided to drop anchor and boil a load of crabs?

I stepped back into the overhang of the trees and worked my way around the left side of the cabin. Then I realized I had not seen everything that was behind it. Desmond's Humvee was parked below the levee, black leaves stuck to the windows, a bullet hole pocked through the windshield on the driver's side.

I took a chance. I was ready to eat a bullet rather than let the situation go south, which I believed was about to happen at any moment. I stood up, the breeze suddenly cool on my face. My finger was curled through the trigger guard on the twelve-gauge, my left hand on the fore-end.

"Iberia Sheriff's Department!" I said. "We don't care who you are or what you're doing, but it's going to stop! Nobody needs to get hurt! We'll work it out!"

There was no response. The last sunlight on the Gulf had turned to pewter. The air was dense with a cold smell like waves bursting on a beach, like piled kelp, like coupling and birth, like a disinterred grave.

"You've got my daughter, you sons of bitches!" I said. "You'll give her back to me or I'll stake you out and send you into the next world one limb at a time!"

I would like to say my words were theatrical. They were not; I meant them. The problem was not ethical. The problem was they did no good.

I saw Clete rise from the grass, the bump-fire stock of his rifle pressed against his shoulder.

The next images were like stained glass breaking on a stone floor and to this day difficult to reconstruct. The first sound I heard was the popping of shells, like a string of firecrackers thrown carelessly from an automobile. At the same time I saw flashes inside the doorway of the cabin. I also thought I saw a tracer round streak from either the levee or the cove and float out over the water like a piece of broken neon.

I saw Clete begin firing into the cabin, the spent cartridges flying from the ejector port of the AR-15, the rounds whanging off the woodstove. I also heard popping from somewhere else, but I didn't know where. I began running at Clete, yelling incoherently, waving my arms. I smashed into him and knocked him to the ground. He stared up at me, his eyes like green Life Savers inside the mud on his face. I grabbed his shirt with both hands and shouted, "You wouldn't listen! You never listen!"

His face dilated with the implication of my words. "Oh, God! Oh, God, Dave! Tell me I didn't do that."

I dropped my cut-down in the grass and pulled the rifle from his hands and threw away the half-spent magazine and inserted the fresh one from my coat pocket into the well. I started running for the cabin door, keeping the cabin between me and the cove and the levee. The flames in the woodstove were blazing brightly because of the holes Clete had drilled in the iron plate. The hatted figure was slumped forward in a chair. The figure next to it had fallen to the floor. I stepped inside the doorway, indifferent to whatever harm might befall me at the hands of Desmond Cormier or Lou Wexler.

The head rolled loose from the figure in the hat. The figures were mannequins. Shell casings were scattered on the floor and the top of the stove. Two were still unfired and inside the skillet that had probably been filled with them. I felt my eyes fill with water, my lungs swell with air that was dense with salt and the coldness of the Gulf.

I turned and went back through the door onto the gallery. "It's not Alafair, Clete!"

He was on his feet now. He grinned at me, my cut-down hanging from his hand. Then there were pops and slashes of light from the darkness, and he went down on both knees, two red flowers blooming on his windbreaker, his jaw dropping, his arms dead at his sides.

Chapter Forty-Three

I WENT OUT THE back door just as the headlights of the Humvee came on and shone directly into my eyes. I raised my hand against the glare and saw Lou Wexler by the side of the Humvee. He had a semi-automatic rifle aimed at the center of my face. Desmond Cormier lay on the ground, his hands wrapped with wire behind him and tied to his ankles, a blue rubber ball strapped in his mouth.

"Lay your piece aside or never see your daughter again," Wexler said.

My eyes were watering in the headlights.

"I'll pop both her and Des right now," he said.

I let the AR-15 drop.

"Back away," he said.

I did as he said. He reached down and picked up the AR-15 by the barrel and flung it into the darkness. "The whore gave me away, did she?"

"Which whore?" I asked.

"The one I had a romp with in City Park," he said.

"Where's Alafair?"

"Snug as a bug in a rug."

"What do you get out of this, Wexler?"

"Tons of fun, and a bit of payback for what you and your ignorant kind did to my uncle in your parish prison."

"Helen Soileau and our friends and I had no part in that."

"Oh, yes, you did, laddie. You pretend to be the knight errant, but you're an ill-bred wog, just like Cormier. I kept his little three-penny opera afloat for years, and bankrupted both myself and that poor sod Butterworth, while the Golden Globes and Academy nominations went to this pitiful puke on the ground."

"Why did you kill Lucinda Arceneaux?"

"I saved her."

"What?"

"She could have been my queen bee. She opted for a life of mediocrity. So I eased her into a role no one around here will ever forget. You have to admit, it's been pretty good theater."

I had no doubt he was mad. But that didn't make his cruelty any the less. Desmond twitched on the ground. Wexler placed his foot on Desmond's neck and squeezed. I could hear the waves starting to hit the cabin cruiser's hull, a steady slap that threw salt spray higher and higher in the air.

"Alafair isn't a player in this," I said. "If you really believe in the ethos of the Templar knight, you have to let her go, Lou."

"On a first-name basis, are we? Get on your knees."

"Is she on the boat?"

"Could be. But let's get back to our biblical lesson. You remember the biblical quotation, don't you? 'Before me every knee shall bow'?"

"Can't do it."

"Maybe this will help."

He fired a round through the top of my foot. I felt a moment of intense pain, as though the bones between ankle and toes had been struck with a ballpeen hammer, then nothing, my shoe filling with blood. I wanted to say something brave or clever, but I could not. My best friend was down and maybe dead, and Alafair might have already suffered the same fate as Hilary Bienville. If she and Clete were gone, I was ready to go also.

"Put the next one between my eyes," I said.

"What was that?"

"Now is your chance. I want you to do it."

"Don't tempt the devil."

"The devil wouldn't let you clean his chamber pot."

He butt-stroked me with his rifle, knocking me to the ground. He pointed the muzzle into my face. "Kiss it."

"Fuck you."

I had to keep him talking. Once he was gone, Alafair would be gone also, probably forever. *Where are you, Bailey? Where are you, Helen?* I held my holy medal, my eyes shut. I was completely powerless and knew that whatever happened next was out of my hands.

I heard Wexler walk away. When I opened my eyes, I saw him step off a small dock onto a boarding plank that hung from the entry port of the cabin cruiser. The hull was dipping deeply into the waves, rocking and hitting the dock and the cypress knees along the bank. He clicked on the cabin light and pulled Alafair from the deck and held her so I could see her face. Blood was leaking from her hair.

I got up from the ground and began limping toward the dock as though half of me had melted. I thought I heard a helicopter droning over water, and I wondered if I had gone back in time to Southeast Asia and the sounds and images from which I had never freed myself. The thropping of the blades was unmistakable.

"You're not going anywhere, bub," I said.

"I'm honoring your war record," he said. "Be humble enough to recognize and accept an act of clemency by a brother-in-arms."

"You taped Bella Delahoussaye's eyes because you couldn't look her in the face while you killed her, you yellow-bellied, sorry sack of shit."

He knotted Alafair's hair in his fist. Her wrists were handcuffed behind her back. I was within fifteen feet of the cruiser now. The waves were bursting against the dock, drenching my hat and face. I saw lights coming in low over the surf in the distance.

"Hear that sound?" I said. "That's the cavalry. They're going to spike your cannon, Wexler. And after they do that, I'm going to kick it up your ass."

"You won't be here to see it. Neither will she."

Alafair's face was white with exhaustion or shock or blood loss; she looked like she had been beaten. Her bottom lip was cut and puffed, her hair matted with blood. I bet she had fought back. No, I knew she had fought back. And I was determined to be no less brave than she. Then, just to the south of the cabin cruiser, I saw a shadow moving through the trees, humped, off balance, leviathan, and unstoppable in its course and purpose.

"Pop me if you want," I said. "I'm no big loss. But before I check out, tell me one thing, will you?"

"I'd be delighted," he replied.

"How'd you get the information about Bailey Ribbons's background?"

"I worked for three government intelligence agencies. But maybe I porked her a couple of times, too. Take your pick."

I came closer and closer to him. He was standing just outside the cabin hatch, holding Alafair by the hair, his rifle butt propped on his hip, the waves swelling under the hull. The boarding plank was hooked to the stern, pulling loose from the bank, half underwater.

"Look at me," I said.

"What for?"

"Sheriff Soileau is in that chopper. She doesn't take prisoners. Make the smart choice. Give me back my daughter and beat feet."

He pulled her to him and kissed the top of her hair. "I might do that. Not tonight. But some night. She'll come around. You'll see. The victors write the history books."

He dropped her and pulled the anchor, sliding it covered with mud over the bow, dropping it hard on the deck. He went back into the cabin and started the engine, looking at me through the glass. My left leg was giving out, my foot squishing inside my shoe. I started toward the boarding plank, although I knew I would not make it. Then I saw Clete Purcel come lumbering out of the trees, the holes in his shoulders or chest draining down his shirt, my cut-down twelve-gauge pump in one hand.

Wexler either didn't care about the boarding plank or had forgotten about it; he was concentrating on backing the cruiser at an angle that prevented the waves from smacking it into the dock or onto the cypress knees.

The aluminum plank bent under Clete's weight, and his shoes clanked on the metal, and the waves sloshed over his ankles as he stumbled up the plank and through the entry port onto the stern.

Wexler turned, at first shocked, then smiling. "You still hanging around? How about another one in the brisket?"

I had seen the two bloody holes in Clete's windbreaker, but I had not realized how badly he was hurt. His left arm hung from the socket like a twisted water-soaked towel. He was trying to lift the cut-down with his right, and having no luck, as though his gyroscope were broken, his mojo gone, his motors in full meltdown. But he kept coming, like a dedicated drunk careening toward the bar, seeking one final sip of his nemesis.

Wexler raised his rifle. "Good try, blimpo. I hope you find a shady place."

Then something happened that was perhaps coincidental, perhaps not. A large bubble of light seemed to surround us all. A tremendous black swell dipped under the cruiser and raised it atop a wave that tilted it at least thirty degrees. Maybe someone in the helicopter had shone a searchlight on us. Maybe a tidal surge from the Gulf was about to strike the coast. Or maybe the ghost of the pilot who'd nailed that Nazi sub wanted to score one more for the good guys.

Wexler was thrown off balance, the wheel spinning as he tried to get his weapon in Clete's face. Clete crashed into him with his full weight, pressing him against the instrument panel. Wexler had his finger inside the trigger guard and was trying to push the barrel down on Clete's feet to get off a crippling shot. Clete shoved my cut-down inside Wexler's trousers.

"This is for Smiley Wimple and Hilary Bienville, asshole," he said. He pulled the trigger.

The number of rents in the cloth left no doubt that the shell in the chamber had been loaded with buckshot. Wexler seemed to be looking straight at me when he realized what had just happened to him. His mouth was puckered like a guppy's, his face shrinking as though it had been miniaturized, his voice locked in his throat as if no sound could adequately express what he was experiencing.

The Plexiglas-like bubble disappeared, and the cruiser settled against the dock, and the waves that had rocked it so violently turned to foam and trailed away in the darkness.

It's funny how your anger goes away when you see a man die, even one who was demonically evil. I adjusted the boarding plank and walked onto the stern and picked up Alafair. I held her against me, and the heat in her body radiated through her clothes. I smelled her hair and the salt on her skin and felt her heart beating when I pressed my hands against her back. Her face was buried in my chest. She didn't speak. She was the same five-year-old Salvadoran girl I had pulled from a submerged plane many years ago. The years between then and now meant absolutely nothing, and I knew that she was my little girl and I was her father and that was the way it would always be, and that Clete Purcel would remain our guardian angel forever, and that we would never change the world, but by the same token, the world would never change us.

Epilogue

NINE MONTHS LATER, the three of us rented a house on stilts just above Bodega Bay, where each evening the waves pounded against the cliffs and coral formations, and the sun left its light under the ocean long after it had disappeared from the sky. Alafair had sold her first film rights to a production company and had contracted to do the adaptation. While she worked at her computer and tried to let go of the deceit and violence and theft of trust that had been visited upon her, Clete and I tooled up and down Highway 1 in his Caddy, our saltwater rods and reels propped in the back seat, the wind cool and warm at the same time, while jeans-and-leather low-riders blasted past us and their badass girls smiled back at us, hair whipping in their faces.

Our wounds healed; our memories did not. Lou Wexler had hurt us in many ways. Oh, yes, the incubus had its origins in the abuse at the jail, but the real cluster of thorns was the suspicion and acrimony we had allowed Wexler to inculcate in us. We had come to distrust one another and lost faith in our institutions and ourselves. I had come to suspect Sean McClain and to quarrel with Helen Soileau and to doubt Bailey Ribbons, who had allowed me to go back in time and believe I could undo age and mortality and, in so doing, erase the mistakes I had made as a young man.

I would always love Bailey, but in a silent and protective way. When she invited Alafair and me to her and Desmond Cormier's wedding out in Arizona, with the vastness of Monument Valley as the backdrop, I made an excuse and decided never to think again about the life I might have had. But the temptation to dream stays with me on a daily basis, not unlike the shimmer inside a bottle of Johnnie Walker Red or the glitter of gin cascading on the rocks.

As far as Desmond was concerned, I believe his dualistic obsession with light and darkness was about the struggle between good and evil. It is not coincidence that in *My Darling Clementine,* the light of oil lamps burns only in the brothels and saloons, while the rest of the desert is governed by darkness. I believe Desmond shut his eyes to Wexler's crimes, including the murder of his half sister, and that his omission, like Butterworth's, would one day lead him to a fatal discovery about himself and a garden he did not want to enter.

The greatest oddity in all of this is that I believe Desmond passed on to me his obsession with light and shadow. I cannot watch the sun course through the heavens and settle into a molten ball without feeling a weakness in my heart, as though God does slay Himself with every leaf that flies and that indeed there is no greater theft than that of time.

But like Wyatt Earp and Henry Fonda, I love the name Clementine. And I love the name Bailey Ribbons. And I love the names Alafair Robicheaux and Clete Purcel. And with those names in my heart, why should I ever fear what tomorrow might bring?

Just the other day, Clete and Alafair and I were at a street dance in Santa Rosa, and I thought about ending this tale with a line about going up the country with Canned Heat, with the martial connotations the allusion implies. Instead I decided it was time to heed other lyrics from other songs. The green republic is still out there, the wheat fields waving, the dust clouds blowing, our mountains and diamond deserts and Gulf Stream waters a votive gift that belongs to us all. And the men who break in and steal by night, who spread self-doubt and fear and acrimony, will eventually fall by the wayside and be unremembered ciphers that disappear like scraps of newspaper in our rearview mirror.

With this thought in mind, Clete and Alafair and I went to a wild celebration among thousands of revelers in downtown Santa Rosa, surrounded by hills that glowed in the sunset with a purple aura under a starry sky, Martha & the Vandellas' "Dancing in the Street" blaring from the loudspeakers.

And that's the way our Manichean tale ends, on a summer night in the land of the free and the home of the brave, trapped between vineyards and the sea and the souls of migrants who come with dust and go with the wind, all of us twirling among young people who wore flowers in their hair, a church bell clanging without stop in a Spanish mission.

Roll on forever, Woody.

Acknowledgments

I would like to thank my wife, Pearl, and my daughter Pamala for their encouragement and support and their suggestions with the manuscript. I would also like to express my appreciation to my publisher Jonathan Karp, my editor Ben Loehnen, my production editor Katie Rizzo, and my copyeditor E. Beth Thomas, whose diligence and commitment have been unflagging.

Thanks also to Jackie Seow and Alison Forner for the lovely jacket, and to Amar Deol and the many other people at Simon & Schuster who believed in my books and stood behind them. Last, thanks to all the gang at the Spitzer Agency: Anne-Lise, Philip and Mary, Lukas Ortiz, and Kim Lombardini. We've made quite a team, and a writer could not ask for more.

About the Author

James Lee Burke is the author of many novels, and the critically-acclaimed, bestselling Detective Dave Robicheaux series. He won the Edgar Award for both *Cimarron Rose* and *Black Cherry Blues*, and *Sunset Limited* was awarded the CWA Gold Dagger. *Two for Texas* was adapted for television, and *Heaven's Prisoners* and *In the Electric Mist* for film. Burke has been a Breadloaf Fellow and Guggenheim Fellow, he has been awarded the Grand Master Award by the Mystery Writers of America and has been nominated for a Pulitzer award. He lives with his wife, Pearl, in Missoula, Montana.

www.jamesleeburke.com

T:@JamesLeeBurke